Paradise

MARC SAVAGE

a perfect crime book
DOUBLEDAY
NEW YORK
LONDON
TORONTO
SYDNEY
AUCKLAND

A PERFECT CRIME BOOK
PUBLISHED BY DOUBLEDAY
A division of Bantam Doubleday Dell Publishing Group, Inc.
1540 Broadway, New York, New York 10036

DOUBLEDAY is a trademark of Doubleday,
a division of Bantam Doubleday Dell
Publishing Group, Inc.

Book design by Claire Vaccaro

Library of Congress Cataloging-in-Publication Data

Savage, Marc.
    Paradise / Marc Savage. — 1st ed.
        p.   cm.
    "A Perfect crime book."
    I. Title.
    PS3569.A827P37   1993
    813'.54—dc20   92-35982
                                    CIP

ISBN 0-385-46770-6
Copyright © 1993 by Marc Savage
All Rights Reserved
Printed in the United States of America
June 1993

FIRST EDITION

10   9   8   7   6   5   4   3   2   1

For Adeline and George

On whom shall we bestow our affection,
And whom shall we confide in, pray?
In whom discover no defection?

—Alexander Pushkin,
Eugene Onegin

Paradise

Misty Carmichael got one of those inspirations that any sane man would recognize to be not only desperate, but suicidal. It happened in a little gray mom-and-pop grocery store on Metropolitan Avenue, in Queens, on one of those August days when the heat and humidity weigh on a person, heavy as a hangover or too many bad memories. Actually, it happened in the back room of the mom-and-pop.

And in that instant Misty Carmichael believed his whole life had been preparing him for this transcendent decision. It was one of the few times in his twenty-seven years of living that he was incontestably correct.

Misty lived with his mother, Molly, in a red shingle two-story row house in Ridgewood; it was long and narrow and the bedrooms were upstairs. There was paneling on the walls and the decor leaned in the direction of department-store Gothic, and the whole place had the dark, still and faintly forbidding aura of a monastery. The title to the house was held by a construction company, the owner of which was a successful contractor who lived in a five-bedroom home in College Point with a view of Powell's Cove and the Whitestone Bridge. The house in College Point had a slate roof and marble floors, a driveway that circled a fountain, and a front lawn that resembled a work of art. The contractor's name was Carl Bellows. He had a wife and three children. He was forty-nine, had forearms that were brown and powerful, a gut that hung over his belt, and he totally believed the fiction Molly spun, that Misty was her younger brother. You had to see Molly to understand how easy was the deception.

She could pass at forty-five for a woman closer to her early thirties, notwithstanding the way the skin faintly puckered at her elbows, the cluster of seams radiating from her cuticles. Since having been enticed by a pretty boy from Hell's Kitchen, and impregnated, Molly had been selective in her lovers and more than stringent with regard to her body. She stayed away from the sun, avoided caffeine, never smoked, and only seldom indulged in alcohol. Her nails were manicured twice a month. She had blue eyes and hair of a lustrous red, almost the color of polished mahogany.

Married once, briefly, to a television weather forecaster whose on-camera persona answered to the name of Doctor Bob, she had little use for commitment, although for the past several years, until Carl Bellows charged into her life, she had enjoyed a comfortable friendship with a Jewish guy who had no more interest in marriage than she did. She earned a living as a realtor, and could have earned much more if not for her insatiable desire to wake up in strange lands. She had spent time in every country in Europe, visited north Africa and various ports in the Orient. Molly preferred to travel alone, although (again before Carl) in recent years she hadn't objected to the company of the Jewish guy, when he could make it. She was, with the exception of her passion for travel, a practical and smart woman with a compact figure that still turned men around to see if she was as lovely going as she was coming. She was.

Misty at birth weighed a healthy eight pounds and was given by his mother a solid, sensible name: John David Carmichael. After his birth, to escape the inevitable frictions, she moved out of her parents' apartment on West Forty-seventh Street, in Manhattan, and found a basement apartment that she could only just barely afford in Elmhurst, near the subway station. When the owner, who lived on the first floor, brought up the subject of a deposit, the amount to equal two months' rent, she stared at him, not saying a thing. He stared back. So they climbed the stairs to his apartment and laid the sleeping infant on the man's plaid couch (he was a widower and it showed) and went into the bedroom.

She was all of eighteen, no skills, and would be living from month to month on food stamps and the small allowance doled out by welfare. Her first order of business, then, once she had moved in her few material possessions from Manhattan, was to wean John David from her breasts, and this she accomplished very quickly, stoically enduring his tears of protest and frustration, although as a consolation to the child she continued to keep him in her bed. Satisfied that her son was weaned, she carried him upstairs one evening after dinner and knocked on the widower's door to ask a favor. She rocked the little one in her arms as she explained her idea, then laid him sleeping on the plaid couch and in the bedroom the widower sucked milk from her as a favor, although it was not the one she had climbed the stairs and laid down in his bed for. He was careful not to hurt her with his teeth. The next morning she found a print shop on Grand Avenue and paid to have one thousand business cards printed. She did not know a great deal about the borough of Queens except that in Rego Park and Forest Hills there lived a great many families quite well off, but not so wealthy as to carry a live-in maid on the payroll, according to the widower.

The morning after she picked up her cards, she arose before six, showered and applied liberal amounts of deodorant, only a faint dab of lipstick and blush, put on pressed blue jeans, a brassiere with gauze pads in the cups in case she leaked, and a snow-white sleeveless blouse. On her feet, white tennis shoes. Her hair was parted in the middle and hung long and straight to a point between her shoulder blades. She lifted John David, still asleep since his last wakeup around four, from her bed and carried him to the kitchen to change him on the wooden table she had picked up at a garage sale. Then she packed a blue-and-white-checked plastic bag with a zippered top and shoulder strap, filling it with diapers, boiled and empty milk bottles, a pacifier, powder, jars of baby food, a spoon, a moist washcloth inside a plastic sack. She would buy the milk as needed in the markets of the neighborhoods she planned to canvass.

It was May, and as she emerged into the sunlight of the early morning with the weight of John David on her back, to say nothing of the burden of purse and baby bag, Molly Carmichael felt the tears stand up in her eyes, although the emotion was less one of self-pity (though there was some of that, to be sure) than the consequence of real pain: from her aching breasts to the effort required of a woman barely five feet two, weighing less than one hundred pounds. But the day at that hour was gorgeous, with the small lawns in the neighborhood deepening in color, the flowers leaping from their buds like stunts of magic. Dogs barked and there were people on the sidewalks and for a young and beautiful mother out with her infant, there were many smiles and even voiced compliments.

She rode the local to a stop in Rego Park. She traveled opposite the general direction of most inhabitants of Queens at that hour, which was toward Manhattan, and as a result found a seat, no problem. The Beatles, together with a whole wave of British bands, especially a raucous bunch by the name of the Rolling Stones, had begun to influence the way men wore their hair. She glanced at high school students, only a year or two younger than she was, the boys' hair inching over their ears and their collars, and ached to experience the freedom they seemed to embody. She climbed the subway steps into the sun. She knocked on the doors of red brick and stone homes, handed out her card, trying to smile with the weight of John David on her. The phone number to call evenings was that of the widower, as a favor.

"Honey," a woman said to her, "I think I should tell you: colored women are asking more than that to clean rooms. Would you like a cup of coffee? Something for the baba?"

The woman's name was Zelda, and while Molly Carmichael sipped the rich black coffee and her child nursed at the bottle, Zelda not only wrote down a list of names, addresses and phone numbers, but told her how much was fair to ask for her services. "Never sell yourself short," Zelda instructed her. Then, looking into the face of the small, gutsy girl, she said, "They hurt that much?" So Zelda phoned her doctor for a prescription to dry out the milk in Molly's breasts.

Most of the names and addresses belonged to homes in Forest Hills and within a short time Molly listed all of them as employers. She dusted, vacuumed, cleaned, polished, scrubbed and waxed, with her child within eyesight, or at the worst, in the next room. When she had saved enough to put down a deposit on a telephone, she began to have a sense of herself as an independent woman. She taught herself how to knit and crochet, how to sew well enough to alter her clothes. She brought home books from the library, many of them romances that took place in foreign locales. She continued to keep John David in her bed and sometimes awoke in the darkness, in a lonely needing hour, with the child clutched to her breasts.

When the widower asked her to marry him, she consulted with one of her clients, who helped her find a second-
floor apartment in Middle Village just north of Metropolitan
Avenue, less than a ten-minute walk to the library. She was
off welfare then and had five women working for her. She
kept no real books and paid them in cash, just as she had
insisted upon being paid when she was on her own. On her
tax forms she described herself as a single, white female
doing business as an independent contractor, her records
neatly documented fictions. She bought a television, because
her son, who was attending school now, told her that it was
all his friends talked about, that without one, he felt like a
foreigner.

There was not any man in her life just then, and she
realized to what depths of emptiness she had plummeted
when she awoke one night with John David sprawled against
her back, his hand groping her breasts, his stiff little member
stirring in the cleft of her buttocks.

Shortly thereafter, she permitted herself to be seduced
by, then wedded to, the husband of one of her clients in
Forest Hills. In reality, the marriage to Doctor Bob lasted
little longer than a station break, but for the sake of her son,
who at last learned to sleep alone, Molly remained married
almost three years.

Misty's name derived from a
condition that might have been treatable with medication,
but neither he nor Molly thought it any big deal: he had
hyperactive lachrymal glands that leaked tears regardless of

his emotional state. He was forever dabbing at his eyes with his knuckles. It was Molly (who else?) who first called him Misty.

In the department of brains, he had clearly inherited whatever amount his one-night father had possessed, along with dark and curly-haired good looks. He was a charmer, no question about it, and even at an early age seemed to have persuaded himself that he had a lock on luck, depended upon it. When he was seventeen, repeating his junior year in high school, Molly came home from a trip to Algeria with a present for him, a small oval wooden thing with a harsh human face carved in it, and something beneath the face that looked like lettering. Molly had purchased it in a market from a man in a saffron robe whose French was considerably better than his English. They haggled over the price, pointing and using their fingers to indicate amounts, and when they had come to terms, the man smiled. His teeth were brownish yellow and gleamed like topaz. The man said, as Molly understood it, that the object was made far away to the south, where the people were even darker than he was and wore little clothing. It was said to be a powerful charm, a protection for its possessor, what the dark people to the south called a grigri. She spelled it for Misty, who didn't listen, so amused was he by the fact that it rhymed with "me-me."

Misty had a friend drill—breaking two bits in the process—a hole through the top of it in shop class and stole from the crafts department a noodle of rawhide eighteen inches in length. The wood of the charm was as smooth as soapstone. It hung from the rawhide in the middle of his chest. The broads loved it.

When he graduated from high school, Misty went through a succession of jobs Molly found for him, seldom lasting six months in any one position, because working conflicted too often with his passions: women and the track. Over the years he drifted into a little b&e, something to do between jobs, going into homes on Long Island for cash or anything that could be easily fenced and transported in the car Molly had bought for him. He worked alone and he worked sober and he held steadfastly to a single rule: once inside the house, you open every door, give yourself every possible avenue of escape.

One night, going into a house with his flashlight and plastic garbage sack, he realized that he was not alone, hearing the escalating *click click click* coming up the hallway. He had entered from the patio through an unlocked sliding glass door, after phoning the house repeatedly from a bar and getting no answer, and found himself standing off a kitchen. In his terror he dropped bag and flashlight, clutched instinctively at his grigri, as if to protect it and his very being, and sprang onto a tiled breakfast bar, then reached down to yank open drawers. When the dog, a snarling German shepherd, came up at him on its hind legs, Misty Carmichael plunged a stainless steel carving knife into the animal's mouth and twisted . . . and twisted.

The next day he traveled to a bar in the Red Hook section of Brooklyn and sat in a wooden booth in back, smelling the fumes of the ammonia tabs attached to the urinals and trying to dicker with a man about a gun. He looked at photographs in a three-ring binder that were arranged like snapshots in a family album. The man didn't dicker; Misty paid his price, dabbing at his eyes. He opted for a .380-caliber semiautomatic, because it practically fit in his palm, or so the man told him. The shells were only slightly smaller than those fired by a nine-millimeter. Then it was necessary to agree upon an intermediary, someone both could trust to hold the money and receive the merchandise. They settled quickly on Anthony "Blitz" Focoso, a money lender for the Scorcese organization, arguably the most powerful crime family on the eastern seaboard.

The man who sold guns and Misty Carmichael rapped their knuckles once on the wood table, sealing the deal, and never saw each other again.

With the gun and an old drinking buddy by the name of Frank Mears, Misty began going into liquor stores and all-night convenience shops wearing a stocking over his head and latex gloves he had coaxed a young nurses' aide he was balling to swipe from Physicians Hospital in Jackson Heights. Frank kept the car running and his eyes open. Misty, always, before leaving the car, caressed the amulet. It wasn't worth shit at the track, where he'd been losing lately big time, but in the crunch, it came through, saved his ass in some tight situations. The way Misty's reasoning ran, all he had to do was score big once, and the grigri would cover his behind. In the meantime, a little armed robbery brought in cash, if not as much as he had anticipated. Most important, it meant he didn't have to go to Blitz Focoso for a loan to carry him through his dry streak.

Which he was certain was about to change soon. Mears had made a connection at Belmont who promised to let him in on a boat race, the absolute thing. Then he could move out from under Molly, that cold bitch, out of that confining, whorish, love lair that Bellows walked into whenever his dick got stiff. That posturing and self-satisfied thug that Molly, even as she ridiculed the decor, treated like a visiting god. As if she didn't have a real man living right under her roof.

Now the thing about armed robbery, you needed a little something in your system to get you through that door: that was Misty Carmichael's philosophy. No way he could enter a store, as he did unoccupied homes, stone-cold sober. Just no way. He believed he did his best work dusted, but if he couldn't score any angel dust, cocaine was a reliable substitute, gave him that edge. And that's why he and Frank Mears spent all of last night sitting in a bar on Metropolitan called Punch's Place, waiting for their guy to show, but he never did, and instead of knocking over a liquor store they had watched for the past few days, the two of them got wasted on salty dogs.

It was nine o'clock in the morning of that August day, four hours to post time for the first race, and fifty dollars is all that stood between Misty and scratch city. Fifty dollars, when he had a sure thing going off in the fifth race, a twelve-to-one shot. Mears's guy at the track had guaranteed this one was a boater. Misty sat in the kitchen at the back of the house in his red jockey shorts, stirring sugar into his coffee and staring out the window at what passed for a backyard: a one-car garage and a patch of cement. Molly parked her new Chrysler LeBaron in there, which she was making payments on, and left Misty the aggravation of trying to find a spot on the street for his eleven-year-old Toyota. He added sugar until the coffee was almost the consistency of syrup. The vodka, ebbing from his system, left him feeling raw and shabby, his head churning like the urinals in the Red Hook bar.

Molly—sweet, snotty little Molly—entered the kitchen dressed immaculately in a black skirt and black heels, a neon blue silk blouse, saucer-shaped earrings to match, and a thin gold watch on her wrist. She was something, his mother: used the TV weatherman to break into real estate, then used the money she made there to desert him, her son, at every opportunity, dumping him in the laps of her parents, who regarded him less as a grandchild than as a spark that ignited an old and vicious war. Thank you, Molly, he thought, for the precious memories. He watched her reach into the refrigerator for a bottle of apple-cranberry juice. The scent of her perfume, Ombre Rose, made him uncomfortably aware of his manhood.

Still not saying a word, she opened a cupboard for a glass and dropped ice cubes into it and poured the cranberry-colored juice over them. The juice was the color of her lipstick.

Idly scratching the hair on his chest, a finger lingering to caress the wooden charm, he said, "Hey, Molly, you know what today is?"

She turned around then, standing at the sink, her pert little face acquiring some color. "The same as every other one is, with me cleaning up your messes. In case you've forgotten, as I'm sure you have, you stood outside my bedroom door in the early hours of this morning and peed on it. It's not how I like to be awakened in my own house."

"Your own house, who you kidding?"

He expected her to throw the glass, but she didn't. She turned to show him her profile and lifted the glass, drained it and put it down firmly next to the sink. Then the eyes over the shoulder. "Oh? Is today the day you're going to take responsibility for your life, find a job all by yourself? Or does Mama need to find something for you?"

A bark of laughter escaped him. "Molly, tell you the truth, you were better off with the Hebe. Take your insults. They were ace stuff."

In spite of the situation, she smiled. She had to admit she missed the Jewish guy a little. He knew what it was to be a stranger, to depend upon artifice, even if he failed to find it romantic, unlike Molly. "He said something about you one time, Izzy did, that I'll never forget. He asked me if I knew the difference between a schlemiel and a schlemozzle. I didn't. So he told me a schlemiel, his first day on the job as a waiter, his first customer, he trips bringing out the soup and dumps it all over the customer. That's a schlemiel. The guy with the soup in his lap is the schlemozzle. He said you reminded him of that guy. But you know what, Misty? I think Izzy was being kind. You're closer to what I'd call a putz, somebody who deserves soup in his lap."

Misty laughed. "Better, Molly. Much better. You on the rag or what?"

She glared at him, her eyes just slices of blue.

"Today," he announced, "I'm hitting the big one."

"You're always going to hit the big one, aren't you?"

"Hey, Molly. Think your boyfriend, Big Daddy Bellows, think he'd like to get down on the action?"

"I have a new listing I'm meeting at ten. You know

what the kids these days say, Misty? It's good advice: get a life."

She strode past him with her black leather attaché case and down steps toward the back door.

"You know what my philosophy is?" he called after her. "The same as yours, Molly. You never want to sell yourself short."

Misty Carmichael drove to Spinelli's and parked the rusted yellow Toyota around the corner, off Metropolitan Avenue. He kept asking himself, what choice did he have? The answer was always the same: zip.

He had shaved and lobbed on the cologne, put mousse in his thick black hair and brushed it back, all but a few curls that he let dangle insouciantly over his forehead. He wore a white knit shirt, light gray slacks and black loafers. He still felt sluggish, and in the heat of that August morning, even from the short drive to Spinelli's, his clothes were already clinging, the weight of them like the grip of his sheets whenever he had a bad dream. He dropped a couple slugs into the parking meter and stopped beside it to lift his shirt away from his pecs. Goddamn. First thing he'd do with his winnings, he'd buy himself a car with an air conditioner.

Inside Spinelli's the light seemed the same day or night, a uniform gray. Both Mr. and Mrs. Spinelli were in there this morning, both looking about one hundred years old behind the refrigerated display case containing cheeses and salamis, barely able to see over the top of the case, either one. Mr.

Spinelli had a fringe of white hair around his head like a cutaway of a Hawaiian hula skirt and liver spots on his shiny pate, and he went around his shop most of the time smiling and singing sotto voce, a sound closer to buzzing than music. He generally kept his hearing aid turned off mornings, so he wouldn't have to listen to the soaps and game shows Mrs. Spinelli watched on a twelve-inch color television resting on a milk crate behind the salamis and cheeses. The old woman tended to be an active participant in these programs, haranguing the characters that displeased her, offering solace and advice to her favorites, even screaming warnings. The old man had confided once to Misty that his wife was worse than useless in the midst of these programs, since she was prone to slice, say, a pound of hard salami, wrap it, slap it on the counter, and sit back down, forgetting to collect any money.

Misty waved at the old ones and said, "Ciao."

Mrs. Spinelli didn't see him, so intent was she upon her drama, and Mr. Spinelli certainly didn't hear him, but he came out from behind the cabinet of meats and cheese smiling and buzzing and said, "I don't see you so long a time, Misty. How you mother? I tell my wife, we been marry sixty-one year, I tell her you don't better take me for granted. I got my eye on Molly Carmichael."

"Yeah?" Misty put his hand on the old man's shoulder, the muscle and bone there having all the substance of a chicken wing. He reached over to flip on the hearing aid. "Mr. Spinelli? Lemme give you a piece of advice, if you got the hots for Molly. Be a bastard. Also, you might want to curb your appetite for garlic."

The old man put a dark, dry hand to his mouth and wrinkles fanned out from the corners of his eyes and he made a faint, gasping sound that was laughter. "Oh," he said, "you Irish, you are the ones with words."

Spinelli's sold long loaves of bread in white paper sacks, as well as condiments, spices, fresh fruits and vegetables, pasta in sealed plastic bags. They sold candy too, and chips, dips, all kinds of junk food. In a refrigerated cabinet opposite the case of salamis and cheeses, there were juices, sodas, and beer. Misty reached into the cooler and removed a bottle of Michelob Dry, paid the old man for it, and ambled toward the rear.

There was in back, to Misty's left, a large door with an unlocked padlock on it, the key in the lock, the door leading to a storage room for the excess inventory that needed to be kept chilled as well as, after closing, the day's take from the store. Opposite it was the door to Blitz Focoso's office, and the door was open, as it usually was, and Blitz was in there behind his dark wooden desk. Brown filing cabinets stood against the wall behind his right shoulder, and behind his left loomed the large black safe with its deep, beveled door askew, and inside the safe sat stack upon stack of Scorcese money, available to the needy and desperate at an interest rate of 4 percent on the principal *per week,* no ifs ands or buts.

Blitz had on a wine-colored silk shirt buttoned to his throat, a gold wedding band, and a diamond on his right pinky finger. There were bags under his eyes and he sported the trademark Focoso nose: a prominent slash of flesh above sensual lips. He was on the phone, but he waved Misty in, pointed to a wooden armchair opposite the desk. There were autographed pictures of baseball players pinned to the paneled walls, along with a few photos of lady rock stars, some others that were actresses that Blitz had explained, in a playful moment, emoted more beneath the waist than above the neck. Blitz winked at Misty, leaned forward to squash an unfiltered Philip Morris in the ashtray, pop a throat lozenge, then went back in his chair, pushed the heel of his hand into a receding hairline. He spoke into the phone: "Yeah yeah yeah. So what the fuck?" Let Misty see him roll his eyes, perform an up-and-down motion with his right fist. There was a radio on in the office, a portable sitting on top of the safe, obviously tuned to an oldies station, because Elton John was funking out the one about the yellow brick road. Misty sat in the uncomfortable armchair imagining old man Spinelli buzzing away on the Elton tune. He unscrewed the cap on the Michelob and let the beer trickle in, dissolving the last raw edges of vodka. He dabbed at his eyes, moved about in the chair trying to achieve comfort. There was nothing short of cancer and taxes, he believed, that a cold beer in the morning couldn't save a man from. That was his philosophy.

Blitz hung up the phone and lit another cigarette and leaned back in his chair. "What's doin' with ya, kid? Stop by to shoot the shit, or you got somethin' real for me? I seen about all the VCRs I wanna see."

"I need a loan," said Misty Carmichael, "very short-term."

Blitz took a drag on his cigarette and looked down, somewhere in the crawl space beneath his desk. "Misty, don't do this. I like you, kid. I can talk to my uncle, see maybe if he can't find some work for you."

"I need a few thou, Blitz. I can handle the vigorish, it comes to that. But it won't. I'll have you squared before the day is out."

"Aw Misty." Blitz shook his head, his great nose moving like a weather vane in a crazy atmosphere. "It's the ponies, ain't it, kid?"

"Blitz? A sure fucking thing in the fifth race. Front me the money, I'll let you in on the action. Swear to crise, it's a boater."

"Who says?"

"Frank Mears. I don't know if you know him, but he's gotta guy inside at Belmont, guy owes him one."

"Mears? Yeah, I know Frankie. The two a you, I think you got ten brain cells between you, know enough not to step in front of a bus and that's about it. Forget about the fuckin' ponies, Misty."

"But Blitz"—Misty stopped to dab at his eyes, which were welling up with real emotion—"Blitz, this is a sure thing!"

Blitz Focoso leaned forward, his arms on the desk, and squinted through smoke. "Let me tell you somethin'. There ain't no such thing as a sure thing, ever. There's work and that's all there is. Now get oudda here. Believe me, I'm doin' you a favor."

And in that instant Misty Carmichael saw clearly what was meant to be, something more certain than a boat race, and reached behind for the .380 stuck in his waistband.

Seeing the gun, Blitz Focoso said, "Don't be a fuckin'

idiot. You touch any this money, the Scorceses will hunt you down like a dog."

Misty Carmichael said nothing, just wagged the pistol, his fingers beneath his shirt caressing the cool, smooth object there. Sighing, Blitz Focoso stood and came around the desk, glanced at the muzzle of the gun, then at Misty. There was no anger in his eyes, or fear—only the dead weight of certainty.

"Misty, you're already meat."

With Blitz Focoso locked in the storage cooler, Misty Carmichael filled two grocery sacks and a briefcase with money from the safe and walked past the cooler with the padlock on it, the key in the lock, the faint sound of pounding from within, and on out through the gray light of Spinelli's.

He thought about calling from a pay phone, let the old farts know what they had in the cooler, but would either one of them even hear the phone ringing? Probably not.

Nah.

CHAPTER 2

Abe Stein tore a chunk from his morning bagel and chewed reflectively, his cup of coffee in the other hand. His kid brother Izzy stood at the window looking down at the street, worrying a thumbnail with his teeth. The kid was a swell dresser, but he ruined the image, the way he bit his nails.

"Will ya stop that awready? I'm gonna buy one a them ointments, sneak into your apartment some night, paint it on your nails."

"What'sa matter, Abe?" Izzy came away from the window, flopped in the chair across the desk from this bear of a brother, ten years his senior, who had raised him from the age of eleven and was still trying to run his life, even if he was forty-five. "Zelda, isn't it?"

Abe chomped another bite from his bagel—never any butter or cream cheese—and chewed for several seconds. "I dunno. What I know is there's more important things to life than work. I got some money set aside."

"He's got some money set aside. Abe, look at me. You stop working, you stop living. I know you. Zelda'd tell you just like I'm telling you."

"I dunno, Izzy. She's running outta steam. Just sits there nights on the end of the couch, the TV on, one cigarette after another, leaning on the arm there."

"Get her to a doctor."

"You think I haven't tried? But she's always got an excuse. That Zelda, she's got some imagination, huh? Bad as you that way."

"Get her to a doctor, Abe."

"I guess it's like she says: it's just something she's going through. Yeah, I guess it is. Like she says, hard as she's worked her whole life, she deserves to relax. What's wrong with a little relaxation?"

Izzy Stein put his head back in the chair, stared at the ceiling of the office he had shared with his brother for—what was it?—the past fourteen years, the same suite of rooms in the Argent Towers.

Izzy said, "Whadda you afraid of, Abe?"

Abe and Izzy Stein (born Abraham and Ishmael, respectively) were the sole stockhold-

ers in a company called Long Arm Legal Services, Inc. Their
suite of rooms consisted of a reception area, a conference
room beyond that, while off to the side of the reception area
(to your left as you entered) was the office shared by Abe
and Izzy and a big gray neutered feline by the name of Balzac. The two desks faced each other across a ten-foot corridor of ratty carpet, at one time Navaho white, but now
closer to the color of kitty litter. On each desk was a telephone with three lines and conference-call capability; on
each as well was a computer with keyboard and monitor
wired to a shared printer and telephone modem. On Abe's
desk there was a commodious glass ashtray for the occasional cigar he permitted himself; also, a beer mug full of
ballpoint pens, a stack of yellow legal pads, bagel crumbs
(soon to be disposed of by Balzac), and a framed photograph of Zelda taken in a studio more than twenty years ago.
Other framed photographs hung on the walls above the filing cabinets. Among them: a wedding picture of their
daughter Naomi and her attorney husband, who now lived
in Cherry Park, New Jersey; a picture of their son Seth and
his second wife and her two children by a previous marriage,
all of them trying to live off a policeman's salary in Miami,
Florida, although Seth had ambitions of striking it rich writing police procedurals. Abe read excerpts from his son's
manuscripts and wrote encouragement, telling him he had
his mother's gift.

On Izzy's desk, all he ever looked at, since removing the
photograph of Molly Carmichael, was a faded five-by-seven
of his parents stretched out on a blanket in the Brooklyn
Botanical Gardens; more precisely, it was his father with a
head of wavy hair who was stretched out, resting on his

elbows, his shoes nearest the camera, his trousers belted just beneath his rib cage, wearing a white T-shirt that showed the definition of his chest and upper arms. There was a jaunty smile on his face, some hint of indescribable bliss. Izzy's mother was wearing a polka-dot dress beneath which her legs were tucked, only her bare feet visible, and she was propped on the palm of her hand, evidently gazing at her husband before the picture was taken, turning at the last instant without losing the expression on her face. She had sharp features that generally gave her an air of severity, although in that instant of time, the arrested emotion conveyed a beauty even the most dispassionate spectator would pause before. The picture, a scratchy black-and-white, had been taken less than a month after his father was mustered out of the service, having spent close to three years fighting in World War II, much of it in the rough and tumble of the Italian campaign. Izzy, who was born just about nine months after the taking of this picture, considered the expressions on his parents' faces to be the measure of human happiness.

For a while there, he thought he detected hints and flickers of this simple, if elusive, emotion in the eyes of Molly Carmichael, especially when the two of them traveled and she could shed the burden of worrying about what new shock or shame her son had in store for her. The rotten little shit (in Izzy's opinion) swilled upon something deep within Molly, where the currents of disgrace and even despair have their origins. And that was where he believed he had erred: by making light of Misty, treating him as the petty criminal he most certainly was, and never addressing the dark hold he had on Molly. Bellows, in his simple, straightforward fashion, had seen Misty clearly and whole as a mortal leech, and had told him to his face to stay away from Molly's money, that there would be no more loans, and that if he even asked for one, he could expect to wake up in a hospital. *If* he woke up. Yes, Izzy admitted to himself, that was how to talk to the Mistys of this world.

And he had blown it. Well, it wasn't the first time.

Long Arm Legal Services operated in an iffy area of the law that sometimes made the work interesting, not to say dangerous: Abe and Izzy Stein were licensed skiptracers—or bounty hunters, as they were known in less polite circles. Much of the business they did originated in the Argent Towers, which boasted a goodly number of bail bondsmen and criminal attorneys, two breeds of business people whose clientele almost by definition were not model citizens. Now it so happened that some of these citizens would depart town unannounced, either from some inherent disinclination to pay the attorneys' fees or because they did not like their chances if they came to trial. Skipping town understandably upset the attorney, who had been anticipating a juicy fee and had already devoted time to the case, to say nothing of the bail bondsman when he had committed himself to cover a sizable bond. (In the bail bondsman's situation, he generally required 10 percent of the sum of the bail from the client, as an assurance that the client would indeed appear for his or her court date, because if the client vanished, the bondsman was liable for 100 percent of the bail, and when the bail ran into six figures, bondsmen got agitated and would pay serious amounts to firms like Long Arm to track down, by whatever means, the scumball who violated a sacred trust.) By whatever means meant different things to Abe and Izzy.

By nature a cautious man, Abe Stein relied upon grim

determination and the assistance of the authorities in whatever jurisdiction he was operating; his pursuit was relentless, if somewhat plodding. It was also certain to drive a man of Izzy Stein's temperament slowly nuts. While he loved his brother, Izzy regarded this methodical approach to their business as something akin to walking a high wire with the net stretched six feet beneath it: what was the point, where the thrill? The fact of the matter was that their profession, thanks to computers and the exponential explosion of data, had become very much a sedentary affair, stalking their quarry down a trail of paper. This development, which at first galled Izzy no end, led to a division of labor within Long Arm that addressed both men's inclinations. Thus, while Abe chased paper by means of their computers and phones, the physical apprehensions, where necessary, became solely Izzy's field of endeavor. Because he was an imaginative man, given to the lure of gambling on occasion, his life had its hairy moments.

To look at him, Izzy, a reasonable man might wonder if he had the equipment to do the job. He stood a slim-waisted five ten, four inches shorter than his brother, his black hair tricked out with threads of gray, high temples and eyebrows that were black inverted vees, sharply ironic hoods over his gray eyes. His nose was slender and speared out from his face. When he smiled, his lips never parted, as if the reason for his amusement was something that could not be entirely revealed. Women found him attractive, but less for his looks than his air of illegitimacy, a sweet taint about him, the scent of risk.

But sooner or later, looking at Izzy Stein, a man would have to notice the shoulders, the powerful chest and the sculpture of his upper arms, and conclude, yes, here was a man who could probably handle himself.

On this August morning he had come directly from a shower at the gym, where he worked out whenever he was in town, wearing bleached jeans, old sneakers with no laces, and a peach-colored T-shirt adhering to his torso. He was there to go through the mail with Abe, and if there were any checks, he would run them to the bank. Then he was planning to drive out to the Hamptons, spend the weekend with friends who owned a house there.

That was the plan, until the receptionist buzzed the intercom and Izzy answered, and was told, "It's Ray Sommer. He wonders if you gotta moment."

Pearl Moss had been the receptionist at Long Arm close to a year, ever since Zelda announced her desire to enjoy life a little, get into Manhattan for Broadway matinees, visit the grandchildren, or just plant her feet on the coffee table with a good history book in her hands. As Pearl understood it, Zelda Stein had developed an uncommon (for a woman) interest in warfare, beginning with Vietnam, and had worked her way through countless volumes of literature on Korea, both world wars, the Russian revolution, and the Spanish-American conflict, and was now wading into the American Civil War.

Married to an accountant laboring so far without distinction in a prestigious firm, Pearl Moss was a short, slight woman, a whiz on a word processor, who combed the tabloids weekly to keep abreast of events in the world. She had once mailed a check for a cream guaranteed to enhance her bust and still spent private time with a chunk of quartz, because she subscribed completely to the notion that certain crystals, handled properly, had benevolent powers. As a woman twenty-five years old, who would entrust her fate to the intelligence of mineral life, Pearl Moss was simply unequipped to deal with a person of Zelda Stein's dimensions. She regarded the statuesque woman with the brusque manner and broad shoulders, the voice that sounded like a rusted pulley hoisting a bucket from the wishing well of hell, as an oddity, a freak of nature. Pearl virtually shivered whenever Zelda dropped by the office, as if she were in the presence of someone who had just stepped off the cover of *The Enquirer.*

Upon being reassured that the Ray Sommer who would shortly arrive at Long Arm was the same Ray Sommer profiled a couple years ago in *People* magazine, Pearl Moss excused herself from the office, spent several minutes in the ladies' room down near the elevators, even contemplated removing her wedding band, but didn't. She loved her husband, within reason.

Back behind her desk, Pearl phoned two of her sisters as well as her next-door neighbor, blurting in a hushed voice, "Guess who's coming to the office?"

When the door opened and a tall, solid man with a dark widow's peak entered, wearing a light gray suit so perfect it looked like silk, Pearl Moss recognized him immediately. There were creases in his face, from the sharp ones that cut south off the wings of his nostrils to the corners of his mouth, to the faint fanning at the corners of his eyes.

Pearl Moss said, "Ray Sommer?"

"Why yes. And you are?"

"Pearl," she gulped. "Pearl Moss."

"Pearl," he said. "How nice a name for so delicate a lady. Do you think I could see Abe or Izzy any time soon?"

Pearl Moss mashed the intercom button and watched the man who had appeared in *People* magazine disappear into the office shared by Abe and Izzy Stein. The most famous detective in Queens, maybe all of New York City, who routinely protected the lives of rock stars and athletes, had stood less than five feet away from her.

She phoned her next-door neighbor. "Marie, he's here. I just talked to him. Ray Sommer, that detective. The one in, you know, that we read about in *People.* He's here, right now. Marie? You know what? He's old. Losing his hair, the whole bit. And he isn't as tall as he looked in the magazine. But God, he's got a way, you know what I mean? Say nothing, you can tell the way he walks, he's got buns'd make your mouth water."

Ray Sommer shook hands with Abe and Izzy Stein before walking over to the window looking down on the street, the small charcoal couch there that had become the exclusive sunning parlor for a fat gray cat. Ray Sommer worked his fingers into the flesh of the cat's neck and said, "How's it going, Balzac? They feeding you enough raw beef?"

Izzy, in his jeans and tight T-shirt, had propped himself on the edge of his desk, and Abe, after igniting a match for a cigar, made himself cozy in a flexible armchair behind his desk.

Izzy said, "What's up, Ray?"

Ray Sommer lifted the cat from beneath its forelegs and rubbed noses with the creature, whispered nonsense to it, then lowered it, left it to its own devices. Turning away from the window, he unbuttoned his jacket, plunged his hands into the pockets of his slacks. He took a step away from the window, evidently reluctant to broach the purpose of his visit. Finally saying, "Izzy, you staying out of the soup, are you?"

"Almost two years now. Since that run-in I had in Tucson, the dentist in Forest Hills that jumped bail."

"Yeah," said Ray, "Cox told me about it, guy in homicide."

"D.J.?"

"That's him. He told me it was an orthodontist would put his patients under, little girls, and while they were out, he'd have sex with them."

Izzy shook his head, remembering. "Pretty pathetic, really. Guy never did that much but peek and sniff. I don't recall there was any instance of penetration. Guy didn't have it in him."

"So what happened?"

Izzy smiled, rather enjoying this part of the memory. "Using the computer, Abe had about worked out a way to access Ma Bell's records, but I did it the old-fashioned way. I went through their garbage every night, three, four in the morning. Wasn't long before I had their phone bill."

"Cute, isn't he, Ray?" said Abe, behind a shredding veil of cigar smoke. "And ripe. Did I mention ripe?"

"There's several billings to the same number in Tucson," continued Izzy, "so we give it a shot, the guy answers, we pretend it's a wrong number. I fly out there, arrange for a hotel suite, hire a local guy for muscle, help me drive the skipper back cross-country. Then I phone our dentist, pretend it's a radio station, his number was drawn randomly, and he has one hour to show up for one thousand dollars in cash. People are suckers for prizes, Ray."

"Something for nothing," said Ray Sommer, "the contemporary Grail."

Izzy turned his hands, palms up. "You got it," he said. "The guy shows up and we incarcerate him with bungee cords, handcuffs, a sock in his mouth with surgical tape. Possibly slightly illegal, but all I got to do is drive the guy back to New York, and my methods are moot."

"Uh-huh," said Ray.

"Possibly slightly," repeated Abe Stein, fanning smoke, his chest rumbling with amusement.

Izzy said, "Up the both of you. How am I supposed to know my muscle, one Aristotle Dukes, has a sister who was raped, and when he hears what we're driving the guy back for, he goes bonkers? Time I got him pried loose from the dentist, the guy looked like afterbirth, and the cops were on the door. Part of the deal we struck, I had to bring the muscle back to New York and keep him here. Evidently Aristotle was suspected of committing a bunch of arsons, but the cops couldn't pin any of them on him and were tired of trying. Abe found him work as a bouncer in a club in Ridgewood. I don't think he's torched any buildings out here, has he, Abe?"

"Not so you'd notice," was Abe's jolly reply.

"You are a sick man," said Izzy, who turned in the direction of Ray Sommer. "This is a sick individual, Ray. So Ray, what brings you to Long Arm—or you just slumming?"

Ray lifted a hand to scratch the back of his neck and cleared his throat. "I've been asked to render a favor. It's a service in which I have no expertise, but you two do. Somebody left town with money that didn't belong to him."

Abe Stein, leaning back in his chair, fanned smoke away from his nose and said, "Whadda the cops sayin'?"

Izzy rose, leaned on his hands over Abe's desk, glanced over his shoulder at Ray Sommer, was satisfied by the level gaze of the man, so said, "Wake up, Abe. This isn't a matter you go to the cops. It's business. I got it right so far, Ray?"

"Dead on, Izzy."

Izzy Stein did not move his face, but continued to look down at his bear of a brother. "I hear you might owe the Scorcese family. This have anything to do with that?"

"I'm not here to shit you."

Abe said, "Wait a minute, Izzy. You aren't even seriously considering—"

"How much we talking about?" snapped Izzy, straightening, ignoring his brother.

Ray Sommer said, "It was in the ballpark of two fifty, three hundred thousand that walked. You'd be looking at ten percent of that."

Izzy Stein emitted a long, low whistle. "What happened?"

"Either you guys know Luigi Vacanza's nephew, Blitz Focoso?"

Abe Stein spoke up. "Yeah. It's a slimy little shark, ain't

it? Does its slimy business in back of a little grocery over to Ridgewood there, on Metropolitan near Fresh Pond Road. Did I forget to mention that this nephew of Luigi Vacanza's is slime?"

Ray Sommer, with his hands in the pockets of his slacks, stared at the off-color carpet.

"No, I think you expressed yourself without much equivocation on the subject, Abe," Izzy Stein answered.

"Ray, I gotta tell ya," said Abe Stein. "If somebody took off Blitz, I'd vote to hang a medal on the fucker. Please tell me that's what happened."

"That's what happened. Yesterday morning. Guy waved a pistol in his face, locked him in a walk-in cooler. Time Spinellis realized he was in there, Blitz had frost on his eyebrows and not a whole lot of feeling in his fingers and toes. His nose, I'm told, was the color of red sauce."

"Good. The fucking wop slime. Izzy, we ain't doin' nothin' about nothin' that concerns the Scorceses. Ray, I'm sorry. I'm sorry you got yourself into whatever you got yourself into, but we don't want Scorcese money."

Ray Sommer raised his face, a certain amount of exhaustion visible in it, and perhaps guilt. "If it's anything you want to consider, the money comes from me. I'm the one accepting money from the Scorceses. Not you, me. This puts you under no obligation to the family. Absolutely none."

Abe Stein leaned forward to tamp ash from his cigar. He had a wide, jovial face with a head of dark, wavy hair parted down the middle that he pushed a hand through now, settling back in his flexible chair and sighing. There was no hint of humor in his face. "Fuck where the money's coming from. Whoever delivers this putz, you and I know what his chances are with the Scorcese family. Ray, I know you twenty years, you are a menschy guy. I will include you in my prayers."

"Try to understand," Izzy interjected. "Abe's on a weird roll today. Earlier he was talking about retirement. You see what I mean?"

Ray Sommer walked back to the couch and leaned over the lazing cat, scruffed about its shoulders, behind its ears, and said, "Keep a clean nose, Balzac. God knows, we try."

"Sorry, Ray," said Abe Stein.

"So who's the bozo," Izzy Stein asked, "who walked with Scorcese money, somebody just released from a clinic or what?"

"Guy by the name of Carmichael. John David, but he also goes by the name of Misty. A punk, from all I've learned. Small-time thief that lives with his mother in a house in Ridgewood."

Izzy locked eyes with the old bear. Abe looked away, saying nothing, clearly nonplussed.

"Ray," said Izzy Stein, "let's you and me step into the conference room. Maybe the two of us have something to talk about."

Ray Sommer stared out the window at the street below, the throb and pulse of activity there. "I suppose," he said, "we could start by talking about Molly, couldn't we?"

CHAPTER 3

The conference room was very much as Ray Sommer remembered it from two years ago—really that long?; yes—and entering it now struck him as tantamount to returning to the scene of the crime: it was here that he had acquiesced in a cover-up that had snowballed on him. There was the same ungainly conference table, its ugly veneer further eroded. The same high-backed chairs that compelled their occupants to sit stiffly erect, as if in a principal's office. The filing cabinets, the small brown couch that three overweight DEA officers had packed themselves into on that long-ago morning looking like aspirants to *Guinness*. The same venetian blinds sliced up what little light crept into the room, and the carpet was the used-up color of dried soapsuds. The few straggly plants that had hung in pots in the window had evidently been taken out somewhere and mercifully shot.

Izzy Stein flipped on the switch for the fluorescent lights, closed the door behind them, and took his pen and yellow pad to the nearest chair, gestured for Ray Sommer to seat himself opposite.

Ray Sommer moved around in his chair and said, "Last time I was in this room, I didn't sit down. Now I know why."

"Yeah? I don't remember that, Ray."

"You wouldn't, because you weren't here. Queens DA appropriated your space for a morning. It was a couple years ago, right after the DeLorio kid got whacked outside my office."

Izzy Stein looked down, exercised his ballpoint on the yellow pad in vigorous vertical strokes. He looked up. "Let it go, Ray. Nothing you coulda done. Everybody knows that except you."

"Oh? His mother doesn't give me particularly high marks, and I just happen to share her opinion."

"Meredith DeLorio, isn't it? What'd I read, something about her getting married recently? Wait a minute: to that Polish pub crawler that writes for the *Crusader*."

Ray Sommer said, "Danny Belinski. Actually, he's Czech. A real believer in the institution of marriage. I think it's his fifth. You wouldn't have anything strong to drink in here, would you?"

"A little early, isn't it?"

"Some days it's never early enough."

"I heard," said Izzy Stein, pushing back his chair. "Lemme see what I can find."

They were drinking vodka and soda from beer mugs at eleven in the morning, two men in their forties who would have no trouble finding excuses for their conduct, even as both recognized the probable consequences. Inviting one's own punishment offered the comfort of accepted ritual. Also, for a while, each might experience a temporary mastery, the illusion of being in control.

"Just so you know," said Izzy Stein, "there's nothing going on with me and Molly Carmichael. She's involved with a guy from College Point."

"I know," said Ray Sommer, chewing on an ice cube. "Married man. Pays the mortgage on her house."

Izzy Stein laughed—a brief, brittle expression of amusement. "Leaves her more money to travel. Molly, that's the real romance in her life: escaping the one she's living."

"I've never met the lady, but I understand she's something to look at."

"Yeah, she's something . . . yeah."

Both men finished their drinks and Izzy Stein took the glasses, added ice and vodka. They sat across from each other once more, neither man speaking, alone with his vodka and thoughts.

Izzy Stein lowered his glass and spoke. "What Abe said, about the Scorceses, it's the truth, isn't it? Misty, he winds up in their hands, he's a done cookie."

Ray Sommer looked directly into his eyes. "I didn't ask. If you don't ask, you don't have to know."

"So you stay clean."

"Call it what you like."

Izzy Stein shook his head sadly and stood up to refill their glasses. "I guess we all of us got our monkeys, huh? The way life is. Tell you this right now: only way I agree to the job is money up front for expenses, whether I find the dummy or not."

"How much you looking for, Iz?"

Izzy Stein parceled out the drinks and sat down, calculated, staring at the ceiling. "Three grand, nonrefundable. Guarantees you two weeks of my exclusive time."

"To be deducted from your ten percent if you do turn him up. And in writing."

"Of course."

Ray Sommer put his palms together, fingers and thumbs perfectly aligned, a steeple of flesh, and brushed his nose with it, staring across the table. "You haven't made up your mind, have you?" he said.

"About what?"

"Oh, you'll find Misty. I'd put money on it. In fact, I *am* putting money on it. But the problem you're having, you don't know what you're going to do with him when you do find him. Because you're still in love with his mother."

"It's got nothing to do with it."

Ray Sommer raised his right hand, palm out, and let it drop. "It's got everything to do with it. But I'm still putting my money on you, Iz."

"Then maybe you better start telling me what you *do* know."

Ray Sommer scooted his chair back a few inches, then leaned forward, forearms on the table, glanced in the direction of the venetian blinds and cleared his throat. "It isn't a whole lot. Misty walked out of Spinelli's with his windfall at eleven o'clock. Mrs. Spinelli is sure of it, because the commercials were on between shows, and she saw him go out. It's not till almost noon that Mr. Spinelli steps in back to take a leak and sees the door open to Blitz's office and the safe door open and no Blitz. First he looks in the can, a logical place, but when he doesn't find Blitz there, he goes back out into the store and dithers around there trying to make sense of the situation, and can't, so he tells the old woman. She goes back, hears this faint, uneven rapping, then notices the lock on the storage cooler is closed, which it never is during the day. Voilà, Blitz."

"So he's in there—what, an hour?"

"A little over that, while the old man wrestled with his confusion. Say an hour and fifteen minutes before Blitz had collected himself and could put in a call to his uncle. Another at least forty-five minutes to get the word out around the city. That adds up to something in the neighborhood of a two-hour jump this punk has got on the family."

"To say nothing of a few friendly law-enforcement types."

Ray Sommer nodded slowly. "Yeah, I don't doubt it."

"Means the family's had close to twenty-four hours. When'd the family bring you aboard?"

"This morning. Had time to make a few calls, that's it. Took a little ride with the old man and his son, Lorenzo. Then here. The airports, railway, bus stations are all covered, and apparently the family's confident he didn't slip out during the two-hour gap. So if he ran, he went by car. A—"

"A yellow Toyota the dumb shit's gone through an engine block, because he's too lazy to check the fluids."

"Lazy or stupid or both?"

Izzy Stein had to think about it. "He's one of these guys, his good looks and luck are all he thinks he needs. Doesn't use his head. Why bother, when you're going to hit the next daily double. One of those guys."

"What do you think: he'd run, or try to tough it out here, go under?"

"Run. He's gotta know there's no place he could hide in this town. Not from the Scorceses. Listen, do you know if they've talked to Molly?"

"I know they talked to somebody by the name of Mears. Some other barflies. Two or three ladies he's been seen with. I don't know about the mother."

Izzy Stein lowered his face, cupped a hand over his hooded eyes. "Listen, Ray, let me talk to her. I want you to get on the phone and make it clear to the proper people that I am working for you *only* as long as they stay the fuck away from Molly. I don't want her getting grief."

Ray Sommer hunched his shoulders forward, his hands on the table. "I'll do my best."

Izzy Stein raised his eyes, the edges of his face sharpening. "You hate 'em as much as me and Abe do, don'cha? Some kinda world we live in."

CHAPTER 4

Without any doubt or hesitation, Misty Carmichael had driven to the nearest service station, checked the oil, the transmission and power-steering fluids, the brake fluid and his belts too, even the water for the windshield wipers, having learned something from his experience. The gas tank filled, he pulled the car over next to the air pumps, reached a pressure gauge from his glove compartment, and checked his tire pressure. With his direction in mind he purchased quarts of antifreeze and lined up the white plastic containers behind the driver's seat.

He figured at best upon an hour to get out of the city.

He drove west on Queens Boulevard to the BQE, took it north into Astoria, swept west and north toward the Triborough Bridge, punishing the tires at speeds of sixty and seventy on the potholed terrain. He crossed the George Washington Bridge into New Jersey ten minutes under his time frame, and after paying the toll, laid a heavy foot on the pedal. The enormity of his actions had begun to compute. He was scared, and at the same time he was beginning to think.

He dodged off Interstate 80 once he was through New Jersey, taking 220 south to Altoona, Pennsylvania, where he found a motel, signed in, then drove to the parking lot of a mall, left the Toyota there, and phoned for a taxi. He watched television the whole night, dining on takeout from Kentucky Fried, the .380 lying flat on his thigh. He slept not in the bed, but on the floor, braced with his back to one side of the door, the pistol in his lap, the safety on, but the action cocked.

The next day he drove the Toyota to an Earl Schieb's, had the rust sanded off, the car painted black and driven next door to have the windshield and windows tinted a shade approaching blue ink. That night, back in the mall parking lot, Misty Carmichael lifted some Pennsylvania plates off an elegant Lincoln.

It was important to steal from money, because the people that had it were unfuckingbelievably slow to realize they were as vulnerable as the next schnook. That was Misty's philosophy.

Misty decided to travel exclusively at night, stay off the interstates, driving at a leisurely pace so as not to attract attention. Eating was an annoyance, because he didn't want to sit inside any public place for the length of a meal, so the first thing he did, upon waking in some motel court, was to drive to a fast-food joint, the drive-thru, and that would be his breakfast. Through the night of driving he would sustain himself on items available in all-night convenience stores—microwave hot dogs, chips, chocolate, a six pack of Budweiser. Mornings it would be another drive-thru for dinner. Then off to find a place to crash. Very quickly the inside of the Toyota contained a harvest of crumpled sacks, cups, cartons, plastic lids and straws, a lode of red, white and blue aluminum, and a general reek of old grease, the definitive exhaust of transience.

It was a night in Gulf Port, Illinois, near the banks of the Mississippi and the Iowa border, that Misty Carmichael slid his hand beneath the white knit shirt to clasp the cool smooth wooden thing, asking himself if he was dreaming, or had he seen the dark blue Buick that was now following him into the drive-thru of a Wendy's only this morning, parked in the street across from his motel room. He had to be dreaming; otherwise, what about the car would have attracted his notice? It came to him as he was speaking into the Oz-like device taking his order of one Big Classic, large fries, and a large portion of chili with a giant strawberry shake. It was almost nine-thirty in the evening, the heat heavy with the damp of the river, and this was his breakfast. What had caught his eye that morning, aside from the glass tinted as darkly as his own, were the New York plates above the rear bumper. As he drew up to the take-out window, Misty Carmichael strained to make out the plates on the grille of the Buick. The young woman handing him his sack of food had to tell him twice what he owed her. Those were New York plates, all right.

Misty eased away from the window with his food, rode over the traffic hump, glanced left and right revving the engine, popped the clutch and was out of there tearing rubber. His headlights showed the avenue he was on to be relatively bare of traffic, so he backed off on the accelerator, watching his rearview mirror. The avenue led to the riverfront where he would pick up U.S. 34 to take the tollbridge into Iowa. As he tried to talk himself down off the ledge of paranoia— now where in hell had he been that someone from the family could possibly have been there too?—bright lights leapt into his rearview mirror. Not only headlights, but flashing red ones. Midwest cops in a Buick? No fucking way. Misty stood on the accelerator to run an amber light. The Buick was forced to slow down, but got through the red with its siren and lights. A slight rise, then a shallow slope, and Misty, with a two-block lead, decided to gamble, braking through a ninety-degree right turn that took him away from his destination and into a district of warehouses, the streets empty, but the air rich with the dankness of the river and the sweet, dark provocation of petroleum. There were no street lamps, and he puttered along with his lights off looking for an alley or cul de sac, some place to conceal himself.

The lights sprang on less than one hundred yards behind him. No siren, no phony cop illumination. Just the big dark car bearing down on him. Misty accelerated, leaving the lights off, taking the first street that presented itself, a left, putting his lights on and shifting into third, giving it gas, another left, revving the rpms to four, to five, hitting fourth gear on target for the entrance to the toll bridge, no lights in his rearview mirror.

Five minutes later he was mingling in the late-night traffic of Burlington, Iowa, no sign of a dark Buick with New York plates.

The Buick caught up with him in Omaha, Nebraska, although this time Misty did not feel the panic of the previous encounter, because in Council Bluffs he had purchased from a pawnshop a pair of double-barreled shotguns, the barrels sawed down to the legal limit, and from a gun shop nearby a box of Winchester Super Double X Field Loads. It was fortunate, for the sake of Misty's confidence, that he did not know that the pawnshop was part of a network of small, innocuous businesses engaged in laundering money for the Scorcese organization.

The loaded twelve-gauges lay beside him, the barrels resting on the floorboard, stocks on the seat, the length of them covered by a blanket he'd lifted from the laundry cart of the motel he was just leaving. He recognized the tinted glass, the air of menace. The Buick was parked across the boulevard, perfectly situated to observe the motel's driveway.

Misty shifted into neutral and idled there, unfolded a map to study it between glances at the Buick. It puzzled him somewhat that whoever was in the Buick had not attempted to accost him in the motel, force their way into his room; unless they had only just arrived. That was a possibility. But there was another and more likely reason, and thinking about it convinced him to change his strategy. Driving the secondary roads in order to avoid recognition seemed pointless now that he was being pursued; furthermore, it played into his pursuers' hands. Alone on a desolate stretch of road, that was precisely how they would like to have him. No witnesses and nowhere to run.

Reaching beneath his shirt for the smooth object there, he smiled, then shifted into first gear, let out the clutch, and emerged from the drive going west on the boulevard, no hurry, sticking to the speed limit. In his rearview mirror he watched the Buick execute a U-turn, its headlights falling in behind him. Two things in Misty Carmichael's favor that he had just figured out: they would not kill him until they had the money, and they could not make a move on him in a public place. He drove down the boulevard and turned off it, to circle a Burger King, feeling a craving for a flame-broiled Whopper. While he waited to place his order, he looked at the map, planning his route to U.S. 80. From now on he'd travel the interstate, make better time, in addition to being safe there.

The dark Buick did not follow him through the drive-thru, but waited, idling, alongside the curb.

Misty Carmichael, confident about his assumptions, saw it there and smirked, handing the girl in the ugly uniform a twenty-dollar bill for his sack of food. That the majority of his assumptions throughout his twenty-seven years had proved to be less than accurate did not give him pause. History, or even reality, had never been his strong suit.

Twenty-five miles outside of Omaha, Misty Carmichael was rudely surprised to discover there wasn't much traffic on the interstate at that hour, not in Nebraska. In fact, as far as he could see either ahead or behind, only two cars occupied the road, his and the big dark one rapidly eating away at the distance between them. He pushed the Toyota for all it was worth, the yellow dashes on the asphalt becoming a single bright thread to steer by. The wind streaming through his open window tossed and flung the debris about in his car; his hand slipped repeatedly, jerking the handle to roll up the window. He flipped off the radio as well to concentrate his thinking, because the big car was gaining, close enough now for him to be sure it was the dark blue Buick. It was less than twenty yards behind him.

Fifteen.

Ten.

Misty saw the highway stretch out ahead of him, rolling in straight easy waves as the Buick pulled out to come abreast. He jerked the handle to bring down the window, then reached for one of the shotguns, resting the end of the barrel on the windowsill. That done, he turned off his lights, touched his brakes and got the stock of the shotgun against his shoulder, just as the Buick swept up beside him, and pulled the triggers. The kick from the discharge knocked him back and away from the window, causing him to yank the wheel to the right, and an instant later, having flung the shotgun to the floorboard, he was fighting to hold the car on the shoulder, downshifting, then with his left hand flailing about to find the light switch, the whole time screaming and not hearing a word, hearing only still the roar of the double explosions, gunpowder fumes gnawing at his nostrils. He brought the Toyota to a stop. He turned off his lights once again and sat beneath the stars, listening. He could hear the ticking from the engine, the radiator gradually cooling. As his eyes adjusted, he could see for what seemed miles nothing but the lonesome swell of the land, the alien fields repeating one another, silvery in the moonlight, blue in the shadows. He felt weak and spent and so alone. A sob, then a succession of them, took him by surprise. He longed for Molly even as he cursed her aloud; even as he sat there encircled by the vast darkness.

He listened awhile longer, then climbed out of the car with the loaded shotgun, the .380 tucked in his waistband. He stayed along the shoulder, prepared to dive into the deep grass that descended away from it. He walked down, then up a rise, down it and up another before he made out the Buick on the far side of the median, sitting broadside in the opposite three lanes. He took his time stealing up on it. Crouching behind a rear bumper, next to the New York license plate, he could hear groaning from within. He moved up the car on the side opposite the driver's seat, poked the barrel through the shattered window in the direction of the groaning, and squeezed the trigger.

Once he had recovered from the concussion, Misty Carmichael stole back up to the Buick and listened. It was quiet in there. Perfectly quiet. He reached for the smooth cool wooden thing beneath his shirt and caressed it with the ball of his thumb. He thought about the man in the saffron robe and the smile on his face when he and Molly had concluded their bargaining, the man's teeth the color of topaz. Misty Carmichael imagined the smile to be much like the one he was enjoying—sly and feral and frankly carnal.

Never sell your boy short, Molly. That would be a mistake. A big mistake. *Bitch!*

CHAPTER 5

Izzy Stein lived upstairs in his own apartment above Abe and Zelda, who had owned the red brick duplex in Rego Park close to three decades. His rent amounted to half the original monthly house payment, although the mortgage had long been retired, but what he paid (since Abe never once asked for an increase) was piddling by today's standards. Three hundred dollars a month for three bedrooms, eat-in kitchen, formal dining and living room with a balcony facing Manhattan: a deal like that was enough to incite persons of the cloth to mayhem, let alone a normal working stiff. So Izzy had no complaints. Many were the nights he and Molly Carmichael had lounged on the balcony—she in her slip, or bra and panties, he in his colored briefs—to watch the parade of lights leading into Manhattan, the ultimate show. Molly's benchmark, that glow in the night. He would tell her she was something, and she would tell him maybe in Queens. She would tell him that almost anywhere she went, she could pretend to be something. But not in the City. In Manhattan you couldn't fake it. You had to have unimpeachable credentials or an aptitude for the outrageous, and she had neither.

So they gazed at it from the balcony in Rego Park. They drank in that dream of limitless possibility even as she steadfastly refused to believe in it for herself, much to Izzy's frustration. "C'mon," Izzy would say to her. "I'll take you to the Plaza. We'll spend the weekend. I'll bring my Armani suits and we'll strut down Fifth Avenue, me and you, knock 'em dead. Take in a Broadway show. Dine at the Four Seasons. Let them see what they been missing."

And she would give him this up-from-under look, her lips shaped less by amusement than irony, and drawl, "Iz, I know my limitations."

"Limitations, schlimitations."

"Shut up and make love to me."

Thus they shared years of amicable dissent leavened by the wonder of passion. They recalled songs together on that balcony and sang them, or attempted to, songs from the sixties like "Turn, Turn, Turn," "Ruby Tuesday," and "Just Like a Woman." Izzy was especially affecting on the Dylan tune about the lady who "fakes just like a woman." Izzy drinking vodka over shaved ice and Molly with her club soda, the two of them engaged in the harmless folly of nostalgia, even as both knew it was a crock.

Once he and Ray Sommer had finished the paperwork, Izzy returned to his apartment for a cold shower, then a hot one, followed that with another brief cold one, and with a towel encompassing his waist, he walked down the carpeted hall to the living room and sat down on the bench before a black Baldwin spinet. His fingers trickled onto the keyboard, feeling their way, his eyes on the ceiling and water dripping from his chin to the hair on his chest, the hair a gun-metal gray. He struck a few chords, and then with his right hand intruded a melody. He sang in a voice closer to a howl, "Nobody feels any pain . . ."

That night, the same night Misty Carmichael left Altoona, Pennsylvania, feeling clever and confident in his newly camouflaged Toyota, Izzy Stein parked his twelve-year-old Ford Mustang in the parking lot of a German restaurant and walked the six blocks in his unlaced sneakers, bleached jeans, a loose cotton shirt with the tails hanging out. Unshaved since yesterday morning, a serious beard was climbing into his face. It was his funky, just-one-of-the-guys look. The shirt he wore was turquoise in color, emphasizing the catlike gray of his eyes.

He walked up the steps and rang the buzzer next to the screen door of the narrow two-story in Ridgewood. Molly Carmichael opened the solid wood door behind the screen one, having identified him through her peephole, and delivered her up-from-under look, her smile for him edged with irony, and said, "This isn't a good idea, Iz."

She was wearing something that appeared to have been

designed for the beach, a raspberry shift with noodle straps over her shoulders, and her luxuriant hair was pulled back severely from her temples. No makeup: her lips pale and the faint spray of freckles beneath her eyes visible even through the screen. Her nipples too, delineated in the raspberry material.

"Molly, how many years we known each other?"

"A lot. Don't forget, we met through Zelda, it was maybe twenty-five years ago."

"I didn't forget. But I was talking about us, you and me."

"Make your point, Iz."

"Then you know when it's business, I'm serious. And this is business."

Molly's eyes fell. "It's Misty, isn't it?"

"Can I come in? Don't worry, I'm not parked anywhere near here. If your friend shows, I'll go out the back. My word on it."

"All right."

He followed her back through the house, the worn carpet and black furniture, a wrought-iron railing where you stepped down into the living-room and dining-room area, through it to the kitchen at the rear with the white wall phone and view of concrete. The motion of her hips beneath the light cotton guided him through the house as if into hypnosis. He took a chair at the table with the black laminate surface and watched Molly Carmichael lean into the refrigerator. "I see some bottles of Michelob," she said, "courtesy of my son. Or there's Dewar's, Iz, I'm sure Carl wouldn't notice."

"Nothing, thanks."

She straightened and turned around, letting the door sift shut. Bringing her eyes up and her lips set in a crippled grin. "No?"

He shook his head. "No. A guy has to know his limitations."

She sauntered over to the table and sat in a chair opposite him, put her hands on the table, her fingers interlocked. The air conditioners in the other room were audible. Molly's perfume swayed in the air of the kitchen.

"Look, I have a good thing going. Maybe as good as it gets for someone like me. You know what I decided about us?"

"Yeah. I made the mistake of believing you wanted a man on your terms."

The smile on her face softened, and she reached across the table to touch his stubbled cheek. "No, Iz. Your *idea* of what my terms were. You would up and leave me, even in the middle of the night, because that was your business. I guess I want a man that *I* can leave . . . and come back to."

"Whoa," he said. "Now there's a fairy tale."

"Oh? Is that what you call what you took for granted for all those years?"

Izzy Stein rested a hand against his forehead, as if to shade his eyes. "I guess it is, isn't it? I guess I'll never win an argument with you, Molly, just like we never walked down Fifth Avenue."

She studied him for some seconds, the crooked grin returning to her face. "Shut up," she said, "and come with me upstairs. I've missed you, Iz. I've really missed you."

Business, thought Izzy Stein, could wait. He pulled her face to his and their lips worked—seeking, exploring, discovering the thrill once more. They held on to the kiss, rising from the table to embrace in the middle of the kitchen, Molly's hands going underneath his shirt, her fingers straining against the back of his ribs. Tears crept from her eyes. He whispered to her, "Same here, Molly. Go ahead. I'll be up in a moment. I need to make a pit stop in your bathroom there."

His eyes followed the motion of her hips out of the kitchen; it was like reading music. From the watch pocket of his jeans he removed a tiny tubular device, shorter than the nail of his pinkie finger and about that color, and attached it, using a screwdriver, inside her wall phone, where it would broadcast every digit dialed out and record every number dialed in. Then he went into the bathroom off the living room and flushed the toilet. Gargled with mouthwash while he was at it.

There was an air conditioner going full tilt in the bedroom window and a good thing too, because Molly Carmichael and Izzy Stein were relentless with one another—grasping, squeezing, demanding, yearning, desperate in their happiness, in the joy of their bodies once more conjoined. Even in the chilled air their skin was slick with sweat as they lay on the sheet, all the covers kicked off, their lips together and hands still groping in the roseate light of the sun descending. Given the years of intimacy they had been frank in their lovemaking and at the same time, because of their separation, there was a certain awkward-ness, the charm of discovery. Molly Carmichael lifted a leg and drew Izzy Stein closer, her calf taut beneath his buttock, her breasts in the damp hair of his chest. "You know what I wish, Iz?"

"You were somewhere else."

She leaned over to chew on his ear and he let his hand roam freely across her fanny.

"Yes," she said. "But with you. You could always make me laugh. Carl wouldn't know if something was funny unless he heard a laugh track."

"Dump him." The words were out of Izzy Stein's mouth faster than he could calculate the ramifications.

She hitched herself up on the heel of her hand to look down at him, her breasts sloping tantalizingly toward his lips, then lowered herself to her elbow, cheek in the palm of her hand. "I think you're serious."

"I think I am," he said.

She moved her face off her hand and placed it on the pillow opposite his. "If you don't mind my asking, what are your intentions, then?"

"If we can't do Fifth Avenue, how about settling for someplace you can always come back to with somebody there waiting."

"Is that marriage you're proposing, Izzy Stein?"

"I guess it is."

"And I'm still free to travel?"

"That's what I said, didn't I?"

"I'll think about it. Now put this back inside me, where it so obviously wants to be."

Molly Carmichael phoned out for Chinese and they sat at the table in the kitchen, Izzy in his briefs and Molly wearing white bikini panties and a short negligee of a blue to match her eyes. The white cartons were lined up in front of them: moo goo gai pan, sweet and sour shrimp, and moo shoo pork, the delicate crepes a tad too moist, but still delicious. And of course a carton of white rice and plastic sack of fortune cookies. Izzy served the food while Molly took care of the drinks—tea for herself, a glass of ice water for Izzy. They sat side by side at the table, poking food into one another's mouths with wooden chopsticks, gabbling about inconsequential matters, and generally behaving like a pair of loons. Both confessed they had not been so happy in a long time.

When they finally admitted to being stuffed, Izzy Stein cleared the table, rinsed the plates and stuck them in the dishwasher along with her cup and his glass. The chopsticks he scrubbed in hot water, then moistened a paper towel with peanut oil to season the sticks. Molly Carmichael sealed what was left in the cartons and put them in the refrigerator.

"Let's get dressed," she said, "and go for a walk. It's not too hot out. C'mon, it'll be good for your digestion."

"*My* digestion? Molly, I'm not an octogenarian."

"Okay. But the two of us together are. It'll do us good."

"Maybe five years ago, sweetheart. This isn't Bellows you're talking to. Forty-five and forty-five adds up to what—a noctogenarian? I think we ought to rent wheelchairs."

"Iz."

"All right. Let's get dressed. It'll certainly make it easier to talk business."

They climbed the stairs to her bedroom to put on their clothes. "Do you remember," she said, as they sorted out their separate pieces of clothing, "the songs we used to sing?"

"Uh-huh."

"That Dylan song you did so well—you really did. But the last stanza, where it says she fakes like a woman, you always leaned on that with your voice. It hurt me when you did that."

He looked at her with his jeans and sneakers on, his shirt in his hands, and said, "Molly? Starting now, just always tell me the truth. Whatever you're feeling, okay? Give me the opportunity to know you."

They walked on the sidewalk beneath street lamps and the broad green crowns of maple trees and ginkgo, the crowns swaying faintly in a breeze that had the smell of approaching rain to it. Izzy walked with his hands in his trouser pockets, his eyes taking in their surroundings, his gait the picture of nonchalance. Molly moved with her arms wrapped beneath her breasts, her hips swaying provocatively, but her torso appeared stiff, unable to follow the music of her hips.

Izzy Stein was saying, "So when Blitz turned him down for a loan, I guess Misty didn't see he had a choice."

Molly Carmichael didn't say anything for several seconds, her half of the conversation consisting of the squeaking of her new L.A. Gear sneakers. Finally she said, "Don't soft-pedal it, Iz. He had a choice. He could have gotten a job. I think we are becoming a country of dreamers, everyone waiting for the big score."

"Well, Misty isn't one of them, not now. He poked a gun in Blitz's face and walked away with a quarter mil in cash, maybe more."

Molly Carmichael put her head down, but kept walking, her pace even a little brisker than before. Izzy Stein could see her shoulders quake and realized that she was crying.

"I'm sorry to be telling you this. What can I say? He's a foolish son of a bitch."

Several steps ahead of him, Molly Carmichael stopped and wheeled, elbows at her ribs and her hands up and apart, pleading, "What can you say? You can begin by explaining where you fit into this. You tell me it's business. Are you working for the Scorcese family now, is that what you're telling me? You're going after my son."

Izzy Stein took ahold of her shoulders, gradually drew her wet face to his chest, stroked the fiercely colored hair. "He's not a little boy anymore, Molly. The reason I'm telling you this is Ray Sommer farmed this job out. The Scorcese family, obviously, they are going to want satisfaction. Now all I'm saying is this: I will do what I can, if I find him, to work a deal. I'm not promising I'll succeed, Molly. But if I'm not looking for him, someone else will be, and they won't give a flying fuck whose son he is. I'll tell you something else: the only reason I took this job is because of who he's the son of. If you want, I haven't cashed Ray's check, say the word, Molly, and I'll walk away from the job."

She pressed her cheek against his chest and said, "Oh, Iz. It feels like my whole life I've been waiting for this to happen. The mess I couldn't clean up. He signed his death warrant, didn't he?"

Izzy Stein pushed his fingers through her hair, pressed his lips to her scalp. "He's going to need a ton of luck, Molly, more than even good people have a right to expect."

It was after midnight when Izzy Stein descended the steps from Molly Carmichael's front door. The air was churning now in anticipation of a storm, the treetops listing and the sky the color of a poorly erased chalkboard. The pinkish light from the street lamps stabbed madly about in the darkness, flailing at the whim of the wind. The air had about it a kind of brutal freshness, like the first blood drawn in a boxing ring. Izzy Stein loosened two buttons on his shirt to let the wind billow it, feeling the air suck round his ribs.

It was several blocks before he was conscious of a car creeping along twenty yards behind him. A few seconds of reflection convinced him it wasn't Carl Bellows, given that gentleman's headfirst approach to matters. And it wasn't the guy he'd hired to sit in his Plymouth all night, monitoring Molly Carmichael's phones (Izzy having planted a transmitter on her bedroom phone as well). So he swung around and stepped into the street; better, he reasoned, if there was going to be a confrontation, to have it within view of his operative in the Plymouth, who presumably would make an effort to assist him.

The car's headlights gradually crowded out the night,

ballooned around him in an eerie glow. Ten feet away the car stopped and the far door swung open, a figure stepped out. The car purred forward and over to park against the curb, shut off its lights. Another figure emerged from the driver's side, a leaner one, both of them approaching now, about the same height, maybe an inch or two taller than Izzy Stein. The stabbing streetlight gave him a glimpse of dark hair and eyes, prominent noses, dark clothing, the heavier one wearing a suit, no tie.

The heavier one spoke when he was a few feet away. "Well, Izzy, you're practically moved in with the lady, aren't you?"

"We've never been introduced, but it's Blitz, isn't it? Ray Sommer explained you had a little problem. Yeah, I been looking into it, see what I can do."

Blitz took a step forward and worked a finger under his collar, as if testing how tightly it fit to his throat. "Yeah? Way I'm told, you spent enough time with her tonight, the two a youse coulda converted Jew to Mick, Mick to Jew, and both a youse to Muslim. Maybe even had time to get laid."

Izzy Stein shrugged. "Whatever it takes to do the job Ray hired me to do."

"Sommer," sneered Blitz Focoso, his tired eyes staring straight into Izzy Stein's, "isn't even in the picture. You wanna say you're working for him, fine. Just remember, that's only sam—what's the word I want?"

The lean guy behind him said, "Samsonite?"

"Semantics," offered Izzy Stein.

"Yeah, it's only a matter of semantics who's paying the freight."

"No," said the lean guy, "that's what Izzy is, is a seman-tic."

"Semite," said Izzy Stein. "Semitic."

"Bennie," said Blitz Focoso, "give it a rest. A guy watches the Saturday-fucking-morning cartoons, I don't ask him for vocabulary lessons. So Izzy, whadda we know?"

"I said I'm working for Ray. Ask him."

Blitz Focoso took two leisurely steps closer, at the same time letting his right hand drag behind him. The right hand sprang up and caught Izzy Stein trying to lean away from it, clipped him across the shell of his right ear with the brass knuckles, dug up his scalp behind it. Izzy Stein stumbled, but steadied himself with the palm of his hand.

"I make myself clear, fuckhead?" said Blitz Focoso.

Izzy Stein spit on the pavement, his fingers feeling the blood, his hearing reverberating, shifting pitches on him. He said, although it sounded like a huge gonging speech, "I see your point of view, Blitz. We'll be in touch."

"We fucking better, Jew boy."

Izzy Stein drove up to the red brick duplex in Rego Park, nursing his ear with a linen nap-kin from the German restaurant he had parked behind. There was an Emergency Medical Service vehicle parked out front, its crimson light pulsing, sloshing an ugly, suggestive color across the brickwork. Rain was beginning to slide from the sky, at first spitting, then gathering strength to slit the darkness, slim panes of driven drops. The shape emerging on the gurney being force-fed the oxygen was familiar. The shade of hair, breadth of shoulders and scope of breasts beneath the white sheet. Zelda.

Izzy Stein charged up the steps and through the open door to the first floor, found his brother in the kitchen hanging up the phone, his maroon bathrobe covered with stains. The big old bear worked a fist in his eye, holding his reading glasses in the other hand. "Abe?"

Abe Stein opened his eyes, as if unable to place the voice, then lunged at his brother, embraced him, sobbing. The robe gave off a sour, visceral smell. "I just called Naomi. It happened so fast, Izzy. She was having some trouble breathing, then she fell asleep there like she does, the end of the couch, and the next thing I know, she's stiff as a six-day-old fish, pitches over onto the coffee table, starts throwing up. I was afraid she'd choke on the vomit. They do, you know. I got 911 on the cellular phone and a ruler between her teeth and just kept her bent face down. I don't know if it was the right thing to do or not. I think I did the Heimlich a couple times to be sure. She's a fighter. She's gonna be okay. That's what I told Naomi. She's a fighter, isn't she, Izzy?"

"She's got more guts'n you and me put together, Abe."

Abe Stein let go of him then, took a step back, blinking tears, brushed his cheek with a paw. His hair looked like a storm-tossed river. "I gotta shower, get dressed, get to the hospital. Could you call Seth?"

"At this hour, Abe?"

"You're right."

"Take your shower. I'll drive you down."

About to take a step, Abe Stein stopped. "Your ear, Izzy. What happened?"

"Somebody entered me in the Vincent van Gogh look-alike contest."

"Who? Vincent who? What, is the world suddenly altogether crazy?"

"Take your shower, Abe. We'll talk about it on the way to the hospital."

"I'm scared, Izzy."

"You ain't alone. Take that shower already."

CHAPTER 6

Stabilized, with an IV affixed to her left arm, tubes up her nostrils, a white triangular pliable rubber mask hanging from an elastic strip around her neck, Zelda Stein reclined in the hospital bed feeling helpless, but not resigned—feeling, if anything, resentment toward her helplessness. The past however many hours, or days, registered as a blur of faces, voices, with only pain and discomfort to give her life definition. Even in her drugged condition, she understood something of what was occurring around her: the tubes, this vile penetration of her throat, had been inserted to draw off fluids that were threatening to fill her lungs; Abe was a constant presence, refusing to leave her side, and there had been visits from Naomi and her husband, the children, Izzy with one of his ears in bandages.

She had tried to speak more than once, but her mouth was full of chalkiness and the effort cost her, so that the nurse, or whomever she attempted to address, pressed the rubber oxygen mask over her mouth until the stress diminished, after which she would lapse into a dreamless sleep.

But this morning (Monday, her third day in the hospital, Abe told her), she could sit up, tilted at a forty-five-degree angle, and even managed to swallow the entirety of her small glass of juice. When she had finished and pointed to the empty glass, her dark brows crimped, Abe told her it was guava-orange. A scraping sound escaped her throat. It was the first time since she had been admitted that she laughed. And it was the first time she managed to speak, her voice sounding like surf heard from a distance.

"Tell Naomi," she gasped, "how fashionable . . . her mother's become . . . in her drinking habits."

The scraping sound again. Abe Stein, his hair uncombed, but his beard shaved, his breath sweet, and his hand infinitely tender, touched her cheek, brushed her forehead with his lips.

Like a big old browsing bear, Zelda thought, exactly how Izzy described him. But he was her bear, her big old sugar bear with a heart as easily breakable as a cookie. Zelda, even drugged, knew what was what. She had sensed its coming. She would just have to walk him through it, step by step; it wasn't all that much different than the preparation for a wedding.

"Laughter is good," he whispered. "Norman Cousins beat the rap with it. So can you, Zelda. Just don't sell yourself short, Zeedee. Okay?"

She lifted the rubber oxygen mask away from her neck,

stretched the elastic, and let it snap back. "This thing," she said, "every time I put it on, I feel like I'm inhaling from some midget's prophylactic."

It was Abe's turn to laugh.

There, thought Zelda, closing her eyes. We've taken the first step.

Monday morning a dark van with porthole windows behind the driver's seat idled in front of a bakery on Metropolitan Avenue. A small man with a face that bespoke antiquity shuffled from the bakery and across the sidewalk, huaraches on his white-stockinged feet, a gray felt hat with a warped brim. A door behind the shotgun side of the van slid open and the small man disappeared behind it. The van eased into the flow of traffic.

It traveled along Metropolitan for a while, then swung to the left into Forest Hills, stopped in front of a stucco row house for a few minutes, until a heavy man with long, thinning red hair emerged. He closed a wood door with stained glass let into it and hobbled along a walkway composed of black flagstone. An ebony cane helped propel him along the walk to the van.

Astride a metallic-blue Yamaha, a 750 cc motorcycle with the kind of acceleration that promoted premature hair loss, Kenny Takimoto felt the engine throb between his thighs, sitting several car lengths behind the van, pretending to concern himself with the chopped style of his hair in a mirror attached to a handlebar. Takimoto was a New York City detective on his day off. He was young for a detective, having earned the gold shield sooner by risking his ass in the trenches, posing as a doper for three years, suffering the strains of a duplicitous life. During that time, his father, a chemist for Hercules in Delaware, had renounced him as a son and died of a heart attack without learning the truth of his mission. And it wasn't clear that his mother would ever forgive him for refusing to reveal that his degradation was only a cover. He had become, in short, at an early age, a man without honor except within a small, acidic coterie: a few real cops like D.J. Cox.

They had been partners now, Cox and Takimoto, for nearly six months, ever since Cox's partner married into money and Takimoto's partner, McClanahan, accidentally electrocuted himself working on a car in his garage. The jolt of energy hadn't killed McClanahan, but it did rearrange his priorities, rendering him ineffectual as a policeman: he spoke in a soft, often quivering voice and followed ladies' tennis tournaments with the fevered, if quiet, intensity one might expect of a stamp collector.

The van pulled out. Kenny Takimoto watched it trundle down the street, waited until it was a full half block away before he engaged the Yamaha's gears. Ever since the attempt on Joe Scorcese's life more than a year ago—the *unexplained* attempt, Kenny Takimoto might add—he had become keenly interested in the little old man with the rumpled hat and creased face, who ran an empire from the back of that van. What had begun as curiosity was developing into something of an obsession, although Kenny Takimoto was intelligent enough to let it go from time to time, just as he was ambitious enough to believe that his persistence might pay dividends. Already he was gaining a reputation within his department as a walking textbook on the Scorcese family, and although he was attached to homicide, it was not unusual for some of the dicks from vice to drop in for the purpose of picking his brain. In an environment where turf and info were fiercely protected, Takimoto freely shared what he knew: even the ones who made dink and gook jokes behind his back respected him for that.

The van was traveling west on Queens Boulevard, adhering strictly to the posted speed limit, which probably meant the man behind the wheel was Cato Dellacroce. Cato looked after the Don, ran errands, and drove vehicles with the studied manner of a driver's-education instructor.

It was hot even at this hour of the morning and Takimoto could feel the sun, smoldering above the ocean, bore into his back. He was wearing a black tank top, cut-off jeans, and rubber thongs on his feet; a nylon fanny pack was strapped to his waist with his shield and a gun zippered in there, snugged against his lean belly. He wore dark glasses and a helmet, only because the law required it, and he juked in and out of traffic with the flair that is the special flag of youth, as if caution and fear were Latin derivatives, words stranded in a dead language. As he accelerated among the cars and trucks and buses, he could feel the air abrade his face, the sweat inching from every pore—only his kneecaps were dry. Dirt and the stench of exhaust assaulted him, but he plunged on at a distance from the van, exhilarated to be doing just this: a cop riding his instincts.

Kenny Takimoto believed in work as an end in itself. It was how you labored to earn forgiveness.

There was a bench seat that faced the porthole window in the sliding door, and on it sat Luigi Vacanza, his hard, brutal hands in his lap, listening to the Don and the fat Jew, the one the younger ones called the Wizard. There was a carpeted partition between the front and the rest of the van, so that the Don communicated with the driver, Cato Dellacroce, by means of a headset. Vacanza, who had twice been the Don's adviser during times of misunderstanding, had been elevated once more, although he was shrewd enough to understand that his position as *consigliere* was nominal. At some point, this honor would devolve to Paul Scorcese, the youngest and cagiest of the sons of the Don. Nevertheless, Vacanza was secure: his daughter was married to the Don's eldest, Angelo, they were living in Phoenix, and a child was on the way.

Because the Wizard was not versed in the language of the island, he and the Don spoke in English. The Wizard had an oxblood leather briefcase open on his lap and plucked from it folder after folder, reading from each one, while the Don sat silently hunched in a corner of the seat, occasionally raising a hand for silence while he spoke into the mouthpiece of the headset. Animation crept into the Don's face when the Wizard commenced reporting on the Las Vegas receipts. It was always so. Las Vegas was now Paul Scorcese's theater of operations, and if Vacanza read the Don's eyes correctly, Paul's efforts there were a matter of great pride to his father.

When the Wizard had finished his recitation concerning

Las Vegas, which the fat Jew with the soft hands was smart enough to save for last, the Don squirmed forward, tugging both on the Wizard's short sleeve (he wore bright, faggy shirts, in Vacanza's opinion, in colors like raspberry, mocha, tangerine, and turquoise) and on the sleeve of Vacanza's black suit, bought for the wedding of his daughter Magda.

"My Pauli," he said, "he's gonna marry a good Catholic girl, this September. Name is Kit, short for Katherine. Her mother play the piano in a symphony orchestra. I have some people look into them. They ain't rich, but they clean. I say to Pauli, forget about it, what do we need with rich? This Kit, she got the charm, she will be an asset to my boy. Whadda ya think, huh? It is a father's good fortune to see all of his sons happily married. Even if that bitch Marybeth, Lorenzo's wife, she give me the fucking heartburn."

The fat Jew embraced the little Don's shoulder, squeezed it, pretending emotion, and murmured something Jewish that sounded as if he were trying to get up a bad oyster.

Vacanza patted the small claw on his sleeve, uttered congratulations in the vowel-rich patois of the island of his birth.

The old man leaned away, releasing them, and spoke into the mouthpiece: "I am a wanna speak to Blitz now."

Cellular phones made business a little less aggravating around the city, because the law couldn't tap them. Anthony Focoso was waiting for the Don's van in a parking lot off Fresh Pond Road, sitting in an air-conditioned, Euroteched white Mercedes, the 500 model, with a white grille, white wheel covers, the rocker panels dropped, a toy spoiler on the trunk, and every bit of glass as darkly tinted as the law permitted. He sat on the front seat, buoyed by the butter-soft leather, wearing a black silk shirt buttoned to his throat and pleated, black silk trousers stylishly, if unnecessarily, held aloft by black suspenders with thin crimson stripes in them. His sport coat, also of silk, a jet matte with specks of crimson, lay folded along the spine of the backseat. Anthony "Blitz" Focoso, thinking about the phone call last night, had reason to feel confident about his meet with the Don. He watched his younger brother Bennie fidgeting with the buttons on the radio, changing stations. Too antsy, that one, too reckless.

Blitz's nephew Ziggy and a sharp driver by the name of Alfred Stedino had caught up with the schmuck Carmichael in Omaha, Nebraska, practically had the slippery fuck in their arms. A tip from a pawnshop in Council Bluffs, Iowa, had brought them in tight on his tailpipe, following him discreetly to a motor court outside Omaha. Blitz instructed his contact (there would be several go-betweens before the message actually reached Ziggy and Alfred Stedino) to tell them to sit tight, until he had spoken to the Don, and by no means should they try to take the guy just the two of them.

The van stopped alongside the Mercedes, on Blitz's side, facing the direction of the toy spoiler. The porthole door slid open, and the smart money guy the Don used climbed out wearing pale brown cotton trousers with plenty of elastic in the waist and kind of a sharp shirt, Blitz Focoso thought, a pullover with a slight turtleneck, a rich pink color with coffee trim on the sleeves and placket. He carried a briefcase and leaned on a black cane, evidently waiting for Blitz to get out of the Mercedes. The man was sweating the moment he hit the morning air.

Blitz felt the heat from the parking lot ignite the soles of his black Bally loafers, a flame of discomfort climbing into his ankles. "I like the shirt, Wiz."

The fat man had a handkerchief in his hand, the brief-case parked between his legs, daubing his moist forehead. "Bought it at Barney's, a fucking fortune like everything else. Bennie, he's not doing anything more important than picking his nose, the Don says he should give me a lift to my office."

Blitz leaned into the Mercedes.

"Thanks," said the Wizard, as Blitz held open the door to the front seat, watched the fat man with the cane deposit himself, arrange his articles.

Blitz Focoso lifted a foot and hoisted himself into the van without any assistance and plopped down on the seat that Joe Scorcese occupied. Vacanza swept the door shut. The van rolled forward.

Blitz Focoso nodded to the Don. "Padrino," he said. "Good news."

"I'm a listen," said the small, shrunken man with no expression whatsoever on his face.

Even as a boy and young man, Blitz Focoso had been a serious, hard-working individual, preferring theft and extortion to the idle pleasures of youth, what the kids on the block devoted themselves to at night:

stickball, hide-and-seek, listening to the radio, spin the bottle, and the one where a group sits in a circle, a sentence is passed in whispers from ear to ear, the final person repeating aloud, usually with hilarious discrepancies, what he or she believed was the message.

Given the number of times Blitz's instructions had to be repeated, what his nephew Ziggy and the driver Alfred Stedino understood their job to be was something entirely different: to pursue and capture the asshole.

The Don, who had been sickly as a child, missing out on the foolishness of that time of life, nevertheless had sufficient imagination not to share Blitz Focoso's confident optimism.

"You tell me good news," said the Don, "but you don't got him, the Misty Carmichael, do you, Blitz?"

"Good as got him, Padrino."

"That is words. How 'bout the money belongs to us: you got that yet?"

"Well. I mean, c'mon. We'll have it."

"More words."

"I thought maybe you'd want some experience out there. Like Vacanza."

"Luigi, I think, is become too tired. Hey, old friend?"

"I am at the Don's disposal at all times."

"You honor me. Blitz, what I think, your nephew and this Stedino fellah, let's see what they are made of. And Blitz? Is a chink on a motorcycle I think is a cop. Find out who he is, where he lives. Take care a some interest you owe on all a missing money. *Capice?*"

"*Sì, capice.*"

The Don flapped his useless hand at him and settled

back in the corner of the seat, evidently exhausted. "Luigi," he murmured, "he will give you the details on a chink."

The small woman with the Irish-sounding name said she was family, and when the supervisory nurse on the floor requested proof, she was instructed to phone Izzy Stein. "Tell him," said the small woman, "it's his fiancée."

Then Molly Carmichael kept walking, found Abe Stein sitting in a vinyl-covered chair that was the color of pureed peas. When Abe stood up, there were slashes visible in the vinyl. "Hi, Abe," she said, putting out her hand, watching it disappear in his. She marveled at the gentleness of his hand, the cool comfort there, like lying down in fresh linen.

Abe put on a game smile for her, stepping aside to offer his chair. "Better," he whispered. "She's been talking today. Got some of the old zip back in her tongue."

Molly Carmichael sat, crossed her legs, looked at the prone figure in the big Stryker bed, the face so pale it gave the impression of threatening to vanish into the pillow. She deposited her purse on the floor beside the chair, rummaged about inside it, and came up with a small black plastic comb.

"Abe? Go ahead, why don't you, stretch your legs, get a drink of water. If you find a mirror, maybe use this on your hair." She shrugged. "Just a thought."

He took the comb, winked at her, leaned over to brush his lips across Zelda's forehead.

There was a television attached to the wall opposite the foot of the bed, the sound turned low, a man and a woman on the screen sharing a long, low desk, each with a sheaf of papers. A local news show. The man and woman were exchanging banter, evidently on the premise that the news was more palatable when delivered by a pair of chirping newlyweds. Molly Carmichael was reminded of the pathetic attempts at humor Doctor Bob inserted into his recitations that always began with a "look at the satellite picture," ghostly swirls above outlines of the states. Doctor Bob might as well have been peering into a crystal ball for all he knew about weather: he relied upon a script and a smile, just like the man and woman chatting between their fifteen-word news flashes. She had seen Doctor Bob not long ago in a commercial for automobile batteries. His acting hadn't improved. He still sounded as if he were talking about thermal depressions and unseasonable highs and the confluence of the elements, and, say, speaking of elements . . . Molly Carmichael distrusted television news, given its reliance upon image and effects, because when you boiled it down, it was a composite of impressions, as balanced and responsible as gossip around a water cooler, maybe less.

Zelda Stein's eyelids fluttered, then opened. "Honey," she said, "please tell me I haven't died and gone to heaven. You look too lovely to be human."

Molly Carmichael rose and leaned over, placed her cheek alongside Zelda's. "Zeedee," she said, "oh Zeedee."

"Look at you," Zelda said. "You look as pure as the day I opened my door a million years ago to this little *shiksa.*"

Molly Carmichael was wearing a white dress with a scoop neck, the shoulders puffed, cut just above the knees, secured up the front with black oval buttons, a strand of onyx beads at her throat and a thin gold watch on one wrist, no other jewelry, not even earrings. She wore no perfume, but after she had bathed, she applied sandalwood oil to her skin, and it was this that Zelda Stein, even with the tubes up her nose, could faintly detect, a smile drifting into her face.

"I must look like perfect hell," Zelda said. "Give me some color, honey. Let me look like a lady for the old bear."

After delving about in her purse, Molly's fingers moved precisely, applying the foundation, powder, accenting Zelda's strong bones with blush. Color was applied to her eyelids, liner deftly drawn, mascara stroked onto the lashes. Zelda spoke as Molly Carmichael worked. Molly brushed her hair. Depilated beneath her chin. Dabbed perfume on Zelda's pulse points. Made her shut up so that she could paint her lips.

Some of what Zelda Stein said she would never forget: "This thing's got me, honey. I know it. I've known it for some time. No reason to bitch and cry about it, since I brought it on myself, smoking like an old locomotive. Do you know how I spent the past year or so? Been reading about men at war. Because war is just another form disease takes. There's no reasoning with it; no escape from it."

Molly Carmichael interrupted. "The holocaust, Zeedee, that was only a disease?"

The woman on the bed shrugged. "You want to dress it up and call it evil, go ahead, I won't object. But the point is, life prevails. It wriggles on. Maybe it isn't always pretty, but it's admirable for its *tenacity,* honey. It's what men at war write large, that fierce desire. God, that's a beautiful thing."

CHAPTER 7

Over the four days, Izzy Stein calculated he had run up several hundred dollars in phone bills and what he got for his money was bupkus. There had been some brief excitement on Sunday when an operative out of a small Baltimore agency found an eleven-year-old yellow Toyota parked outside a Wendy's, even had New York plates on it, but the op phoned back fifteen minutes later to report that the car belonged to a kid from Long Island on his way home from visiting a girlfriend in Charlottesville.

Izzy, who hated eating alone almost as much as he hated hospitals, had been trying Molly's phone number since five-thirty. He dialed her number once more a little before seven, and when her message machine engaged, he said, "Izzy Stein calling for Molly Carmichael. Izzy Stein calling for Molly Carmichael. Miss Carmichael, pick up the white phone please. . . . Darling, it's almost seven o'clock. If you get this message any time soon, how about joining me for dinner at Flamingos? I'm in the mood for swordfish, Cajun style. And other things."

He hung up and dialed the number of St. John's Hospital and was patched through to Zelda's room, Abe picking up on the first ring.

"Abe, it's Izzy. How's our lady?"

"Sharp as ten tacks."

"Really? But that's great. Put her on, lemme give her a hard time."

"She's kinda taking a nap right now. But if you wanna try later."

"I might. Any chance Molly's there?"

"Left about a half hour ago. You two back together?"

"Say where she was going, Abe?"

"Yeah, as a matter of fact, something about dinner with her mother, someplace on Third Avenue, in the city."

"Shit. Her mother. That's all she needs, the walking guilt clinic. You eaten yet?"

"The cafeteria downstairs while Molly was visiting. They gotta pretty good goulash."

"And you've got brass knuckles for taste buds. I'm going to Flamingos, you need to reach me the next hour or so. Then I think I'll revisit some friends of Misty's. Monday night I think I know where I can find at least one of them."

"In other words, you ain't learned zip."

"About the size of it. You be in tomorrow?"

Abe Stein chuckled. "Zeedee threatened to have every bone in my body busted if I wasn't."

Izzy Stein found a spot for his Mustang around the corner from Flamingos and stepped out of it, stretched. The car was riddled with dings and nicks and creases, and bearded along the rear wheel walls with patches of rust, but the V-8 engine beneath the hood hummed as sweetly as any doo-whop chorus, thanks to the ministrations of Marcus Littlejohn, who had a shop on Eliot Avenue. Izzy and Marcus treated the engine like an only child.

Flamingos was filling fast, the crowd already two deep along the bar, but after removing his eyeglasses to study the papers on his lectern, Mario, the host, said the wait for a table for two would be no more than fifteen, twenty minutes.

Izzy stood, sipping a Heineken, watching videotape of memorable pitches, plays, and at-bats from the day games on one of the large-screen televisions. A waiter circulated among the patrons with a platter of deep-fried onion rings, free for the asking. The waiter was an accomplished whistler, and as he stopped in front of Izzy, he performed a lusty rendition of "Take Me out to the Ball Game." Izzy stuck a dollar in the waiter's shirt pocket, snagged a couple of onion rings, and received a snappy *"Grazie!"*

A woman addressed him from a bar stool. "Having any luck, Mr. Stein?"

The woman was blond, somewhere in her twenties,

wearing bleached jeans with strategic rips in them, peeps of firm flesh, and cowboy boots of a color that appeared to be lavender; a white halter top, which did not make a mystery out of her topside dimensions, something only a tent might have accomplished; a white headband and her hair tied in a ponytail; a pretty face in the party-doll mode, and it would probably stay that way for another ten years. She was, or had been, Misty Carmichael's main squeeze, a nurses' aide at Physicians Hospital in Jackson Heights by the name of Karen Santiago.

"Karen," said Izzy, squeezing closer to her, "nice to see you. Heard from Misty?"

Her legs crossed, her back to the bar, she lifted a stemmed glass, a straw poked into what looked like a margarita, and drew some of the drink in before answering. She wagged an index finger. "Always business, this one. Trish, Izzy Stein."

Trish, evidently, was the dark, smaller woman next to her, a face hinting of a Caribbean heritage beneath a wide-brimmed straw hat with a rounded crown. Trish too wore a halter top, if not with so much abundance to advertise, but there was a sinewy quality about her, bones and flesh more in harmony, that Izzy found attractive. She wore a flowing skirt of some crinkled material that fell over her calves, wheat-colored like the halter. Leather thongs on her small dark feet. Sunglasses on her face even in the dim atmosphere of Flamingos.

Izzy put out his hand and felt a warm, dry grip. "Nice to meet you, Trish."

"Likewise, Izzy Stein."

"Onion ring?"

"No, thank you."

"Karen?"

"What, so I can have BO breath? Fahgeddaboudit."

Izzy chomped into the sweet, succulent treat, washed it down with his Heineken.

Leaning forward to run a finger behind his ear, Karen Santiago said, "You shoulda had stitches there. What happened?"

Izzy put his lips close to her, to compensate for the cranked-up volume of music alerting the patrons to the imminence of the ball game. "What happened," he said, "is I got in the way of the people that Misty ripped off. You know, I might just be the only chance he has to stay alive. No fucking around, Karen. If you want him dead, keep freezing me out."

"Whadda ya mean?"

"Talk to his mother. You know Molly?"

"I met her."

"Ask her who she'd want to find Misty first, me or somebody connected with the Scorcese family."

Sucking on her straw, Karen Santiago said nothing. Izzy moved his eyes in Trish's direction. "A guy in trouble, who are you going to trust, his mother or a bunch of mob guys?"

The attractive dark lady called Trish said, "I trust no one, baby. Not even a man I like, like I like you."

"Karen?"

"I haven't heard from him, all right? Honest. Was just making small talk. On account you were standing there and Trish said you looked halfway interesting for a white guy, something about—whaddid you call it?"

There was a smile for him beneath the dark glasses.

"Your aura, baby. The way you stand, your eyes, how you wear your clothes."

"And I go, like, hey, I know the guy. He's a private investor."

"Investigator. Skiptracer, you want to get technical."

"Like I thought," said Trish, "trouble."

Mario signaled to him that a table was available, and Izzy Stein uttered his apologies. Trish said maybe she'd see him around, trailing a fingertip for a moment down his necktie, just enough pressure for him to feel it passing the neighborhood of his heart. Approaching Mario's lectern, he recognized the black man moving his way in the dark suit, white shirt, and hand-painted silk tie. They nodded, laid hands on shoulders, and kept moving. The black man's name was Elvis, and as far as Izzy understood it, he was the brains behind Flamingos. They had bullshitted once over the Darryl Strawberry trade, and that was about the extent of their friendship. At the threshold to the dining area, Izzy Stein stopped to glance over his shoulder. Two young and brawny gentlemen in tight white tennis shorts and Ralph Lauren knits, the shirts with the little polo player on the breast, whose tongues had practically dangled over Izzy's shoulder as he spoke to the women, now vied to impress Karen Santiago. The lady named Trish was greeting Elvis with a kiss on the lips, her dark glasses in the hand that stroked the back of his neck.

Izzy Stein sat in a small booth toward the rear of Flamingos watching the opening inning of the Mets game on a small-screen television projected out from the wall on an apparatus much like the one in Zelda's hospital room. The comparison gave him no more pleasure than dining alone did, but the ball game began with offensive fireworks in both halves of the inning, distracting him enough so that he actually enjoyed the basket of crab legs dipped in garlic butter, followed by an endive salad with lemon juice. He polished off the blackened swordfish, the rice pilaf and braised broccoli, passed on coffee or dessert, but relaxed with a tall glass of ice water. He left a tip in cash and handed his Gold MasterCard to the waiter. He filled in the chit, signed his name, tore off his copy, and left with the Mets in front in the fourth inning. They led by a run.

Karen and Trish were nowhere to be seen.

Emerging from Flamingos, thinking about how he might approach Mears, he was accosted by two men who evidently had been waiting on either side of the door. They were men with meat on their bones, and the older one looked especially mean.

"Izzy?" he said.

"I don't believe we've met."

"We're meeting now. I give the little wop that keeps track of the tables ten bucks to point you out," said the older one with the piston-shaped wrists, pushing his face into Izzy's, "but what I'd like to know, what's this fucking stuff you put on Molly's message machine? I don't think I like your trend of thought, Slim."

The face had blunted edges, a thick head of hair, eyes that suggested that thickness was not an exclusive property of the hair.

The traffic on Queens Boulevard hurtled past, wave upon wave of droning, the insistence of it oddly reassuring, a sign of some fundamental vitality. The street lamps were on, the illumination from them seeping into the night, shedding a shade of bubble-bath pink on the faces of the men on the sidewalk.

"Carl, isn't it?" said Izzy.

"Who the fuck are you, call up my little lady, leave a message like that?"

"An old friend."

"Oh. It's a joke then."

Izzy Stein glanced past Carl's shoulder at the younger one, who was probably an employee, which didn't in any way diminish his potential as a bone breaker. There seemed to be a new style in trouble. From Izzy's experience, instead of threes, it seemed to be traveling in deuces. He made a decision.

"No joke."

"Whadda ya mean? You boffing her?"

"That question is too stupid to dignify with a reply."

The older man looked over his shoulder. "Take a hike, Milt. Won't be but a minute." Then, facing Izzy Stein, he said, "Slim, you look like a bright guy, so I shouldn't have to say this, but I tell you what, go near Molly Carmichael, and your fucking ass will land in a hospital or morgue, one the other."

Izzy stared into the man's eyes, holding his attention. "That kind of threat might work on Misty, but to me, you sound like a sack of shit. Pardon my French."

Carl Bellows waded in then, grabbed Izzy by the throat

of his shirt, the knot of his tie, and pushed his face into Izzy's, his nostrils distended and a vein crawling away from his eye toward his temple. Izzy completed the dance by yanking Bellows even closer, his hands on the material stretched across the bigger man's pectorals, delivering a headbutt to his chin in the instant he pumped a knee into his groin, pushing off from the deadweight, backpedaling, diving into Flamingos.

Mario, after listening to his explanation and looking at the face of a twenty-dollar bill, arranged for his exit from the door off the kitchen. Mario hadn't done badly off him tonight, thought Izzy Stein, striding along the alley. Ten from Bellows, twenty from him. He damn well ought to get a better table next time.

Punch's Place was large for a neighborhood bar in that it could accommodate a full-sized pool table. There was a jukebox, a beautiful old Wurlitzer bathed in golden light, that sat opposite the bar about the middle of the wall. As you entered, the bar was on the left, a long smooth sweep of wood that looked almost butterscotch. The stools were covered in a black vinyl. There were tables for two and four, and in the rear to the right, partitioned off from the doors to the bathrooms, was an area for dart enthusiasts. Around nine o'clock, with the Mets on SportsChannel, it was loud in there. It smelled of smoke, spilled beer and peanuts.

Twenty-four-inch color televisions were mounted at an angle facing down from the ends of the bar, affording those on the stools and those at the tables a view, if not always a great one, of the game.

Tending bar was Iris, Punch Bichler's second wife. Hans "Punch" Bichler had boxed professionally for several years after the war in the late forties, a light heavyweight with an awesome right hand, but a sense of timing so poor that the U.S. mail could have done a better job of delivering his punches. But he was an affable guy, and not without some intelligence, so after an undistinguished career in the ring, he joined his father in the burgeoning business of television sales and repair. While the business made him a rich man, or at least a rich man by Middle Village standards, he gained legendary status as a corner man for the best amateur boxer ever to emerge from Queens, Sal DeLorio. It was Sal's loss in the Golden Gloves finals on points, a decision disputed all over the borough, that prompted Punch to open the bar on Metropolitan Avenue. It was in its own rough way a kind of salon for unreconstructed DeLorio supporters. Twenty-some years later, on the heels of his son's murder, Sal too died violently (a suicide, the police argued, but the coroner demurred), and a wake was held in Punch's. All drinks were a buck. Iris had worked the bar, slamming down drinks and trying to console Punch, who didn't really stop blubbering until he passed out.

Now she pinched a cigarette from the corner of her mouth and exhaled, her overpainted eyes at first narrow, then widening. "Hello there. You were in here, what, last Saturday?"

Straddling a stool, Izzy Stein cocked his head. "Memory like a steel trap. How are you, Iris?"

"Can't complain. Not so good a memory really. But when a man leaves a nice tip."

"How about a cold Heineken? I don't need a glass."

He admired the economy of her moves, the flair with which she snapped the cap. She was a bottle blond, her hair the hue of a trombone, and she looked to be a generous, hearty woman at least twenty years younger than Punch, though about the same weight. She placed the sweating green bottle on a paper napkin and picked up his tenspot. She fanned the bills of his change, stacked three quarters on the paper, and winked. "Next one's on the house."

"It's a deal," he said.

She looked at him, as if hesitating about something.

"Anything the matter?" he inquired.

She put her hands on the bar. They were reddish, and the nails were scarlet and curved like talons, every one of them. "I guess I forgot how good a man looks in a suit and tie. We don't get much a that in here."

He reached over and patted a fine slab of flesh above her elbow. "Iris, don't you be trying to sweet-talk me out of my free drink."

Iris tucked her chin and shook with girlish laughter, something like a locomotive trying to build momentum.

"Shameless hussy," Izzy added.

"Stop," she said, "or I'm gonna pee my pants."

"Brazen slut," he said, just loud enough for her to hear, laughing himself now as she waved one of her taloned hands at him, dabbing at the corner of an eye and waddling off to take the waitress's order.

It had felt good to kid around with the big woman, a

way to ease down off the adrenaline surge from the run-in with Carl Bellows. The skin still stung where he had butted the man's chin, but his head was clear: the front of a man's skull is considerably more durable than a fist. He moved the cold bottle over his forehead. It was safe to assume that Bellows, when his balls stopped throbbing, would not return gracefully to a life of monogamy, which meant that Izzy had simply won the first round. He had a license to carry a concealed weapon and given the drift of Bellows's thinking, he tried to remember the last time he had fired it. Not in at least six months. He needed to get to the range, pump off a hundred or more rounds, then break it and clean it. Abe, who had been a marine, had taught him that: keep a clean piece. It can be the difference.

It was the sixth inning when Izzy, enjoying his house beer, spotted Frank Mears coming through the doorway. There was a young woman with him. Izzy turned his attention to the game to let Mears get comfortable.

The Mets were up by two runs, but the Dodgers had men on first and third, one out, and Strawberry was stepping into the batter's box. The patrons were hurling insults at the Dodgers in general and Darryl Strawberry in particular, calling him everything from a whore to a prima donna. Having so few of them, Queens hangs on to its heroes, even the ones it hates.

Frank Mears had a habit of reaching behind his neck to stroke his long blond tresses, especially when he had drunk too much. From mornings at the beach and afternoons at the track, there was a deep bronze glow to his skin, and he was lean and looked fit except for a swollen left eye, a result of Bennie Focoso not appreciating the answers Frank had for him. The pop in the eye came about from Bennie's short temper, but it also came as a form of relief, since prior to the punch, Bennie had been smacking him in the lower back with the yellow pages, *A* through *L.* Frank Mears had pissed blood for two days.

He still did not feel 100 percent, although the company of his lady friend, Anna, and the three salty dogs he had had at her place contributed to a mood of confidence. Watching Strawberry go down swinging only added to it.

He and Anna took a table toward the rear beyond the jukebox, chairs side by side against the wall with the table in front of them so that they could see one of the television screens. When the waitress arrived, he stuck with salty dogs, but Anna, who had had one at her apartment, switched to light beer. She was a smart chick, Anna, always watched how much she drank. Worked as a dental technician, a steady income there. Frank Mears had met her at Riis Park Beach one Sunday, standing behind her in line waiting to order a knish, striking up a conversation by complimenting her upon the small rose tattooed on her left breast. A few minutes later Frank and Misty Carmichael moved the blanket they were sunning themselves on next to where Anna and her girlfriend, Meryl, were lying on their tummies, their bikini bras undone. Frank went for beer and Misty Carmichael scooched next to Meryl on the blanket, lying on his hip, and asked her if she knew what his philosophy was. Misty was full of philosophy, but the broads seemed to eat it up. It didn't hurt that he had a good body and good tan to go with it. By noon all of them were a little drunk. Misty led Meryl down to the ocean, and they bobbed around out there, looking pretty animated, which was fine with Frank, since it gave him time to put some moves on Anna, although what really loosened her up was the sight of Misty clowning around on the shoreline, twirling his suit on his finger and wearing Meryl's bottoms, his business practically bursting through the fabric. Misty could be a crack-up, no question about it.

Anna bumped her head lazily against his shoulder. "What's so funny?"

"Just thinking about that first day I met you," he said, taking a sip of his drink, his eyes on the television. "Fucking Misty in Meryl's bikini."

"That was rotten," Anna said, but laughed in spite of her sentiments. "Poor Meryl almost drowned waiting for him to stop goofing around."

"Fucking Misty. I miss the bastard already."

"I'm glad to hear that, Frank," said someone dragging a chair up beside him, "because he's a guy that needs all the friends he can get."

Frank Mears eyed the intruder as he curled some of the long blond hair at his nape around a finger. "You," he said to Izzy Stein. "Look, hair ball, I don't know nothin' more'n I didn't know the last time you hassled my ass."

"Maybe you forgot something the last time. After all, you had a lot on your mind: that beautiful eye of yours, for one. And I heard that wasn't the only place you got smacked. Guy with sore kidneys, I could excuse a guy like that if he forgot something. C'mon. Buy you and the lady a drink? I'm sorry, miss, but we haven't been introduced. The name's Izzy Stein."

The young woman with dark hair leaned forward, but did not smile, commit herself. "Anna," she said. "You pardon me, I have to visit the ladies'."

As she strolled away toward the bathrooms, Izzy signaled to the waitress, ordered a round for the table. Frank Mears slouched in his chair, eyes on the television, toying with his hair.

"You see me whacking you with any phone books? No. I'm buying you a drink, trying to be civil."

Frank Mears finished his salty and moved his eyes, saying nothing, staring impatiently in the direction of the waitress.

"Frank, all the facts, or at least the ones I know, support the idea it was impulsive, what Misty pulled off, and not something he planned. Okay? I'm on your side: no way did you know anything about it." Izzy kept his voice low and pleasant, full of reassurance. "Now, Misty plays the horses, he's a believer in the big score. You're a horse player yourself. The two of you, you must've talked, bullshitted around, what you would do if you hit it big. Frank, I'm talking to you."

"I'm listening."

"Good. We're making progress. Now try to work some thinking into your act. Two guys dreaming aloud. What did Misty talk about doing if he scored?"

Anna had returned to the table just as Izzy asked the question.

Frank Mears, one hand playing with his hair, the other

embracing Anna, said, "I told you. All kindsa shit. You asked me that question last time."

"No, I didn't. I asked you what *you* thought he might do. My mistake."

The drinks arrived, were distributed, and Izzy paid for them. Frank Mears dived into his salty dog. Anna lit a cigarette. She leaned forward. "Izzy?" she said. "Frank's a little trashed. But if it's any help, the first time I met him, he told this girlfriend of mine, Misty said if he hit it, he'd go someplace where the sun was, like some island, or maybe Mexico, where it was cheap. Follow the sun, he said, that was his philosophy."

Frank Mears leaned toward her and snarled, "Why don't you shut the fuck up?"

Izzy Stein reached over and grabbed the abundance of blond hair on Frank Mears's neck, cranked a handful of it hard and down, and said, "Frank, I don't know if it's lack of manners or lack of sense, but it's a wonder you get through a day without someone kicking your dumb ass. You and Misty, you're a matched set."

Izzy Stein finished his beer at the bar as an alternative to dragging Frank Mears outside and knocking him around for the sheer pleasure of the exercise. Besides, he had become reconciled to the view that if Misty Carmichael had left any clue as to his predispositions, Frank Mears was simply too fucking stupid to have registered it. At least Anna had given him a glimpse of Misty's thinking. The idiot could be headed toward Florida, the Caribbean, Mexico, or the southwest. Cut a few degrees off the compass of his search, probably reduced it to no more than a few million square miles.

Outside, in the warm, damp air, the armpit feel of it, Izzy Stein was about to climb into the Mustang when the beeper on his belt was activated. He read the phone number to be called and recognized it as belonging to the operative in the Plymouth. He reentered Punch's Place, asked Iris if he could use the phone, and she plunked it on the bar with the stipulation that he stay on it no longer than a minute, or he owed her a kiss. He leaned across the bar and pecked her on the mouth and said, "How about if I pay in advance?"

She emitted more girlish laughter and pushed a hand through her trombone hair, thoroughly enjoying the razzing up and down the bar.

The voice at the other end of the line sounded tense with excitement. "It's him. Calling from—lemme see—area code three-oh-three. Give me a minute I'll look it—"

"Settle, Harvey. Settle. You recording?" It was one of the most common and maddening flubs: operatives, sitting for days on a tap, bored out of their skulls, become almost anesthetized by the routine, prone to getting caught with their pants down. "Harve?"

"Shit!"

"I was afraid of that. Recording now though, aren't you?"

"I am, yes, now I am. Izzy, goddammit, I'm sorry."

Izzy Stein tried to keep the anger out of his voice. "Should be there no more than ten minutes."

He put the receiver down carefully, took a deep breath,

and thanked Iris for the use of her phone. Outside he walked to the Mustang without haste. He would let Harvey repeat the part of the conversation that wasn't on tape, then listen to the recording. Yes, that's what he would do. Spy upon the woman he loved, who trusted him. But it was for her own good. Sure it was.

Then he would drive back to the apartment in Rego Park and take a long, hot shower.

CHAPTER 8

The Plymouth smelled of hot coffee and sandwich material going stale, of old fruit and too many cigarettes; but strongest was the reek of urine. Izzy Stein noticed the half-gallon milk carton leaned against the transmission hump when he climbed into the car, and even though Harvey emptied it after employing it, a residue—and hence, an odor—clung to the carton. The air of uncleanliness suited Izzy's frame of mind.

Harvey Wendt had grown up on Flatbush Avenue in Brooklyn, a scrappy little Jewish guy who still said "dese" and "dem" even as he peppered his conversation with comments upon the likes of Spinoza and the Stoics, Rabelais, the

Nihilists and Rosicrucians. He had married a girl from Elmhurst, Queens, living upstairs from her parents in a row house for five years, then moved into a house of their own one block over. He drove a bus for twenty-three years until the day a glue-sniffing punk, a skinny *shvartzer* with a gold stud earring embedded in his right nostril, climbed aboard and stuck a handgun in his face, demanding not only his wallet, but his goddamn sneakers—name-brand types his eldest daughter had bought him for a birthday less than a week before. It had blown him out that the kid was more serious about his shoes than the contents of his wallet. All he could say to the police who questioned him after was, "You believe the mentality? I don't fucking believe it." He submitted his resignation, effective immediately, and took his pension, then found a job delivering dry cleaning. He worked four days a week, and the hours were flexible, because the owner of the dry cleaner's was a first cousin of Zelda Stein. Abe and Izzy, if not steady employers, paid better, and Harvey Wendt enjoyed the secretive nature of his work, anything not to be exposed to a nutzoid public.

Harvey sat in the heat and humidity in a tank top, shorts, what looked like bedroom slippers, his flesh pale in the darkness, shins narrow and bright as knife blades. A black yarmulke rested on his crown and a Marlboro light between his lips. He was a terrier of a man with snakelike muscles in his upper arms.

Light filled the window in Molly's bedroom, but the rest of the house was dark, its high, narrow profile accentuating its air of vulnerability. Izzy Stein slumped in the seat, his eyes focused upon the light in the window, as if it were in the power of yearning to elicit some sign of forgiveness. He was stalling, and he knew it. Whether from modesty or out of some deep dread, Izzy had always been reluctant to probe the relationship between Molly and her son.

His silence was making Harvey Wendt uncomfortable, and the small man tossed his cigarette out the window and squirmed on the seat. "Iz, I'm really goddamn sorry—" He stopped, seeing the gesture from Izzy, a lazy swipe of his hand in the air.

"It happened. It's done." His voice sounded to him flat, distant. Still watching the light in the window, he said, "Tell me what you heard the best you can up to when you started recording. Don't summarize. Their words, not yours."

"You got it. Dat area code? It's Colorado, mosta Colorado. Guy's prob'ly, be my guess, in Denver."

"Harve? Just what you heard, okay?"

"Hey, no problem." The small man shook a cigarette from the pack lying on the dash, flipped open a lighter for it, and settled into the corner formed by the seat and door. Smoke threaded away from his lips. "It's him. I hear him first," putting Flatbush spin on the word, transforming it into *foist.* "He's sayin', 'You know who dis is?' And dere's dis silence. She don't say nuttin. He goes, 'Molly, you dere?' She goes, 'Yes.' He goes somethin' like, I don't remember the exact words: 'Try not to get too fuckin' excited about it.' She goes, 'Where are you? Are you all right?' He goes, 'Great. For just about gettin' fuckin' killed.' And she goes, somethin' like, 'What'd you expect?' And right den you called me, so I coulda missed a few tings in dere. You want I should start the tape?"

Izzy Stein shook his head and closed his eyes, willing himself not to look at the light. "No, just a minute. He said he was just about killed. He didn't say he *could* be killed?"

The small man was adamant. "No. No way."

The Scorcese family, with its network of eyes and ears, evidently had a sizable jump on Izzy Stein. And if they caught up with Misty before he did, disposing of him in their usual brisk fashion, then Ray Sommer wouldn't see a penny of the ten percent finder's fee, meaning the three grand he'd already paid would come out of his pocket. Tough shit, Ray. It's the world we live in.

Izzy Stein's gaze returned to the light in the bedroom window. Molly's bedroom. The woman he loved. He was hauling quite a load of guilt tonight. Maybe what he'd do, he'd return the three thou, less the cost of his phone calls. Yeah, that lightened the load a little. Not much, but a little.

"All right, Harve, let's hear the tape."

Harvey Wendt, in Izzy's considered opinion, had missed more than a few things.

Izzy recognized Misty's voice immediately.

". . . to me there. That shouldn't be too difficult."

Then Molly's voice, weary and edged with sorrow. Or was it resignation?

"No. You're right. Then what?"

"Kinduva switch, huh? Me dumping you. Now you got nothing to run away from."

"That isn't true and that isn't fair." (Something unintelligible that Izzy suspected were sobs.) ". . . isn't fair."

"Blow it out your ass, Molly. You don't have an audience, it's just me. Save it for Bellows."

(More sobs.)

"Just keep your mind focused on the money. Ten grand. I bet you can fly anywhere, stay pretty fancy for ten grand."

(More sobs.)

"Gimme a break," Misty Carmichael said, and hung up.

Izzy Stein listened to the tape, still turning, still recording the sound of Molly Carmichael crying. He searched his memory and couldn't recall having ever heard her this broken, this utterly shaken. Sitting there, his eyes burning, the sound of her desolation released something profound in him: he discovered he just might be capable of killing Misty Carmichael.

Izzy asked Harvey Wendt to rewind and replay the tape. They listened to it twice more. A rendezvous had been agreed upon, wherever "there" was— that much Izzy was willing to believe. And evidently, for her trouble, there was money in it for Molly. Ten thousand dollars. Not, from his knowledge, that she would have asked for it. No, that was Misty rubbing her face in it, manipulating and at the same time insulting her. The son of a bitch never did pass up an opportunity to piss on her.

Izzy Stein, fumbling for the handle to extricate himself from the Plymouth, realized his hands were shaking.

"Sit tight, Harve. You did good."

"Thanks. It won't happen again. I'm here till two den?"

Izzy glanced at his watch, saw it was almost eleven o'clock. "Stay here as long as the light's on up there. You'll still be paid a full shift."

"Hey," Harvey Wendt objected, "no—"

The red light on the computerized phone intercept blinked, registering an outgoing call. The digits being dialed appeared on a small silver screen, about the width and length of a bandage for a razor nick. Izzy Stein recognized the phone number Molly Carmichael was trying to reach. It was his.

There was a two-car garage beneath one half of the red brick duplex in Rego Park and Abe's car was there, a three-year-old Buick Riviera with seats like a sultan's throne. Izzy punched a button on a plastic dingus that transmitted a pulse to the mechanism that closed the garage door. There was a ten-second delay, time enough for him to emerge, to hike up the drive in the pale moonlight. Winters, it could be a pain entering and departing that garage. It was a short drive and the slope approached forty-five degrees. And whenever there was a sudden melt, the garage was transformed into a wading pool. Same story with heavy rains. An odor presided in there that Izzy associated with the residences of old people, specifically the basement quarters of his mother's parents, who had lived in a brownstone on Manhattan's upper west side. The cloying aroma of gentle deterioration.

He stood at the summit of the drive, between sidewalks, and arched his back, yawning, fingers locked behind his head. Street lamps showered the block with comforting light, with shadows as delicate as lace. Shrubs and flowers that he couldn't readily identify filled the abbreviated front yards with soft dark shapes. Sirens could be heard, and he listened to them with no particular emotion, hearing them only as testimony to the city's ferment, a minor theme in a symphony played day and night throughout his life. He stood there, feeling empty without Molly in his arms, but at the same time reviewing what he had heard on the tape. The fact of the matter being, Molly had never refused Misty's money, only cried about it. Had never committed one way or the other. Commitment not being at the top of Molly's list.

Lights came on, and a car glided up abreast of the drive. Blitz Focoso stepped out of the white Mercedes. "All night I'm looking for you."

Izzy Stein let his hands drop, moved his shoulders.

"Relax, Izzy. We're onna same team."

Izzy brought a hand up, pointed behind his ear. "So you told me."

The taller man shrugged. He was dressed all in black, and darkness crept up one side of his face, shadow from the street lamp. Blitz did not smile exactly, merely looked a little less glum. "You weren't paying attention, so I hadda get your attention."

"Uh-huh."

"You makin' any progress?"

"Some." Izzy would risk a beating before he would implicate Molly. "First, from this girlfriend of Frank Mears, I learn it's a good bet Misty's going either south or west. Tonight, a little while ago as a matter of fact, I get word he was spotted in Colorado."

Nothing changed in Blitz's face. He regarded Izzy with his sunken sad eyes and pulled on his chin, thinking about things. "Spotted. What's this spotted business?"

"It's what I've been doing the past few days, Blitz, is phoning other agencies, faxing them a picture of Misty that I got from his mother. Some agent spotted him in the vicinity of Denver, but apparently lost him."

"Lost him. And just how did you get word? I been by your office coupla times tonight and you ain't there."

"This is the telecom age, Blitz. Gotta recording machine in the office that I can call in for my messages, or Abe can. He checked the machine, I guess it was a half hour, forty-five minutes ago, took the message, and got me on the beeper. I was just leaving Punch's Place. I was there because I thought if I made nice to Frank Mears, his memory might improve. It didn't. He's just stone dumb, in my opinion. But like I say, his girlfriend gave me a little something."

Blitz moved his hand over his chin some more. "You're lucky you're making sense, because something about this sounds like you're jerking me around. I don't like being jerked around."

"I don't like it myself. That's why I don't do it."

Blitz's gaze held for a moment, then descended to study the ground between them. "This dumb fuck Misty took out two of our people, sometime last night. State troopers found 'em on the interstate, somewhere outside of Omaha. One of 'em was my sister's son. Me, I didn't hear about it till this afternoon, after I told the Don I could deliver the dummy. So now not only do I gotta go to the Don with my thumb up my ass, this *buffone* has got the law looking for him too. Suppose they gotta witness? Suppose they find him with the money before we do? You gotta sense for what I'm sayin' here?"

"Blitz, I'm giving it my best shot."

The taller man ceased pulling on his chin, leaned toward Izzy, his face half in shadow but clearly desperate, clearly ruthless. "Your best is rapidly becoming not good enough, Iz. I hope you appreciate what I'm tellin' ya."

Without waiting for a response, Anthony Focoso drifted off toward the big white car, the door swinging open for him, and folded himself onto the front seat, closing the door all by himself. The big car murmured off down the block, stately and quiet and full of purpose, like a shark in familiar waters. A breeze of little consequence mucked about with the hot night air, brushed against Izzy Stein's face, as refreshing as grease.

From beneath the door to Zelda and Abe's place, light seeped onto the darkened landing, about the color and depth of a mustache of milk on a child's upper lip. Izzy hesitated, letting his eyes adjust. Abe in his bathrobe was probably hunkered over the coffee table in the living room, a cigar going along with a glass of apple juice on ice, the chessboard out, following that day's match printed in *The New York Times*. Sitting in there grunting, "Huh. Now how . . . ?" Abe had contracted a fascination for chess in the Bobby Fischer era, and its intricacy had become his evening pacifier. Izzy had never observed his brother complete a question in all the years that he carried on this murmured dialogue with himself, sitting alone, thrilled and amazed as the various strategies unfolded. With its implacable logic and structure, but with the possibility of inspired improvisation, chess was to Abe what music did for Izzy. There was a glint of order in the universe neither of them routinely encountered.

The light fanned out across the landing, catching Izzy's heels as he made his way to the stairs.

Abe said, "I saw the slime out there with his fancy car and his fancy clothes. You okay, kid?"

"Don't worry about me. Get some sleep. Keep your strength up."

"Don't worry about you? What's to worry?" From a pocket of his bathrobe he lifted the .357 Magnum he continued to target shoot on a bimonthly basis. "Slime puts a finger on you, and I'd've put a hole through him, you coulda stuck an egg roll in it."

Izzy turned and took a step toward him. "Abe?"

"And if he wasn't carrying, I'da stuck an untraceable piece in his hand. You think you're the only one thinks about emergencies?"

Izzy took another step. "Well, no, I don't think that. It's just . . . you go by the book, Abe."

Abe Stein brushed at his eyes with the gun in his hand. "Try threatening the ones I love."

Izzy took one more step and embraced his brother. He felt the lump of the Magnum dropped back into the pocket against his groin. Abe smelled of fruit and smoke, a combination vaguely like incense.

"How's she doing?" said Izzy.

"Good. Good. We watched part of that preseason Giants game on Monday-night football. She said she'd divorce me tomorrow for Phil Simms. Something about his tenacity."

Upstairs, after a shower, holding a Stoli on shaved ice, Izzy Stein punched a button on his phone to retrieve his messages, and sitting on the side of his bed, heard Molly's voice, the fifth one on the tape.

"It's me, Iz. Molly. You there? I guess not. Iz? It's a little past eleven. I'm sorry I missed you for dinner. If you are home any time soon and get this message, call me. I don't like it here. I want to spend the night with you. There in Rego Park. Is the piano tuned?"

Izzy Stein listened to the rest of his messages, snugged the towel round his waist, and strolled toward the front of the apartment, the balcony, watched the shuttle of lights across the Queensboro Bridge, to and fro, the circuitry between Queens and the City. The sky ranged from a bluish charcoal around Manhattan to jeweler's black velvet up in the stars. In the air the smell of cooked asphalt still lingered, crosscut by the warm sweet scent of recently mowed lawn and the perfume of mysterious flowers. The balcony sufficed to accommodate two plastic folding lounge chairs, some standing space, and room for a hibachi.

There was an extension cord on the phone attached to a wall in the kitchen, and it was on this that Izzy returned the call from Molly Carmichael.

He waited through the message on her machine as she had for his.

"Molly," he said, when the machine beeped, "it's me, Iz."

She picked up before he could finish identifying himself. "Is it okay?" she asked.

"You mean to spend the night? That's not something you should have to ask. Molly, you all right?"

"While I was waiting for you to call, you know who I was listening to?"

Izzy didn't know, but of one thing he was certain: the false air of gaiety probably issued from the bottle of Dewar's belonging to Carl Bellows. It wouldn't have taken much, given Molly's general abstinence. He suspected some of it was shock as well, the one gift Misty was so generous about giving. He heard her saying, ". . . a genius. The one that starts out 'I am a child'?"

"Neil Young, darling."

"Yes. I just said that. You know the line I love?"

"Tell me."

" 'You can't conceive of the pleasure in my smile.' "

"It's a good line," Izzy conceded.

"It's what I could have told you a thousand times over, Iz, but I didn't know the words. And then, we didn't seem to be going anywhere. My fault, I know."

"Both our faults. We thought we were so smart. Owed nobody and nobody owned us."

"I scrubbed floors for your family and friends of your family."

"Not that again," said Izzy Stein. "So you worked on your knees. It was honest work."

"Yes." The voice came down the line, dull and tainted with disgust. "Molly Carmichael can always do what's necessary."

"I'll be there in fifteen minutes," said Izzy.

"No. I'm sorry. My mother still can do a number. I'll call a cab. I may want a drink though, is that all right?"

"I'll be watching for you from the balcony. I'm drinking Stolichnaya, but whatever you're in the mood for, I can arrange for it."

There was silence for a few seconds.

"Molly?"

"I'm going to love you like you've never had it before."

It was past one in the morning when the two of them, having showered together and fixed drinks, opened the sliding glass door and stood on the balcony. It was a little cooler now.

They were quiet for a while watching the lights rippling across the night, hearing the sounds of the night: footsteps down the block, a car door slamming, an agitated dog, sirens in the distance, a squeal of girlish amusement that prompted Molly to put an arm around Izzy's waist, press her cheek into his chest.

There had not been much in the way of talk from the moment they crossed the threshold of his apartment. She had dropped her overnight bag beside the piano, pulled his face to hers for a deep kiss, and with her free hand found the sash of his robe. She was wearing a beach shift similar to the one she had worn the night they had renewed their passion, and beneath it she was wearing nothing except perfume. They had gotten a little crazy right there against the piano, then gone on to the bedroom to prolong what they had, the giving and the taking, the sweet, slow savoring. Then laid there face-to-face, murmuring, until the decision was made to get up and shower.

Now on the balcony they made themselves comfortable on the lounge chairs. Each of them was wrapped in a forest-green bath towel, testimony to a redecorating project Molly had undertaken several years ago. Though he had a certain flair for dressing, Izzy was indifferent to his surroundings, having accumulated before Molly's make-over a collection of amenities that might kindly have been described as eclectic, or as Molly judged them, unfit for human consumption.

Molly took a sip of Scotch and made a face.

"The booze," said Izzy. "What's the occasion?"

"Maybe see what I've been missing."

He pursed his lips and stared out at the stars, not for a minute believing her. "I ran into a friend of yours tonight. Literally," he said.

"A friend?" Then: "Carl?"

"The man himself. Evidently he has a key to your place and no scruples about checking out your phone messages." Izzy stopped, hearing with a heavy sense of irony what he had just said. Tapping her phone, and here he was waxing indignant about the guy's absence of manners. Iz, how do you do it? "Anyway," he finished lamely, "he didn't like the ones I left for you."

Molly had swung her legs off the lounge chair and was

sitting sideways on it, her face pale, intent. "Izzy, he could be a dangerous man."

"So he informed me. He and a friend—somebody he called Milt—were waiting for me when I walked out of Flamingos. He said if I tried to see you, I'd wind up in a hospital, if I was lucky."

"What did you say?"

"Say? I didn't see much point in talking. I kicked him in the stones and got out of there."

"It isn't funny, Iz."

"It wasn't then, that's for sure. Listen, if he's got a key to your place—"

"His place. He owns it."

"That's right. I heard that from someone."

"I don't know if it's age, but it's become easier to write off pride as excess baggage."

Izzy set his drink on the cement and sat up, swiveling to face Molly Carmichael, take her face in his hands. "First, you let your mother beat up on you, then you take up the job. No, Molly. Nobody beats up on you in my presence. Not even you." He eased his fingers into her hair and leaned forward to feel her lips upon his. They took strength and comfort from each other; then he said, "I think we ought to arrange moving you in here. I don't want that guy coming back at you for something I did. The sooner the better, Molly."

With her forehead pressed against his clavicle, she murmured, "Let me think about it. So much . . . There's so much going on in my life right now. I mean, my son. I can't simply abandon him, can I?"

He held her while she cried, wanting to tell her the dumb son of a bitch wasn't worth it. She quieted down, began to hiccup softly, unevenly. He padded to the kitchen, found a roll of paper toweling, brought it out to the balcony, tore off a section, and handed it to her to blow her nose.

After a good deal of honking and dabbing at her eyes, she said, "Oh, Iz. You've got to find him first. Have you any leads or clues or whatever it is you call it?"

"Not much, unless there's something you can tell me."

"Me?"

"If you don't know, I'll tell you. He's heading west. And outside of Omaha, he killed two Scorcese people who were on his tail. It seems the bad guys are way ahead of me."

Molly's eyes became all watery again. "Killed? He killed someone?"

"Two people for the family that were following him wind up dead. So far no witnesses, but the presumption being Misty had something to do with it. They find him, there won't be any sophisticated interrogation."

Molly studied his face, her eyes leaking tears, but said nothing, shutting him out of what she knew about Misty. After a while he suggested they go inside, enjoy the air conditioning. She drew out the piano bench and lifted the cover from the keys. He sat beside her after refreshing his drink, let his fingers drift over the ivory. She settled her head against his shoulder.

" 'I am a child,' " he sang softly, " 'I last awhile . . .' "

Thinking that they were both cheating, selling the other short, and all in the name of love. It was effing sad, he thought, how the two of them had managed to bitch things up.

Molly poured herself another Scotch and they sang some more songs—softly for Abe's sake—and then Molly went into the bathroom to be sick over the toilet.

CHAPTER 9

Tuesday morning, a bright and hot one, Misty Carmichael had fetched up in Cortez, Colorado, having taken U.S. 25 south out of Denver through some pretty tall passes (he thought he saw a sign at one point announcing an elevation above ten thousand feet), then rode 160 west into this sleepy little burg perched more than six thousand feet above sea level, to the Pinecone Motor Court. He had used up two liters of antifreeze alone, not taking any chances with the radiator, to scale the passes, and as he studied the map in his log-cabin-looking room on one of the double beds, the coverlet smelling of air freshener, he reminded himself to purchase more antifreeze for the trek tomorrow. One more day, and then he'd be on a plane far, far away.

Around noon he put on a straw hat with a wide floppy brim that he bought in Denver and a pair of dark glasses, along with some high-heel gray leather cowboy boots he had picked up an hour or so ago in a shop in Durango, and strolled out for some breakfast (in reality, his supper). The heat of the day surprised him, having driven through the night—the air at that altitude capable of cutting to the bone, the threat of snow in it. By daylight he had never seen such lush and intimidating foliage. The spruce and straggly jack pine, the aspen and birch that lined the sudden cavities in the slopes, where even in the day the temperature dropped dramatically, the air imparting the bracing sensation of ice water, this was all new to Misty, and a little dizzying.

He looked up at it now and decided he hated it. It was too quiet, and the shadowy slopes—even in the sunlight there were patches of blue and black and tremulous grays—perpetuated an atmosphere of brooding, of dark and ancient antagonisms. There was enough on Misty's plate without the towering silhouettes of the conifers together with the alien silence. He stroked the hard smooth comforting thing next to his heart.

In Small's Cafe, the one recommended by the lady manager of the Pinecone Motor Court, everyone wore a kind of cowboy hat, even the fucking obvious Indians with their metallic skin and glittering eyes, those flat, abrupt features. Some had feathers stuck in their hatbands, but what Misty couldn't understand was why they would want to try to look like cowboys, their sworn enemies. It didn't make sense. Even the women in here wore the curved brim hats. Boy, everyone wants to be a cowboy. It gave Misty Carmichael the willies.

He sat at the counter on a stool nearest the entrance with the .380 stuck in the waist of his gray trousers, beneath the purple cotton pullover he had purchased in Denver. The white knit shirt had begun to show the effects of his crude laundering, and the black loafers kind of stuck out in this part of the country, or at least that was the excuse he gave himself for spending close to three hundred bucks on the boots. He fancied the high heels, the extra height. Wearing them on the walk to Small's, he felt they conferred that edge that guys like Clint Eastwood had, or that new one with the catlike moves had, the one with the long straight hair and little tail, his name sounded like a bird. On the stool with one hand lolling near his waist, Misty Carmichael tried squinting behind his sunglasses. Seagull was as close as he could come, the name of the new dude with the ponytail.

He ordered a rib eye medium with eggs over easy and home fries, ascertaining that they would be real potatoes and not something nuked out of a box, then ordered a Coors to start the ball rolling. The waitress, a plump little thing in a salmon-colored dress, the standard uniform in here, gave him a look, but scuttled off. She wore a name tag on her left tit that identified her as Meg. Shooting the goops from the Scorcese family (he didn't think it took too much in the way of smarts to figure out who the inhabitants of the dark Buick were) gave him a sense of temporary security. Enough so that he thought the risk minimal of enjoying a real sit-down meal. Man, all that fast food going through you, after a while your mouth got to tasting like recycled grease.

The waitress Meg brought him a cold longneck of Coors and a Coke glass still hot from the dishwasher. He drank from the bottle and kept an eye on the front door.

Seagal, he thought to himself, and grinned. Not Seagull. It was Steven Seagal that was the tall whiplike dude with the martial-arts moves.

Speaking of moves, Misty felt the old familiar squirm, and realized, as a man unaccustomed to the experience, that he hadn't been laid in—how many days was it? Five? A frigging lifetime.

Each of the booths was equipped with a tabletop juke-box, and in the one behind Misty, three women were anguishing over what to select with their quarters. Misty, who was already sitting at an angle to the counter, the better to watch the door, moved his chin onto his shoulder, took them in through his dark glasses. Each wore a white cowboy hat, much smaller than a man's, of course, and the cutest and youngest of the bunch wore jeans and boots and a tie-dyed tank top that showed she had nice, perky ones, not in the same league as Karen Santiago's, but they were there all right, the sweet fruit to be plucked. The other two wore blue-jean skirts and a lot of makeup, and blouses—one with mother-of-pearl snaps, the other with a V of fringe that met between her titties, with more fringe that ran from elbow to wrist. It was the one with the fringe and the overmade mouth (it reminded Misty of the Rolling Stones logo) that turned a bright, expectant face in his direction.

"You there. You handsome thing." *Thang* it sounded like to Misty. "Don't Hank Williams, Junior, just about break every bone in your heart?"

Misty Carmichael said, "Who?"

Fringe turned to her companions across the table. "Will you listen to him? Girls, we got ourselves a bona fide comedian."

Mother-of-pearl, who sat a head higher than little tie-dye, gave him a wink. "Randy Travis, right? Or how 'bout Garth Brooks?"

The way they were sitting, Fringe by herself across from Mother-of-pearl, who was sitting to the inside of the cutie, gave Misty an idea. "Ladies," he said, working up a warm, faintly flirtatious grin, "you got me at a disadvantage. But maybe if I joined you, I'd get an education."

The young, cute one spoke up then: "You're not from around these parts, are you?"

Snatching his glasses from his eyes, Misty Carmichael accepted that as an invitation, stepped away from the stool, and squeezed into the booth next to Fringe with a perfect view of the door, and better yet, he was looking directly into the face of the cutie. She had nice teeth, a nice smile, and she was giving him 100 percent of it. Big round blue eyes and skin so clear, he could imagine she'd just washed it in one of those mountain springwater streams they show you in the Coors commercials. Face a perfect oval, pure and without guile, unlike Molly Carmichael's. Or any broad from Queens for that matter. Dark hair, what he could see of it, cut short so she wouldn't have to mess with it for the interminable time it seemed to take a Queens broad to do it. Karen Santiago, take one example, spent half her free waking time doing something or other with her miles of artificially colored hair. He set the bottle of Coors in front of him, extended his hand, and said, "I'm Johnny Davidson."

"Les," said the cutie, taking his hand. "Short for Leslie."

Mother-of-pearl turned out to be Audrey and Fringe

was Renee. "French," she said, "so there's three *e*'s." Audrey and Les worked in the same office as travel agents, and sometimes conducted Jeep tours into Mesa Verde National Park to visit the cliff dwellings, show the tourists the three- and four-story adobe residences built by the Pueblo Indians inside shallow cliff caves. Les, who had been on the job only a few months, told him most of it, how the Indians climbed ladders every day to the tableland ("that's what *mesa* means, you know, table") to do their farming and how sometime in the thirteenth century this whole civilization suddenly picked up and split, a mystery why to this day. Audrey interrupted at that point to say, "Why hells-bells, girl, it was some icky old famine, no mystery about it, not enough rain made 'em go. Scientologists more less agree." Renee, rapping Misty on the arm and rolling her eyes, chimed in with, "Ancient history, huh Johnny?" But Misty moved his eyes back to meet Les's and told her it was fascinating. Maybe, after her lunch, she could give him a personalized tour. Was that possible?

Her smile exceeded 100 percent. "Johnny," she said, "I'd be delighted. But a personalized tour for one, I have to warn you, is kinda expensive."

"Why don't you let me worry about that."

"Okeydokey."

Misty turned back to Renee, in case there were some ruffled feathers there. "So Renee, you didn't say what it is you do, all dressed up that way." Her eyebrows danced with appreciation. She was Audrey's best friend going back to when they were in fifth grade, her husband was a state senator, and besides raising three good children, she operated a

burgeoning homemade fudge company. As the recitation
wore on, Misty had to combat a desire to restore the sunglasses to his face, in order to close his eyes. Finally, the
woman shut her trap.

Misty Carmichael dumped the rest of his beer down his
throat and put his elbows on the table, leaned forward toward Leslie. "I been on the road a lot recently, seeing different parts of the country. Les, you know what my philosophy
is?"

If he hadn't felt so horny and
stirred by the looks little Leslie was giving him, he'd never
have proposed this trip up to the mesa, because in the first
place, the meal and two bottles of beer left him pleasantly
drowsy, ready for some serious sleep, and the other reason
had to do with the fact that he didn't give a particular shit
about some old Indians and where they didn't live anymore.
But sitting beside her, watching the profile of her face as
they zipped along in the open Jeep, he congratulated himself
for peeling off the hundred-dollar bill, sealing the arrangement. The only problem as they sped through the curves up
the forested slope, the air cool and green in here: it was next
to impossible to talk, you had to shout to say anything. Not
the ideal situation for putting the moves on a lady.

There were signs to follow once they'd gained the summit, and Leslie whipped the pink Jeep expertly over the
asphalt and braked where the sign told them to. They
walked a hard clay trail the color of parchment through
splotches of light, wherever the sun eluded the tall piercing

shapes of the trees. The air smelled dry and piney, and Leslie, with binoculars hanging from a strap round her neck, pointed here and there, identifying the junipers and the piñon pines, and brought his attention to the wildflowers in the distance away from the trail, splashes of faded color. She pointed again. "The juniper there? It produces a blue berry, they use it to make gin. For the flavoring. Or you can use them in the preparation of venison to remove the gamy taste."

Misty Carmichael had to work in his new boots to keep up with her. "Hell's venison?" he said.

She stopped and gave him a smile, nothing sarcastic or arch about it. What a sweet, pure thing she was. "I'm sorry, Johnny. Us country folk take a lotta stuff for granted. Venison is deer meat."

"Lotta deer up here?" he said, not because he cared, but to keep her talking, standing still where he could use his eyes and smile on her instead of tagging along breathlessly behind her.

"Deer, yes, but you can't hunt them. Also a few bears, some mountain lions. But they're more scared of you than anything."

"Snakes?"

"Why heavens yes. But they don't generally come out till night, for the rodents and such."

Misty reached beneath his purple cotton pullover, showed her the pistol in the flat of his hand. "Let me know if you spot one. I'm not comfortable in the presence of snakes."

Leslie looked at the gun, then looked in his eyes.

"That's a concealed weapon. You can do time for that in this state, unless you have a license. Are you in the law-enforcement business, Mr. Johnny Davidson?" Not nervous at all, almost conspiratorial. She shrugged and started walking. "Oh, well. As long as you don't intend to use it on me."

"No," he said, tucking it away and hastening to catch up with her, "it's definitely not my weapon of choice. To use on you."

If she understood or appreciated the innuendo, she showed no indication of it. Kept walking, pointing out things. Juniper again. "The Pueblos probably used it for medicinal purposes, as a diuretic. Clean out the system."

Looking at her ass, the nice arch to it, he thought of various ways he'd like to clean out her system.

They came to a modest railing, something that wouldn't stop a determined child, to peer across a chasm. Several hundred yards away, looking out from where Leslie was pointing, there in the gape of a cliff were crowded structures composed of rocks and adobe, a sandy yellow in color, that reminded Misty Carmichael of a tenement for midgets. Of course, it was far away, and distance can be deceiving, but it looked damned cramped, even by tenement standards. Leslie lifted the binoculars away from her neck and handed them to him. "Here. Have a better look."

"You mean, we can't walk through it, this is as close as we get?"

"Now it is. It used to be you could walk through them, but because the whole thing's so fragile, only archaeologists get in there now."

"Those scientologists have all the fun, huh?" Misty Carmichael fitted the glasses to his eyes, brought the ancient dwellings up close, a few yards away it felt like. They looked at once sophisticated and vulnerable, the kind of elaborate things that kids built from sand at Riis Park. Such a sign of industry, so ultimately doomed. Misty came as close as he ever did to admiring something other than himself.

"Scientologists," Leslie said, "I was kinda hoping you didn't pick up on that. Audrey's a sweetheart, but in some respects—make that most respects—she's dumb as a box of rocks. I hope you don't think, coming from New York and all, that everyone this way is a complete hick."

Talk about a perfect moment. Misty said, "You? Not a chance. I was just thinking how much I'd like to get to know you better. Really know you."

She turned on that sweet smile and took hold of his elbow, started striding away. "You want to walk through something, I can show you the ruins of a kiva."

They climbed into the Jeep and drove across the mesa to a place of scrub and yellow grass bowing faintly to the prevailing wind. There Leslie led him to a shallow ruin enclosed by blackened stones and bits of earth, a narrow protuberance at one end that Leslie explained was where the chimney would have risen. It was a place where the men of the tribe came for important ceremonials, purifying themselves in the confined heat. Again Misty was struck by a sense of the diminutive. Give him some running room, and he felt he could have broad jumped the whole ceremonial space. "Christ," he said, "I think I seen mattresses in Macy's bigger'n this."

"Macy's," said Leslie, "that has the Thanksgiving parade on television before football?"

"That's the one," said Misty, "before it went belly-up."

Facing him alongside the kiva, her hands on her hips, Leslie leaned forward from the waist, the wind stirring what of her hair the cowboy hat didn't hide, and said, "Mattresses, Johnny? You keep making remarks I think you have bed on the brain. Or am I just a hopeless hick?"

He grasped her shoulders gently. "Not in this boy's book."

"Then why don't you offer to take me someplace comfortable, because I'm sure not into fucking in the woods."

See? Wasn't she a precious thing?

Late-afternoon sun laid ribs of buttery light across the brown coverlet on the bed nearest the door. In the far bed, stripped of coverlet, blanket and topsheet, Leslie Rice lay spraddled atop Misty, her cheek beached upon his shoulder as the spasms still twitched through her, damp and feeling absolutely weak as the dry mesa grass in the wind. He had surprised and pleased her by his expertise, his patience, nothing like the usual young guy, you were lucky if he had enough sensitivity to remove his hat. Slam bam, thank you, ma'am. That's why, as a rule, she liked an older man in his forties, even fifties, a guy who has just about given up all hope of feeling himself inside a taut, fresh body, and is so grateful to be there he just keeps giving, wanting it to last. Also, the money was better.

Leslie Rice, recently turned twenty-one, had attended school for two years at the University of Texas at El Paso, majoring in having fun, spent a year with a professor that appreciated her education from the *Kama Sutra,* hacking at vines and breaking her fingernails digging about in the Yuca-

tán, then went off in search of her father, who over the
formative years had written her colorful and amusing letters
from a prison in Florence, Arizona, his place of residence for
almost seven years due to repeated episodes of forgery and
violence. She found him in a small casino in Reno, Nevada,
dealing twenty-one for the house and glad to get it.

She made it clear, when her father floated the idea, that
no way would she move back to Glendale, Arizona, to live
with her mother, a pretty enough woman, but with all the
spirit of a dishrag, and a Mormon to boot. So it was her
father's advice to go stay with her aunt Audrey, who was a
twice-divorced good old gal, always full of ideas, until he
could put together something that would set them up for
life, her father and her.

Earl Warren Rice wasn't doing terrible, pulling down
almost six hundred a week, but it was money the IRS got to
root around in, and so by the time he saw it, it was pigdew,
the way he explained it to Leslie. Which is why he didn't
have any he could send her. But their ship'd come in, she'd
see. In the meantime . . .

She moved a little, a labial caress upon his diminishing
member, and raised her face, her breasts, from his chest, and
peered down at him. "What's this round thing?"

"A grigri," he said, "from someplace in Africa. Supposed to be a kinda charm. My—a woman I know bought it
for me over there in Algeria. I might visit there, find out
what this lettering means. See it there beneath the face? Nobody can tell me what it says. Smooth, huh?"

She held it, moving the ball of her thumb over it. "Very.
It's got some weight to it too."

"Tell you what, that wood, whatever it is, it's harder'n

shit. Whoever carved in it had to have some sharp frigging tools, or a lotta time on their hands."

"It might be worth something," she said, looking from it to him.

"No might about it, Sugarcheeks. It *is*. This baby's been there for me in some tight-ass situations."

She nestled the grigri among the hairs on his chest, touched the tip of his nose with an index finger, gave him her sweet springwater smile. "Such as?"

He shifted beneath her, gently rolling her off, so that he could get out of bed. He pointed at her. "Stay there, I have to take a whiz. Don't move. I don't even want to see a pubic hair outta place."

She smiled. The moment she heard the bathroom door shut, she was off the bed. His trousers were on the floor and she fished the wallet from it, flipped it open and spread the leather panels with her thumbs. A guesstimate: fifteen hundred to two thousand in hundreds. She didn't touch a one. Slipped the wallet back where it belonged and rearranged herself on the bed and thought about what she had seen. A guy with a pistol and lots of cash. A guy, by the way he talked, all the traveling he had done and was going to do, who had a lot more than what she had seen. She called out to him there behind the door, in the sound of a faucet running, "Hurry up, Johnny. I'm not one of those professional models. I think a pube moved."

He came out of the bathroom with a towel in his hands, rubbing it over the skin beneath his Adam's apple, a happy leer on his face. He was a handsome boy, all right. Cocksure. Didn't even stop to check for his wallet. Had probably never paid for it in his life, and had no anticipation of doing so now. Maybe he wouldn't have to. Not right away, that is. She'd let things ride, see where they took her.

He put a knee on the bed, leaned over, put his lips between her legs and did things that made her close her eyes and begin to feel all sweet inside, the way she did a long time ago when her daddy would spank her and then be filled with remorse.

A voice from far away filtered into her consciousness: "Leslie?"

Her eyelids fluttered. "Call me Leslie Ann."

"Leslie Ann." He kissed her navel, kissed beneath her breast and over it, kissed the other one in the same fashion. "Leslie Ann, you like to travel?"

"I like to travel?" Still coming back, approaching, not yet entirely there. "That what you said?"

"It's what I said, Sugarcheeks."

There. "Well, of course, silly, why else become a travel agent?"

He leaned down from above her, kissed her on her lips. "See, I have this idea. Here we are just getting to know each other, having some fun together, and I got to take this business trip tomorrow, fly out of Phoenix. Now I'm thinking to myself I haven't had much sleep, and it's a long drive, much easier for two than one, and a whole lot more pleasurable. How'd you like to see Hawaii?"

"You serious?"

"As a heart attack." He grinned. "Hey, you're the travel agent, get on down there and make us some reservations. Lemme give you some money."

At the agency Leslie Rice booked them on an America West flight direct to Oahu leaving shortly before noon, which meant that they'd have to start driving soon, in order to reach Phoenix with a comfortable cushion of time. She paid for the tickets in cash, using the money Johnny Davidson had given her from his wallet. Then she phoned a number in Nevada.

"That you, Earl?" she said when a man answered.

"Leslie Ann," the man said, "I'm your father, not some John. I got feelings, you know."

"Daddy? Is that better?"

"Much. How you doing there, little girl?"

"I think our ship's come in."

"You little angel."

"If you can purchase a ticket to Oahu, Hawaii, I'll give you the name of the hotel. But it'll have to be your money, Earl, because after taxes, all I take home is pigdew."

CHAPTER 10

The first time Izzy Stein awoke, it wasn't even light out, the dials on his clock glowing. He rolled onto his back, let his hand drift beneath the sheet to touch Molly there in the dark, his hand at rest on her hip, her skin smooth and warm, and listened to her breathing. Poor kid knocked out by a few cocktails. He glanced at the clock again, computing the difference in time zones, and told himself to go back to sleep, there was nothing he could do until—when?—probably nine at the earliest. So go back to sleep.

Sure.

Scratching around in his private parts, Izzy padded barefoot out to the kitchen and drank from a carton of milk.

He stood in the light of the open refrigerator, the carton in his hand, and gazed numbly at nothing. A thought flickered and died, the milk lubricating his drowsiness. He put it away and went back to bed.

The second time he was awakened by Molly having a bad dream, her leg jerking, crying out what sounded like, "I can't!" There was a faint light in the sky now and he could see her face, her eyes clenched, and he leaned over her, stroking her hair, whispering it was okay, she was okay, and then she was quiet, her respiration nice and easy.

The last time was no more than a half hour later, when he was jerked from sleep by the memory of the conversation between Misty and Molly. The ten thousand. What did Molly have to do for ten thousand dollars? He had assumed Misty's words implied a rendezvous, but why was that? It was easier, less risky, to pull off a transaction (what it sounded like: ". . . to me there" linked to a payoff) through the mail, or even by telephone. Or suppose they use an intermediary. He had been thinking these things last night waiting for Molly to arrive in the taxicab, and then later, after she had been sick and passed out and he had carried her, laid her gently on the bed. Lifted her to remove the big green towel. Kissed her on the forehead, the smell of sickness on her breath. What was it the goyim vows were? Something like *in sickness and in health . . .* Give them credit, they knew a little something about love.

The thought flickered once more, the one he had had standing in front of the open refrigerator, only this time it lingered long enough for him to look it over: *No, it has to be a rendezvous between the two of them, because there is nothing left of trust or respect.*

He got up and showered, started the coffee, took a quick inventory of the contents of the refrigerator, slipped on shorts to fetch the paper. It was seven o'clock. He popped vitamins, sipped coffee, skimming the paper, then pulled on clean sweats. Drove to the gym in Forest Hills to stretch and pump iron for ninety minutes, then returned to the apartment to shower.

Molly was gone.

There was a note on the table in the kitchen:

Iz,
Sorry I conked out. Guess I can't carry off the image of the Irish. May I make up for it with dinner this evening my place sixish?

Underneath the note lay a key to the front door, admitting Izzy Stein to the house in Ridgewood.

It wasn't until nine-thirty that anyone answered at the Denver branch of the Pinkerton Agency. Izzy Stein had decided to go for broke. He sat in the office in the Argent Towers looking across desks at his brother, on the phone about a contractor evidently accused of dabbling in extortion, the guy had jumped a hundred-thousand-dollar bond.

The voice of a woman at the other end of the phone said, "This is the Pinkertons. How may we help you?"

"My name is Izzy Stein, and I'm with Long Arm Legal Services outta New York. You gotta guy there name of Phil Fall? He should remember me."

"Your name again please."

What, he wondered, are they all doing the first time you say it, at work on a cure for cancer? He told her again.

"Let me check."

Minutes passed.

"Izzy? This is Phil. How can I help you, partner?"

"I gotta skipper, Phil, traced him to a Colorado area code as of about twelve hours ago. Lemme give you the number, maybe you guys can nail it down. How much to hire two your guys on a daily basis?"

"Give me the number," said the voice in Colorado, and after Izzy read it off to him, he said, "Five hundred the day, Izzy, best I can do. But I can deal you a pair of aces."

Izzy Stein didn't hesitate. "Do it, Phil. I'll fax you a photo of the guy along with his social security number."

"Any chance the guy is wearing a disguise?"

"I doubt it. Loves himself too much the way he is. He may be driving a yellow Toyota, eleven years old, pretty beat to shit, but I wouldn't bank on it. He's probably stolen or bought a new set of wheels by now. But the thing I want you to get across to your guys—two things, I should say. One, he's armed and it looks like he popped a couple guys back in Nebraska. The other thing, he's probably headed toward sunshine, either Mexico or the Coast, so that's where they should concentrate their energy."

"You say so," said Phil Fall in Colorado. "I seem to remember you always did like to roll the dice."

"That's what my brother tells me, but the way I see it, sometimes you gotta go on instinct. Get your aces on it and keep me posted."

"You got it, partner."

Izzy Stein put down the receiver and watched his older brother, listening patiently, hanging in there, in that way he had that drove Izzy crazy.

Izzy stood up to take off his coat. He was wearing a pale suit today, white shirt, loafers the color of wheat, and a silk tie swimming in impressionist hues. He also wore in a holster clipped to his waist, behind his right hip, a nine-millimeter Smith & Wesson, which he removed and laid on the desk next to his phone. Seeing it, Abe Stein lifted his eyes, listening to the contractor's wife on the other end feeding him a line of shit. Abe wore a white shirt, no tie, and three Panamanian cigars racked in the pocket over his heart.

Izzy went over to the window to wrestle with Balzac, keep the big neuter's blood moving. Tugged on its cheeks and the cat brought its teeth to bear on the fat of his palm, a warning, no skin broken, and that was that. Balzac shot off and out the open door to the area where Pearl Moss presided.

And nearly gave her a heart attack.

Poor Pearl, divulging to a cousin the details of the visit from Ray Sommer, saw from the corner of her eye a streak of color, felt claws on her ankles, shrieked, imagining herself the victim of some tabloid creature attack.

Abe Stein hung up the phone, consulted his watch, decided it was time to enjoy a cigar, burn off the air of mendacity he had been breathing, listening to the contractor's wife. When he had it stoked up, he used the cigar to point in the direction of his brother's desk. "Going to the range?" he said amiably.

In his chair, chewing on a nail, Izzy said, "Might."

Abe thought about that. "This have anything to do with the visit from the slime last night?"

"No. Focoso's got more to worry about than me. Anyway, what's he gonna do, besides give me a buncha shit?"

Abe thought about that too. "This is something else then, nothing to do with that kid a Molly's?"

"No. Nothing."

"You gonna tell me?"

"Don't be a kibitzer."

"Kibitzer? Kibitzer he calls me, my own brother."

"Nosy old fart." But Izzy was grinning.

"Nosy? Sure I'm nosy. It's a good nose I got too; it can smell shit clear over in College Point."

"College Point. What's over there?"

"The contractor's wife I was just talking to. Her husband, this *khazer,* doesn't show up for a discovery proceeding yesterday, guy been milking his subs for kickbacks, prob'ly doing it for years. Guy's missing along with some files that were subpoenaed, and the little woman can't imagine where he could be. 'This just isn't like him, Mr. Stein. Carl never ran from anything a day in his life.' "

Izzy Stein thought: no. "Abe, you said the man's name was Carl. Is that what you said?"

Fanning smoke with his free hand, Abe Stein said, "Yeah. Some putz contractor by the name of Carl Bellows."

Then Abe Stein said, "So I said something funny?"

A little after four o'clock Abe
Stein announced that he was packing it in, going to see
Zelda in the hospital, take her the Bruce Catton volumes on
the Civil War that she said she felt well enough to continue
reading. Bellows's wife, he had learned, had family in Wil-
mington, Delaware, and he had arranged for an agency
down there to stake out the house. If Bellows was indeed
staying there, then Izzy would fly down with pleasure to
handle the physical apprehension.

Abe Stein, after going to the window to give Balzac a
good scratching, walked out of the office with a briefcase
containing the Catton volumes and a portfolio of his invest-
ments to review later in the evening. His shoulders and the
small of his back ached, and he was hungry, having eaten
only the one tuna on rye from the deli, the big dill that came
with it, and the diet soda that Zeedee insisted he drink.
What was diet soda anyway, but wet air? He said good night
to Pearl, that little bit of a thing still looking like she'd encountered the Creature from the Black Lagoon.

Going down the hall to the elevator, shaking his head,
he had to laugh at himself. Creature from the Black Lagoon.
There had been a movie by that name when he was nineteen,
twenty, in the service then, and the female lead had been an
actress by the name of Julia Adams. A redhead. Redheads
had a good run in the early fifties. There were a bunch of
them then, but Julia Adams was the one he would remember, because he was in love with her. There in that white
bathing suit floating around in the lagoon, as vulnerable as

only a B-movie maiden would be so brainless as to be. Zelda's hair was a deep shade of red when he met her, and with a certain amount of imagination, one could have said she bore a vague resemblance to the actress: broader shoulders, bigger breasts, nose, a manner that suggested she wouldn't scream at the sight of a mouse—or a lagoon creature, for that matter. No, Zeedee had entirely too much grit to play the shrieking actress part. Closer to a Barbara Stanwyck, a Bette Davis.

At the hospital, walking into his wife's private room, Abe Stein was greeted by Zelda's personal physician, Dr. Betz, Howie to Abe. Betz in the white coat, stethoscope, chart on a clipboard, walking away from the foot of Zelda's bed, index finger wagging, signaling silence. Abe backed out the door and waited for the doctor.

Howie Betz stood about five seven, five eight, wore black-rimmed Trotsky glasses, had the hands of a classical pianist, fingers that made you think of wingspread, and spoke in quick bursts of words, as if on the verge of hyperventilation. Dr. Betz drew the door closed behind him and ushered Abe Stein down the hall, into a lounge area, gray furniture, pastel works of art on the wall. A soda-and-juice machine. Two television sets mounted in the far corners of the room, a game show on one and Geraldo Rivera on the other. Abe Stein registered these details as a means of grounding himself, because a walk to the lounge remained a vivid memory. After his parents, one a professor at Columbia University and the other a high-school teacher in Harlem, were found shot in the lobby of the brownstone where they lived, he had waited outside the operating theater, waited and waited and waited, then been led by the surgeon who hadn't changed out of his surgical garb, the blood of his parents all over him, to a lounge just like this. Told him both had suffered traumas to the brain stem, shot in the back of the head, and neither probably felt much, although Abe had to ask himself how much they felt while the surgeon was doing whatever it was that bloodied him. His parents, shot by assailants unknown, for reasons unknown, unless for kicks. No money stolen. Or because they were Jews. That possibility remained, although a faint one, since killing Semites was generally something someone would brag about. Or, and this had to be considered too, possibly they were victims of mistaken identity, dying for someone else.

Howie said, "Get you some juice, a soda?"

Abe Stein waved a hand, wearily brushing off the offer. "No, nothing. What's going on, Howie?"

The doctor removed his glasses, used his white cotton jacket to polish the lenses, then fitted them back on his face. "Long and short of it, Abe, I'm not sure. . . . The cell activity is consistent with the presence of a tumor, but . . . nothing shows up in her X rays . . . an imperfect tool to be sure. . . . But with fluid continuing to be produced . . . my recommendation would be to do an exploratory . . . locate the culprit. . . ."

"Surgery, that's what you're recommending?"

"One of the best thoracic surgeons in the country . . . right here on staff."

"Jesus, Howie. Tumor you said: is it malignant?"

"That's what the biopsy's for, Abe . . . and I think the sooner we move on this, the better. . . . You'll want to talk it over alone of course . . . but if Zelda has any questions for me . . ."

The public-address system erupted with a request for Dr. Betz, in another wing of the hospital. The physician with the Trotsky glasses apologized for the abruptness of his departure and sped off.

Abe Stein stood there. His body ached. His heart was reeling. Where his brother would have stepped back to slide some Stoli into his system, Abe trudged to the elevator, rode it down to the cafeteria to buy himself a cup of coffee, black.

A voice behind him in the cafeteria line said, "It's been a while, Abe. I almost hate to ask."

Abe Stein recognized the gritty, somber face, the fat man in the natty suit, the shirt and tie and shoes all synchronized: Lieutenant D. James Cox, a Queens homicide detective. The man putting out a hand to shake even as he slipped something into his mouth with the other hand.

"Yeah," said Abe Stein, glad for the human contact, "how are you, Lieutenant?"

"What's good in here, anything?"

"Try the goulash."

"Makes me feel like I'm in high school."

"You asked."

"Gimme the goulash, darling." Then: "How things going? Last I heard Izzy hasn't been cutting any corners, or at least that anybody caught him at."

"Yeah. Who knows, maybe is coming the second Resurrection."

The two men approached the cashier, Abe with his cup of coffee, Lieutenant D. James Cox with his goulash, slice of apple pie, glass of milk, and coffee, and Lieutenant Cox said, "Lemme take care of it. We can sit down and shoot the shit."

"You won't get much for the price of a cup, D.J."

The police officer said, "Abe, you wound me with the insinuation."

"I'm looking, I don't see you bleeding."

Abe Stein respected the detective, even liked him so far as he knew the man, but he was wary, sensed a play being run. He chose a table in the middle of the cafeteria, for its lack of privacy. It becomes part of a private operator's psyche, after very little experience in the business, that any friendly overture from a so-called public servant ought to be treated as something akin to the shell game, or three-card monte. He sipped his coffee, watching the detective prod a load of goulash onto his fork, and heard his own stomach emit a rumble of protest.

Finished chewing, the lieutenant poked around his mouth with a paper napkin, pronounced himself satisfied with the taste, and shoveled several more forkfuls before reaching for his glass of milk. The cafeteria was crowded and loud at this hour, almost evenly divided between visitors and members of the staff at the end of their shift, or on break. The din of health depressed Abe Stein, the unfairness of it percolating beneath the floors of the injured and ill. Resentment welled up in him that would not have occurred to Zelda, who would be more inclined to fix her thoughts upon the floors devoted to birth and recovery.

He slapped his cup down, slopping coffee onto the plastic saucer.

"You okay, Abe?"

"Am I okay? My wife's got fluid in her lungs, the docs can't drain it off fast enough. A tumor of some kind. They want to open her up, you ask if I'm okay."

Lieutenant D. James Cox laid down his fork and touched the corners of his mouth. "I didn't know," he said. "I'm sorry. I met Zelda a few times, funerals for cops she knew. She's good people. Jesus, I'm sorry."

The cop with a face carved from gristle laid a hand on the back of Abe Stein's hand. The touch was warm, sincere, brief. Abe Stein finished his coffee with little relish and said, "So maybe I believe you. If you are not a *gonef,* explain to me please how you just happen to be here, this hospital. It shouldn't be too difficult if it's the truth."

"It ain't. My partner, his day off, I think—I don't know —he spent most of it tailing somebody in the Scorcese organization. Name is Kenny Takimoto. Gonna make a name for himself becoming the authority on the Baker's family. A for-real cop, not a clock puncher."

"Okay," said Abe Stein, "so he's a good boy."

"Little fucker doesn't weigh even a hundred fifty pounds, two guys jumped him in the foyer of his apartment last night, never said a word, but they kicked the shit out of him, beat him on the kidneys with his own yellow pages. See him he's sucking oxygen, his eyes look like he pissed off Mike Tyson." Lieutenant D. James Cox lowered his face, stared at his plate a few seconds, then brought his eyes up to meet Abe Stein's. "Joe Scorcese," he said, "you look at him, here's this harmless little old guy, knock him over with a flyswatter. Don't you believe it. He's one ruthless son of a bitch."

"Your partner's condition, what do the doctors say?"

"They upgraded it from serious to fair. Big fucking deal. Kenny's still gotta have surgery to rebuild a cheek."

Abe Stein expressed his sympathy.

The police officer resumed eating. "When the anesthesia wore off some," Lieutenant Cox said, "Kenny kinda muttered in my ear, something about a rumor Blitz Focoso got taken off by some punk last week. The amount mentioned was in the six figures. Blitz is in the Scorcese fold, that much is a fact, and word has it so is a private operator by the name of Ray Sommer. Got an itty-bitty drinking problem, but otherwise a stand-up guy. Who, the day after Blitz has this little misfortune, someone observed paying you a visit, shortly after climbing out of a van registered to a company in Brooklyn that consists of a telephone receptionist. Am I putting anything together here, Abe, or just stringing beads?"

Abe Stein stared at the dregs in his coffee cup. "So he comes to see us. We know Ray a long time, done work for him. So what's the big deal?"

"Anthony 'Blitz' Focoso, he lends money for the Scorcese family, works out of a grocery on Metropolitan, I guess you know that much."

"I live in the borough, keep my eyes open, sure."

"Sommer's visit to your office, the day after Focoso got ripped off, right after he's seen getting out of old Joe's van, you want me to believe it's all just coincidence?"

Abe Stein watched the detective finish chewing the last bite of apple pie and reach for his coffee. "Do I want you to believe it's just coincidence? I don't want you to believe nothing you don't want to believe."

At a table to one side of them, somebody had evidently told a successful joke, and laughter lapped over them. Neither man was in the mood for it, scowls standing up in their worn faces, sharp as the claws of opposing bears.

It was Lieutenant D.J. Cox who broke the hostile silence between them. "I guess I heard wrong," he said, "that you were the half of Long Arm, if I put my cards on the table, you'd be willing to play. But you might as well be Izzy, always trying to shuffle the deck. Let me tell you something: what I think is you believe you're looking out for Izzy, because if what I hear is true, that the piece a shit that took off Blitz is the son of Molly Carmichael, then it would be straight out of the Scorcese handbook, send Molly's lover, the professional skiptracer, after the asshole. How can he refuse?"

Abe Stein pushed his chair back, clutched his briefcase, about to rise. "Next lunch will be on me, D.J."

"Oh?" The detective palmed a dark reddish wafer, slipped it between his pale lips. Sipped his coffee. "Does your conscience come that cheap, Abe, or do you have some other bookkeeping formula?"

"I don't know what to tell you."

"You can't tell me nothing, you can't tell me nothing.

But you tell Izzy, running errands for the Scorcese people, a guy gets real dirty real fast. You might also want to mention the existence of the Witness Protection Program. Carmichael kid might know enough about Blitz's operation to interest the feds. Of course that still leaves Izzy's ass hanging out there, don't it?"

"Not if it wasn't out there in the first place."

Lieutenant D.J. Cox lumbered to his feet, made some minor adjustments to the brim of his pale straw fedora. "There's times," he said, "when I'm happy to be wrong. This would be one of them. My regards to Zelda, Abe. I'll see my wife includes her in her prayers."

The two men made their way out of the cafeteria without another word.

Izzy Stein nuzzled the Mustang against the curb directly in front of Molly Carmichael's house. Once again he caught himself grinning at the prospect of Carl Bellows on the run from the law. That was juicy. Only thing better would be having the opportunity to put the cuffs on him personally.

It was almost a quarter to six, people coming and going on the sidewalks, most of them commuters on their way home from work, to judge from their faces, anticipation awakening in them, and relief too. As he sat there, the car idling, the air conditioner laboring, a boxy, baby-blue Plymouth four-door coasted to a stop beside the curb several car lengths ahead of him and on the opposite side of the street, Harvey Wendt arriving early for his six to two stint. Another guy by the name of Moon Humphries, a retired cop living off a disability pension, took over at two and covered the house until Molly left in the morning. Izzy Stein climbed out of the Mustang slowly, to give Harvey Wendt every opportunity to spot him, locked his door and walked around the front of the car to the passenger door, reached in for the bouquet of gladioli (Molly's favorites) and the sack with the bottle of vodka and two quarts of club soda in it. Molly disdained all the elegant brands of sparkling water, having once described Perrier as "pricey pee, fit only for a princess." A remark that had the saucy ring of something Zelda Stein might say.

The sky at this hour was an indefinite blue-gray streaked with cirrus, the sunlight flaring from somewhere over New Jersey, casting an ashen light on the underbelly of the clouds. It was hot and the air was limp and the leaves of the trees on the street drooped, exuding a smear of faint green color against the sky. The people climbing the steps to their homes exhibited, if tepidly, that burst of energy of a runner approaching the finish line.

When a second press of the buzzer went unanswered, Izzy Stein used the key Molly had left him to enter. With all the curtains drawn to assist the air conditioners, it was shadowy inside, and he had to fumble about for light switches. As he found one and proceeded toward the kitchen, the phone started ringing. He flipped on the kitchen light and opened the refrigerator to deposit the club soda, stick the vodka in the freezer. The machine had engaged and Molly's voice explained that she was presently unavailable, but if the caller wished to leave a message, she would respond as soon as possible. Izzy flipped open cupboard doors, searching for the crystal vase he knew she possessed, because he had bought it for her, a Waterford, in London. Located it and began to fill it with tap water when the voice of the person calling was broadcast:

"Molly, it's me, Vick. About ten to six. Listen, hon, I got you booked out on Northwest, for your WorldPerks card. You pay a little bit of a penalty for the urgency, since you were booked for three weeks from now, but it's minimal. You'll be flying direct to San Francisco this Saturday, from there to Oahu, a layover of ninety minutes, then Maui. I am so-o-o-o envious. Call me when you have a moment, we'll go over the times. Ciao."

Adjusting and readjusting the long stems with the tissue-thin, flared, trombone-shaped flowers of scarlet and white, Izzy Stein recognized the voice of Molly's travel agent, and wondered if Molly, when she came home and monitored her calls, would mention anything about Maui to him.

He poured a Stoli on ice, steered the needle on the phonograph to a Neil Young cut, folded himself on a chair beneath the kitchen table. Ten, maybe fifteen, minutes later Molly came through the door with a large shopping bag looped over one hand and the smell of fresh vegetables and seafood emanating from the bag cradled in her arm.

She dropped the merchandise on the table in order to free her arms to embrace him. They kissed, lingering over it, giving the flow of feeling time to complete the circuit. Then she saw the vase full of glads and they had at it some more, kissing like newlyweds. When they parted, Izzy said, "I've been running around most of the afternoon, various errands. You mind if I take a shower?"

Molly cocked her head, and then light danced in her

eyes. "Alone? Or did you need someone to scrub your back?"

"Now there's an idea," he said, and grinned.

"Let me put this stuff away."

"I'll get the water all adjusted." Izzy Stein started from the kitchen, but turned around in the doorway. "Remind me to tell you a story I heard today about an old friend of yours."

CHAPTER 11

Late August in Phoenix, the days staggered through triple-digit heat, and the prospect of sudden rain murked up the sky, the sun disappearing behind a metallic overcast. But all that generally happened was that the air grew stickier throughout the day, and no rain fell, and the night was enormous, the stars arranged up there like God's own diamond district. It was when the sky turned a muddy brown that you had to watch out. Then the rain might fall in torrents, the streets flooding within an hour, so that vehicles still on the road risked riding to unintended destinations, or being altogether swamped. It was the monsoon season in Phoenix, when the prevailing winds swept west and somewhat north out of the Gulf of Mexico, weighted with warm moisture. It was the season that gave the lie to the community boosters' boast about the dry heat in Phoenix, so superior to that found in Miami or any other coastal oasis.

Sitting beneath his patio, overlooking his pool in Paradise Valley, Angelo Scorcese watched along with the red-haired Dutch nanny the younger children of his union with Mai Lee Scorcese, his deceased French Vietnamese wife. His current wife, Magda, six months pregnant, remained within the air-conditioned house, watching game shows on the bedroom television.

Angelo Scorcese was the eldest of Joe Scorcese's three sons, and from his base in Phoenix he ran the family business in the southwest, with the singular exception of Las Vegas. The business there—the hotels and casinos, the loan-sharking and prostitution, the sports wires—belonged to the youngest brother, Paul, the star of the family in the old man's eyes. Angelo did not begrudge Paul his position of ascendancy, attributing it to a difference of luck. That was putting it mildly. Paul had not had the misfortune to be married to Mai Lee, a stunning but ambitious lady, always giving Angelo little hints and nudges, never coming right out and telling him what they both knew: that the old man would never relinquish the power in the family to Angelo, that the only way for him to achieve what they both lusted after was to become man enough to take the power. Taking over had been his and Mai Lee's euphemism for whacking the old guy. Even today Angelo believed he had set up the hit beautifully. The shooters, some lowlifes he had recruited from the South Bronx, nailed the old guy with shotguns as he sat in his bakery on Metropolitan Avenue, and the shooters, in turn, were blown to pieces by the crew that occupied rooms above Luigi Vacanza's fruit-and-vegetable market across the street from the bakery. It had gone smooth as silk, nobody alive to trace the hit to him. Except somehow the old man survived. You believe it? Armed with two twelve-gauge double-barreled shotguns, the goddamn spic lowlifes couldn't take out a guy in his seventies. Talk about bum luck.

Of course, it was true that Mai Lee's luck was considerably worse, having long ago earned the Don's enmity not so much for seducing his son as for having triumphed, however temporarily, over the old man's wishes by convincing Angelo to marry her, to father children by her. So that when the Don had fully recovered from the attempt on his life, it was Mai Lee who incurred the brunt of his wrath, her beautiful body left mutilated in a scandalous situation and Angelo an object of snickering in the bars and social clubs from Howard Beach to Long Island City.

And the snickering, once a brief period of mourning had been observed, swelled to an uproar of derision when it was announced that Angelo Scorcese would wed Magda Vacanza. It came as no surprise to him. Magda stood not quite six feet, possessed a tongue and bearing that had backed down more than one teamster. She was not so much slovenly as indifferent to the norms (to say nothing of the nuances) of feminine charm. If she had an itch, it got scratched regardless of its location or in whose company she happened to be. She was loud, opinionated, sarcastic, and intimidating, and she ran her father's market (had run it for eleven years) with the unchallenged authority of a drill sergeant. In the presence of Angelo her black eyes almost flared, as if from the intensity of her longing, and she became awkward, diffident, a victim of inexperience. On their wedding night, alone at last in the bridal suite, Angelo had persuaded her to watch pornographic movies with him, as he explained it, for her own education. He said nothing about requiring the stimulation to block out the reality of what he was about to do, what he had to do to save his skin. Marriage to and children by Magda Vacanza satisfied part of the deal he had struck with the Don, in exchange for his life.

The other part of the deal had been his virtual exile to the southwest. It was a toss-up as to which aspect of the arrangement he loathed more. If it weren't for the surreptitious hours he spent with the nubile nanny, Gretta, he was convinced he'd go completely off his nut, fly back to New York, and whack the old bastard personally.

For Angelo Scorcese hated Phoenix. It was the bottom of the world to him, almost another planet. He hated the rawboned, cowboy mentality that prevailed. Anybody white that wasn't a family member he dismissed as a retard, an Okie, or as white bread, and that was when he was in the mood to be polite. He hated the jigs and beaners, the gooks, the dinks, the slopes, and was especially vexed by the Indians because he knew no term of scorn for them. He hated the heat and the desert. He hated turquoise jewelry. He hated the absence of neighborhood bars and the bland food in restaurants and the lame nightclubs with their little-kid curfews. In one of his more grandiloquent exercises in self-pity, he compared himself to Nixon at San Clemente, a leader isolated from the world he knew, exiled (in Angelo's instance) to a place that in summers even the locals admitted was little farther than a few blocks from hell.

The morning wore on beneath a sky the color of sheet metal. The children splashed in the shallow end of the pool, and Angelo and Gretta, stretched out on lounge chairs side by side, conversed about this and that, nothing important, Gretta rising from time to time to tend to a child or answer the phone for Angelo or rub sun lotion onto his shoulders, a task to which she brought the same subtle pressures as she did when they made love. The Mexican maid, Consuelo, emerged from the house from time to time to announce a visitor, one of the various connected people around the valley with access to the Scorcese residence. Most of the people that needed to speak to Angelo met with him later in the evening in automobiles or in public places—the dog track, bars, parking lots, the ballpark where the Phoenix Firebirds generally crashed and burned. The last to visit the house that morning were a couple of guys from Paul's old crew, left behind when Paul moved to Las Vegas: Louis Lippi and Vincent "the Surgeon" Lament. They had remained in Phoenix at Paul's request, to ease the transition of power, to bring Angelo up to speed on the spectrum of the family's involvement; but most of all, because Paul was not privy to the reasons behind the shake-up, he wanted loyal people inside Angelo's camp to report to him.

Lippi and Lament were both solid guys, and over the months, closing in on a year now, Angelo Scorcese had grown to appreciate Paul's legacy. He didn't particularly trust them, because he trusted no one, but he enjoyed their company. They were guys from his old neighborhood, their voices were the sounds of his youth.

Louis Lippi was the only guy in the Phoenix crew to wear a suit year round. He wore the suit for the simple reason that where he came from, men of responsibility wore suits. It might be 105 degrees in the shade, but here was Lips, suit and tie, dark shoes. A brick.

As Lips's driver, Vincent Lament also stepped onto the patio, but hung back. He was not yet a player in the family, but simply salaried help, earning $350 a week for a no-show position as a cook at Sport Time Lounge. A small, wiry guy with thick wrists and black hair crawling out to the last knuckle of his fingers, Vincent Lament stood to one side of the French doors, his eyes behind dark glasses and thinning hair beneath a ten-gallon straw hat, a jean jacket with the sleeves turned to his elbows, no shirt, a pair of bleached-out Levi's bunched in accordion pleats on his white leather boots. Vincent, unlike Louis Lippi or Angelo Scorcese, had gone completely native. If it weren't for the delicious mayhem perpetrated upon the English language by his Queens accent, Vincent would be just another whitebread in Angelo's eyes. As things stood, he was still not a made guy, still not a player, but had proved his usefulness and potential as a skilled carver of corpses, hence his nickname. He gave new meaning to the expression, "dearly departed."

The thing Angelo admired in Louis Lippi was the professionalism. The stout and sweating guy with the fireplug physique was conscious of business at all times. Angelo Scorcese watched him, before uttering a word, move his eyes behind dark glasses over the coral-and-white cliffs that prodded the sky to the east, looking for the little blip of light that might indicate the sun's reflection off a lens, the intrusion of federal surveillance. Lips knew enough about that sort of operation to be the obvious choice as the man in charge of watching the air terminals, in the event Misty Carmichael thought he could make his run through Phoenix. That was why he was reporting personally to Angelo this morning. From New York they had learned that Misty, as of a day or two ago, was in Denver, so close to Angelo's turf that he could taste the asshole. He had ordered Louis Lippi to redouble his efforts at the airport in Phoenix, make the watch so tight, they'd know who farted anywhere in any one of the four terminals. Louis Lippi had nodded.

And that was the other aspect of Lips's style: even if he didn't spot the enemy, he didn't give anything away. So many of the young guys were prone to blab openly, even in public places, so that if their words couldn't be recorded, they could still be understood by a competent lip reader. Not Louis. It was a carefully developed habit of his, when he spoke to Angelo, regardless of where they were standing, to rest the arch of his hand beneath his nose, the palm shading his lips. And even the words they exchanged were couched in shadows, the vagueness of what they said clarified by looks, previous understanding, or something scribbled on a notepad and burned. Thus the entire conversation on the patio between Angelo Scorcese and Louis Lippi concerning the situation at Sky Harbor Airport consisted of the following:

Angelo, in his black bikini briefs that shopped his business so obviously that Louis Lippi was embarrassed by it, strolled to the diving board at the deep end of the pool: "How we doin', you know, on the thing?"

Shuffling beside him, head averted and hand over mouth, Louis Lippi said, "Nuttin' so far. But it's papered."

"Fuckin' better be. The uh . . . the old guy is hot."

"Look. I said it's papered." Louis Lippi had seen to it that Misty Carmichael's picture had been circulated to every baggage handler and ticket clerk within the four terminals, along with the promise of a thousand dollars in cash for the first person to recognize the putz.

Angelo Scorcese stepped onto the diving board, walked to the end of it to flex his legs, the board dipping beneath his weight. He backed up, took several lumbering steps and was airborne off the board, the children screaming with delight. It was not a graceful dive. His chest struck the water in the same instant his chin did and water exploded into the air from the impact and the children screamed even louder and clapped their hands, thoroughly enjoying their father's antics.

Angelo Scorcese traveled the length of the pool underwater, surfacing at the steps in the shallow end, Gretta hovering above him with a bath towel, and next to her Louis Lippi staring impassively down. Angelo climbed the steps, took the towel and mopped it over his face, held it just above his lips to say, "That little spud sucker comes through here, the surgeon's gonna be a busy boy."

Louis Lippi nodded.

Consuelo emerged from the house. "A phone call," she said. "Is for Mr. Lippi."

The somber man in the suit followed her into the house and lifted the receiver next to the sink. "Yeah?"

"Bingo."

This Leslie Ann was a perfect treasure. Not only had she arranged for the tickets, obtaining a discount, but she had encouraged him to sleep for several hours while she packed and settled matters with her aunt, then had done most of the driving through the night. They arrived in Phoenix around eight-thirty in the morning, enjoyed a leisurely breakfast at a Denny's restaurant waiting for the Metrocenter shopping mall to open. Inside the mall Misty Carmichael purchased a fiberglass suitcase with a digital combination lock, a black Delsey with wheels that emerged for dragging it through airports. He found a shop that sold prints and lithographs and convinced the salesclerk to sell him a length of clear bubbled plastic wrapping for a price that approached extortion. While Leslie Ann shopped for swimsuits and other beach accessories, Misty sat in the hot parking lot breaking down the .380, wrapping each component in plastic and stashing it amidst the cash in the black suitcase.

When Leslie Ann arrived with her shopping bags, Misty was hot, edgy, eager to be moving. They followed I-17 to I-10 and from there to the airport, Misty maneuvering the Toyota into a parking space at the east end of the Barry M. Goldwater terminal. They entered the lower level, an expanse of mocha-colored carpet with a faint pattern worked into it, silvery baggage carousels flanked by service desks for auto rentals. Misty was surprised at how quiet it all seemed, fewer than a hundred travelers milling about, redcaps standing around with no one needing their services. Seeing Misty towing his new black Delsey, a garment bag over a shoulder, and trucking along with Leslie Ann's suitcase in the other hand, a cap started toward him, but peeled away before Misty could rebuff him. Despite the locking mechanism, Misty wasn't going to relinquish the Delsey until he absolutely had to. They found an escalator that delivered them to the check-in area and the lines that are the immutable aggravation of air travel, the inchworm pace of them evidently modeled after the scheduling practices of modern medicine. The shuffling gait of the line almost cost Misty his life.

He saw them, or in any event sensed them, just as he was depositing their bags on the scales. He checked out three of them, two in jogging outfits, shorts and nifty sneakers, both wearing loose cotton warm-up jackets, and the third one in a flowery short-sleeved shirt, casual khaki-colored trousers, his long hair slicked back and tied in a ponytail. All of them in dark glasses and moving across the mocha carpet with easy purpose, a kind of lazy menace. Flowers was running the show, Misty was certain, and wouldn't be carrying; but the other two would be. He fought back the taste of panic. He watched the bags snatched up and tagged. Leslie Ann was completing the paperwork with the America West clerk, when Misty leaned over her ear and whispered, "I know you can act, Sugarcheeks. Throw a fit, right now. You're a diabetic. Do it for chrissake, or we're gonna be dead. But hang on to our boarding passes."

Leslie Ann didn't say a word, just stumbled forward clutching the passes, drooling down her chin, her eyelids fluttering, hanging by one hand to the service desk as she crumpled, Misty Carmichael imploring the clerk to roust up some assistance for his diabetic girlfriend. At his feet Leslie

Ann began to shudder and mutter incomprehensibly. A crowd gathered, and within moments a police officer was tunneling her way through the spectators. The three guys in dark glasses drifted off to hover on the periphery, exchanging shrugs, stymied by the police presence. The young woman cop started to kneel next to Leslie, but Misty said, "I can handle this. Please, officer, if you could just back off the crowd, her medication's in her purse here, then if you would just help me walk her to the gate, there's so little time."

The cop laid a hand on his shoulder, a gesture of reassurance, said, "Certainly."

Misty Carmichael pretended to fumble about in the purse, pretended to find and push past Leslie Ann's slobbering lips some form of medication. He called for water. An ashen-faced America West attendant crouched beside him with a paper cup as the cop explained to the spectators that the show was over, please disperse. Leslie Ann, her head cradled in Misty's arm, swallowed dutifully and quickly ceased to shake and slobber, giving the cop and the attendant and Misty a weak smile of gratitude tinged with embarrassment. "I'm so sorry," she uttered in the tiniest of voices, "so sorry to have caused everyone . . ."

"That's all right, darling," said Misty Carmichael, helping her to her feet, "you've been under a lotta stress, lately." He glanced down at the policewoman, who had assumed a position of support on the other side of Leslie Ann, one hand beneath her arm, the other guiding her wrist. "She lost her father," he lied to the officer. "It was a close relationship. The stress. I suspect she's been neglecting her medication."

"I understand," said the officer.

Leslie Ann, that pure gem of a lady, commenced to sob over the loss of her daddy. The police officer, a stout black woman by the name of Cerise Turner, accompanied them to the boarding ramp, waited while they passed through the metal detector and had their carry-on scanned by X ray, and never tumbled to the anxious presence of three guys in dark glasses, whose pursuit of Misty Carmichael had been foiled. Misty watched them stomp off, and his heart slowed down enough to permit the recording of other sensations, like the smell of his own sweat congealing or the pressure of Leslie Ann's fingernails digging into the flesh beneath his rib cage. He wanted to lean over and love up his priceless Leslie on the spot, but Cerise Turner insisted upon guiding them to their proper gate, and when they got there, had found a seat for Leslie, Misty shook the officer's hand, and abruptly raised it.

"Sir, please!"

He kissed her knuckles anyway.

Magda slept a lot. Generally she conked out around four in the afternoon to doze for a couple of hours before dinner. This was a period of the day when there was plenty on television to amuse the children, if they weren't otherwise occupied by Nintendo or rental movies. It was also the part of the day that very often Angelo and Gretta tried to enjoy some privacy, either within the house or at a nearby watering hole.

Less than five minutes from the house by limo, La Posada, a rather exclusive resort complex, had become one of their favorite retreats, especially one of the bars there that brewed several beers of its own. Gretta, having read about it in the *New Times,* introduced him to the place, and while Angelo had never had much tolerance for alcohol, he came to appreciate the house malts almost as much as Gretta did. She liked her beer, did Gretta, and Angelo liked the shine of polished woods and brass, the friendly clamor of the place, and the general air of camaraderie. It was a kind of neighborhood bar, but severely upscale, nobody hollering out double negative remarks, although even the ladies in their Moschino jeans, tennis togs, and Ellen Tracy casuals dropped the occasional *fuck* into a conversation, so that there was no mistaking their sophisticated, feminist pedigrees. Angelo Scorcese had watched and listened to these pampered ladies and wondered if a one of them had had a proper lay even once in her life. They couldn't touch Mai Lee. And as far as that went, next to the delectable Gretta, he didn't think there was enough juice among them to fill a teaspoon.

They were sitting in a thickly padded booth, plenty of shrubbery all around them, across from the bar when Angelo spotted Louis Lippi standing at the entrance, his shaded eyes moving over the room. Angelo raised a hand, and Lips moved among the patrons, all the loud and happy people, and took up a seat in the booth across from Angelo and Gretta.

"Louis," cried Gretta, "you are being a movie star, always with the dark glasses, yes?"

Louis, who had spent the afternoon struggling to keep a cap on his rage, to say nothing of his dread of this moment, leaned his elbows on the table, hand over his mouth as he said, "There's good news and there's bad."

Angelo removed his arm from Gretta and edged forward, lifted his Mets cap to run his fingers through his hair, then spoke in the dialect of the island from which his and Lippi's parents had emigrated. "This a fuckin' joke you're tellin' or what?"

It was no joke, as Louis Lippi's explanation made clear. Angelo Scorcese said quietly, "Gimme the glasses you're wearing, Louis," holding out his hand for them, then sat back snapping the plastic into smaller and smaller pieces.

Gretta sipped her beer, to make it last, and stared back at the table of idiot ladies, all staring their way. She bet if she closed her eyes, the popping plastic would sound just like a big roaring fire in the fireplace. She could almost feel the heat of it licking over her.

CHAPTER 12

Zelda made the decision, and Abe complied, to have the exploratory performed as soon as possible, and not to notify the children until there was something concrete to tell them. Whether she had absorbed it from her reading or developed the position on her own, she expressed an aversion to any theatrics over the issue of her life or death. And one more thing she wanted Abe to promise: under no circumstances would she agree to live as a vegetable. She patted his cheek saying this, telling him she had better things to be doing.

Then she asked him to call Molly Carmichael, to see if she could come by after the biopsy, once Zelda was out from under the anesthesia, to make her look pretty for Abe. Zelda told Abe that Molly could mold mud into a bouquet of flowers, such was the little *shiksa's* spirit.

"I shall call," he said to her, kissing her on both cheeks before touching her lips, and added not only gallantly, but partly truthfully, "I think you are women cut from the same cloth. Looking at one another, you look into mirrors. Shame on you, my darling. Vanity does not become you."

"Vanity-shmanity. As long as I look beautiful."

Surgery was scheduled for seven-thirty that Wednesday morning, so Zelda was awakened at six-thirty to be prepped, given her initial sedation, and transferred to a gurney, in order to move her to an operating room. A small, shapely woman with deep red hair and an imperious manner that the nurses resented flashed a note with Dr. Betz's letterhead and signature stating that Molly Carmichael, with identification, had permission to stay with the patient up until surgery, and again immediately after. She stood next to the gurney in the cool tiled corridor, one of her manicured hands grasping the benumbed one of Zelda, her nasal passages trying to accommodate odors she wasn't prepared for. From her purse she extracted a tissue to employ against a sampler of perfume, something tossed in with a purchase, pressed the tissue to her nose, and swore on the spot to buy Lancôme's new scent by the pint.

She had considered wearing heels for the authority height conveyed, but opted for comfort—her size-six sneakers and a forest-green pullover top of sueded silk with matching trousers that tapered to her ankles. She wore gold hooped earrings and a heavy gold necklace that looked almost liquid the way the light trickled over it. On her wrist was a thin gold watch, a knockoff of a Rolex, that even so had not been cheap.

At seven thirty-five on her watch, Molly Carmichael marched over to the nurses' station to inquire why no one had come for Zelda, her operation was scheduled for seven-thirty. The three nurses there looked at her as if she had made an obscene request. One of them, by the looks of her the senior member, hung a clipboard on a peg, swiveled out of her chair, and strode up to the desk. She gave Molly a weary smile that might have been tinged with a hint of condescension. "You're the lady with Dr. Betz's patient, scheduled for a biopsy?"

"I'm the lady," said Molly.

The nurse shuffled clipboards behind the desk, then picked up one to study. "Ah. The presiding surgeon will be Colin McDermott. You couldn't ask for better, Miss—Carmichael, is it?"

"Carmichael," said Molly. "And I think it's wonderful he's such a dandy man with a knife, so what I wonder is, why Mrs. Stein isn't benefiting from his expertise."

The nurse gave Molly the smile again, although this time there was not a hint of condescension, there was a dollop. "Miss Carmichael, the operating theater is not like the movies, with a predictable running time. Schedules are approximated estimates. I see here the anesthesiologist and Dr. McDermott are both in the midst of procedures. Surely you do not expect them to walk away from one patient in the middle of surgery to begin surgery on another patient, simply to begin operating on schedule."

"Surely," said Molly, retreating from the nurses' station, and murmuring to herself, "Approximated estimates?"

She spent the next hour and fifteen minutes standing on her feet beside Zelda turning the pages of a paperback she had brought in her purse, her eyes rising expectantly whenever rubber soles squeaked in the corridor. Finally, two male attendants arrived; one of them skimmed the chart dangling from the foot of Zelda's gurney, then winked at Molly. "Show time," he said, and the two attendants wheeled off with Zelda.

When Molly found Abe—forearms on thighs, staring at nothing—he virtually leapt at her, his hands gripping her shoulders with some strength. "How is she?" he cried. "Did Howie tell you anything?"

She smiled, tried to make it a soothing smile, and put a hand on his cheek. "Please don't kill the messenger before you've heard the message. She was just now admitted for surgery. Operating times evidently are modeled after third-world train schedules. I'm sorry."

When he had absorbed what Molly had told him, he drew her tenderly to his chest, castigating himself for his abruptness even as he threatened to suffocate her in the wealth of his apology. Fortunately for her, Iz discovered them in the embrace. He put a hand on each of their shoulders, asking quietly, "What do we know?"

Releasing Molly, Abe hugged his younger brother. "Nothing yet. Molly just—" Abe fumbled a handkerchief from a pocket on the seat of his pants and used it on his eyes.

Molly, suppressing her desire to have Izzy's arms around her, trailed a hand down his arm. She said, "There was a delay. The great thoracic surgeon has just begun."

Izzy brought an arm around to include her in the circle, kissing her just on the hairline. "It's a start," he said.

Then said, "I spoke to Rabbi Horovitz, Abe. He's on his way. A stand-up guy, the rabbi."

"I didn't ask," protested Abe.

"I know," said Izzy. "I did. What can it hurt?"

The climb from coma progressed from hallucinations to childhood memories to the amassing of lists, Zelda creeping from the fog of anesthesia compiling the roll call of states to secede from the Union: Virginia, North Carolina, South Carolina (an easy one), Georgia, Alabama, Arkansas, Louisiana, Texas (she was almost there), Tennessee, Mississippi . . . Mississippi, Mississippi: what a hypnotic chant it was, the music of it distracting, elemental.

But she was certain there was one more. She drifted up, recognizing faces now: Molly's first, because she was near, and speaking words that eluded Zelda like small bright fish skittering away from a swimmer. Then she saw Abe, his dark rolling hair and jowls, his gentle fingers on her face. And Izzy back there, the sweet slenderness of his profile, his eyes on Abe, and on Molly too. In Izzy she recognized what she had always suspected, and that was the deepest sort of compassion: his thinking already tuned toward the survivors.

At last she understood something Molly was saying.

What Molly said was, "I love you."

So it was as bad as all that.

Zelda's lips hissed, dry and bloated and useless. She moved them, and they felt as distant as kites.

Tears squeezed from her eyes.

Again she tried to speak, to convey the sudden, simple delight that was in her heart, and the word emerged, scratchy but audible: "Florida."

That was the rebel state she was forgetting. The confederacy: a union of the proud and brilliant and foolish and doomed. She closed her eyes and she could see them: all those men, those men and boys, marching into hell bent upon surviving. In blue, in gray, and in rags. How they hung in there was a mystery maybe even God Himself puzzled over. Who could say?

Molly sat on a chair in the private room reading and watching Zelda sleep, a state she had been in since her brief moment of lucidity around noon. While she and Izzy remained dubious, Abe had convinced himself that her single utterance was the expression of her desire to move to Miami, to spend what was left of her life nearer to Seth, who had the gift of her imagination, to say nothing of the grit. Seth had recently accepted an under-cover assignment, the nature of which he would not share even with his wife, much less his parents. It had required the better part of the afternoon before the details reached Zelda's son. He called the hospital after five, spoke to Izzy, and delivered a terse explanation of why his wife and children were already aboard a flight, but he wasn't: there were lives on the line.

Izzy said, "Zeedee and Abe can handle that. You stay careful. You gotta wife doesn't want to read about you, and parents the same thing. You hearing me?"

"Hearing you?" said Seth, standing in a phone booth. "Take off the gloves, already."

"*Sholem,* Seth."

"Yeah. Back at you."

With Naomi and Abe to watch over Zelda, Izzy and Molly offered to give the rabbi a lift to his home in Flushing, after which they drove, neither of them saying much, to Molly's place in Ridgewood. Hot, tired commuters moped along the sidewalk. Several car lengths up the block a baby-blue Plymouth was parked, a small figure inside it. Another August day: heat unrelieved by any breeze, the air congealing upon one's skin. Izzy followed Molly up the steps, held the screen door for her while she fiddled with her keys.

Inside, without a word being said, they walked straight to the kitchen at the rear of the house, Molly crouching to retrieve the bottle of Scotch while Izzy plucked two tumblers from a cabinet next to the sink and filled them with ice cubes. Molly poured them each a generous portion of Dewar's. They sat across the table from one another with their drinks, Molly hefting hers with two hands and closing her eyes, clenching her teeth as the heat of the Scotch climbed her throat. Izzy put a hand on one of hers.

"I want to go to sleep," she said, "and wake up, find out this is all a bad dream. No good, huh?"

"Abe said the doctor told him the tumor was the size of his fist. You hear that?"

She nodded. "And the way it's metastasizing." She raised his hand in both of hers, brushed her lips over his knuckles. "The bad dream isn't a dream at all, it's the way it is."

Izzy poured more Scotch down his throat. "Zeedee's been dodging the bullet for a long time."

"Did Abe make a decision yet, whether to try radiation?"

He shook his head. "Going to talk it over with Zeedee. Betz didn't recommend it with much enthusiasm."

"How much, if they don't . . . did the doctor . . . ?"

"Time? Three to six weeks. Or it could be tomorrow."

Molly closed her eyes and moved her head slowly from side to side, a gesture less of denial than of utter, weary surrender. "I feel so tired," she said, "I feel so dead inside. Iz, I have to ask you something."

"So ask."

"I had made plans, a short trip, before all this happened. Would it . . . would you think me awful if I went away for a few days?"

Izzy reached for her hand and smiled, even if that was not the emotion he was experiencing. "To be the lady of mystery, to be yourself? Molly, you are something, I don't care what you say. You're happy anywhere in the world as long as it isn't your home. You are the antithesis of a Jew. You have the soul of an expatriate. And I love you as you are. Go, darling. Do what it is you need to do."

She looked at him, blinking back tears, and hoisted the tumbler of Scotch. It was agreed that she would nap for an hour while he went to the office, and they would meet eight-thirtyish for dinner at Flamingos. They kissed good-bye at the door, and Izzy Stein descended the steps, his heart divided by the fact that Molly never mentioned her destination.

It was a little past seven when Izzy stepped off the elevator in the Argent Towers. The Pinkertons were an efficient outfit, not as infallible as they liked to portray themselves, but in the assignments he'd thrown them over the years, they had acquitted themselves respectably. However, given the trend of the day's events, he approached the office without that squirm of anticipation that connotes any real optimism. His heels echoed in the empty hallway. Listening to them, he heard the measure of his own exhaustion, realized he almost didn't give an eff one way or the other as to the investigation of Misty Carmichael.

A tall, lean man that he recognized as Bennie Focoso was resting a shoulder on the door to his office. Bennie was standing there as if he had all the time in the world and seemed to have adopted Blitz's style of dressing: he was wearing a loose, light double-breasted jacket, a dark shirt buttoned to his throat. A guy in sneakers moved up behind Izzy as he reached the door, a guy who smelled of cigarettes and cheap after-shave. Something hard poked him in the spine, and a voice told him to place his hands flat on the wall. Izzy did that, looking at Bennie Focoso, who was cracking his knuckles, his eyes stony and unreadable in the light of the silent corridor. A hand went up and down Izzy's legs, around his waist, and under his arms, then the hand went away and with it, the hard pressure on his spine.

"He ain't got weight," said the guy with the cheap after-shave.

Bennie Focoso lifted his chin. "C'mon, Iz. Let's go riding."

Izzy took his hands off the wall. "How about we step in the office, talk there? I could fix some highballs."

As he brought the keys out of his pocket, Bennie stepped in front of the doorknob. "You gotta choice," he said. "You can go riding, or Billy the Deuce can make you go riding."

"Your car or mine?" said Izzy, his tongue feeling thick as he uttered the words, trying to fight back the light-headedness of fear.

"Relax, Iz. Blitz just wants to see the channels of communication are kept open. This isn't the sorta thing can be done over the phone, know what I'm saying?"

Izzy Stein nodded, telling himself to stay focused, use the adrenaline instead of being used by it. That was the trick. His hands still shook faintly as he stepped onto the elevator, but he didn't think Bennie or the Deuce guy noticed. He concentrated upon his breathing, bringing himself under control. Crossing the lobby, odd details leapt out at him— the precise color of the chairs off to one side in a conversation pit, the decorative shrubbery, the somber gray curtains —as if he were seeing them all for the first time. They filled him with a bizarre elation, which was simply recognition of how passionately he wanted still to live.

Beyond the double-doored entrance the big white Mercedes waited.

Izzy was invited to climb in back, where Blitz Focoso was sitting, his fingers interlaced over a knee as he watched the progress of a Mets-Dodgers game on a small television attached to the back of the front seat. When the door was closed, Blitz said by way of greeting, "I got ten large on the Mets this game, you think Fernandez can find the fucking plate? Not even with a searchlight, he couldn't."

"Nice to see you too, Blitz."

"Not even with a fucking seeing-eye dog, he couldn't," the loan shark with the tired eyes continued to grumble.

The Deuce got behind the wheel of the idling Mercedes, and Bennie rode shotgun. Within minutes the Mercedes was gliding through the twilight on Metropolitan Avenue, although from inside the automobile, given the tinted windows, it was difficult to differentiate broad daylight from twilight. When the Deuce guided the car south onto Woodhaven Boulevard, and still not a word out of Blitz, Izzy commenced reverting to square one—pure and utter panic. At the intersection with Rockaway Boulevard, Woodhaven turned into Cross Bay, and Izzy began to have an idea of their destination. It did nothing to alleviate his condition.

He forced saliva into his mouth and said, "I thought we were going to have a conversation. I got things to do other than watch baseball."

"Jesus," said Blitz, "when is Torborg gonna yank this guy? My sister's gotta better arm."

"The reason I mention it, Blitz, is I got a couple of Pinkertons working on Misty's whereabouts. Hired 'em this morning. And uh, before Bennie intercepted me, I was on my way to find out what they knew. While we're out here riding, we could be missing out on stuff you and I'd both like to know. You follow me? Blitz?"

The car merged onto the Shore Parkway.

Blitz Focoso raised a hand, a plastic transmitter in it, and the television screen faded to gray. He worked the index finger beneath the throat of his shirt. "So whadda ya know, Izzy?"

"That's what I was trying to tell you. Bennie and his friend, they got in the way of me finding out."

Blitz massaged himself beneath his eyes. "Got in the way of finding out what, Iz?"

"Misty. The last I heard, that's who we're talking about."

"The little shputz."

"Him. I gotta pair of Pinkertons working on him in Colorado, and I might've had something to tell you, if Bennie and the Deuce hadn't been so brain dead. Blitz, you gotta teach your people to think."

"No, I don't think so, Iz." A sigh unreeling from the words, the weary shark letting his hair down. "No, what I think I gotta do is, I gotta have a conversation with Misty's hot little mama that you are poking on a regular basis, but haven't come up with jack shit. It's been almost a week we let you poke and stroke. There's other methods is what I'm saying."

The Deuce maneuvered the Mercedes off the beltway exactly where Izzy Stein anticipated they were headed. A phalanx of apartment complexes to the right, their tall blunt shapes like enormous coffins driven vertically into the earth, nail heads of light hammered up and down the flanks of them, the sky that framed them a voluptuous shade of shadowy blue. Something he should be sharing with Molly, who was enamored of sunsets, instead of riding inside this graceful brute of an automobile toward what might be his last few minutes.

In spite of the sealed windows and air-conditioning, the smell intruded, the rank festering of the landfill on the far side of the beltway, opposite the apartment towers. This was where they were headed now, toward a landscape of waste, mound upon mound of it rolling, it seemed, straight for the shore. Beyond it, Jamaica Bay looked inviting by comparison, a smooth dark sheen filled with winking lights. The car left macadam and slithered along dirt, the tires crunching the earth smoothly, a sound that to Izzy was oddly reassuring where nothing else about his predicament was. The Mercedes, its lights off now, crept to a stop. Izzy could make out a sturdy storm fence, strands of heavy-gauge steel carving the air to a height of ten feet in a pattern of diamond shapes. Atop it, and canted away from the landfill, three strands of wickedly adorned wire, almost certainly pulsing with electrical current, were meant to discourage all but the terminally stupid from trying to scale the fence. This city, thought Izzy with a touch of rue, if it isn't nailed down or locked up, it becomes the property of whoever snatches it first. Even our garbage.

Which was correct as far as it went, although the

Scorcese family had a more compelling reason than securing the expensive heavy equipment parked on the grounds: privacy.

The Mercedes was stopped in front of a gate that required the muscle of both Bennie and the Deuce to shove open, and once they were all inside, to shut and lock. The sour air marched forcefully into the Mercedes along with Bennie and the Deuce, both of them panting, Bennie expressing himself without much imagination, inserting the eff expletive about every third word. He was not happy to be here.

Neither was Izzy Stein. Surreptitiously, while the punks were struggling with the gate, he had tried the door handle beside him and found it locked, evidently something controlled by the driver. So the option of running did not exist. Not now.

But later? He reasoned if he was going to be offed, it wouldn't be inside this fancy car. Blitz wouldn't want blood or vomit or feces, depending upon the style of execution, all over this luxurious leather and carpet. People like Blitz valued their toys more than their women.

So if it happened, it was going to happen outside, someplace within the maze of dungheaps where even sounds of screaming or gunfire would be swallowed up in the high walls of stinking waste. The Mercedes inched along a corridor flanked by the giant ripples of garbage.

"Billy," said Blitz Focoso, "I think any time now."

They stopped. The Deuce ran his window down, stuck out his head to back the Mercedes between mounds of garbage. Mounds that climbed twenty, thirty feet into the sky. Izzy thought: the fucking Wall of China wearing Russian perfume. Funny, Iz, very funny. Perhaps you should share your little bon mot with Blitz over tea and scones. Sugar, Blitz? Cream? Ducky outfit you're wearing there. . . .

Goddammit! Stay focused. You don't want to die, do you? Not here, not like this. Not at the whim of some two-bit hood. You are not going to be a victim. You are not! No!

Stay close to Blitz. If he was going to be hit, it would be Blitz's call. Stay next to the decision maker and act accordingly. Either gouge out his eyes or use him as a shield.

The Deuce switched off the engine and silence pressed in upon them.

"Billy," said Blitz, "if you would." There was a muted click within each door, the sound of the locks being released. Something hard prodded Izzy Stein's rib cage. "Let's you and me have a conversation, Jewboy."

Bennie Focoso opened the door for Izzy and stood beside it, his eyes unreadable in the moonlight.

They walked several yards from the car, Izzy taking step after step backward, the gun clearly visible now in Blitz's right hand, Blitz poking him with it to make him move. The garbage rose on either side of them, black at the base to nearly silvery where the moonlight struck. Izzy stumbled, lost his balance several times, but managed to stay close to Blitz, enough so to see his eyes. Abe had told him that up close if a man is going to shoot you, he will telegraph it by narrowing his eyes. Never having had the opportunity to test the theory empirically, Izzy Stein trusted it now implicitly. As if he had a choice.

The sound of an airliner's jets intruded, lights blinking

red off its wingtips and tail, the plane probably waiting for permission to land at JFK. It floated up there like a dream, an impossible hope.

Izzy said, "Look, Blitz, if the point of this is to scare the shit out of me, you're doing it. Other than that I don't see the point."

"The point is maybe we haven't applied enough leverage. It occurs to me you don't understand how serious I am. How serious is this business of some street fuck walking off with family money."

"You think I don't know it's serious?"

"I don't see any results is what I don't see."

"Standing out here in this fucking landfill, how'm I gonna produce results?"

"You gotta brother, don't you? What's he doin' all this time?"

With his elbows at his rib cage, Izzy opened his hands, palms up. "Whadda ya want? His wife's in intensive. Got inoperable cancer. Lymph nodes. He's doin' good, he can answer a phone call without falling apart. C'mon, Blitz."

Blitz Focoso's expression didn't change: he still looked tired, almost bored with the business at hand. He pushed back the slide on his gun, chambering a round. The sound of it seemed enormous in this valley of death, just as its echo did. Izzy, rooted where he was, not five feet from Blitz, realized he had just lost a crucial opportunity. He had assumed the gun was already prepared to fire. He tensed himself. An automatic, when a round is manually chambered, remains in a double-action mode, unless the hammer is cocked, and Izzy didn't hear the telltale ratchet of the cocking mechanism. The amount of time he had to disable Blitz depended upon the strength of the man's index finger. But better in double mode than single, thought Izzy, taking a step forward.

"You disappoint me, Iz," said Blitz, almost sleepily, as he brought the gun up, waving it in the direction of Izzy's chest. "Maybe if you're gone, your brother and your girlfriend will take things more seriously. Whadda you think?"

Before Izzy could answer, there were explosions—two of them to be exact—and Izzy hit the ground rolling, scrambling across slime and stink, slipping as he tried to get to his feet, to turn, to see . . .

The figure sprawled in the dirt wore a dark mask from his eyes down. A mask of blood. Worn beneath his sightless eyes as a result of the second round, a round that Bennie Focoso had not intended to fire, the first one had done the job, and anything more was an insult. Of all people he would not want to insult his brother. But he had never fired this auto before (nor would ever again) and was unfamiliar with the action and so by reflex squeezed off the second round without even realizing it. Squeezed it off and blew Blitz Focoso's nose clean off his face, annihilated it.

Izzy moved closer. He could see now in the moonlight where the other slug entered, just behind the ear, and where a chunk of Blitz's skull had landed, about seven feet up the mound, nestled next to a bright orange plastic container for laundry detergent. The inside of the skull glistened, a composition of bone and topaz ooze—brain, the so-called gray matter. Izzy backed away, turned around, and clasped his legs just above the knees . . . and vomited between his shoes.

Crouching next to his older brother, Bennie Focoso

tucked the automatic beneath his jacket, in a shoulder holster there. He kissed his fingertips and placed them on his brother's forehead. "You fucked up, bro'," he told the corpse. "I didn't have no choice. It's business."

Then he stood up and approached Izzy. "Somebody thought this might give you some idea what's expected."

Izzy raised his face, but could not summon words. He nodded.

The lean man with the stabbing nose suddenly coiled up, his eyes burning into Izzy's. "You think I'm not hurting? Fuck up, you'll pay for what I'm feeling."

There was no stopping it, Izzy Stein ralphed again, this time on Bennie Focoso's double-breasted jacket.

CHAPTER 13

For the flight to Hawaii, Leslie Ann Rice had requested a window seat, which, after an hour of it, she decided was a highly overrated experience, there being little to see except endless acres of cumulus. Relentless sunlight filled the window, and her face began to throb from the heat, so that she finally lowered the shade, snuggled her face next to Misty, and asked if he wouldn't order a light beer for her. "And a glass with some ice cubes in it? I want to taste it really cold."

He lowered the magazine he was reading and nuzzled the top of her head, inhaling the scent of her hair. "We get to our hotel room, Sugarcheeks, we'll have champagne over shaved ice, about half the glass, and the rest is brandy, what they call Brown Sugars. And we'll get naked. How's that sound?"

She closed her eyes and shivered, then reached up to peck him on the cheek. "I can't wait," she whispered.

"That's my girl," he said, and hailed a stewardess. In addition to the beer he ordered a vodka martini for himself, and when they had their drinks in hand, he complimented her once more upon her acting ability, proposing a toast: "You were so good, I halfway believed it myself. You sure the name's Leslie Ann and not Meryl Streep?"

"I'm sure." She tasted her beer. "But I'm kinda wondering if your name is really John Davidson."

Misty dabbed at an eye. He seemed amused. "Oh? And why's that?"

She tasted more of her beer before answering, getting it straight in her mind. "You said we'd be dead if I didn't do what I did. Which means you're in some sort of trouble. And people in trouble don't always go by their real names." She shrugged. "Long as it's not the police, I guess it's your own business what you tell me. I knew the moment you started talking, there was something different about you, and when you took out that buncha hundreds, that clinched it. That and the gun. So it isn't like I walked into this with my eyes closed."

There. She had got that out. Better to play it this way than to pass herself off as a mindless jump.

"Well well well," he said. But he slid an arm around her shoulders, his hand dangling, just touching her breast. He gave it a brief, gentle pat. "I guess I got to watch you every moment. You could probably tell me my own social-security number." He hesitated, but only for a moment. "The name's John David Carmichael, but everyone calls me Misty, on account of my eyes."

"I thought maybe it was an allergy or all the cigarette smoke."

"Smoke doesn't help, but that's the way they are."

"Misty," she said. "Misty Carmichael. It's got a nice ring. And what sort of trouble are you in, Misty? You didn't steal the pope's precious jewels or anything like that, did you?"

He grinned. "You know somethin'? You sound just like your aunt and her friend Renee. *Thang. Any-thang.*"

She smiled back at him. "I guess it's the hick in me. You know, you can take the hick out of the country, but you can't take the country out of the hick."

He squeezed her breast again and said, "I wouldn't have you any other way."

"So did you rob the pope or what?"

"No," he said, "not the pope. This guy kinda works the other side of the street."

The wing of the 747 dropped away as the plane banked beyond Mamala Bay and seemed to rotate above the jewelry hues of the ocean—the sapphire of the deep, the patches of emerald, the inviting aquamarine that embraced the shores. Inland, the coastal tans gave way to the lush verdancy that Misty associated with exotic lands; the network of rivers and streams cut sinuous, stark lines in the terrain and reminded him of photographs he'd seen of the canals on Mars. This sense of remoteness appealed to him, not as it did in Molly's case, for its aspect of liberation, but rather for the security it offered, the distance from the terrifying world he knew. The captain's voice on the intercom called their attention to the appearance of Diamond Head to the east, and then the wing rose and a tremendous racket unfolded beneath them, the landing gear descending, and Misty kept moving his jaws, trying to unplug his ears. Leslie Ann said something to him that sounded like a fly trapped in a jar, and the 747 stood on its wing once more, then leveled off for the final approach. Misty Carmichael closed his eyes, glad for having imbibed the four vodka martinis. Takeoffs and landings scared him shitless.

As the plane taxied to the terminal at Honolulu International Airport, the captain's voice could be heard again welcoming them to the island of Oahu and informing the passengers that it was a little before two in the afternoon and that the temperature was a balmy eighty degrees.

Emerging from the plane into the spacious confines of the terminal, Misty gripped Leslie Ann above the elbow, guided her to one side at the flight gate, his eyes moving over the sparse crowd of people waiting to greet someone from the plane.

Leslie Ann tried to see what it was he was seeing, and failing that, muttered from the corner of her mouth, "What? You see somebody you recognize?"

"No."

"Well, shoot then, let's go grab us our luggage and begin to have some fun."

But he stood rooted to the polished floor. "Where's the

broads in grass skirts? You come to Hawaii, there's supposed to be hula girls greet you with leis. This might as well be fucking La Guardia."

"C'mon, hon. Maybe the hula girls are somewheres else. And don't you be talking to any girls except me about lays."

They spent Wednesday and Thursday on Waikiki Beach during the sunlit hours doing little more than flopping in the sun's path and immersing themselves in the joyous warmth and tumble of the Pacific. She read magazines. He found a bookie that serviced the beach. Inside the vinyl beach bag that Misty slung over his shoulder, among the lotions, the munchies, and magazines, was the reconstructed pistol. Wrapped in the bubbled plastic, it had escaped detection, if indeed the suitcase had been monitored. The Scorcese money rested in a safety deposit box provided by the hotel. Leslie Ann frolicked in the ocean with the uncontained glee of a child, time and again begging Misty to join her, but secure as he might feel, he thought it prudent to err on the side of caution. Hence, the meals they enjoyed he had delivered by room service. Hence, the name and gold MasterCard under which they were registered at the hotel belonged to Carl Bellows, Misty gambling that the credit card he had filched almost three weeks ago with no precise purpose in mind, except that it was there, had not been reported stolen, since the man had virtually a library of cards in his wallet. Hence the practice of Misty to sit stretched out on the rental lounger, his body shimmer-

ing in sun lotion that Leslie had applied, his right hand resting inside the open beach bag in close proximity to the
.380.

After two days of sunning themselves, Leslie had acquired some color, enough to define the exact dimensions of
her bikini when she was naked, and Misty, who had fre-
quented the beaches all summer, was waxed almost walnut.
Pleading a cosmetic need for relief from the sun, Leslie persuaded Misty to sign them up for a tour bus on the morning
of the third day, a Friday. He agreed, having purchased a
fanny-pak for himself, the main pouch perfectly suited for
the pistol. Belted around his waist, the concealed piece was
just a zipper away.

The bus arrived at the hotel at nine A.M. sharp, the
driver hunched over the wheel and smiling, a big Polynesian
who might have flunked out of a sumo wrestler's school for
lack of malice, and the tour guide, a pert and tiny lady of
Oriental heritage outfitted in a charcoal blazer and skirt, a
collarless white blouse that had been ironed so many times,
it was approaching transparency. Even in her tired black
pumps she stood barely higher than the back of the seats on
the bus. Her name was Alice, she informed them over the
microphone, and later, responding to one of Leslie's endless
questions, she explained that she had grown up in Hong
Kong, but her family—parents, three brothers, a sister, and
an unmarried uncle—had saved nearly ten years in order to
emigrate to the United States. All of the family, except for
herself and her sister, lived in Seattle. She said it was a crazy
business living on the island, so expensive everything was,
but at least she didn't have to live with the fear of commu-

nists taking over, stupid bureaucrats and worse running her life. Leslie was smitten by the girl, her spunk and abilities (she spoke five languages), while Misty was of the opinion that Alice was a titless dink.

He was not particularly enjoying himself on the tour. The crowd that had boarded at their hotel typified the demographics on the bus. A smattering of old white folks in funny outfits, the old guys in weenie hats and women with broad butts and big, hashslinger voices; Japs of all ages with cameras dangling and hollering exuberant gutturals, as if they were trying to converse and pump iron at the same time; and the boomers now pushing fifty, mostly but not exclusively white, with children in tow, most of them in need of a corrective back of the hand. Misty recognized no one his and Leslie's age, although by the same token, he didn't see anyone that gave him reason to be nervous. Dressed in new peach shorts and a matching halter top, a tri-color gold necklace at her throat and pale leather sandals on her feet, Leslie was the stunner of the bus, and the geezers, the male Japs, and boomers devised all kinds of strategies to get a glimpse of her. It was so obvious that even the hashslingers were joking loudly about it halfway into the tour.

When the bus stopped at Pearl Harbor, a certain solemnity overtook the group. Alice led them onto a white concrete-and-steel canopy that embraced the U.S.S. *Arizona,* submerged in the sweet blue inviting water, as if the beauty of the gravesite could atone for the horror perpetrated there. Some of the people wept, mainly the Japs and geezers. An old fart with muscled arms and crude tattoos on them approached Leslie with one of the oldest lines in the book, asking her if she knew what time it was. Misty paid little attention as she stepped away from him, so engrossed was he in the size of the entombed battleship, trying to associate it with a television memory of the movie, *From Here to Eternity*. What's his name, Montgomery Clift, trying to make it back to the base during the attack. Did he? Misty couldn't remember. All he remembered was how totally the country was caught with its pants down, how people died from not keeping their eyes open. It wouldn't happen to Misty Carmichael, that was his philosophy.

As the group gathered to return to the bus, Leslie introduced Misty to the old guy with the tattoos on his arms. He said his name was Earl. He was dressed in sunshine-yellow polyester trousers, dun-colored boots with heels that raised him to a height commensurate with the bridge of Misty's nose, and a short-sleeve shirt full of flowery flourishes. He suggested an almost unthinkable mix of big-rig driver and golf enthusiast, a union man in Republican pants. He had a ruddy face with a delicate nose, scar tissue over his eyes suggesting a boxer's past, and the general air of someone who would sell acreage in swampland or a used automobile with egg yolk in the crankcase. He combed his mustard-colored hair straight back, trimmed neatly at the nape, and sported sideburns to the base of his earlobes. Up close, Misty revised his estimate of the man's age down some, to the middle forties, a boomer. A boomer with the lightest blue eyes Misty had ever seen, about the shade of the sea that the warship sat beneath. Grinning, the man extended his hand, offered a strong, dry grip. Said to Misty, "So you folks are moving on to Maui?"

And Leslie chimed in, "It's Earl's favorite island, he was telling me. Says we'll love it."

"Tomorrow," said Misty. He had the impression suddenly of having seen the guy somewhere, but couldn't place him. "So Earl, you live out here, or you a tourist like us?"

"Tourist like you, son. Couldn't afford to live here unless they legalize gambling." Addressing the frown on Misty's face, he went on, "I'm a dealer in Vegas. And since I'm a die-hard bachelor, I do manage to put away a penny or two, so I'm free to visit the islands time to time. Come here to restore my batteries is what it is."

From the bottom step of the bus, little Alice chided them: "Misser and Misses Bellows, please, is a whole bus waiting."

Leslie touched Misty lightly on the wrist. "We should be going," she said. "But Earl? Maybe we could meet you later, buy you a drink in exchange for what you can tell us about Maui. Whadda you say, Carl?"

"It sounds like a plan," said Misty, and he watched the guy in the flamboyant pants give Leslie the name of his hotel, the room number, and agree to a time to call. The guy seemed utterly straightforward, just someone happy to hook up with friendly people in a strange place. But it didn't change the fact that Misty had experienced, however vague, a gnawing sense of recognition. But where?

The good news, which Louis Lippi was finally permitted to deliver once Angelo Scorcese had broken his dark glasses into pieces barely the size of croutons, had to do with the fact that they had identified Misty Carmichael's departure gate, and from that, his destination. But two days of secretive inquiry on the island by friends of the family turned up nothing, and Angelo, frustrated by the limitations of talking over the phone, drafted Lippi to fly with him to Oahu, to conduct the search personally. It was a gamble, but the way Angelo figured it, nailing this scum might be a bridge back into his father's heart— what the fuck, maybe even his ticket back to New York. Angelo did not discuss his decision with the Don, because that would have required an explanation of how Misty eluded them in Phoenix, a maneuver that would not exactly shed a favorable spotlight on the way things were done under his jurisdiction.

So, wearing a Jets jersey, gray cotton shorts, black hightops, and his Mets cap on backward, the bill pointing down his back, Angelo Scorcese boarded a Northwest flight nonstop to Oahu accompanied by Louis Lippi in a gray suit, black shirt, and black shoes. Louis, by means of a flight attendant on the family payroll, had on his person a nine-millimeter Smith & Wesson, and in the luggage of the 747's hold there was a sawed-off twelve-gauge with a burl grip, a container of plastique, and a pair of silencer-equipped .22-caliber Colts, one of them with a scope for night vision. Also a folder filled with photographs of Misty Carmichael, as well as a description of the woman traveling with him, everything the three schlubs who'd messed up at the airport could remember.

Angelo Scorcese and Louis Lippi were greeted in Oahu by a fat, smiling, brown man by the name of Larry Lee, a gentle giant in a tank top, his belly hanging over the waist of his cut-off jeans, rubber thongs on his feet. Lee was a gofer and sometime driver for Moe Wiseman, who had made inquiries on the island as a favor to Angelo. Moe, although not always on paper, owned sizable pieces of several hotels in Honolulu, as well as some on the sister islands, but two days of spreading the word had come up with zip on Misty Carmichael. Angelo Scorcese was convinced to a certainty that if the little creep had eluded Moe's informants, it had to be that he was using phony identification. He cursed himself for not forwarding the photos to Moe: living in Phoenix with the heat, the dummies, and Magda had dulled his instincts. Acting, maybe killing the slimeball with his bare hands, that would sharpen them. He wanted to feel blood on his hands, feel alive once more, explode from this coma he'd been living in since the loss of Mai Lee.

The fat Hawaiian gofer said, "If you will follow me, sirs, to the baggage carousel, I will collect your luggage. Mr. Wiseman say I to drive you to the Prince Lane, a suite is there registered for you. I am to be your driver this evening for wherever it is you wish to go. I know many good restaurants if you are hungry. I would especially recommend you try the mahimahi while you are with us. It is a delightful fish."

Angelo grunted and said, "Louis, I guess we oughta be happier'n pigs in shit. Not only we got a driver, we got fucking Craig Claiborne to show us around."

It was early evening, a tender shade of blue gathering in the sky as the sun trekked west, a breeze sifting in off the ocean, and as Larry Lee loaded the luggage into the trunk of a forest-green Mercedes, a big sedan in the 500 series, Misty Carmichael and his precious Leslie were greeting their new friend, Earl, in a cozy piano bar called Mellow Eddie's.

A young black lady with short hair, a single spiraling braid dangling down beyond her nape, had fingers that moved liquidly over the keyboard, a voice rich in texture and capable of belting out a song like "My Man" with authority, unintimidated by anyone's memory of Billie Holiday. Even Misty Carmichael could appreciate the silken inflections, the magic of the woman's talent.

Earl was saying, "One of the movers on the island is a guy by the name of Moe Wiseman. He's got a piece of the action here is the way I hear it, and the little colored girl is one of his—uh, he's showcasing her here. Name is Mariah Riggs. Ain't she got a voice?"

"In spades," said Misty.

Sitting across the table, Earl took a pull from a longneck of Coors and winked. "In spades, you say. That's good. Ain't no moss under your feet, is there?"

Misty dabbed at his eyes, the expression on his face sober and unamused. "Not the last time I looked," he said quietly. It was Earl's hair that bothered him, the bleached shade that might have been a consequence of days spent in the sun, but although he had some color, it wasn't nearly enough to extinguish his true casino pallor. So it must be a dye job: vanity. There was nothing a vain man like Misty detected sooner than symptoms of his own disease. The man, he decided, bore watching.

Leslie Ann, who was sitting between them and daintily sipping a mai tai through a straw, lifted her face to look at them both, as if to gauge how they were getting on. She had changed outfits. She wore a clinging white cotton shift, basically a T-shirt for a tall man, with the sleeves rolled over twice, no bra beneath it, a belt that looked like woven hemp cinched on her tummy by a turquoise clasp. When she walked, the material hugged her flanks, revealed precisely the definition of her silk thong panties. Her nipples stared out as well, like veiled eyes. Turquoise earrings dripped tear-shaped pendants. Her dark hair was cut and combed in such a fashion that she was perpetually catching a swath of it in the crotch of her hand to lift it away from her left eye. A dry scent on her skin that Misty associated with fresh strawberries, a freshness in her face that made the world around her brand new and brimming with promise. Listening to her now, Misty could just eat her alive, she seemed so delicious. "I hope you don't mind, Earl, but I'm about busting to hear about Maui."

Earl grinned, took another tug from the longneck before saying anything. "Not at all, ma'am," he said. "I'd be most happy to tell you."

As he described the island's virtues, its points of beauty and what they shouldn't miss, the shops, the restaurants, the best beaches, day tours, and all the rest of it, Misty found his attention wandering. The guy sounded like a travelogue.

Mellow Eddie's was tricked out with a lot of fishnet and cork, a mural of a swordfish dancing on its tail across the wall to the rear, a circular bar employing two bartenders, the amber lights low except for the spot on the singer. A fairly good crowd, the noise level up there, everybody feeling happy. Earl was leaning over the table to make himself heard. Even in the dim lighting Misty could make out the tattoo on Earl's right forearm, a blue bucking bronco with the legend beneath it: *Ride 'em Hard.* Motto of an old circuit rider? The man talked on. The black singer was working her way into "Red Sails in the Sunset," and Misty could almost picture it, the tableau of hull and filled sails, the swanlike grace of the vessel, the bloody shimmer of light on the water from the dying sun. The water.

The water in sunlight.

A man with hair bleached a mustard yellow in the Waikiki surf yesterday. Misty thought about it, certain it was him now, and a stab of panic made his eyes smart. He reached for his salty dog and poured some of it down his windpipe, his fit of coughing drawing a bland smile from Earl and clucks of sympathy from Leslie. He apologized for the interruption. Leslie caught the shock of hair falling over her eye and lifted it away, her face shining with tenderness.

"Better, hon?"

"I'll live."

"Get you another salty there, son? Make up for the one went the wrong way."

"No. I'm good. I still got some."

"So Earl, Lanai's where the great shops and galleries are?"

"No, ma'am. That's a little island. Lanai is where they grow all the pineapple. *Lahaina* is where your shops are, tons of 'em, and painter galleries, and restaurants, lemme tell you . . ."

The man droned on. Misty used the time to reason with his attack of nerves. Earl's hotel, for one thing, was not that far from the one where they were staying, so it was not implausible for him to wind up bathing on the same beach they had chosen. It was a coincidence, quite possibly a meaningless one. Then, too, there was the sedation factor. The more Misty listened to the guy, the stronger became his opinion that the only thing he had to fear from him was death by boredom.

Still.

Leslie seemed perfectly enchanted, peppering the guy with questions. First, the dink Alice, now this Earl.

Still.

Misty slipped a hand beneath the royal-blue knit shirt Leslie had bought for him in the Metrocenter in Phoenix and stroked the smooth cool shape against his chest.

Still, he thought, the shock of recognition had opened his eyes, and whether what he saw was threat or mere coincidence, prudence dictated mobility. What that meant to him was simply acknowledging the merit of an old rule, something learned from his days of breaking and entering: expand the avenues of escape.

He finished his salty dog and dropped a pair of twenties on the table. "This should pay for the drinks until I get back," he said, skidding his chair across the dark plank flooring. He leaned next to Leslie's ear to whisper, "Business, Sugarcheeks. Shouldn't be more'n an hour." And to Earl he said, "If you'll watch over the little woman, Earl, I'll be right back. Dinner's on me. I was just thinking, we could drop by the Galley Inn the bus driver recommended; remember that, darling? Said the mahimahi was out of this world."

Having watched the dark oak door, the entrance of Mellow Eddie's, close behind Misty Carmichael, Leslie Ann Rice returned her attention to Earl, taking time before she spoke to scoop the swath of hair away from her eye. "Daddy," she said, "have you been taking lessons from Mother?"

His eyes narrowed. "Just meaning what, little girl?"

"All that bullshit about Maui, you sounded like some of those folks on public television. I swear. I like to've nodded off."

He shook his head ruefully, raising a hand to catch the waitress's eye, order himself another longneck. "Hell, girl, you give me such short notice. All I had time to do was watch this buttass video about three times and bone up on some travel books, some freebie pamphlet called *This Week: Maui.* I don't think your daddy did half-bad. He looked impressed, you ask me."

Leslie sucked on her straw and it made a snorkeling sound, indicating that she was at the bottom of her mai tai. "I do hope so," she said, "because he's gotta whole suitcase stuffed with money and all of it's in a hotel safe deposit box. Ain't no way we can touch it there."

One of Earl's strong hands drifted over, squeezed Leslie's. "You just leave it to Daddy."

"Not if you're going to be so dumb as to be indiscreet," sniffed Leslie. "Get it, please, through that horny skull of yours that we are strangers."

"Leslie Ann, I love you when you are on fire," he said, his hand gripping hers hard, jerking her toward him, his dry lips searing hers, and his free hand moving freely over her.

CHAPTER 14

Some choice tail there, Robert Martin thought. He could not believe how abruptly she'd shot him down. Women did not do things like that to Robert Martin. Not if they were in their right minds.

Robert Martin owned an import auto salon located in Forest Hills. He was thirty-six years old, happily divorced, tanned and fit (jogging every morning and tennis three times a week), owned a summer residence on Fire Island and a yacht berthed in the Hamptons. He had a fine head of wavy brown hair, bedroom eyes, and a smile he was told that made a woman twitch in her secret parts.

But here he was standing with his drink in hand (a dry Tanqueray martini with a scroll of lemon peel in it) across from the bar in Flamingos, trying to mask his surprise and disappointment, some anger creeping in as well, over the turndown. Who did that juicy little slut think she was— royalty?

"There you are, Boppo." It was Colin Cavanaugh, only son of the owner of Cavanaugh's Fine Furniture, established on Park Avenue South, in Manhattan, with branches in Westchester and Forest Hills. Cavanaugh was Robert Martin's customary tennis opponent, a shorter man with long, simian arms capable of lashing serves and wicked ground strokes. He was a toucher, looped a long arm over anyone nearby to draw them closer to his smile. His favorite expression was, "Would I lie?" He encouraged people to address him by his initials, C.C., and he was the only person of Robert Martin's acquaintance to call him Boppo. He could not recall how it started, and there were times, like now, when Robert Martin wanted to tell Colin Cavanaugh that if he uttered the word again, ever in his lifetime, he would brain him senseless with his own custom Johnnie Mac racket. Cavanaugh was saying now, "Last I saw, when I went to the head, you were putting the moves on little blue eyes."

"She has herpes," said Robert Martin, taking a sip from his martini and still not believing it.

Colin Cavanaugh swung around to check out the shapely redhead sitting alone at the bar, sipping a club soda. He put a hand on Robert Martin's shoulder. "What?"

"It's what she said, C.C."

Both men stood there in tight tennis shorts and Ralph Lauren knit shirts, holding their drinks, scanning the length of the bar with practiced eyes and egos accustomed to success. Robert Martin spotted the guy first, the guy a little taller than C.C., and even with a sport coat on, a muscled torso was evident. Robert Martin recognized him from two nights ago, the guy bullshitting at the bar with the black chick and . . . Kristen? No, Karen. With the Spanish-sounding last name. She didn't look or talk Spanish. Not with that pile of blond hair (a nest of blond pubes too) and those magnificent breasts—no silicone in those babies, just nature gone exuberant. Karen. Radiant with genetic generosity, but no class. Zip. The little blue eyes, even as she grossed him out, somehow managed to convey a quality of hauteur that Karen could never pull off. But Karen, give the lady her due, had fucked him six ways from Saturday. He wondered though about those pubes, being almost *too* blond: a dye job?

And as he wondered, he watched the guy, something about him suggesting a nefarious background. Noting the guy's jeans and sneakers, he could see him as a distributor of nose candy, or as a midlevel person in the Scorcese family. More than a few of the people to frequent Flamingos fell into that category. And what was this?

The guy approached the little piece of delicious, who had shot him down, and they went at it, embracing and kissing and murmuring and kissing some more, enough so it made Robert Martin wince over his Tanqueray martini. A fucking sleazy hood like that getting her action. This guy had some kind of luck with the ladies, or else he was their dealer. That was it. He was just a schmuck feeding the ladies' habits.

Colin Cavanaugh said, "Boppo, you see what I'm seeing? I don't believe it, she told you she had herpes."

Robert Martin said, "C.C.? Would I lie?"

"**W**hat is it, Iz?"

"In a minute, okay? Sorry I'm late." He caught the bartender's attention. "Vincent? A Stoli on ice, Vincent, make it a double." Then to Molly: "You give Mario a name yet for a table?"

"I was waiting for you. Something's wrong. I mean, besides Zelda. I can see it all over you."

Izzy had driven home from the Argent Towers, where the Deuce dropped him, and showered, changed clothes to remove the stink of fear. He had poured himself a drink there, but couldn't remember if he'd drunk it. The drive to Flamingos was a blur. He wasn't shivering anymore, but the vision of the chunk of Blitz's skull shining next to the empty Tide container remained vivid. Along with Bennie Focoso's warning.

Izzy pushed a twenty across the bar in exchange for the double vodka. He took a sip, then dumped almost half of what remained down his throat in an effort to wash away the remnants of what he had witnessed. Had witnessed, but could no way prove to the satisfaction of the law. That being what the execution of Blitz Focoso had been arranged to illustrate.

A tall guy with a lot of chin that Izzy thought he vaguely remembered shouldered his way between them, resting his brawn on the bar, his face turned toward Molly. "You tell your friend here you're a walking center for communicable disease? Or did you want to apologize for misleading me, maybe accept my offer of a drink? I don't think you realize how much fun you might have this weekend, if you'd join me on my yacht."

Molly Carmichael looked at him thinking there must be a machine somewhere that stamps them out. Assholes were all the same: they believed implicitly that wherever they walked, there traveled the center of the universe. And her anger flared as she realized this was a fair definition of her own son.

Izzy wrenched the taller man around by the shoulder and squeezed between him and the bar, stood chest to chest with the guy. He recognized him now as one of the two preppy types who moved in on Karen Santiago and her friend Trish the other night in here, and then he saw the guy's pal in those sporty shorts they both wore, his hip cocked against a low partition and a well-oiled smirk on his face. "You always barge into conversations," said Izzy, "or is this your first day in assertiveness training?"

Robert Martin smiled, although it was not the way he smiled for a hot prospect—no, this was a look laced with indulgence, something to be used on social outcasts and mental defectives. "Pardon me," he said, "but I believe I was speaking to the lady. With whom I had been conversing earlier. So if anyone is interrupting, it would seem to be you."

"Look, slick"—this from Molly, swiveling on her stool —"I don't know who you are, or what your problem is, but if you don't disappear, I'm going to call the bartender, and let the bartender call the bouncer, and that'll be one more problem for you in what I have to assume is a rather large inventory of them."

"Why you little slu—"

Izzy Stein punched Robert Martin cleanly in the testicles, plucked the martini from his hand before he dropped it, and steered him gasping toward the short guy in the knit shirt and tennis pants. Izzy said, "I think this is a friend of yours," and handed him the martini.

The short guy was staring at Robert Martin, bent over now, tears streaming from his eyes, still trying to catch his breath.

"Don't worry," said Izzy, "he'll live. But you ought to look into a better class of friends."

Izzy's name was called in less than five minutes. They followed their waiter—his name was Arturo—to their table, which was on a landing, and it turned out to be a superb location for viewing any of the cable networks programmed for sports. The maître d', Mario, had not forgotten Izzy's largesse, which meant an outrageous tip would be in order.

When they were seated, and Izzy had ordered a second double vodka for himself, another club soda for Molly, he opened his tall menu with the flamingos' profiles in the middle of the cover, two pink shapes arranged in a feathery yin and yang configuration, to scan the list of hors d'oeuvres. Turn the menu upside down, and you could read the lunch offerings.

Molly said, "Iz."

He said, "How about some calamari to start?"

"Iz, what happened?"

He told her.

They sat with Abe in the downstairs apartment for more than an hour. The chessboard was out, all the figurines arranged for the contest, but neither white nor black had advanced so much as a pawn. There was a glass of apple juice beside the board, the ice dissolving in it. Abe was in his bathrobe. He talked, as people so often do when faced with the prospect of losing a spouse, almost as if in a trance. He let loose what was in his mind, because he had an audience. First his parents; now another assassin was stalking someone he loved. Knowing the assassin's name did not make it any easier in light of his helplessness to intercede. This was knowledge that loomed large in his thoughts tonight. This utter and final helplessness.

But in there as he spoke were glimmerings, a sudden joyous memory, even something amusing that caused them all to laugh for a moment, to back down the tension of their mutual sorrow. A moment's grace.

Because Zelda was going to die.

Going to die soon.

No escape.

"You love someone," said Abe, in the midst of one of his soliloquies, "you'd kill to save them, no question. But this is something you can't kill."

As Iz and Molly climbed the stairs to the second floor, Molly was remembering the first half of the equation.

You love someone, you'd kill to . . .

There was no music that night. No piano keys struck. No attempt to harmonize.

No Young, no Dylan.

No poignant words.

Just a man and a woman facing each other on a bed in a room lit with moonlight. They touched one another. Hands moved tenderly over bare skin, as if enacting a process of discovery. He thought, as they slipped into bed, that they might be able to lose themselves for a while in desire, but he had been wrong. At least, he could not. Nevertheless, putting his hand here and here and over here, and *there,* yes there oh especially there, afforded them both a measure of satisfaction and relief. Simply gaining the knowledge of one another's flesh was something to hang on to, for tenderness at times can be every bit the equal of passion.

After a while, after more kisses and murmured sentiments, he was asleep, or at least she believed he was, breathing easily, curled away from her on his hip.

She lay on her back, her eyes open. She was thinking the light in the room was something like the backgrounds in those Matthew Brady Civil War photographs Zelda had shown her, the solemn air draped with the mystery of death. She rolled her face to one side. The muscle fanning away from Izzy's spine shone in the light, the hard washed color of a seashell, and she pressed a fingertip there, to reassure herself.

He felt it, the gentle, insistent pressure behind him, prodding him like a conscience, driving him deeper into solitude. He hadn't told her everything. He had told her about the ride, the threats, but he hadn't told her about the dead loan shark, his blood watering a wasteland. That part of the nightmare was his, to sleep with by himself.

Friday afternoon broke with the parade of sunshine-filled days. Still hot, miserably hot, but an armada of slate-colored clouds sailed in during the morning to shut out the sun, then a little past noon a downpour commenced, swollen drops falling at such a velocity that they bounced off the sidewalks, virtually blinded drivers in their vehicles trying to navigate Metropolitan Avenue. It was no better being parked on the avenue, insofar as trying to conduct discreet observation.

To the fat man sitting behind the wheel of a stationary Buick Regal, the shitty weather was something to be expected. It was his day off, what else happens? Normally, the fat man would be spending his down time at home, shuffling through the deadwood, murders still unsolved or not solved to his satisfaction—washes, laundromat specials—probing the records and more recent reports by means of his IBM-compatible computer equipped with a modem, gather info over the phone anywhere he wanted. His wife would bring him sandwiches, garlic dills sliced lengthwise between slabs of pumpernickel dressed with mayo—his kind of mayo, Miracle Whip, that he had grown up on. And an occasional dark beer, a stout chilled for an American taste, not the room-warm brew he had tasted up in Montreal once and realized he *really was* in another country. The cost of the phone service was something he incurred, not the department. Answers, a whiff of the truth, happened to be a private obsession, and not necessarily something to dock the taxpayers for. As any politician would be quick to point out.

But this afternoon in the driving rain, he was borrowing a page from his young partner's book, shadowing a dark van registered to a nonadvertising business in Brooklyn. The business, S & S & Sons, listed as an address a PO box, and the phone number was answered by a gum-chewing babe out of a flat in Brooklyn Heights, who received messages between nine A.M. and four P.M. That's what the tape-recorded voice said, if you missed the time frame. Whatever the lady did in her free time, it wasn't lessons in elocution.

He was sweating so much behind the beaded wind-shield, even with the air-conditioning on, that he removed his pale straw fedora. He helped himself to a disc of dried plum, then dipped a freckled paw into the ice that remained in his fast-food jumbo drink and mopped his brow, cleansed his fingers of ketchup and hamburger grease. A man of his weight, his wife would tell him, shouldn't be filling himself with hamburgs, but as he patiently tried to explain to her, it wasn't like he could find a Jenny Craig's on every corner.

Lieutenant D. James Cox had sworn to his partner, Kenny Takimoto, swathed in plaster of Paris, plastic, and adhesive bandages, IVs in his forearm, that he would pursue the cocksuckers Kenny had been shadowing, that had turned the tables, jumping him in his own apartment. An additional incentive: if Kenny was correct about a family shark being taken off, it represented a fissure in the Don's empire. A faint one, to be sure, but if it wasn't quickly rectified, there would be blood in the streets. Family blood. The price of failure. Lieutenant D. James Cox harbored the dream of being there when the price was paid. And sticking close to the van that transported Joseph Vincent Scorcese hither and yon throughout the boroughs of New York City seemed a reasonable beginning.

The van occupied a spot just in front of a fireplug, directly across the spattering sidewalk from the entrance to the bakery. It had been sitting there for nearly an hour, nobody emerging from it or entering. Not that this discouraged Cox. He was a man who had spent close to eleven hours under brush within spitting distance of the Ho Chi Minh Trail, surviving on dehydrated chocolate, foliage, and whatever insects he could identify. Department wags informed rookies that Cox could outwait the inhabitants of a cemetery. And while that was stretching the point unto absurdity, the fact remained that he had single handedly waxed an entire patrol of Charlie coming down Ho's Freeway, had accomplished it with a flamethrower and thirty round clips in his M-16. Patience had its rewards.

He watched the sharply attired lady work the broad black umbrella open as she stepped out of the bakery. He had noticed her walking in several minutes earlier, and the view had been no less enjoyable. But something tripped his curiosity: she had emerged as empty-handed as she had entered, only a purse hanging from a strap on her shoulder and the umbrella. People did not walk out a bakery as famous for its pastries as the Scorcese one on Metropolitan without a purchase in a snow-white sack. It didn't happen.

The woman wore a deep-blue dress with black diamond shapes running transversely down the front, obscuring the buttons there, and black patent pumps, a black hat with a shallow round crown and wide brim that turned down. Her appearance was at once demure and enticing, something that might knock a doubting priest right out of the diocese, but was still perfectly acceptable for an audience with the pope. Cox, much as he loved his wife, could not help but envy the man who enjoyed this woman's favors. He fitted the zoom lens of Kenny Takimoto's camera to his eyes. The closer she came the better she looked. Her hair was chestnut, or maybe a deep red; it was difficult to tell in the lousy light, say nothing of the shadow of the brim. Blue eyes, perfect skin. No wedding band. Now why the fuck was that important to a man like himself? Except as fodder for fantasy . . . Which was about as good as it got for a man in his condition and position in this, the fifty-second year of his life.

The lady stood there beneath the awning, beneath the black canopy of her umbrella, until the glass door swung out once more, this time ahead of a huge guy with an abbreviated mustache and a small guy behind him who touched the woman in black and blue between her shoulders, indicating she should follow the big man in khaki trousers wearing a white knit collarless shirt with a placat front, something that appeared to have been inspired by the top half of somebody's turn-of-the-century long johns. The little man that followed her to the van wore a rain-stained gray fedora, the brim bent every which way, over an implacable face filled with creases, its swarthy cast enriched by long winter holidays on the beaches of the Caribbean.

He recognized the men. The big one was muscle, a combination gofer and body watcher by the name of Cato Dellacroce. The little one was the Don, Joseph Vincent Scorcese, the man known across the country, to the people who made it a point to be informed of such things, as the Baker. It was the very lack of embellishment to his aka that established him as a man of distinction.

But the woman, the woman with the siren shape and dark hair visible beneath the black hat, the woman climbing into the back of the van along with the Baker, she wasn't anyone Lieutenant D. James Cox had encountered before, much to his regret. Even with the benefit of the zoom lens he could not make her. The camera was an expensive German or Swiss model—Takimoto had confused him rattling on as he had vis-à-vis lenses, filters, film, and camera—something called a Hasselblad, a very pricey item capable of reproducing just about everything but human life. Cox snapped away in the rain, trying to keep the mystery lady in the yellow frame of the viewfinder, and hoped to God that Kenny was correct, the camera was a no-brainer. The rain continued to slash down creating thin silver slats in the afternoon, the lady in black and blue moving through them and out of them, as if casually strolling a cell block. Vanishing into a dark van with the Baker.

He drew his upper lip beneath his bottom lip watching the van, watched it back up, stop. He cranked over the ignition, forgetting the engine was on, and cringed as the starter grated loudly. The van eased into the traffic moving east on Metropolitan Avenue, Lieutenant D. James Cox in the Buick Regal right behind it. The van had its lights on in the rain.

Cox plucked a wafer of dried plum from his coat pocket, snicked it between his lips, and thought about the lady in the van. Could be somebody Joe enjoyed on the side, although she didn't look like a whore.

That was stupid.

There were plenty of whores who didn't look like whores, like the stable of them that Seven Sisters broad had run a few years ago, what'd they call her? She had grown up with old East Coast money and breeding, gone to the best schools, then used the skills she had acquired earning an M.B.A. from Vassar to open an escort service. Some service: gorgeous ladies tricked out to look like debutantes who would gobble richard in the rear of the limo, swallow every last drop, and still be able to smile for the camera, nothing mussed, as they entered some gala opening or premiere on the arm of the distinguished gentleman who was paying for her company and a blow job, and who knew what else as the gossamer evening spun wildly on. Broads made anywhere from five hundred to a thou a night, split fifty-fifty with the Vassar lady, which was a whole better percentage than they'd see from a pimp in any city in the civilized world. If that wasn't a contradiction in terms. What was her name?

Evangeline Marie Leeds-Bennington. Preferred to be called Eve, the original woman. Nice touch. Eve Leeds-Bennington, the Aristocrat of Amour. The Vassar Vixen. The papers had had a ball. The Eve of Erection. So had the guys in homicide.

Lieutenant D. James Cox was thinking it was a crazy world in which high-priced hookers dressed to look respectable and the teenaged daughters of men his age and younger outfitted themselves to look like hookers, taking their cue from rock singers. Probably neither the rockers nor the teenaged daughters of the men he worked with knew what a richard was: a hard, therefore longer, dick. He hoped not, but maybe he was being stupid again.

After all, one of the most active devotees of whore couture promoted herself as Madonna. You wonder why kids didn't know what was what, when all you had to do was watch the real world stealing all their reference points. Eve's become a madam. Madonna sings in her underwear. In the ghetto, *bad* is something to aspire to.

And for this, thought Lieutenant D. James Cox, I put my ass on the line every day.

No maybe about it. I *am* stupid.

He fed himself another wafer of dried plum and accelerated, pulled up tight on the van's ass. If they were fucking in there, he was going to be close enough to feel the heat. All he wanted was a measure of revenge for Kenny, and then he'd submit his resignation, go to work for Ray Sommer's security service. Become a high-priced bodyguard for the fast-lane set—who knows, maybe even meet Madonna. Tell her to grow up and get dressed.

He said: "You love this man so much?"

She said nothing. She just looked at him.

"Let me see how much."

She said nothing.

"I need proof, before I agree to what it is you suggesting. Matter of trust."

"Trust? I told you what I will do."

"That is the future. This is now."

"What?" she said.

"Take it off."

"What?"

"The dress. I want to see you without the dress before I decide if I should trust you."

"You think I'm wired or some kind of dumb cop thing? Is that what you think?"

"I think you are a beautiful lady. I think you owe it to me to show me."

She wanted to, but did not sigh, as that would have been evidence of reluctance, a signal of weakness. She loosened the buttons down the front of her dress, shrugged out of the sleeves and sat on the seat in her black slip, black panties, and black brassiere, displaying her breasts and nipples behind a faint, extruded veil. "See? No wires."

The van swung sharply right, pitching her into him, into the old man's arms, a smell of cloves about him as he burrowed his almost raisin-colored face between her breasts. She could feel his lips on her bare skin, dry, with the ticklish roughness of a cat's tongue, moving over her exposed breasts now as his right hand, the one with bent fingers, crawled beneath her slip to touch her.

She put her hand on the hand beneath her slip, stopping it. "This is not the business we were discussing," she said.

"You are very beautiful," he said, trying to remember one so astonishing as this one even when he was young. Surely there must have been some. Surely. But none could he remember wanting so desperately as he now wanted this one.

But she was leaning away from him, tucking those creamy breasts inside the cups of her brassiere.

"Beautiful," he said, "and brave. So at least you speak. But do you got what it takes?"

"I can do what's necessary. I always have."

"Show me."

"What?"

"You can do what is necessary."

"I'm sorry. I don't—"

"To earn my trust."

"I thought—"

"Take off the panties," he said brutally. "Take off every goddamn thing. And do not insult me by making excuses."

She stared at him, narrowing her eyes.

"The hat, too," he said, staring right back.

She reached behind her back for the clasp to her brassiere, her hand trembling with rage. She pulled off her hat and flung it. She wriggled out of her panties and slip and knelt between his legs, her deep red hair falling, spreading over her pale shoulders. Already she was envisioning an opportunity, a means of revenge. Already she was thinking about killing this one too. She did not doubt for an instant that she had what it took. Not for an instant.

But not yet. Not now.

The old man's penis jumped to attention the moment she touched it, stiff as a strutting schoolboy. She dreamed of someplace far away, a paradise, and focused on that dream.

CHAPTER 15

It took Misty Carmichael longer than he had anticipated, but this was because he decided on the way back to the hotel to exercise several precautions—changing taxis, for one. At the airport, he rode up and down the escalators scanning the terminal for a tail. So nearly two hours had elapsed before the final taxicab deposited him in front of Mellow Eddie's. Inside he found a ticked-off Leslie, and Earl, who looked well on his way to oblivion, a big sloppy smile sloshing around in his face. He wanted to shake Misty's hand, then seemed reluctant to let go. Old Earl, the longer you got to know him, seemed more and more harmless.

The black singer was nowhere to be seen, a jukebox on

the far side of the bar undertaking the chore of entertaining the still boisterous clientele.

Earl hung on to his hand. "See what it is, little girl got her head stuck in a hornets' nest, thinkin' where was you. I tole her and I tole her: a man's business comes before his pleasure. Is what I tole her."

And Leslie, her arms folded snug and tight beneath her breasts, wouldn't look at him. "I was worried sick," she said, staring into the fresh mai tai the waitress had brought only moments before Misty stepped through the door of Mellow Eddie's. "I *was.* You said it'd be only a hour and it's . . . what'd you say it was, Earl?"

"Quarter of. But look here, little girl, a man's business—"

"Almost two hours. I was worried sick." She guided the straw to her lips and assuaged her anxiety, sipping primly.

"Earl, could I have my hand back?"

"Just *sick.*"

"Is what I tole her."

The waitress came over, a robust blond with sweat on her smiling upper lip. "Get you something, sir?"

"Salty dog," Misty said, and glanced down at the grinning Earl. "And a fucking locksmith to free my hand."

In many respects (most people might argue all respects), Angelo Scorcese led a carefree existence, more or less his own boss and no job to report to on a regular basis. Oh, he had a wife he loathed, but what spouse didn't generally despise the other after a while? Besides, he had a luscious live-in mistress. Hard to feel pity for a guy in his position.

But Angelo was doing a good job of it, feeling sorry for himself, after several hours of fruitless inquiry, flashing photostats of Misty Carmichael at every front desk of every hotel they could find in downtown Honolulu. He and Louis marching grimly in, while Larry Lee kept the Mercedes idling in the no-parking zone, introducing themselves to the smiling, usually youthful desk clerks as private eyes, identifying Misty Carmichael as an armed and dangerous embezzler. Upon request, they could both provide phony licenses with their pictures on them, something Angelo had had the foresight to arrange for in Phoenix. Only a piddling few had the temerity to ask for proof of who they said they were. That was the good news. The bad news was that not one of the personnel they confronted could remotely remember seeing anyone that resembled Misty Carmichael.

It was coming up on seven o'clock when they settled on the backseat of the Mercedes, both of them admitting to hunger, and Angelo leaned forward and thumped the fat Hawaiian on the shoulder with a thick forefinger: "Larry. You said somethin' about a good fish dinner."

Larry Lee looked back at him in the rearview mirror, grinning broadly. "But of course," he said in his jovial voice. "I did say. If the gentlemen hungry, I recommend the mahimahi. I take you now?"

"Take us where?"

Larry Lee slowed the Mercedes as they approached an intersection, estimating locations and distances, and said, "No question. It is the Galley Inn. The very best in Honolulu. It is what I tell everyone."

"Yeah? Well, we don't feel like standin' in no line."

"Is no problem. Mr. Moe Wiseman, he is a very major investor I think. I think if I phone ahead, here on the car phone, the gentlemen don't hafta wait."

"Well, shit," said Angelo Scorcese. "Service here's as good as Queens. Get on the horn, Lare, get 'er done. Lips and me, we're hungry enough to start gnawing on the upholstery here."

They were so hungry, in fact, that they didn't bother to glance at the mob lined up outside the Galley Inn, just followed the fat Hawaiian through the lobby across scarlet-and-gray carpet to the comely hostess with a plumeria blossom fastened behind her ear. Had they not been so intent upon their appetites, Louis Lippi or Angelo Scorcese might have noticed the pretty boy with the sprinkle of black curls adorning his forehead raising a clamor toward the front of the line over the snailish pace of admission. The pretty boy with the pouting girl in white and the tattooed redneck with the beatific smile, the aspect of a tenant farmer trying to pass himself off as the Dalai Lama.

But all things said and done, the delay stimulated an improvement in Earl's condition. He sobered up remarkably. Misty thought, almost magically. Almost *too* magically.

They were seated in a padded booth with a view of most of the restaurant, especially the entrance, which Misty appreciated. Hors d'oeuvres arrived speedily at their table, which Misty also appreciated, hungry as he was. Old Earl seemed to be behaving himself, politely ordering a rib-eye steak medium well. And a baked potato, please, with sour cream. And Leslie, at last, was coming around, scooching closer to him, a hand slinking over his leg to grope him beneath the tablecloth. After the waitress brought their drinks and distributed them (Earl slapping her hand away when she tried to pour the contents of his longneck Coors into a glass), Leslie lifted the swath of hair away from her eye and proposed a toast: "Tomorrow, Maui," she said. "More fun, more sun . . . and, who knows?"

A little fetching sidelong grin for Misty that seemed radiant with erotic promise.

Touching her glass, he said, "I'll drink to that."

"And I'll drink to the both a ya," said Earl, the goofy grin reappearing in his face.

"And to our good friend Earl, for all the help you've given us."

"Sure, why not? To old Earl, the walking encyclopedia."

"Carl."

"What?"

"Old . . . and . . . and encyclopedia."

"What's wrong with that?"

"It sounds . . . I dunno. Earl, he didn't mean anything by it."

"Well shoot, I know that. We're all Americans here," he said, as if that explained matters.

While around a corner of the room, at the far end of the restaurant, where the booths were elevated three steps from the floor and the view of moonlight and bobbing hulls on the water was truly spectacular, Angelo Scorcese was congratulating himself for having invited the fat Hawaiian to dine with them. That the food he was devouring was superb only contributed to his sense of satisfaction, as though he were somehow responsible for its preparation.

"Take your time," said Angelo Scorcese, the advice resonant with amiability, his little porcine eyes glittering.

Larry Lee was sitting between them in the horseshoe-shaped booth with his back to the ocean, one hand idly scratching his voluminous belly as he squinted at the photostat, moving it away above his plate (actually, his second helping of mahimahi). Louis Lippi, finished with his meal as well, had pushed his plate away and was using the tablecloth to polish the lenses of his new designer sunglasses. From recessed speakers music issued softly over the table, steel guitars for the most part mooning away as the crooners sang of love and sunshine and heartbreak and sand. Evidently the hot topics on the island.

Larry Lee held the photostat at arm's length, squinting and murmuring, "Lessee . . . lessee . . ."

"Lare," said Angelo Scorcese, leaning over the table, "you want Lips here, take the picture across the fuckin' room, so you can see it better?"

Larry Lee wagged his other hand—no, no—treating the sarcasm as if it had been a polite, but unnecessary, offer. "It was today I am for certain. I think was this morning, the early tour. With Alice."

"Alice?"

"The lady conducting the tour. Little tiny thing she is."

"The guide."

"Yes, the guide. Lessee . . . We picked up at three hotels, yes, all out on Waikiki Beach. That is why you have had no luck, because we have only visited downtown Hono-lulu. Of course"—and Larry Lee grinned hugely—"now we are getting to someplace, huh?"

Angelo Scorcese lifted the Mets cap off his hair to run his fingers over his scalp. "I dunno, Lare. You tell me."

"The hotels I remember. Was the Point, the Golden Sands, and . . . lessee . . . the Surf Regency. Yeah, that was the tour. I be hones' with you, I don't remember pa'ticular hotel, one they stayin' at, but Alice maybe might. She is a real smart little girl."

"Can we get a phone at a table?" said Angelo.

"But of course we can."

"Good. Let's talk to this Alice."

Larry Lee lowered his face. "I don't know her number. We have to go through the agency. You know, that arrange the tour."

"So do it."

"Umm."

"You meditating, Lare?"

"No. But agency's not open. Not open till tomorrow, seven in the morning."

"Okay," said Angelo Scorcese, cuffing the helpful Ha-waiian on the shoulder, "what the fuck. You drive us out to the hotels. One outta three ain't bad odds. Hey, Lare?"

"Yes?"

"Don't get all bent. You done a helluva job so far. I'll mention it to Moe Wiseman. The honest truth."

"Really?"

Angelo Scorcese produced his wallet, shoved three one-hundred bills at Larry Lee. "Take care a dinner, know whaddamean? Check, tip, whatever's left is yours. Let's us visit those hotels. Be inna Mercedes, soon as you take care a business. Fair?"

"I think so, yes. Surf Regency, Point, or Golden Sands, I swear is one of them."

Waiting for the parking valet to arrive with the Mercedes, Angelo inquired of Louis Lippi: "So whatta we carrying?"

Louis Lippi was wearing his designer dark glasses even in the night. "Got the nine-mil Smith beneath my arm. Got the silenced two-two in the trunk along with the sawed-off. Twelve-gauge has a clip of five, gotta broad buckshot spread, at least tag him, maybe slow him down."

"You guys with your two-twos," muttered Angelo. "A fucking nine will knock a guy down. Ain't that what we're looking to do?"

Louis Lippi, whose business this was, tried to be patient. "You want to defend yourself, yeah, a nine-millimeter, that's a good caliber to carry. Also a three fifty-seven, a forty-five, a ten-millimeter, any a those. Sound alone prob'ly make most assholes change their mind. But if you hit the guy, chances are, it's gonna be a through and through, like goin' through butter. But your twenty-two, it goes in, it don't have that kinda power, but it kicks up one helluva mess bouncing around in there. So what it does is, it actually causes more damage. You see what I'm saying?"

Angelo Scorcese rotated the bill of his Mets cap from the back to the front of his head as the Mercedes rolled into view. "Okay," he said, "you're the expert. But tell me one thing."

Louis Lippi held the back door open for Angelo Scorcese. "Yeah?"

"How inna fuck you gonna see to hit anything wearing shades in the night?"

Earl drank three more long-necks with dinner and became momentarily belligerent when Misty Carmichael tried to pick up the tab. He speared a twenty from his wallet and launched it across the table at Misty, insisting he could pay his own way (even if the twenty, not counting a gratuity, came to barely half what his meal and drinks added up to). "We're all Americans here," he said, whatever in hell that meant, "and old Earl, by God, he's good for it."

One thing cheered Misty: the look of distress, or maybe disgust, that fleetingly appeared in Leslie Ann's face. Even she, evidently, had lost her enthusiasm for the old bonehead. Good. Because as they progressed through the courses of their meal, Misty had developed the apprehension that she would invite this windbag back to their hotel for a nightcap. The salty dogs and scrumptious cooking had precipitated a mood better suited to a party of two, of the opposite sex, preferably naked. So as he graciously permitted Earl to cough up a pittance of the tab, he did so in anticipation of feeling Leslie Ann's flesh next to his, the taste of champagne and brandy on her lips, the sweet resilience of her erected nipples as he descended her body with kisses.

Outside the Galley Inn he slipped one of the parking valets a five-dollar bill to whistle down a taxicab. Old Earl was leaning on Leslie Ann to keep from falling on his puss, one arm flung over her shoulder, his hand precariously close to her breast. Once, as they waited on the sidewalk in the comfortable night air, Misty thought he caught from the corner of his eye old Earl copping a feel, but let it go, figuring it would be the highlight of the old fart's night, and what the hell, looking at Leslie there in her snug white costume, those perky breasts saying talk to me, what man with blood in his veins wouldn't ache to answer the call. He knew he did. Go for the gusto, Earl.

After they had piled onto the backseat of the taxicab, and Misty Carmichael had given the driver their destinations —the Point, where they were staying, and the Golden Sands, a little farther down the shore—he put his arm around Leslie Ann, who was sitting between them, and leaned forward to look at Earl. "Say Earl," he said, "how you doing?"

"Doing great," he said.

The taxicab accelerated away from the curb.

Light and darkness flickered over them. From the driver's radio they could hear the taxi service dispatcher between blats of static. Christ in plastic was being crucified on the dashboard. The light flickered over Him showing the blood drops, and a face decidedly swarthy.

"Earl?"

"Yeah?"

"You Italian?"

"I sure ain't, son."

"I was just wondering, on account a your Roman fingers."

"Huh?"

"Kinda take your goddamn hand off my wife's thigh."

"Carl."

"Oh, did I . . . ? Sorry, son. Just tryin' to keep my balance is all. Didn't realize."

"He's tipsy, darling."

"Probably. I just didn't want him to fall all the way into your lap."

"Carl."

"We're all Americans here, son."

"Ain't that the truth. Yo, cabbie."

"Sir?"

"That the Point coming up there on the right?"

"That's the Point, sir."

The taxi swung into an illuminated circular drive and stopped where a royal blue-and-gold carpet ran from the curb to double plate-glass doors. A doorman wearing white gloves and a blue uniform with gold epaulets snatched open the door. The wrong door, as it turned out, because it was the side where Earl was sitting. Had been sitting. Prior to taking up residence on the blue-and-gold carpet, shaking his head and staring up the doorman's creased trousers.

Leslie Ann assisted the doorman in returning Earl to the seat, while Misty Carmichael leaned in the open window to inform the driver: "Thanks, bud. The guy in back'll take good care a you."

The driver glanced into his rearview mirror, a dubious expression on his face. "Guy don't look in too gooda shape."

"That? Oh, he'll do anything for a laugh. Regular comedian, old Earl. Yo, Earl, you cut that out now. Knock off the clowning. Earl?"

"We're all Americans here."

"See?"

Misty Carmichael waved as the taxi rolled off, swinging out to pass the big green Mercedes hugging the curb just ahead. Glancing around at the other cars parked or idling in the turnaround, he counted a half-dozen Benzes, a BMW sedan, a white Porsche Cabriolet, two Caddies, a Ford Taurus (a *Ford?*), and a sunshine-yellow Bentley with a uniformed driver bending over the front of it, assiduously polishing the chrome grille. Leslie Ann waited for him on the curb. She was hugging her elbows as if to ward off a chill, and perhaps she was chilled, because her nips were sticking right out there in her white costume, two little chunks of chalk. He put his arm around her waist just as a van roared up the drive and braked hard, the driver spilling out a second later with a bouquet of red roses in his fist, bolting past them toward the double plate-glass doors, the uniformed doorman hastening to swing one open. They stood to watch the boy in the bright orange shorts and T-shirt bolt through the door, practically high kicking as he plunged into the lobby.

"You think he's afraid the flowers'll wilt?" said Leslie Ann.

"Asshole even left his van running," observed Misty. "Serve him right if someone swiped it."

Leslie tilted her head back and sighed. "God, it's so beautiful here."

"Not half as beautiful as you are going to look without your clothes on."

She let her hand drop, patted him on the ass. "You're only saying that 'cause you're horny."

"And I'm horny because it's true."

The doorman, a skinny bird with watery eyes, a pronounced Adam's apple, and what Misty believed to be a British accent, dipped his head an inch, no more, greeting them as he did every night, "Evenin' mum, sir."

And they entered the lobby with the white marble floor, the steps straight ahead to a sunken conversation area filled with stuffed chairs and divans to enjoy a cocktail at leisure, or simply to sit and drink in the vision of beach and surf and sky. While off to their left—

Louis Lippi had grown up in Queens, New York, in a working-class neighborhood in Woodside so close to the Brooklyn Queens Expressway, families joked about what octane they were breathing when they gathered in their cramped backyards for summer barbecues, big sausage-and-pasta feasts that frequently dissolved into quarrels, old nurtured wounds surfacing, accusations flung, somebody waking the next day with a shiner, a shaky tooth, or the vague memory of initiating a sexual faux pas. And like most of the young men in his neighborhood, or with whom he associated, he got to the beach regularly in the summer, either Riis Park, Far Rockaway, or the Hamptons. (Coney Island, even twenty years ago, was considered a dump, fit only for the niggers and spics, human turds washing up on the shore, broken glass all over the beach, and clap-infested hookers that would do a guy beneath the boardwalk, just lift their tight skirts and bend over, here doggy, here doggy.) The last almost ten years of his life he had spent in Phoenix, working under Paul Scorcese most of the time, this last nine or so months under Paul's older brother Angelo. In all that time he had never been to a shore. And now here he was in Hawaii, beaches everywhere and hardly not a spic or jig on the island, no wonder he was beginning to feel he was in paradise. A lot of the Polynesians, like Larry Lee, were porkers, they did seem to run to fat, but they were polite, that was the thing, and the women that looked after themselves, and Louis Lippi had checked out a number of them in his few hours on the island, those women knocked him out. The big dark eyes and the hair that looked like polished black glass.

Louis Lippi, as sober and businesslike as he continued to try to be, was a man captivated, infatuated, and distracted. When he and Angelo Scorcese walked into the hotel that night, his enchantment underwent another jolt: nowhere that they had inquired that day quite prepared him for the sumptuousness of the Point. Chandeliers of faceted crystal hung from a ceiling three stories high, the facets scattering light that seemed a blend of rose and aqua. The sun was just descending as they approached the lobby, a huge blush above the black water. Ahead of them as they passed through the glass doors fitted with bronze inset handles, there was an area down some steps where couples and groups lounged, enjoying the sunset and a drink, their voices discreet and melodious, altogether alien from the pitch of conversation that he had grown up with in the backyards of Woodside. This was class, he thought. These were people with style. These were people who didn't belch out loud and fart and say fuck every five words and walk around in public like sixteen-year-olds with a baseball cap on backward and bust up someone's Foster Grant shades in public to demonstrate displeasure. Louis Lippi listened to the sound of his sober black leather shoes striking the polished marble floor as they crossed toward the reception desk, heels and toes creating something alluring, like the rhythm of castanets.

Even the help, to whom he usually paid no attention, charmed him. They were dressed in black and white, white blouses and shirts, black ties for the boys, black trousers and skirts. And every one of them that Angelo queried spoke with the flat, clear articulation of network anchorpersons. And furthermore, all the boys and girls at the reception desk recognized the photostat of Misty Carmichael, just as all expressed their shock that the gentleman known as Mr. Carl Bellows could be involved in any criminal enterprise. Such a warm and friendly couple, especially the Mrs., the Bellowses.

During the peak hours the reception area could accommodate six lines of guests checking in, two receptionists per line, but at this hour only two desks were operating, neither of them doing more than fielding the occasional question from a perplexed or curious guest. Beyond this area was a booth where the money-exchange rates were posted daily, and where guests could arrange for a tour, change currency, complete the paperwork for a safe deposit box.

They did not interview either of the pleasant-looking young ladies in the booth, not right away, since Angelo Scorcese was antsy to check out the location of the suite. He rudely rebuffed an offer to ring the suite from the front desk. The reception area faced a bank of elevators, and they crossed first marble, then carpet (a soft gray with a rose pattern worked into it), which began at the elevators. The elevator doors, four on each side, had the aspect of old pewter with intaglio figures worked into them, small mermaids flirting about the four corners and a bearded hemaid or merman—whatever an underwater guy fish was called—posing as if about to hurl his trident. Must have cost a bunch, the doors alone: probably had to commission some faggot artist.

And look at this: carpet inside the elevator is the rose of the pattern outside, and in gray letters on the floor, it read— *Have a Nice Friday.* The exact day it was. Talk about class.

Angelo Scorcese exercised his knuckles on the door of the suite, it must've been close to five minutes, before he listened to reason. They returned to the lobby, enjoyed a drink (at least Louis enjoyed his, a Scotch and soda, while Angelo opted for Pepsi) in the sunken area with a view of the ocean amidst all the discreet conversation, Louis praying Angelo wouldn't ruin the mood with a stupendous release of flatulence. He didn't, but to make up for this lapse into good manners, he insisted upon dragging Louis away before he had finished the Scotch and soda, in order to quiz the girls in the money-changing booth.

The girls both looked Polynesian with the dark hair, the richly hued skin, and modest figures (either could have been a model for the mermaids engraved in the elevator doors), figures Louis Lippi would have been happy tapping any day of the week. Not for any opulence of flesh, which neither possessed, but because of a kind of shy intelligence in their faces, something completely foreign to his experience. He did not want to leave this part of the world, ever.

It was the one who identified herself as Miriam who

looked up from the unfolded photostat and said, "Of course, Mr. Bellows. He used two of our largest-size safety deposit boxes."

"*Used?*" said Angelo Scorcese.

"Yes." She smiled. It was all Louis Lippi could do, his eyes hiding behind the dark glasses, not to lean over and start chewing on Miriam's smile. "Why there he is now, with his wife. Aren't they a beautiful couple?"

—even forty, fifty feet away, he recognized Angelo Scorcese, whirling in the brilliant light, his dumb jock costume famous all over Queens before he left with that sow of a new wife, laughed out of the borough the way he'd heard it. And he knew in the instant of recognition that the oldest son of the Don wasn't standing in the Point by coincidence.

The tears in his eyes weren't simply the product of an affliction, they registered real emotion. He was seized by panic.

He snatched Leslie's hand.

Snatched it so abruptly, he almost pulled her off her feet.

He hit the brass in the plate-glass door with the heel of his hand, and they were out of the lobby, moving. To Leslie's credit, she yelled "What?" only once, then was moving with him, scampering down the broad walk of blue-and-gold carpet as best she could in her tight shift and fragile leather sandals.

The bright orange van with the stylized profile of a bouquet of flowers beneath the logo—*Petals by Metal*—loomed up before them, the sound of its idling engine especially enticing.

They dived into it.

In the driver's seat, digging his left foot into the clutch, Misty Carmichael breathed just a bit easier, however unhappy he was with the neon coloring of the van. Another precaution was paying off. As he popped the clutch, barreling past the green Mercedes, he liberated the .380 auto from his waistband.

Angelo Scorcese was not a particularly subtle man, but even he enjoyed, however briefly, the irony of shouting, "Stop! Police!"

And saw the asshole and the girl (tasty, that one, he'd give her the option of being diddled or offed, before she was offed) go out the door as if they had launched themselves from sprinters' blocks. He beat Louis Lippi to the sidewalk, but he was unarmed, and by the time Lippi arrived, the taillights of the van were nearly swallowed up in night, heading, if Angelo had his directions correct, east. East and somewhat north. Toward Diamond Head. And more hotels.

They sped toward the green Mercedes.

Flung themselves onto the backseat.

Angelo Scorcese said, "You see that van go by, Lare?"

"Yes, I see it. Like a big lump of sherbet."

"See where it went?"

"Of course I do."

"Then, step on it, Lare."

The thing about even a big Mercedes on asphalt warmed all day by a tropical sun, jump on the accelerator and the tires will scream, as they did in front of the Point, the big sedan fishtailing away from the five-star premises, smoke unfurling, wafting the stink of burnt rubber against the double plate-glass doors.

CHAPTER 16

They wouldn't get far trying to outrun anyone in this. The van was a dog. Old ladies in walkers would be passing them soon. He strained over the wheel, sighting lights, a small constellation of them, ahead on their right. He glanced in the rearview mirror. The road curved and dipped along the coast, affording little consistent visibility either in front or in back, only glimpses. Their pursuers could be a mile behind them or just beyond the last curve. One thing for certain: it wouldn't be much longer before whatever was behind them was on them like stink on shit.

"Up there on the right." He pointed. Her eyes, her face, all focused on him, had a harsh orange cast to them from the lights on the dashboard. "Look! To the right. Hotel."

She looked. Then looked back at him, her eyes glinting as if in the reflection of firelight.

"Maybe Earl's hotel. The Golden Sands."

"Maybe Earl's . . . ?" she said, letting her voice die. Was she in shock?

"We gotta dump this piece a garbage."

There it was, around the next bend, a sign indicating a turn-off, and sure enough, maybe a hundred yards farther, a smaller road appeared, still asphalt, but trickling north away from the main highway. Misty Carmichael slowed the van and turned left, cutting his lights to drive by starlight. The road wound through what appeared to be dense vegetation, trunks of trees and bushes appearing blue and charcoal in the faint light. He had no idea of the terrain, but he also believed he had little time, and he turned the van off the asphalt, ordering Leslie Ann to get out, wait for him on the shoulder of the road. She did so and stood there hugging her arms.

"You see any light coming up the road," he said, "get your ass outta sight."

"Misty?" she said. "What's—"

"Just do what I'm telling you," he said, instinctively stroking the smooth cool object under his shirt, "you'll be okay."

He eased the clutch, touched the accelerator, and rode the van bumping amongst bush and broad leaves, through vines too, until he was satisfied the van could not be seen from the road. He hiked back to the shoulder and found Leslie, crouched and aware in her tight white shift.

She grasped his right hand, the one holding the .380. "Misty? I don't know as I'm ready to die just yet."

Just, he thought, like it was a joke: *jest.*

"You aren't going to." He switched the gun to his other hand and took hold of hers. "Come on."

They walked upright along the side of the road, albeit not as lovers out for a late-night stroll, but rather more like a parent with a recalcitrant child. The problem was her sandals; they were too flimsy for the terrain. Trying to keep up with Misty, Leslie lost her balance on loose gravel, stumbled over roots, once cutting her knee, and twice had to stop to retrieve a sandal. To his credit, though he doggedly urged her on, he recognized that the fault was not hers, and rather than rebuke her, he was always quick to retreat to her assistance.

They were both winded and sweaty by the time they had retraced their way to the coast road. They crouched close to the intersection. The road appeared to be empty as far as they could see in either direction. They listened. There was plenty to listen to, cries and calls neither was equipped to identify, but of the sounds they could hear, none resembled the menacing growl of an engine.

This was the tricky part, crossing the highway here, because they would not only be exposed on the road, but for another fifty or sixty yards across neatly trimmed lawn before reaching the relative protection of a tree line.

Misty drew Leslie back into deeper shadow and looked her over. The white shift flared up even in the darkness; it had to go. He stuck the pistol in his waistband, then pulled the royal-blue knit shirt over his head. "Here," he said, "put this on. No, first tuck the hem of this thing in your belt."

Her white thong panties didn't amount to much, but he was going to take them off, until he realized his shirt hung to the middle of her thighs.

"Good," he said. "You okay?"

She lifted a swath of hair away from her eye. "With a bloody knee and about forty-seven insect bites? I'm having the time of my life. A night every girl dreams of."

"That's better. That's my girl."

At the edge of the road they stopped, and Leslie removed the sandals. The air was cool and refreshing. Misty drank it in in deep breaths. There was faintly the scent of moist grass. They would be vulnerable for thirty seconds, maybe less. Probably less.

No headlights visible in either direction.

No engine sounds.

"You ready, Sugarcheeks?"

She squeezed his hand, his left one. In his right was the .380.

They bolted up the bank and onto the asphalt, Misty restraining his pace to match hers, not wanting to yank her off balance. Without a shirt on, the grigri bounced and stung his chest. He could hear her breaths as if they were being torn from her. Down the far bank and onto the grass, it was slippery going, but they covered ten yards, fifteen, before lights leapt out at them from the east, sweeping around a curve.

Nothing to do but run. Run. Run.

They had driven at speeds in excess of ninety miles per hour along the coast past the

Golden Sands, and beyond it the Surf Regency and several miles more in the direction of Diamond Head before Angelo Scorcese ordered them to turn around.

"No way," he said, "could a van outrun a Mercedes this far. The hotels. They gotta turned off."

And so they had wheeled west along the winding asphalt that the big car had hugged so securely at ninety, prowled the entrance and parking areas of the Surf Regency, no sign of a neon orange van, and proceeded on toward the Golden Sands. Angelo and Lips sat pressed against opposite sides of the backseat, Angelo behind the driver, everyone in the car straining for a glimpse of the asshole or the girl or the brightly painted vehicle. Louis Lippi, without waiting for Angelo to suggest it, had long ago tucked his designer dark glasses away.

Larry Lee said, "What's 'at?"

Angelo Scorcese, sitting behind him, his vision partially obscured, leaned forward. "What?"

"Up ahead on the left. I dunno. I thought I saw . . . I dunno."

"What? What the fuck did you think you saw?"

"Over there. I dunno. Just movement. There where you see those trees."

"Slow down. Isn't that the entrance to the Sands?"

"Yes, it is."

"You see anything now?"

"No."

"Me neither. Louis?"

"No. Ain't seen a thing."

The car swung in at the entrance and stopped there at Angelo Scorcese's request. He peered into the wall of palm trees, seeing nothing. "All right. Here's what we're gonna do."

Louis Lippi emerged from the Mercedes and took up a post next to the entrance. Angelo rummaged around beneath the popped trunk for the .22 with the silencer. He closed the trunk and touched fists with Lippi and climbed back into the car. The Mercedes glided down the asphalt drive to the hotel portico, where Angelo got out, holding a black attaché case with the silenced .22 inside.

It was a simple plan, and in its simplicity almost elegant. Angelo Scorcese thought so at any rate. While the fat Hawaiian cruised the parking areas scouting for the van, Lippi would work his way through the palm trees, in case whatever it was Larry Lee had maybe seen happened to be the asshole and the girl. It was a tactic Angelo had recalled learning from a compromised Harvard Jew by the name of Metzenbaum, the Wizard. Big sweaty guy with a bald pate and fringe of red hair, brilliant where it came to moving family money, walked with a cane and talked better than anyone of Angelo's acquaintance. The tactic employed tonight was called flushing the quail.

Angelo Scorcese stood on the curb watching Larry Lee motor off to search the covered garage for an orange van. The Golden Sands, like the Point, enjoyed a reputation for world-class cuisine (harboring on its grounds a sushi bar, French restaurant, a bakery and coffee shop, and a grill that imported mesquite for the barbecuing of freshly landed fish and beef from Argentina), which attracted guests from not only around the world, but wealthy locals as well. A farther star in its firmament, and an additional island draw, was its bistro facing out over the Pacific, famous for showcasing up-and-coming talent. There was a sandwich board set up outside the hotel, greeting its guests with pictures and the information that a singer by the name of Mariah Riggs would be featured from eight o'clock to nine thirty, then would appear once again from ten to eleven. Angelo Scorcese had never heard of her, although from the photographs, he thought he might like to meet her, try some of that dark meat. The Golden Sands had a series of three glass doors that slid open upon breaking an electronic beam, and as Angelo patrolled the terraced front of the hotel, he set off door upon door. The costumed doormen just touched their caps and smiled: obviously an eccentric guest waiting for a lady friend or business associate. After a few minutes, he returned to the curb. Lippi was nowhere visible on the slope. A few seconds passed before he made out the headlights of the Mercedes moving slowly through the parking garage. Then not moving. Stopped. Of course: the fat Hawaiian had discovered the van. And now it was moving again, the lights were moving.

The concrete structure was about the size of a football field with ramps at either end leading to the roof. The staff, be it the hotel manager or a bellhop, a chef or concierge, parked their vehicles on the roof; to do otherwise, not to abide by the rules, invited instant dismissal. The area below, in spaces clearly delineated by yellow paint, was reserved for guests of the hotel, whether there for a week or an evening.

Down here, sheltered from the elements, were parked row upon row of luxury automobiles, a sea of waxed surfaces. As they made their way among the polished vehicles, their compressed shadows a reflection of caution, Misty Carmichael experienced, against all logic, a surge of confidence. It was as if the conspicuous evidence of wealth, all by itself, provided sanctuary.

The garage was illuminated—not brilliantly, but sufficiently—by floodlights in mesh cages. Amidst the pampered showroom shine of the automobiles, the rank scent of petroleum oozed into their nostrils. The stink of a Lamborghini was no less than that of a Plymouth.

Parking spaces ran round the perimeter of the garage, as well as a double row down the center of the area. Misty and Leslie Ann, crouched between a Buick and a Corvette, in the double row, watched the green Mercedes, with Larry Lee at the wheel, purr by. Squeezed between the grilles of the two cars, he glanced at her, a puzzled turn to his brow.

"He's familiar," he whispered, "isn't he?"

"I didn't get that good a look."

"Okay. But that green Mercedes. I think it was parked —make that I'm *sure* it was parked at the Point, just ahead of the van. You remember it?"

"C'mon. Men look at cars. Women don't."

"I'm sure of it. A green Mercedes sedan. We drove right past it at the Point."

They were in the garage because Misty had several times covered Frank Mears, watched him steal cars from the circular Macy's parking lot on Queens Boulevard. General Motors ignitions were easy ones to punch out once you got inside, and the white '78 Corvette was just sitting there, its doors unlocked, freedom just a few seconds and the contents of Leslie Ann's purse away.

But the green Mercedes, which he observed continuing to ignore open slots to park, possibly presented something more to be desired. The Mercedes was at the far end of the garage. Misty removed the knit shirt from Leslie Ann. They traded whispered ideas, then Misty moved away between the opposing grilles of the pricey autos, remaining crouched, as the Mercedes slowly wheeled around and slowly rolled their way.

Its headlights were on.

The headlights were really unnecessary in the garage, but they did illuminate to good effect the pear-shaped flanks of a woman in white, evidently bent over to retrieve the contents of her purse. Stupid broad probably didn't know which end was up. As the Mercedes purred forward, Larry Lee began to realize this was some exquisite ass he was looking at. He slowed down. And not only the ass. The lady wasn't wearing panties. She was bent over and showing him the family fur flared out over her thighs, the sweet dark mystery dead ahead.

Larry Lee had never heard of a code of gallantry, but it was in that spirit—and perhaps out of an even older urge— that he braked the Mercedes and opened the door.

Misty Carmichael crept away from the rear fender of a

champagne-pink Lexus and put the barrel of the .380 Colt in Larry Lee's ear.

"I don't want to kill you," he said, "but I will. Nothing personal. It's just my philosophy. You care to hear about it, or you want to die?"

Larry Lee allowed as how he had an open mind.

Told to lie in the trunk of the Mercedes and keep his mouth shut, in exchange for the opportunity to go on living, Larry Lee complied eagerly. It was not comfortable in there for a man his size. Indeed he was miserable. But he liked his chances, as the cute boy with the black curls explained it, better where he was with Angelo possibly putting rounds into the trunk with a .22 than inviting a .380 to do its damnedest rattling around inside his cranium.

The trunk of a Mercedes, strongly built though it is, can be penetrated by a .22 slug, which can do some damage, no question about it. But Larry Lee had read somewhere that the velocity of a .22 passing through a silencer was considerably reduced, and he had recognized the tubular device. So, given the probabilities, Larry Lee was content to suffer the discomfort and indignity of riding where he was right past the nose of Angelo Scorcese.

Which he estimated they were about to do, feeling and hearing the acceleration in the blackness of his surroundings. Almost as a reaction to the thrust that rolled him backward, he inhaled suddenly and belched, releasing some of the pent-up gases from his rich meal. The sound of this normal and necessary bodily function coincided with the impact on the windshield of the first bullet out of Angelo's silenced .22. Slugs splattered along the length of the speeding Mercedes. It sounded like a brief afternoon torrent, a staccato of comforting weather he had grown up with, a tropical lullaby. And then something rocked him, sickened him, the factor that he had not taken into account, that skewed the probabilities: Louis Lippi emerging from the palm trees and laying down more than half a dozen hasty nine-millimeter rounds with full metal jackets, two of which slammed through the trunk and slammed into Larry Lee. Caught him in the gut and in the throat. Gave him maybe sixty seconds to hang on to the wonder of life—the taste of mahimahi, of a woman's lips, of warm rain in the afternoon.

CHAPTER 17

Because she had acted in several plays in high school and had a plum part her freshman year in college as Maggie in *Cat on a Hot Tin Roof*—and also because she was a woman who like every other woman had given her share of performances in bed to reassure that most fragile of entities, the male ego—she had not in the least been inhibited by the situation in the airport, nor frightened by it in retrospect. It was just another job of acting, given some spice, it was true, by Misty telling her their lives depended upon it, although she chalked some of it up to a taste for melodrama on his part. But not anymore.

Not when lead slugs slapped the windshield and tore along the length of the car, Misty shouting at her to keep her fucking head down, and then those explosions—she was too terrified to count them—one of which shattered the window above her, showering glass all over her and Misty. He made her lie there the longest time listening to the engine strain and Misty curse, the car hurtling through the night. Gingerly she touched her hair and could feel sharp particles everywhere. Some of the glass must have cut her too, as the taste of blood seeped into the corner of her mouth.

Leslie Ann Rice was beginning to believe there were easier scores than this guy Misty Carmichael, no matter how many thousands in cash he was carrying. Her life, after all, was worth something too, wasn't it?

And when they had driven the riddled automobile all the way to the airport parking lot, and sprung the trunk to find the fat guy (she recognized him now as the bus driver on their tour this morning), curled in a fetal position with blood everywhere and a raw smell enveloping him, she knew she wanted out.

The craziness was accelerating out of control.

Until Misty Carmichael shut the trunk of the Mercedes and said, "Fucking wasn't us that shot him. Listen, Sugarcheeks, you have old Earl's phone number?"

"I think so."

"You thank so?"

"Don't make fun," she said, but without any heat to it. She was in fact trembling and felt a giddy sensation in her stomach, as if on the verge of throwing up.

"Let me look at you. Uh-huh. You gotta few nicks, but nothing that's gonna scar that beautiful face of yours."

He removed his knit shirt for the second time that night and along with saliva, managed to clean her face. Then he kissed her, settling one hand on her ass, squeezing it. He ground his hips momentarily into her and she nearly fainted from the hot, foul scent of his sweat, the slick residue of panic.

"You wait here in the garage," he said. "I'll get a rent-a-car. We'll find a phone booth somewhere and see what percentage of Earl is bullshit."

She nodded her head in agreement meekly.

Then slumped down flat against the fender, her feet in front of her, her ass flat on the oil-soaked concrete. She wanted her daddy. She wanted her daddy to tell her everything would work out fine.

Not only had he removed the .380 from their suite upon returning there earlier in the evening, but he had brought out clothing as well as the contents of the safe deposit boxes, and secured them in lock boxes throughout the airport. He had expanded his avenues of escape, adhering to a philosophy that had served him well over the years. From one of the lockers he extracted a black knit shirt and changed into it in the men's.

Now, inside the airport with the light resonating off the marble floors, all the weary travelers dragged themselves across the expanse as if participants in a solemn, if mysterious, processional. Misty Carmichael found a portly white woman standing behind a waist-high booth with a sign on top of it that read: *Information*. She was yakking at an Oriental couple, the man with a pair of cameras slung bandolier style from his small shoulders, and because the couple evinced some confusion as to what they were being told, the white woman, to clarify matters, kept raising her voice. The white woman had to be in her fifties and was built in the grand, operatic mode, a perfect battleship of a lady. Wore a white blouse with ruffles cascading over her turrets, a red plaid skirt over the hull of her hips—an outfit that suggested she had doseyed when she should have doed, mistakenly boarding the flight to Hawaii, instead of the one to Iowa for the international polka competitions. She wore too much rouge and her home perm was wilting. When she had at last shouted the perplexed Oriental couple into submission and they were retreating, heads nodding, expressing their appreciation for what, to Misty, appeared to be a monumental cultural misunderstanding, she smiled at him, her hands hitched to her hips, and said, "I bet you speak American, don't you, honey? How can I help you?"

Ten minutes later he was standing in front of a Hertz desk finishing the paperwork, in order to rent a Chevrolet Beretta. He inscribed the name of Carl Bellows, that fine and generous American, and was given a copy of the rental agreement and the key to the car, a dark-blue coupe to which he would be delivered by bus. The agent thanked him for thinking of Hertz. He told her he would never think of anyone else, and winked, going out the glass door to wait at the curb for the bus.

The agent, a slim brown lady in her early twenties who had grown up on Oahu, turned to her uniformed co-worker, also a lady, but a recent arrival from Nebraska with her husband, a dentist, and said to the corn-fed blond, "Do you know the easiest way to recognize assholes?"

"Assholes?" said the sweetheart from the breadbasket of the nation.

"Yeah, assholes. Pricks. Bastards. Son-of-a-bitches. Take your pick. You know how?"

"No," said Nebraska, her eyes big and blue.

"They make the same stupid jokes. You know how many times I've heard that bright remark?"

"What remark?"

"About never thinking of anyone but us. Delivered with the cute leer."

"I don't understand."

That's when the slim brown lady behind the Hertz desk felt like saying gobble, gobble. But didn't. She would spell it out for her co-worker, using small words. Maybe the Midwest occupied territory formerly known as Eden. Where all the little girls grew up to be virgins. Maybe. But something inside her, her relatively brief experience of the carnival called living, suggested to her that Eden was a dreamed-about place. It was a yearning ground. And her co-worker from Nebraska was simply a landlocked turkey.

The Beretta had strange door-handles; they were nowhere on the door, but on the frame that enclosed the windows, more evidence of Detroit's aspiration to build something with European flair, if not European quality. But once Misty Carmichael turned over the ignition, engaged gears, the little V-6 displayed real spunk.

Maybe Detroit was ready to play in the big leagues once more.

He pulled up behind the punctured Mercedes, saw Leslie Ann sitting rigidly against the fender. He touched the horn. She turned her face slowly in his direction, then wearily climbed to her feet. Poor thing had been through it. He had tried to explain on the way to the airport how they had the grigri going for them, saved his ass so many times he had lost count, but he didn't believe she shared his confidence. He leaned across the seat and pushed the door open for her.

"Sugarcheeks," he said.

She slumped in the seat, yanking the door shut. She strapped herself in with the seat belt, sighed, showed him her eyes. "You ain't even one little bit scared, are you?"

"No time for it now. We got to get off this island."

"I don't think I ever met anyone quite like you. You're either crazy or you got more balls'n any man I ever met."

"You haven't done so bad yourself."

"Really?"

"Really."

She thought about that, staring straight ahead as Misty Carmichael accelerated out of the parking garage, guiding the Beretta back to the heart of Oahu. "I don't know if I should be telling you this," she said, as they moved through the darkness, "but I think I'm in love with you. Is that going to be a problem?"

"You precious thing. I wouldn't have it any other way."

"Really?"

"Really."

Her daddy Earl, the more she thought about it, was

becoming the odd man out. Much as she was inscrutably attracted to him, she had not appreciated the display of arrogance in Mellow Eddie's, running his hands all over her. It violated the tacit equality between them as conspirators. Misty Carmichael, on the other hand, while not a genius, had at least looked out for her, asked much of her, yes, but had demonstrated concern, too. So as they rode through the night, she made the decision to align herself with Misty, not only for the practical reasons that he was younger and already possessed the swag, but because of a deeper response, resentment at being demeaned. It was as if a fever had broken. Her concern now was how to accomplish the switch of allegiance without sacrificing Earl on the one hand, or alerting Misty on the other that anything like a switch had occurred. There was some major acting ahead for Leslie Ann Rice. Of the kind that truly tested an actor. Pure improvisation.

Flying by the seat of the pants.

When they had found an outdoor phone booth in downtown Honolulu, Misty Carmichael instructed Leslie Ann to dial old Earl's number, get him on the line. When Earl answered, groggy from the night's pleasures, Leslie Ann passed the phone to Misty.

"Earl," he said, "this is Carl. Carl Bellows. We had dinner together tonight. My wife's Leslie. You might remember her better. How you doing, Earl?"

"Carl, is it?"

"Carl. Yes."

"Doing just fine, Carl. How's your wife?"

"She's fine, thanks for asking. Earl, the reason I'm calling, you seem to know your way around this part of the world."

"Flatter on, son. Flatter on."

"What are the possibilities of renting a boat, to sail to one of the other islands?"

"A boat?"

"A boat."

"To one the other islands, huh?"

"Yeah."

"You'd want a big boat, something seaworthy."

"That's what I'd want all right."

"Kinda romantic, going by boat."

"Discretion is more what I had in mind."

"Huh?"

Standing behind Misty in her greasy, blood-smeared shift, the breeze rising off the harbor to chill her clean sober, Leslie Ann Rice suddenly awoke from the drained condition into which terror had plunged her, awoke as if she had discovered herself sleeping naked on a frozen lake. Realized where Misty was going with this conversation and glanced at her watch. It was not nine o'clock. She believed she saw the crack in her dilemma; it was big enough for the both of them to walk through—fly through, to be more precise. She pulled on his arm.

He shook her off. "Earl, you there?"

"I'm thinking, son."

She pulled savagely this time. "Misty, goddammit," she said.

"Hang on a moment, Earl, will you?" He clamped a hand over the mouthpiece, his moist eyes on the verge of steaming. "What's a matter with you? I'm trying to get us off this fucking island alive."

He had not shouted, but there were people on the sidewalk, people strolling slowly, in no hurry, people gazing into shop windows, and some of them swung their attention in the direction of the phone booth, alarm plainly inscribed on their faces.

Misty Carmichael recognized it and tried to defuse it with a smile and a shrug. For the most part he succeeded. With effort, he squeezed the words out softly: "What is it, Sugarcheeks?"

"We don't need Earl," she said, hugging herself.

"Oh? There's no more flights tonight, I checked. By tomorrow those bastards will have the airport blanketed. Boat's the only way out, unless you know about a subway runs between islands."

"Misty, listen to me." She felt her confidence resurfacing and poured all of it into her smile. "I'm a travel agent. I'm paid to know how to get from here to there."

He held up his hand, moved the receiver to his face. "You still there, Earl?"

"Son, I think I got—"

"Hang on to that thought. And hang on to the phone." He covered the mouthpiece once more. "Go on," he said, interested now.

"First, it depends how much money you have."

"Oh? How about if I have a credit card?"

"That's right. Sure. Then it's no problem."

"What's no problem, Sugarcheeks?"

"Getting off the island now, tonight. Listen. Tell Earl we'll call him in the morning. No, wait. Tell him you changed your mind. We're flying back to Phoenix tomorrow."

Misty grinned. "I can see those little wheels turning. I just don't know where they're headed."

"To Maui, silly. Isn't that where you need to get to?"

"It is, but I don't feature myself swimming there. Which if we aren't going by boat and can't go by plane—"

"By helicopter," she said, and showed him her hands, palms up, a smile on her cut-up face that he wanted to suck on, like a peach. "We can charter a helicopter. Those ol' boys'll fly anytime for the right amount of money."

"Earl, you still there?"

"Son, I about thought—"

"See the thing of it is, we changed our minds. I think we're gettin' island fever. We're gonna catch the first flight back to Phoenix tomorrow."

"Phoenix? What inna world you want to do that for?"

"Nostalgia. Hey, Earl, it was great making your acquaintance. And Earl? Keep a clean pecker."

When he hung up, Leslie Ann Rice punched him, not hard, on the shoulder. "Misty."

"What?"

"Saying that to Earl, about his pecker."

"What? I was just having a little fun with the old fart."

"He's not so old."

"What're you, his publicity agent?"

She averted her eyes. "No."

"Fifteen minutes ago you're saying how you're in love with me, but you know what? I think you and the old fart had something going on while I was gone, there at Mellow Eddie's. I didn't say anything, but there was something looked a lot like lipstick on the side of his mouth. Maybe something he forgot to wipe off, it was too dark in there to see. Whadda you say about that?"

She brought her eyes up to meet his, no hesitation. "If it was lipstick, it wasn't mine. I admit in the taxi his hand was on my leg, and I'll tell you something else. While we were waiting for the taxi, he tried to fondle my breast. Well, he did in fact. But I didn't want to make an issue of it, because I didn't want you to get all bent outta shape. Besides, he was just a drunk old man."

"Oh, so now he's old."

She took a step toward him and wrapped her arms around him, her cheek against his chest, and said, "He's whatever you say he is. Let's just please find a phone book and get off this island. What do you think?"

"I think you are my very own precious thing," he said, pronouncing the last word *thang*.

Louis Lippi's ears hurt, even minutes later, as he and Angelo Scorcese sat in the hotel manager's office explaining to the director of security that they were private detectives on the trail of a bad type from the mainland, no need to call the police. The manager of the Golden Sands was a tall, elegant lad with waves in his hair and smoothly shaven pink cheeks, who seemed perfectly willing, even eager, to believe their story. The director of security was not so compliant. He was lean, also closely shaven, with a boyish face colored by stubbornness and a by-the-book attitude shaped by his beliefs as a Mormon. His blond hair was neatly combed. His name was Wayne Millwood. He had an extremely small mouth, little wider than the wings of his slender nose, and he used it to say, "I'll ask you again, Mr. Scorcese, may I see the pistol inside your case there? From what the doormen described, I am tempted to deduce that it has a silencer. Please prove me wrong."

Angelo Scorcese moved his eyes to confront the hotel manager, a gentleman by the name of Evan Burgoyne. He wore a black suit pin-striped in charcoal, a red carnation in his lapel. A real carnation, Louis Lippi was certain. In a hotel like this, almost the equal of the Point, they did things up right. No phony flowers for this bird.

"Evan," said Angelo Scorcese, "where'd you find this guy?"

"Mr. Millwood," Burgoyne replied, with a touch of huffiness, "I repeat, Mr. Millwood is a top-notch security man. While I personally—"

"Stuff a sock in it," said Angelo Scorcese amiably. "Either you pissants want a drink? 'Cause I sure could use one. How 'bout you, Lips?"

"Scotch and soda."

The office, like so much of the hotel, was anchored by the driftwood motif: an ash-gray dado on the walls, the panels unevenly turned; the manager's desk of the same washed-out hue with weathered fittings on the corners, the same weathered alloy on the handles of the drawers; a carpet the color of the beach that could be seen by starlight out the spread of plate glass behind the manager's chair. The backs of the aqua-colored stuffed chairs were supported by spines and ribs of driftwood. So too the identical couches on either side of the room. There were pictures of smiling entertainers in driftwood frames on the walls. Conch shells, the coral heart of them turned out, adorned ash-gray sconces around the room. From a concealed sound system came the strains of Peggy Lee grinding her musical hips through the song, "Fever." Even Louis Lippi, his ears aching from the concussions of a nine-millimeter pistol, felt himself momentarily derailed, the toe of his right shoe taking up the beat.

Standing to the right of Burgoyne's desk, Wayne Millwood continued to glare at them out of his bone-white face. His tiny lips looked like ghostly smears. He tried again. "I don't know who you think you are, but until—"

Angelo Scorcese came out of his chair, all two hundred and some odd hard pounds of him, and slammed the palms of his hands on Burgoyne's desk with such force that the manager shrunk in his fancy chair and the heat seemed to evaporate from Wayne Millwood's face. "I know perfectly fucking well who I am. Either you beauties know who Moe Wiseman is?"

Burgoyne moved his neck around and touched the knot of his tie. "Yes," he said. His voice changed pitches delivering the single syllable. "He's a very respected, very influential—"

"He can squash you like a bug, Burgoyne, is what he is. You too, Millwood. Like a fucking bug. See, what I am is a personal acquaintance of Mr. Wiseman. His home phone number is Aloha 7-4223. Now, if you can't get us a decent drink and a taxi in jig time, I'll ring him up, let him know what a pair of beauties you are, interfering with a serious investigation. How'd that be?"

Burgoyne's mouth moved, but nothing emerged, not a sound. He just sat there like an elegant puddle. Millwood fixed his hot little eyes on a corner of the ceiling, possibly wondering whatever happened to good old divine intervention.

Burgoyne found his voice. "That was Scotch and soda? And you, Mr. Scorcese?"

"Bring me a Pepsi."

"Well, Mr. Millwood, I think we ah . . . you have ah . . ."

"Certainly," snapped Millwood. He stalked to the door, flung it open, stalked out, his shoulders stiff with fury.

Louis Lippi rose to retrieve the door and close it. His ears felt better. Sammy Davis, Jr., was singing a catchy tune, something about a candy man. Louis Lippi sat down to wait for his drink, while Angelo Scorcese used one of the manager's phones to call their hotel for messages. All by itself, it seemed, the toe of Louis Lippi's shoe began to bounce.

The taxicab, at Angelo's instruction, drove them directly to the Point, where they learned that, no, the couple posing as Mr. and Mrs. Bellows had not returned since they were last seen sprinting from the premises. And also learned, yes, that Mr. Bellows had removed the contents from his safe deposit boxes earlier in the evening and relinquished the keys to them. Angelo Scorcese foisted twenty-dollar bills upon every member of the staff there, along with the promise of considerably more for the first person to phone him at the hotel with valid information on the couple. They left a trail of smiles in their wake, an air of good feeling that was not the customary effect of a visit from Angelo Scorcese.

Their next destination was the airport. It was a little before nine o'clock.

They split up there, each with a sheaf of photostats of Misty Carmichael. Ten minutes later Angelo Scorcese approached a big broad in a white blouse, a plaid skirt, who was talking loudly to a party of dinks. The island was crawling with them. He had never seen so many dinks outside his stay in Vietnam. Not that there was anything wrong with that. His first wife had been a dink. Not pure dink, because there was French blood in her, and that's what contributed to the distinctive blue eyes, the sharp, thin nose. She had been one in a million, Mai Lee, and before he knew it or had any inkling of the emotion, he could feel the tears stand up in his eyes. He blotted them with the back of his hand and listened to the broad bellowing and the dinks exchanging haltingly articulated questions among themselves, in an attempt to translate the white woman's words.

There were five of them, an older man and woman, and three girls with girlish figures, neatly dressed and not a one of them could fill an *A* cup. He saw braces on what appeared to be the youngest one. He stepped into the fray, a gigantic, unsmiling figure, and requested from the broad a pen, folded one of his photostats face in, and said, "You trying to find the Surf Regency?"

The man in the group nodded furiously. "Yes? Yes? Soofegency. Yes. You know?"

Angelo Scorcese printed the name of the hotel on the back of the flyer, handed it to the little man, and gripped the man's shoulder, while he scanned the airport. Catching sight of Louis Lippi, he affixed thumb and midfinger to his lips and produced a whistle that would be the envy of a New York City doorman. He asked the dink his name, and when Louis Lippi came up, he introduced the two. Then said, "Help them at the baggage carousel and see them to a taxi, would you?"

"You're the boss," said Louis Lippi, clearly mystified.

The little girls in their neat blouses and neat skirts curtsied and the older woman, the wife, blinked, and the man, the husband, inserted his hand in Angelo's paw and jerked it once, and bowed, and smiled, and said, "Sank you. Sank you."

And the big old broad in the white blouse and red plaid skirt said, "Well, ain't you a knight in funny armor. How can I help you?"

The slim brown girl at the Hertz desk recognized the picture of Misty Carmichael, but looking into the face of Angelo Scorcese, she was reluctant to admit to it. The face in the picture belonged to the asshole, no question about it; however, Angelo Scorcese did not strike her as a prize human being either.

"Sweetheart, it coulda been only thirty, forty minutes ago. The broad at information gave him directions. The guy come here or what?"

At which point her co-worker, Kim, returned from the bathroom and glanced over her shoulder, saw the photostat, and tittered, "Isn't that? You know, isn't that?"

Angelo Scorcese leaned on his forearms. "Yo, blondie, you recognize the guy?"

And Kim, the blue-eyed sweetheart of the Great Plains, said, "Isn't that the asshole you were just explaining to me how you could tell them immediately?"

The slim brown girl closed her eyes for a moment. "It could be," she said, her eyes fluttering open. "They all look alike after a while."

"What kinda car he rent?"

"I'm sorry, Mr.—"

"It was a Beretta," chimed in Kim. "I just did the paperwork. A blue Beretta. Lessee, do you need the license number?"

"It would help."

"Hold on," said the slim brown girl. "I need some identification to give out that information."

Angelo Scorcese permitted his predatory smile to surface. "But of course." He extracted his wallet, let it flop open to show the phony private investigator's license.

"Would you please remove it from the wallet?" the slim brown girl requested.

"What is this?"

"Regulations."

Kim with the big blue eyes said, "Jeez, Laura, I musta missed that."

For the second time in less than an hour Laura experienced the impulse to mutter gobble, gobble.

She studied the phony document, but was only stalling, as she was untrained to distinguish legitimate documents from something false. But in so doing, she unwittingly distracted Angelo Scorcese long enough for Misty Carmichael and Leslie Ann Rice to empty several storage lockers in the airport and traipse down to the helicopter pad to meet Wescott Page, their pilot, an Englishman qualified to fly them by virtue of the fact he had consumed only three gin martinis. He greeted them graciously.

"Up for a spot of heli riding, are we?"

CHAPTER 18

Saturday, six A.M., Molly Car-
michael awoke from an anguished night to see Izzy Stein on
a chair pulled up next to the bed, sipping coffee, a pot of
tea, a cup, and a jar of honey for her on the nightstand. Izzy
was wearing a pair of plum-colored shorts that made the
hairs on his bare chest look the hue of iron filings. Behind
him the curtains were drawn open to admit the frail morning
light, a suggestion of sunshine today as opposed to the
storming of yesterday, part of which she had spent on her
knees and then her back for that wretched little monster in a
van, in exchange for an agreement. The experience of which
had slithered through her sleep, sliming every dream.

Izzy smiled at her in that way he had, his lips lifting at

the corners, but never fully revealing his teeth, as if holding something in reserve. The gray eyes that she loved to look into frightened her a little this morning; whether from guilt over the terms of yesterday's bargain or the cold cast of speculation she imagined seeing there, she could not say. But she pulled the sheet closer to her throat and said, "I'm sorry."

Izzy cocked his head, apparently not understanding.

"About last night," she said. Then: "I'm sorry I didn't . . . I couldn't . . . I'm sorry we didn't, it didn't happen."

Izzy Stein smiled once more, the same smile that bespoke constraint, then touched a fingertip to his lips and drew it slowly across her mouth. "It happened," he said, "even if we didn't fill in all the blanks. We were together. Tea, my dear? Some honey?"

She rested a cheek in her hand, her elbow on the pillow, and said, "How out of the multitude of rotten jerks out there, especially at my age, have I got someone like you?"

"The Irish aren't famous for their luck."

"You. A spoonful, please."

He unscrewed the jar, lifted the quivering topaz substance on a silver spoon.

"Not for my tea, Iz, for me." She leaned forward to suck the honey from the spoon. Moved her tongue around behind her lips.

He said, "Your plane leaves at eight-forty. I thought if I got your tea ready, we'd have a good cushion on getting to the airport."

"Not until you come over here and kiss me. Let me love you before I leave. Make up for last night."

He moved next to her, sat on the edge of the bed, stroked her hair. "No making up required," he said.

"How about desired?" she said, pulling the sheet away to draw him down upon her bare body.

They brushed lips.

Then went back for more.

"Molly," he murmured, "you and I, in spite of whatever—"

"Oh. There. There, yes. Oh." Molly Carmichael opened her eyes. "Iz, I don't want to hear a speech. Just be with me. Please? Just be with me."

And when her pleasure peaked, so intense she felt herself buffeted by it, she was washed by sobs, tears that not so much cleansed her of yesterday's experience, but at least released her to hope. While above her, oh gentle man, Izzy brought himself into her, brought himself, brought himself, every time an affirmation, every time a promise . . .

Oh, God, they were good together.

He braked the Mustang against the curb beneath the sign for departures at La Guardia. Lifted her suitcase from the trunk and handed it to the redcap. The black man said, "This it?"

He had a warm smile that the scar on the side of his throat tended to shed a chill upon. The scar was pink and traveled from just beneath his jaw to the base of his throat, one vivid seam with fainter transverse lines, like railroad ties.

Izzy Stein thrust a dollar bill in the man's hand and said, "Yeah, that's it."

The cap's eyes moved as Molly emerged from the Mustang, then moved back to meet Izzy's. "Man," he said softly, "I ought to be tipping you."

Only it sounded to Izzy like *Mahn* and *tippeen,* the lilt definitely Caribbean, probably Jamaican. Although could he distinguish that from, say, Haitian? It seemed like every third taxi driver in the city these days hailed from Haiti. Maybe they were invading as well the ranks of the redcaps. He slammed the trunk shut. What he was doing, he realized, was prolonging the moment of separation, when he was certain she would walk away without volunteering her destination—she with her secret, he left with his.

She came into his arms then, the stink and din of traffic all around them, and she told him she loved him, to please give Zeedee and Abe a kiss for her.

"Write me?" he said.

"I'm not going to be gone that long."

"Call me?"

"You promise to be there?"

"I'll try," he said, although it was not an answer to her question so much as a promise to himself.

She leaned into him, her lips on his, and then, as if the wind or some other elemental force had swept her from him, she was moving toward the waiting redcap, clad in a sleeveless yellow dress, sunshine-colored heels to match, her hips weaving music. Her hair shifted in the morning air like a lazy flag and the waiting redcap touched his hat. A smile so bright you'd never notice the scar on his throat.

Dressed in the plum shorts, a gray T-shirt, his comfortable Reeboks, Izzy Stein lifted his suitcase and matching charcoal carryon from the trunk of the Mustang. The suitcase was equipped with wheels and a strap, so that it could be dragged. Inside the carryon was his nine-millimeter Smith that he was going to have to clear, which was why he had arranged for nearly a three-hour gap between Molly's flight and his. He left the Mustang in the long-term parking lot.

From his conversation with Phil Fall yesterday, he learned that the Pinkertons had a definite trace on Misty Carmichael in Cortez, Colorado, a waitress and travel agent that could place him several days ago in a diner there. The travel agent did even better than that. With a little encouragement (compliments upon her appearance, professionalism, and manners, for example, plus both Pinkertons raving over the music of Randy Travis), she volunteered the information that someone looking very much like Misty Carmichael had left Cortez in the company of her niece bound for Phoenix, Arizona. And they had purchased airline tickets. Paid cash for them.

Oh? And wouldn't there be a record?

Audrey told the agent but of course there would. Who did he think he was dealing with, a bunch of hicks?

"Hawaii," Phil Fall had told him. "The island of Oahu. Tickets for two. You want me to contact somebody there?"

"Yes," Izzy Stein had said, at about the same time Molly Carmichael was spreading her legs to admit the flesh of Joe Scorcese. "But what I'd like you to arrange, there's a Northwest flight out of La Guardia tomorrow, an eight-forty morning flight, goes through Frisco, then on to Oahu, find out the earliest shuttle after that to Maui, and have someone on that shuttle."

"For this Misty and his lady?"

"No. For Misty's mother. I'll fax you photos. I'll spring for two Pinkertons, but leave one at the airport in Maui to meet me. It's not a big island. One pink ought to be able to sit her until I get there, no?"

Phil Fall didn't say anything for several seconds. Then: "Climb down offa your New York horse, Stein. One pink in a place like that will not only sit her, but discreetly wipe her ass if you so desire."

"Thank you."

"You inna hurry, I think we accept MasterCard or Visa, either one."

Izzy Stein had grinned in spite of himself. "Fuck you, Phil."

"Kinky, kinky," said the voice in Denver, the man named Phil Fall sitting in a twelve-by-twelve office behind a cheap desk of laminated walnut, the block walls adorned with pictures of scenic Colorado that in his four years there he had never yet had enough paid leave to visit.

Phil Fall was married, a father of three, blond hair receding over the horizon faster than any man deserved. He was thirty-five years of age, developing a paunch. He thought New Yorkers were pushy bastards, but he had to admit they generally got the job done. And he liked this Izzy, even if he was a Jew. He liked the man's guts and he liked the sense of humor.

Maybe he'd share with him, the next time they talked,

his observation that after thirty-five, the fastest thing that grew was not your waist, but the hairs in your nose.

"Hey Izzy," he had said, "how old are you anyways?"

"Why?" drawled Izzy Stein. "Do I get a senior's discount?"

"You ain't that old."

"Today I am. I aged a lot this past week. Listen. I got an eleven-thirty flight out of La Guardia, puts me in Oahu around five o'clock there. I should be in Maui no later than six-thirty, seven. It'll be flight number—lemme see—flight number two four five. Got it?"

"Roger."

"Thanks."

"Nothing to it, partner."

That was yesterday. Today, finished with the paperwork required to transport his weapon and with still more than an hour before his flight left, Izzy phoned the hospital, asked for Zelda's extension. Abe answered.

"How's our lady this morning?"

"She slept good, the nurse said."

"Keep up her strength."

"Yeah."

"You don't sound so good."

"Me? No, me, I'm good. Zeedee, she's lookin' good."

"I'm glad to hear that, Abe. Give her a kiss for me. And Molly too. She said for me to tell you."

"You get her to the airport okay?"

"Uh-huh."

"I still don't like it."

"What? What don't you like?"

"The situation you're in, the whole schmear. Did I tell you that conversation I had with that cop, that Cox?"

"You told me, Abe. About a half dozen times yesterday I think. I know the words and music by heart."

"Yeah, yeah. Such a smart guy you are, you sneak around behind the woman you love for a buncha *khazers.*"

"I don't see I have a choice. It's a lousy situation and I gotta deal with it and I can't begin till I find that fuckin' idiot son of hers, which I then hafta figure out a way to cover his worthless ass."

"But you didn't tell *her* that, Molly."

"No. And she didn't tell me where he is either. She doesn't trust me that far, I guess."

"You're a pair of lovebirds, you are."

"We got off on the wrong foot, that's all. We'll work it out. Once this is over, we'll work it out."

"I don't like it. I don't care what you say, Izzy. Nothing good ever gets done behind somebody's back. Zeedee'd say the same thing if she could."

Izzy Stein glanced at his watch.

"Any leads on our friend, Mr. Bellows?"

"You are changing the subject."

"I'm changing the subject."

"Iz, listen to the words I'm saying. Behind a person's back, nothing good comes of it."

Izzy Stein said he wasn't going to argue, things would work out, words to that effect. He didn't remember exactly.

Abe was saying there was nothing new on Bellows, but he'd turn up, a guy like him had had his own way so long, he was spoiled. Abe promised to save all the guy's garbage for Izzy for when he got back. But Izzy Stein wasn't thinking about Bellows. To hell with Bellows. Izzy was thinking that Abe was right. Molly had said in bed that morning that she didn't want to hear a speech, but he should have gone ahead. He should have squared it with her, told her that whatever mistakes may have been made, they were mistakes of love. Even people in love made mistakes. Maybe especially people in love.

Izzy wasn't airborne long before he decided to upgrade his ticket to first class for the return flight. He knew he should sleep, but could not, regardless of how he screwed himself around in the cramped seat. Next to him in the middle and window seats were a smiling couple, looked to be in their middle fifties—she a lanky lady with muddy brown hair parted severely to one side, brown eyes, a distracting number of black hairs on her upper lip; he a tall, pear-shaped fellow in a plaid leisure suit, white hair slicked back, a round red face that looked as if it might ignite at any moment—German tourists, it turned out, from Munich. He managed an automobile dealership, which had enjoyed another banner year. A trip to New York City for seven days, six nights had been his reward. All expenses paid. And since they had come this far, the wife went on to explain, they were extending their visit an additional week to visit relatives in San Francisco and go to Disneyland. Her husband had wanted to go to Detroit to tour General Motors and Chrysler and Ford, but wasn't it true the whole city was blacks now?

She called them "blacksfolken." In a voice that the pilot very well could have heard.

Izzy squirmed in his aisle seat in an effort to scan their neighbors, saw no one black, and said, "I'm not that familiar with the city. I know there's a black mayor. But so is there one in New York, in D.C., in Los Angeles." He shrugged. "And a ton of other cities. We're a mixed bag, as countries go."

The woman, who was sitting beside the window, leaned over her husband. "Excuse me. Mixed bag is meaning confusion, yes? You are in confusion?"

"Well, we are, as a matter of fact. But no, what I meant, we are a country of great diversity. Many different people."

At which point the benevolently smiling husband chimed in, "So long as they all buy Mercedes," and nudged Izzy with a beefy elbow.

But the wife wasn't satisfied. "Sebastian, do not make small of the issue. I think it must be very much confusing to live in this country. The cities, especial. So much—what is the word? Undesirable. Undesirable contact."

Izzy thought he saw it coming and stiffened. Stiffened as everything in his life had trained him to expect. He pushed a fraudulent smile into his face and said, "I'm not certain what you mean by undesirable."

"I am meaning only what I can see in the, the journals of news, that how you call them, the moogers."

"Muggers," said Izzy, surprised. "But not all blacks are muggers, nor are all muggers black."

The woman's eyes widened. "This is true?"

Izzy Stein said, "Yes."

And the husband poked him with an elbow. "Just so long as they buy Mercedes, is no matter who is their color."

The Humboldts, husband and wife, had two martinis apiece, because they could not tolerate the weak American beers or, they declared in voices loud enough to be heard in the rearmost seat in smoking, any of the watery imports. Then they fell asleep. The Humboldts, husband and wife, snored. Izzy Stein was reminded of the movie "Deliverance," the scene that featured the dueling banjos.

But at least their sleeping relieved him of his tour-guide duty. Alone with his thoughts he realized rather quickly how little he relished the situation. Because he had concentrated the past week upon the single object of locating Misty Carmichael and not upon the more complicated issue of what he was going to do with the creep once he found him. He would not have the luxury, he was convinced, of dodging that bullet much longer.

All right. Stand and face it. He was going to use—no other word for it—Molly to lead him to her son. Then . . . the matter of Misty's sleazy personality to one side, he still did not want to have to shoot the dirtball. Simply show him the Smith & Wesson and explain how it was in his interests to surrender the money he had taken from the Scorcese family, and how it might also be in his interests to change his appearance as much as possible and get out of the country for a . . . Of course. There could be one very good reason for Molly traveling so far. Because the heist had all the earmarks of something carried out by the seat of the pants, Misty Carmichael had not prepared for the consequences of his act, although he must have quickly perceived what was absolutely vital to his success: washing up somewhere outside the Scorcese sphere of influence. But to leave the country he needed—his passport. *That* was what Molly had agreed to meet him for.

Once abroad, it would be safe for him, after some discreet inquiries, to purchase phony documentation. Izzy Stein was confident that someone with Misty's affinity for low life would gravitate toward the people who could help him, for a price. Izzy thought about that for a while and decided to let the kid run with twenty-five thousand. Seed money. It amounted to the 10 percent recovery fee promised him, which he was betting the Scorcese family had no intention of honoring in any event. So, up them.

But returning the money—*most* of the money—addressed only half of his predicament. How to account for Misty Carmichael? First of all, steer clear of melodrama; he'd be suspect immediately. Keep it simple. Tell the whole thing like it was, the Pinkertons tracking him to Phoenix, there learning he was bound for Hawaii. No mention of Molly going there. Okay. Now tell them about the arrangements for the two Pinkertons in Oahu (he'd solidify this story with Phil Fall over the phone before he returned to New York), deviating from the truth only in so far as to say that they were assigned to track Misty, not Molly. Simple so far. Then that he, Izzy, flew out to Maui to nail young Carmichael, confronted him in his quarters (wherever that turned out to be), and that in the process of toting up the money, the kid had blindsided him (he'd have one of the Pinks suckerpunch him) and gone out the door. While he might have had a shot at him, no amount of money was worth the possibility of taking a fall. If the family wanted him pursued further, he would say, that was their option, but he had at least salvaged the bulk of their money. That was his story, Izzy Stein decided, and he would stand by it. He wasn't a goddamn paid assassin.

He looked his story over as the Humboldts snored in uneven counterpoint, and while it wasn't a flawless vehicle of exposition, it had the virtue of eliminating any mention of Molly Carmichael.

Izzy's flight touched down in Oahu a little after five o'clock in the afternoon (it was ten p.m. Izzy's body time) and all he saw of the airport was a couple of sand-colored outbuildings, not the main terminus. Between the runways the grass looked parched and tough as straw. He deplaned with the strap of his carryon slung over a shoulder, into pleasantly warm air as contrasted to the oppressive heat of Queens in August. He enjoyed the walking, the opportunity to exercise his muscles. As he found his way to the building from which the flights to Maui departed, the air invigorated him, and much as he dreaded explaining his presence to Molly, when the time came, he longed for the opportunity to do just that, if only to look into her eyes in a place like this, which he sensed was as near to paradise as man and woman were granted the chance to experience.

Landing in Maui an hour later only reinforced this impression.

Sitting there in a sea of blue diamonds, with a volcano in its heart, jungle as lush as anything Rousseau painted, beaches of blindingly white sand (and black sand too, although these were considerably less than advertised), the island possessed all the ingredients to cast a spell, to instantly charm. A man in Izzy Stein's occupation could lose his edge here, easily.

CHAPTER 19

Martin Combs had never aspired to work in law enforcement. His father Wendell had been a Pinkerton, and if there was a career he wasn't going to pursue, it was as a Pinkerton. His father was one of the grayest individuals he had ever known, practically colorless, which was probably the reason that after six years of marriage, his mother walked out on them, just woke up one morning and walked out the front door with her purse and the clothes on her back and disappeared from the face of the earth. (Knock, knock. Who's there? Wendell. Wendell who? Wendell you think Combs will find his wife?) No, what Martin Combs had in mind for himself was a career in baseball. When he graduated from the University of Miami, sporting a lusty .345 batting average, he was an early-round draft choice of the San Francisco Giants. After knocking around five years in the minors, he wound up just a step away from the bigs, playing for a triple-A farm club, the Phoenix Fire-birds. He played one-half inning in the outfield in the first game and got beaned by the first pitch in his first at bat. After that, he just couldn't see the old pill as well; his timing was gone, his rhythm, his entire beautiful swing—vanished as suddenly and completely as his mother.

So he became a Pinkerton.

Charlie Bolton, on the other hand, almost from the instant he could articulate words, had wanted to be involved in law enforcement. In kindergarten he had caused something of a sensation by announcing that when he grew up he intended to become a black police officer—an ambition miraculous for its innocence, insofar as young Charlie was a skinny, freckled white boy with hair so pale as to be almost transparent. But Charlie did grow up to become a police officer in Detroit, then a detective, and a fairly good one too, until his fundamental innocence rose up in revulsion at what he had to witness and wade through day after day. Charlie Bolton burned out. He was granted medical leave, and with his wife and child of several months, he drove west away from the grinding spectacle of slums and gang wars and drug dealers and twelve-year-old pregnant hookers and sorrow and waste . . . west where the air was clear and clean, one of the few surviving cherished myths. He too became a Pinkerton, not with a sense of resignation, as was the case with Martin Combs, but because he loved the challenge of investigation, and this the job offered, along with the opportunity to travel—and for the most part, to stay out of police stations, which for him reeked of too many memories.

They had flown out from San Francisco that morning. Martin Combs, approaching his thirty-fifth birthday, had become a little thick at the waist, but still had the powerful arms of an athlete and alert eyes, even if they couldn't pick up an 85 mph fastball until it was virtually sitting on his knuckles. He had a pleasant face and plenty of hair on his arms, most of which were showing because he was wearing a gray San Francisco Giants T-shirt. Cut-off jeans and rubber thongs on his feet. Dark glasses and a brown beard purchased in a Berkeley costume shop. The beard looked good; even Bolton had complimented him on it. The beachcomber look all the way. Charlie Bolton was much too earnest to attempt that sort of disguise. A lean, blond man almost six feet tall, Charlie Bolton looked like an apprentice accountant who sang in the church choir Sundays, a perfect pitch tenor. He had in fact killed one man in the line of duty, as well as getting shot in the thigh (almost dying from loss of blood), slashed, stabbed, bludgeoned by a ball bat, and struck on the knee by a brick. He was dressed in long pants and a madras shirt, and not one of his scars was visible. On his feet were black penny loafers.

Both men had permits to carry concealed weapons. Charlie Bolton still had his service revolver, a .38-caliber Colt. Martin Combs, who had never shot an individual in his life, packed a nine-millimeter Ruger, a semiautomatic with a fifteen-round clip in it, as well as one in the chamber. It would not pay to fuck with either man, as both were dead shots on the range, although as Bolton could have told Combs, the surge of adrenaline in a real-life situation can reduce a marksman to silly putty.

Their guns were not on their persons, but in carry-on luggage that rested at their feet as they compared watches at the bar in the Oahu airport, sipping sodas.

Charlie Bolton volunteered to walk down the corridor to check the monitor for time of arrival. When he returned, Martin Combs was unfolding the photostat of Molly Carmichael.

Bolton put a hand on his shoulder. "Marty, you're just supposed to follow the lady, not make love to her."

"The flight still on time?"

"Fifteen minutes from right now."

"Jesus. This could be the high point of my career as a Pinkerton. I'm talking if the lady looks even half as good as this picture."

Charlie Bolton glanced at Molly Carmichael's face once more over Combs's shoulder. Because he was a married man, a father of two, a boy and a girl, and an essentially innocent man still, all Charlie Bolton would admit was, "Gosh, if I weren't a married man."

Martin Combs, who had never been married, who never would be married, said, "I wouldn't give a shit. I'd walk out the door at high noon naked right over my wife, the minister, and the whole congregation for the opportunity to fuck that woman."

Martin Combs had never been known for his delicacy around women. He laid a lot of them, because he was glib and good-looking, not at all the gray figure his father was, but none of the ladies stayed. Martin Combs told himself he liked it that way.

They watched her—Combs from behind dark glasses—emerge from the Northwest ramp and pause to study the monitors, the directional signs. Then the two men converged at a distance of twenty-five feet behind her, seemingly by accident.

Combs said, "Jesus, Charlie."

Bolton swallowed saliva. "I know. She's one pretty lady."

"Pretty? *Pretty?* She's the most gorgeous piece of ass ever to walk through my life. You call her pretty."

"Well, you know."

"Jesus, Charlie, you must've gone straight from virginity to marriage, come up with a lame-ass word like pretty. I can think of a hundred. Unbelievable. Scrumptious. Elegant. Edible."

"She's a beautiful lady, all right."

"Hitting the nail on the head, that's you, Charlie. So when we get to Maui, I vote you wait for the New York Jew at the airport, I'll dedicate myself to staying close to the quiff. How about it?"

Innocent as he looked, Charlie Bolton was not about to lie down for any wise guy. "I'll tell you what, Marty, we'll flip for it."

And they did.

Charlie Bolton won, and when they deplaned in Maui, it was Charlie Bolton who rented the wine-colored Chrysler from Avis, in order to tail Molly Carmichael. Martin Combs offered him one hundred dollars if he would forget about the decision the coin had made for them. Charlie Bolton refused on the grounds that of the two, he would be the more detached.

Charlie Bolton, married, the father of a girl and a boy, had told himself and his partner one great big whopper.

Combs stayed with her to the baggage carousel, watched the redcap, a white guy (can you believe it, a white guy permitted to work in the service industry?), touch his cap politely, murmur words at her to which she nodded. The cap lunged, rescued her suitcase, and delivered it to her. Along with a small package wrapped in brown plastic. There didn't seem to be anything else. After fitting the brown plastic package in her capacious purse, Molly Carmichael followed the redcap out to the curb to hail a taxicab. That was unusual. Most visitors to the islands, especially Americans, preferred the freedom of a rental car for their stay.

Martin Combs found himself in a pleasant quandary: if his partner didn't show up damn quick, he'd have to choose between honoring their coin toss or jumping into a cab to follow Molly Carmichael.

Gee.

Nowhere on the concrete island where the rental-car buses stopped was there anyone resembling Charlie Bolton. So he must have already caught a bus. Which meant that he was probably filling out the paperwork. Now. Even as the redcap waved down a taxi and Molly Carmichael in her snug yellow dress approached the curb, turning to address the redcap. My God, those eyes, those lips, the way the lady carried herself: there was about her an air of such complete integration, as if she had had not a few decades, but thousands of years on the earth to perfect her act. Looking at her behind dark glasses and amidst the turmoil of arriving tourists, Martin Combs experienced, perhaps for the first time in his life, the clutching sensation of intimidation. Was it possible? Marty Combs not sharp enough, or witty enough, or absolutely off the wall enough to tease some interest out of the lady?

He would never know.

Because in that instant a wine-colored Chrysler cut across three lanes of traffic and glided gently to the curb with Charlie Bolton behind the wheel grinning.

Combs shuffled over in his rubber thongs, the beachcomber bum with his carryon, and tossed the carryon into the Chrysler.

"Okay," said Bolton, still grinning, "so I'm not so good at adjectives. But you can't say I don't have a sense of timing. I'll stay glued to her."

"Yeah. Glued, hued, and tattooed."

"Whatever that means."

"We'll be sitting in the bar, next to the phone, soon as the New York Jew shows up."

"I'll try to ring you every half hour."

"Charlie?"

"What?"

"Two hundred bucks, Charlie."

"See what I mean? You're too emotional about the lady."

"Three, you bastard."

The power window climbed in front of him, reflected his smooth, frustrated good looks. Charlie Bolton grinned inside the Chrysler, touched his fingertips to his eyebrow to cast off a salute. Charlie Bolton was a disgusting example of a human being.

The Jewish guy was all right. Not that Martin Combs could claim an extensive knowledge of the people or the religion. Having grown up in Florida, his experience led him to believe they were all past seventy with whiny voices and money to burn, but with which they would not part without the equivalent of a Senate debate. He didn't meet many playing baseball except for reporters and betters. And as a Pinkerton, he saw them only as reflections of his experience as a youth. Something for nothing. What is this, highway robbery, in a suit yet? Stuff like that. So a level guy like Izzy Stein came at him as something of a surprise.

Walking up to him in his purple shorts, a tough-bastard build but not throwing it around, just in a soft voice with this queer little smile saying, "Combs? Or is it Bolton?"

"Marty Combs."

They shook hands.

"Izzy Stein. What's the program?"

"Suppose we stroll on over to my office. It'll look a lot like a bar, but that's just part of the disguise."

"Happy to. Molly landed?"

"You see my partner anywhere? For that matter, if I could have concocted a legitimate excuse, you wouldn't be seeing me here, either. That answer your question?"

Izzy Stein said, "It's almost seven o'clock. I bet you could use something stronger than a soda. And since I'm buying . . ."

"You know," said Martin Combs, "you're all right."

Izzy Stein bought Martin Combs Wild Turkey, a double on the rocks with water on the side, a Stoli over ice for himself, then trotted off to retrieve his luggage, a single suitcase. When he returned, Combs told him he had just heard from his partner, who had ascertained that Molly Carmichael was staying in a fifth-floor condominium overlooking South Kihei Road and beyond it Kamaole Beach, almost directly across the island from the airport. Izzy sipped his vodka and said, "I appreciate it. You Pinks have always been good to me."

"We try."

"I'll finish this and go rent a car. As long as I'm paying for your services today, I'll let you earn your money. Stake her out for the night, okay? I don't think it'll be too challenging, since she's probably as wiped as I am. Must be midnight, close to one in the morning our body time."

"Funny thing about her."

"What's that, Monty?"

"Marty."

"That's right. I *am* out of it. Marty. What's funny?"

The package wrapped in brown plastic, that Molly Carmichael deposited in her bag, meant nothing to Martin Combs, intrigued him not in the least. He said, "The lady rented a taxi."

"I'm sorry, Marty, it's the exhaustion. What's funny about that?"

"Taking a taxi. Americans are drivers, not riders."

A weak smile crept into Izzy Stein's face.

"She grew up in New York City. If there's anywhere in the world you don't want to have to drive, it's there. She hates driving."

Izzy rented a convertible, what the hell, and followed the rental agency's directions to Kihei, which when they arrived had the feel less of a town than a village, a single main street through it tracing the outline of the shore. They found Charlie Bolton in his wine-colored rental car with a pair of good binoculars in his lap, the car atop a parking garage for the residents of the condominium complex. Charlie passed the glasses to Izzy Stein and pointed to the westernmost balcony, the top floor overlooking the water. Within his circular perspective, Izzy Stein could see Molly Carmichael standing at the railing. There must have been a breeze up there because her hair trailed behind her head. She stood with her elbows on the railing, her hands clasped and her chin on top of her hands. As if she were appealing to the sea, or something equally ancient. He ached for her, longed to touch her. What he said was, "Monty, let's you and me go find a place for me to eat and bunk. The two of you work out schedules."

"Marty," said Combs.

"Yeah," said Izzy Stein, still watching Molly through the lenses, "Marty. I apologize."

He continued to watch Molly through the glasses, mesmerized by the vision of her up there alone in the night, her beautiful white face given a bronze cast by the patio lights, there in a strange land, in her element. The patio lights filled her red hair with shifting gold tints.

CHAPTER 20

When they explained to the pilot where it was they wanted to stay, Wescott Page had recommended a hotel and condo complex right on the beach in Kihei. Leslie Ann Rice worried aloud over the fact they were flying in late on a Friday night, wouldn't the hotels all be booked up? Wescott Page had shouted into the noise of the helicopter: "This time of year? Love, you have to be kidding. Not a bloody chance."

And he was right.

At the airport they had phoned the hotel and gotten a two-bedroom ground-floor condo with cooking facilities, walk out the front door and you were on the beach. No problem.

She loved it, looking out over the waves the next morning, the sea air sweet and rattling the leaves in the palm trees, a group of small children diligently digging in the sand directly in front of her. Even Misty relaxed some and agreed to come with her for an early-morning swim. On the patio, right outside the sliding glass door, sat two plastic lounge chairs provided by the hotel. The chairs were striped in coral and white and looked cool and inviting in the morning shade. They dropped their towels on the loungers and walked across newly mown grass holding hands and down into the white sand that was rapidly heating and into the water. Though the tide was beginning to recede, there was an active surf out there, the waves breaking in thunderclaps and dispersing, shooting sheets of water up at them to lick their ankles. The water was as warm as a puppy's tongue. They stood in the shallows for a while taking in the spectacle of color and light and sound. Leslie Ann was wearing a purple one-piece that arched up from her crotch to give maximum exposure to her derriere, had almost no back to speak of, and a front that plunged precariously, designed in such a way that one or both breasts might escape at any moment. With the sun on her shoulders, on almost her entire back to within a fraction of an inch of the crack of her ass, and on her bare haunches, Leslie Ann felt a sense of delightfully erotic anticipation, a swimming sweetness within her. She tugged on Misty's hand and said, "Let's get wet, baby. If I stand here much longer, feeling the way I feel, I'll tear off your trunks in broad daylight."

"Funny about that," he said. "I was just having similar thoughts. You know what my philosophy is? When you feel it, act on it. Go with the flow."

They started running then, straight into the sea, and

sure enough, Leslie Ann Rice had to stop before they hit the breakers in order to tuck in a breast. Misty plunged into the foot of a wave and surfaced on the far side laughing, his black curls shining in the sun. He was a beautiful man, she thought, beautiful and unafraid of anything. She swam out to him and they stood in the deeper water, beyond where the waves were breaking, face-to-face, and she pulled away the crotch of her bathing suit so that he could enter her there in the water, in the deep water just the two of them moving in sync, in the rhythms of paradise.

Later they shopped for groceries, feeling pleasantly stunned after spending the entire morning either in the water or on the lounge chairs, which they moved down to the beach. With the groceries they returned to the condominium, mixed up a batch of salty dogs, ate lunch, cleaned up, and retired to the bedroom to make love again, then slept until almost four in the afternoon. They awoke and showered together and Misty said, "How about this, Sugarcheeks: how about we drive up to Lahaina, have dinner on Front Street, that fish joint Earl was telling us about?"

"The Pearl?"

"Yeah, that's it. My contact is flying in today, but what the hell, this is the weekend. Let's enjoy ourselves."

"You and this mysterious contact."

They were toweling off together in the steamy bathroom.

"Business."

"What is this business anyway, Misty? I mean, do I

have to think about the possibility I'm going to be shot at on Maui too?"

He snugged his towel around his waist and leaned over to kiss her full on the mouth. "You brought your passport like I told you to?"

"Where we going?"

"Wherever we feel like, as long as it's far from here."

She searched his eyes. "Are you serious?"

"It doesn't get much better. You and I, we've got real possibilities as a team. I can show you some things."

She nudged the grigri on his chest with her index finger. "I bet they aren't entirely legitimate, are they, Misty Carmichael?"

"You know what I read somewhere? There isn't a fortune that's been made in this world that you won't find a crime committed somewhere along the way to making it. So what it boils down to, if you have the balls to go after it. I do. And watching you in action, I see nerve there. Real fucking brass. That's why I think we could be a team. Whadda you think?"

"I think we should get dressed and drive to—where is it?"

"Lahaina."

"There. Where the Pearl is. And have a feast. I think I could devour a whole side of a whale."

"Partners?"

"Well of course, silly."

The road to Lahaina for the most part wound along the coast, taking them first north, then curving west around a spur of the island, then resuming the northerly direction. It was high tide and the sea was a steel blue, and in Maalaea Bay the waves were tall and creamy at their peaks, and beneath them, crouched on their big boards, countless surfers waited for the water to gather and thrust them shooting from the force of the ocean. The boards were bright in the sun and neon-colored, and the surfers, all of them boys or young men, in most cases favored snug-fitting trunks that stopped just short of the knees, although they were too far out in the water for Leslie Ann Rice to check them out.

It was about a twenty-minute drive and she had her eyes open the whole way. A stand of Norfolk Island pine cut short her view of the surfers, the trees rising thirty, forty feet and their thick needles blue in the late afternoon, their branches drooping with the symmetry of pagoda rooftops. Because it was warm and pleasant, the windows were down and the scent of pine washed over her and it seemed to be the very aroma of innocence, of a time she could not quite remember, but was certain had existed.

"Can you smell it?" she said to Misty.

"I can smell your gorgeous perfume if that's what you mean."

"No, the trees. Can't you smell the pine?"

"Yeah, so?"

"It makes me feel like early-morning rain makes me feel when I'm lying in bed, and the sheets are clean and cool. Kind of makes me feel pure and . . . I don't know. Like the world is a good place and not filled with all the shit it's filled with."

He glanced at her, a grin on his face, and brushed her

cheek with the knuckles of his hand. "You get all that from smelling a tree, I am definitely going to keep you away from the hashish. You'd start spouting like fucking Walt Whitman."

She cuddled close to him. "Who's that?"

"Just a poet my mother used to read out loud to me that I found out later was a fruit. She used to read all kinds of stuff to me, a lot of poetry. You think she was trying to turn me into a fruit?"

"If she was, I think she failed. What's she like, your mother?"

He stared straight ahead at the highway and didn't say a thing, not right away. They were climbing as they rounded the spur of the island and behind them stretched a sugarcane plantation, the fields tumescent with seven-foot stalks, the cane lean and yellow-green. In the distance a thin column of smoke quivered in the blue sky, and Leslie Ann, gazing back at it, was reminded by the motion of it of the dust devils that would swarm and dance in the summertime, when she was growing up in Arizona. A field of cane was being harvested by fire, and the ashes that rose with the smoke and were dispersed by the wind were known locally as Maui snow.

The land climbed steeply on either side of them and there were signs warning of rock slides. A network of cables had been strung across the landward slope, presumably to inhibit any slide from gathering momentum. She turned to study his face in profile.

"If you don't want to talk about it," she said, or started to say.

"No," he said, "I was just thinking is all. Molly—that's her name—you want to know what she's like, the word is *remote.* Off somewhere. Probably a real dead fish in the sack."

Leslie Ann Rice blinked. "That's funny."

"What?" He jerked his face in her direction. "What's so fucking funny?"

"I only meant you saying what she's probably like in bed. I didn't think sons thought of their mothers that way. You know, they're all supposed to be rehabilitated virgins or something."

He squeezed the wheel of the rental car and stared straight ahead. "I don't know what you mean."

"It's nothing," she said. "It's just you sounded like you'd considered it, like you would with any other woman."

"Molly isn't any other woman," said Misty Carmichael, "she's Pygmalion's ivory statue *before* it came to life."

"Pig who?"

He fumbled with the knobs above the ashtray. "Isn't there a fucking decent radio station on this island?"

It was a little after five o'clock when Misty Carmichael and Leslie Ann Rice found a parking spot just off Front Street. At the time he was locking the rental car, another Beretta, Molly Carmichael was letting herself into the fifth-floor condominium using keys that were waiting for her at the front desk. The condo was every bit as lovely as she expected it to be.

As you entered, there was a dining area and living room

dead ahead, and off to the left was a spacious kitchen with a white tile floor, plenty of cabinets all faced in bleached wood, a double-door refrigerator finished to blend with the cabinets. There was a breakfast-bar island covered with white tile, four bar stools on one side and more cabinet space on the other. A bedroom to the right with its own balcony and the master bedroom off the living room that shared a balcony with the living room. Peach-colored carpet throughout except for the two bathrooms and kitchen. Predominant colors were pastels: the peach together with aqua, rose, a pale plum. There were plenty of books on the shelves opposite the living-room couch.

Upon closing the door, Molly Carmichael parked her suitcase next to the breakfast island and leaned on it to remove her heels. Then she conducted a survey of the cabinets to learn what was where, finding a tall glass for herself in the process. Finishing her inventory, she went to the refrigerator, filled her glass with ice cubes, added water from the tap, drank deeply from her glass, refilled it, and did a walk-through of her quarters.

Then she opened both the glass door and the screen door off the master bedroom to step onto the patio. Touched by the late-afternoon sun, the concrete was warm beneath her feet, but by no means unpleasant. She stepped back inside, leaving her glass on the patio table, and walked on the plush carpet to a spot behind the curtains, then lifted the hem of her dress so that she could pull off her pantyhose. She hesitated, then shrugged, and pulled off her panties as well, dropped the hem of her dress and smoothed it just above her knees.

Now she could truly feel the heat of the sun rising from the concrete and the stir of island air whispering between her legs and the newness of this new place rubbing up against her, caressing her senses with the promise of a new world. It was a promise she needed desperately to believe in, now more than ever, because inside her purse, inside a package wrapped in plastic, lay a gun she was being paid to use.

The condominium was owned by a semiretired attorney, Sidney Simon, and his third wife, Claire, a tall, gorgeous lady whose face had adorned magazines like *Vogue, Elle, Cosmo,* and *Harper's Bazaar,* and who once confided in Molly Carmichael that she, Molly, was the sort of woman who could walk into a room of people and silence it with her beauty. Molly Carmichael had been instrumental in locating and negotiating a home for them in the Hamptons several years ago, shortly before they were married, and periodically kept in touch with them. When last year the Simons purchased the condo on Maui as a place to recuperate from the holidays, Claire had telephoned Molly, knowing her penchant for travel, and offered her run of the place anytime she could make it to Hawaii, outside of January and February.

Everything that Molly needed was there—bedding, towels, condiments, spices, liquor, pots and pans—but no food. She had watched on the way through Kihei for restaurants and had noted several within walking distance. She finished her glass of water on the balcony and turned her attention away from the ocean with the sun high and bright above it and looked north. She could see the cedar-shake rooftop of the nearest restaurant, the Carpe Diem, if she remembered correctly. It appeared as she had passed in the taxi that its outside bar did a lively business, a throng of casually dressed men and women in there leaning on the railings, the restaurant enclosed to the left and presumably not so rowdy. She would try it tonight, maybe shop for groceries tomorrow. It depended upon when her son contacted her. He had the phone number.

She glanced east, but she was on the wrong side of the building to see the imposing profile of Haleakala, the ten-thousand-foot volcano that had lapsed into silence for two hundred years now. All she could see was a bit of the volcano's flank and another complex of condominiums and the parking facilities and a single purple or wine-colored automobile on the roof of the parking area. She noticed it only because it appeared to be the same model she owned, a Chrysler LeBaron. She thought it an odd place to park, unless the covered sector below was filled. Possibly that was it. Although Claire had told her that during the summer months close to 70 percent of the condos were vacant.

Molly Carmichael closed the screen and glass doors behind her and emptied the diminished ice cubes in the kitchen sink. She was hungry. She hauled her suitcase into the master bedroom, opened it, and found her L.A. Gear sneakers, snugged her bare feet into them. To hell with her pantyhose and panties. She went into the bathroom and washed her face thoroughly, applied fresh makeup and perfume. Then addressed the package wrapped in brown plastic. Her face in the mirror, if she was any judge of faces, looked scared. It surprised her, because whatever dread she experienced, she felt more strongly a sense of determination. She believed she would do, could do, anything for Iz. She loved him that much.

She took the package and her purse into the kitchen to find something sharp enough to cut the brown plastic tape. She used a paring knife. Moments later she was looking at a Dan Wesson .22-caliber revolver with a two-and-a-half-inch barrel, weight of only thirty-two ounces, with a walnut grip and blued steel and smelling sweetly of oil. Molly Carmichael had never fired a gun in her life, and there were no instructions. She regretted then refusing the many invitations Iz had issued to join him on the gun range.

But she did remember the times she had watched Abe Stein breaking down his nine-millimeter and his .357, and so she searched first for the safety, found it, then located the mechanism to spring free the chamber. It was loaded, six slugs sitting in there, bright as newly minted coins. She returned the revolver to her purse and let herself out of her quarters. Rode the elevator to the ground floor. Waved to the man and woman who presided over the lobby desk and pushed through the glass doors that after eight P.M. would lock out anyone who didn't possess a condo key.

The air was a delight. It swarmed off the ocean and lifted her hair and stroked her skin. Red hibiscus flourished alongside the building as well as white and pink roses, although some of the roses, the white ones especially, appeared bedraggled. There was a divider down the drive to the main street, condominiums on either side of the drive, and in the divider a column of stately palms stood like tranquil sentries, their crowns shifting gently in the breeze. Molly Carmichael stopped beside one of the trees, let her hand drift over the virile, abraded surface of it, and watched the sunlight playing on the ocean.

At the base of the drive she turned around to enjoy the view of the volcano and noticed the blond, gangly man in sunglasses standing about where she had stopped. He bent over quickly to fuss with a shoe. The slope of the volcano was dark, rising from green to a shade approaching the color of a bruise, its peak enshrouded by thick white clouds that gave it the aspect of fuming. It looked cold up there, and forbidding.

She waited for a break in the traffic, then scampered across the main street clutching her purse to her hip. Shallow dunes presided over the beach, and parched grass struggled to maintain a foothold on them. There were also thickets of suckers punctuated by violet, trumpet-shaped flowers that Molly Carmichael believed were heliotropes. She removed her shoes to walk in the sand down to the shoreline. The breeze was lustier here and she parted her legs. She closed her eyes, feeling its thrust and insistence, tempted to return to the condo to phone Izzy Stein that instant, for the pleasure of his voice.

Behind her and in the direction of the Carpe Diem stood an outdoor shower, a tree of piping with four shower heads and four taps, and she stopped there to rinse the sand off her feet, then walked in the yellowing grass until they were dry.

The Carpe Diem, at least the open bar part of it, was noisy and festive, the music loud and the waitresses tunnel-

ing precariously through the mob of revelers. Steps led up to
the bar, and there was a lectern before the entrance, and a
young woman behind the lectern protruded her bottom lip
to blow her bangs off her forehead. She wore a white blouse
and a brown skirt over broad hips; a pleasant face with
brown eyes that seemed to hold the light of mischief. As
Molly Carmichael approached, she leaned away from the
lectern, telegraphing her assumption that there must be
someone escorting this woman. Then pulled back and put
on a smile. "Hiya," she said. "Welcome to the Carpe Diem.
You come for happy hour?"

"No," said Molly, "I was thinking more of dinner."

"Smart move." The woman leaned forward to confide.
"Honey, you go in there, a woman with your looks, it'd be
like walking into the lions' den. You'd get grab-assed till you
were black and blue."

Molly thanked her and said, "What's worth trying on
the menu?"

The woman stepped out from the lectern and took
Molly by the arm and hollered for someone named Wanda.
"Trust me, honey. If anyone knows what's delicious tonight,
it's Wanda."

Wanda appeared, a big brown woman with beautiful
skin, breathing as if she suffered from asthma, although it
was probably from the effort required to cart about 235
pounds on a five-foot, five-inch frame.

Wanda, with menus pressed to her bosom, led Molly
into the restaurant and over to a table for two, overlooking
the ocean. "Is there a gentleman along later?" she asked,
when Molly was seated.

"No. It's just me."

The ambience of the restaurant was one of studied indifference toward the tastes of the carriage trade. There were wooden booths with hard wooden seats and round wooden tables, sans tablecloths, that, from the way the tabletops shifted, suggested no two table legs agreed in length. Lanterns hung from wrought-iron chains and wrought-iron brackets, shedding overlapping pools of golden light. The floor was composed of gray hardwood planks and did not look inviting to someone in bare feet. Molly studied the menu thinking how much Iz would be at ease in a place like this. A goodly number of the tables and booths were occupied, and while it was not nearly so loud as the outdoor bar, the cumulative buzz of conversation intensified Molly's solitude. But she had to admit that in a way she enjoyed it, this being here in a new place naked beneath her dress, the isolation and privacy of it as well as the element of . . . stepping out on a ledge?

She guessed that was so. She guessed there wasn't a better description of a forty-five-year-old woman in a strange land with a loaded gun in her purse.

When Wanda waddled up to ask if she had made up her mind, Molly closed the menu and said, "I thought I might ask you what you would recommend."

"Well, darling." Wanda licked her lips and rolled her eyes. "A thin little thing like you, how many days it been since you had a bite to eat?"

"Not days, believe me, just hours."

"Sure sure sure. No wonder you don't have a man tonight. Darling child, you are too skinny by half. Now, what I suggest . . ."

Molly Carmichael ordered a fraction of the courses Wanda proposed. When the shrimp cocktail arrived, she thought she recognized the slim blond man across the room, the one fiddling with the straw in his drink, who seemed almost to be blushing, but that could have been the lantern light. The blond man did not look much older than her son . . . who . . . in that instant she realized . . . was the same age now that his father was the night he looked into her eyes and said, "It's going to be good, Molly. Believe me when I tell you: it's going to feel so good." The lying, useless bastard.

CHAPTER 21

There was a staircase of lacquered wood to the right as you entered the Pearl, bathrooms beyond the staircase, and ahead you were greeted by a lissome blond in a skimpy white costume who said, "Hi, I'm Kim. Upstairs or down tonight?"

Misty Carmichael said, "How about you give us the best table in the joint?"

Kim said, "Right this way," and led them up the stairs, introduced them to another waitress in a skimpy white outfit named Brit, a name that instantly intrigued Leslie Ann Rice, who, once she was seated, prodded the girl into explaining her full name was Bridgette, but she had hated it from day one. Brit was a nickname given her by an older brother, and she had never relinquished it. She was a sky diver and had ambitions as a poet, asked them if they had ever heard of Sylvia Plath or W. B. Yeats.

Misty Carmichael may have surprised her when he said, " 'Turning and turning in the widening gyre,' " uttering the words in a believable brogue, " 'The falcon cannot hear the falconer.' That the Yeats guy you're talking about?"

"That was beautiful," said Brit, and Leslie Ann Rice looked at him with genuine admiration. "You Irish?" asked Brit.

Misty laughed. "With a name like Carmichael? But I'll tell you something, Brit, because I don't like to mislead a pretty lady. My mother once brought home a record of Yeats readings, and that's where I picked up the accent, or whatever you call it."

Brit said, "It's music, you know that? Pure as music. Oh, to be able to put words together like that."

Misty Carmichael glanced at Leslie Ann Rice and winked. "I hate to break it to you, Brit, but there's no money in it."

Leslie Ann reached over and slapped the back of his hand. "There's other things besides money."

"Sure there is. But let me ask Brit. Brit, it says here the red snapper broiled, an entree goes for fourteen ninety-five. How much is that roughly in iambic pentameter?"

The young woman named Brit grinned at him—showing beautiful teeth—and said, "You are a character," then turned to Leslie Ann. "He's a handful, isn't he, or does he have his dull moments?"

A lazy, sensual smile surfaced in Leslie Ann's face as she

lifted a swath of dark hair away from her eye. "Not so far," she drawled.

The two women enjoyed a bawdy chuckle, and then Brit took their drink orders and swayed off between the tables of diners.

Plants in pots had been strategically arranged to offer a modicum of privacy to each table—bromeliads with big, broad, waxy leaves, and yucca with bent, sword-shaped leaves, their thickish trunks the color of driftwood, and then too there was the startling beauty of birds of paradise, the flowers shaped like vases, the hues running from deep or-ange to purple. White fans hung on stalks from the ceiling and abetted the breeze off the ocean. An enormous bar that appeared to have been finished in mahogany filled a good deal of the wall opposite the water and maybe a half-dozen patrons lolled on stools there, waiting for a table. Daylight provided all the illumination the upstairs needed except be-hind the bar, where several spots assisted the bartender, who wore a flowery short-sleeved shirt and a gold pendant of some sort in his left earlobe. The tables were round, had a burled mahogany veneer, and the chairs had comfortable cushions. There were no windows between them and the sea. The sunlight conspired with the water at that hour to create the illusion of diamonds shifting about on dusky satin. A tour boat was motoring inland out of the sun filled with fished-out fishermen, and beyond it, in the distance, a skier was crossing the blue sky hoisted by a kitelike structure. Leslie Ann Rice said, "I might try that. But I sure don't hanker to ever sky dive, like Brit does. Do you?"

And Misty said, "If I'm going to put my ass on the line, it better be for money. That's my philosophy."

They shared an order of oysters Rockefeller, then each enjoyed a bowl of conch chowder. The sky was deepening over the ocean, filling with a rose color and with clouds swollen to the hue of prunes. The water was becoming black ink. The fans churned overhead, spilling the cooling ocean air over the patrons. Even finishing the bowl of conch, Leslie Ann Rice shivered, clutched her elbows. "Misty?" she said. "How can a person be chilled in August on Maui? But you know I am. Does that make me a wimp?"

He had been scanning the restaurant, but brought his eyes back to focus on Leslie Ann. "More hot food," he said, "that's the ticket."

"I hope so," she murmured demurely. "I think I'll visit the ladies'."

"Another salty dog? You're about dry."

"Sure. Why not."

Leslie Ann Rice maneuvered her way through the tables to the head of the stairs, and descended them. Turned right onto deep plum carpet and felt a hand behind her, strongly grasping her tricep. She knew immediately.

"Daddy?"

It was Earl all right, his bleached hair combed back flat to his skull and his eyebrows bristling and his lips closer to snarling than smiling. "I thought someone was shitting me," he said, "and I figured you got to eat somewheres, and this is the only place I mentioned. Lucky for you, your boyfriend don't lie too good. In my opinion he's just a punk. But that's just one man's opinion."

She thrust herself upon him, her arms beneath his, hands on his back and lips on his lips. "Oh, daddy," she said, "I'd about given up hope."

"Say," he said, touching her cheek, "what happened here, you run into some barbwire?"

Leslie Ann Rice said to Misty Carmichael, "You believe who I bumped into? Small world, isn't it?" There was pleading in her eyes.

"Why Earl," said Misty Carmichael, rising from his chair to put out a hand to shake the older man's, "hell brings you to Maui?"

They shook and Earl pulled out a chair between them and sat down. "Must be serendipity, you know that? You tell me last night you ain't comin' here, you're headed for Phoenix, danged if I just didn't feel so bad you'd miss the chance to see this island that I got downright nostalgic. Caught a flight this morning. I can't tell you how damned glad I am you two kids changed your mind. Is this about the most beautiful place on the face of the earth or what? Look at that ocean."

Misty Carmichael said, "A sight for sore eyes. Join us for dinner, Earl?"

"Yes," said Leslie Ann Rice, "we'd love for you to join us." Again the pleading eyes for Misty's benefit.

"Well, I guess we're all Americans here," said Earl.

"Say," said Misty Carmichael, "I was reading some of the tourist crap they hand out—remember that stand out in front of the Rainbow Mall, Sugarcheeks?—and I was kinda intrigued by the Iao Valley. Is that how you pronounce it?"

"Yep. Ee-ah-o. About every danged letter gets pronounced in Hawaiian."

"Ever been there?"

"Not in a coon's age, son."

"I was thinking—"

It was the waitress, Brit. "Excuse me. I noticed the
gentleman. Did he wish a . . . drink or something?"

Earl didn't hesitate. "Bring me a Coors. You got
Coors?"

"Yes, we have Coors. And Coors light."

"I don't want none a that girl beer. Bring me a Coors
and a plateful of whatever these folks are having. Just the
bottle, no glass."

Brit turned to Misty Carmichael. "It . . . because I already turned in your orders, they might be ready a little
sooner than your friend's. I can have them held back, kept
heated, but I can't promise—"

Earl again jumped in. "Bring 'em when they're ready,
little girl. If I have to wait, that's okay, I ain't the king of
England. Just you bring on the beer and I'll live off that."

Brit looked at Earl an instant longer, her eyes clearly
intent upon identifying what specimen of humanity this was,
and clearly failing. Brit smiled weakly and wandered off.

"You were saying, son?"

"Iao Valley. I was thinking tomorrow Leslie Ann and I,
we'd drive up that way. I mean, if you'd care to join us."

"Well . . ."

"Sure, Earl," added Leslie Ann Rice, "long as you're
here."

"If you folks are serious."

"Of course we're serious," said Misty. "Darling, how

about we'll have a picnic up there, buy us a cooler and stuff it full of beers and sandwiches. You like tuna fish, Earl?"

"Is the pope Polish?"

"We'll get some tomatoes and lettuce. I love a tuna-fish sandwich with a slice of tomato, some lettuce on it. And we'll bring chips, good greasy chips."

Leslie Ann Rice said, "Mist—Carl, did you see the price of tomatoes, when we were shopping this afternoon? Lady ahead of us in line bought two of 'em, wasn't either one as big as my fist. Cost her almost three dollars."

"Welcome to the islands, sugarcheeks. Weren't you listening to the dink tour guide, how expensive everything was?"

"Alice? She was a sweetheart."

"If your taste runs to dwarfs. You saw her, didn't you, Earl? Little thing that yelled at us from the bus there in Pearl Harbor. Shtupping her, you'd feel like a child molester."

Earl, for once, was at a loss for words.

"Honey, that's not nice. She was a sweetheart, Earl. Speaks five languages."

But Misty Carmichael was on a roll, at least thought himself to be. "Yeah, but that's not what you get in the sack to do—talk."

Leslie Ann Rice flopped back in her chair, her eyes on the ceiling. "You're hopeless," she said.

And Earl said, "Well, here comes little miss cupcake titties with my Coors. Danged if I wasn't beginning to think she had to go all the way to Colorado for it."

The waves ran southeast against the shore at Kihei, and Molly watched them breaking for a while from the sidewalk, walking slowly after her dinner, feeling pleasantly drowsy, and in a lazy sort of way longing for Iz, for his hip bumping against hers, his arm around her. To the west the sky was rose and the rest of the sky was a crystalline black, stars beginning to shimmer in it. The temperature was dropping. Traffic on the street was heavy and slow moving; the sound of loud music and shouts from car to car—razzing, flirtatious invitations—made her smile. The pure joy of it. Two cars stopped, blocking traffic in both directions, in order for the occupants to exchange remarks, and when someone honked, one of the passengers in the stopped cars extended an arm out the window, wiggled his pinkie and index finger, signaling both apology and an appeal to lay back, relax. Molly walked on, laughing to herself, thinking here she was, an old broad and beginning to feel what it is to be twenty for the first time in her life. This was the gift Iz had given her by coming back into her life, coming back seriously for her as she was, and not how he might like her to be.

Entering her quarters on the fifth floor, she settled her purse on the breakfast bar, and while she had not had a cocktail or glass of wine in the Carpe Diem, she felt a desire for a taste of something strong now. She found among the liquor a bottle of Stolichnaya and poured some over ice the way Iz drank it, and walked over to the shelves of books. Studying titles on spines, she sipped at her drink, concluding it was not a flavor she would lean toward, but enjoying it as something Iz enjoyed.

She finished the vodka and emptied the ice cubes in the sink and rinsed out the glass. The light in the room was soft and she felt like sinking into bed, but believed, with the liquor in her system, it would do her well to experience the sobering winds off the ocean. She went into the bathroom first and washed her face clean of makeup, then rubbed in a moisturizer. She removed the sneakers. Then slid back the glass and screen doors to step onto the patio. There was a tremulous sliver of violet light lingering on the horizon, the sun's adieu, and the water moved beneath the starlight like liquid slate. The palms in the drive looked ancient and confident as warriors. Molly Carmichael stood beneath the lights of the patio with her elbows on the railing, her fingers linked, chin on her hands, and thought about Iz. How badly she ached for him. How early she would rise the next morning in order to phone him.

It was around seven in the evening, island time. From a certain distance there were sparks of gold shifting about in her hair.

Then the phone rang.

Calling from a booth in Lahaina, Misty Carmichael recognized his mother's voice and listened to her say hello three, maybe four times before he hung up.

Good, he thought. Stick around, bitch, I have some business to deal with, then you and I, we can settle up. Fair is fair.

No sense selling either of ourselves short.

Molly was certain the silence
at the other end of the line was Misty. Who else could it be?

She undressed and showered to wash the day's accumu-
lation from her—the strain of traveling, the anxiety of preparing herself for what was necessary. She raised the temperature of the water until the heat stung, then closed her eyes
to soap up, lather her skin in a fragrant residue. She moved
soapy fingers between her legs, made it slick there, and a
smile climbed into her face, a clean, clear expression of anticipation. She rinsed off in the still-stinging water, then
dried herself, wrapped a large aqua bath towel over her
breasts and a smaller one around her mahogany hair and
exited the steamed-up bathroom. She flipped off the lights
in the master bedroom and sat on the patio outside in the
amber wash of light there. The sky was radiant with stars.
The breeze was dying and the palms in the drive were practically rigid. She rubbed the towel over her hair, shook her
tresses, worked the towel into them some more. She had
made a decision.

Tomorrow, as soon as she woke up, she would telephone Iz. Invite him to join her, if he had the time. Hint that
maybe she had a line on her son. That way he would earn
points with the Scorcese family, when she brought Misty
down, or the money in.

That was how she framed it to herself, at any rate.
When the simple truth of the matter happened to be that the
beauty of the island cried out for someone to share it with.

She glanced over her shoulder and there it was on top

of the parking garage, the profile of the Chrysler LeBaron, the car that had been sitting there for hours. The funny thing about it was, although she didn't give it a great deal of thought, there seemed to be a light inside it that gained intensity periodically.

Molly, because she had never smoked, did not even think that somebody might be inside the wine-colored Chrysler on top of the parking garage, smoking out of boredom.

Unhitching the towel that covered her breasts, she opened it to expose her torso, put her feet up on the chair opposite, and let the current of air from the ocean move over her. She closed her eyes for a bit and dreamed it was Iz breathing as he loved her, moving over her as he did, like a shading cloud in summer, cool and gentle relief. Oh, and the sweet promise of him there between her legs.

She didn't see it, but a tumbling spark of light arced out of the automobile parked atop the parking structure.

The blond man with the binoculars pressed to his eyes, the smell of nicotine on his fingers, said out loud, in the solitude of his vigil, "You pretty lady. Martin, eat your heart out. Show me some more, pretty lady. That's it. What are you do—oh my lord . . ."

CHAPTER 22

When Molly Carmichael awoke at a little before seven in the morning, the sky above the ocean wore a milky cast. Her sleep had been restless and threaded with ominous imagery, fragments of which she was trying to shake off as she walked to the bathroom to relieve herself, to wash her face and brush her teeth. There was coffee in the kitchen and she put a fresh pot on to perk, then drifted over to the bookshelves and lingered there, wearing a cotton shift and nothing else. The titles she recognized ranged from popular fiction to pop psychology (one of Claire's avocations), from poetry to history, from the antic humor of Dave Barry to the sober reflections of (really?)

Henry Miller. She had read the *Tropic of Cancer* long ago, and while she did not much sympathize with Miller's portrayal of women, she was struck by the energy, the candor, the vitality of the writing. She plucked down a volume with a blue cover and began to read and within minutes slammed it shut and stared out into the morning, wondering if she would ever have the strength to say, as the author had written: *I mean that I have made my peace with suffering.* Or was it only verbiage? She would settle for making her peace with the past.

The coffee had ceased to perk, so she returned the book to the shelf and poured herself a cup. She drank it black with some sugar and made a mental note to pick up juices at the grocery store, so that she would not have to drink coffee.

She took cup and saucer into the bedroom and set them on the nightstand, lifted the receiver from the phone there, and gave the operator her credit-card number. It would be a little past noon in New York. Izzy's phone rang several times before the answering machine engaged; after the message, Molly said, "Iz? Molly. I'm calling from Hawaii, Iz. It's just after seven in the morning here. You rascal, where are you? Let me give you the number here. . . ."

She put down the phone and took a sip of coffee, and the unease that followed her from sleep stirred once more, the fragment of a scene repeating itself. She would be all right once she heard his voice.

When she dialed Long Arm on the off chance Izzy was there doing paperwork, the answering service picked up. No, she said, there was no message. Two swings, two strikes.

At the hospital Abe Stein answered when the phone rang beside Zelda's bed.

"Hi, Abe. How's Zeedee?"

"Molly? That you, doll? She's good. Well, you know. Holding her own. We gotta funny connection or something, you sound like you're halfway around the world."

"Just about. Hawaii. You happen to know where your brother is? I've tried the house, the office."

"Izzy, yeah. Yeah, he's out of town," said Abe. "It came up kinda sudden."

Molly sighed. "It must have. I'll give you my number. If he calls, would you give it to him?"

"First thing, doll. First thing."

"Now tell me about Zeedee."

There was a stretch of static on the line, then Abe said, "What's to tell?"

When she hung up the phone, Molly Carmichael remained perched on the side of the bed, finishing her coffee and trying to wrestle the last bit of her troubled night into oblivion: the image of Izzy Stein bursting into a room where something terrible waited.

It was the something terrible that she could not recollect, that eluded her, and that she would just as soon forget.

They bought two Styrofoam coolers and packed one with beer and ice, the other with ice and sandwiches wrapped in Baggies, a plastic container of deli potato salad, plates, forks, garlic dills wrapped in foil, tomato slices and lettuce in separate Baggies. A bag of chips was tossed in the back on top of the cooler on the floor behind Leslie Ann Rice. It was a little past eleven when they picked up Earl in Lahaina. Leslie Ann scrambled in back, behind Misty, and Earl occupied the shotgun seat.

Earl said, "Looks like we're packin' for bear."

"Nope," said Misty, "just a little party. All of us Americans—right, Earl?"

"You got 'er there, son."

It was a windy but clear morning except at the summit of Haleakala, where the air was gray and swarming. The road on which they were traveling, Highway 30, was also known as the Honoapililani Highway and Leslie Ann Rice challenged Earl to pronounce that three times quickly. Earl gave it a game shot, sputtering on until Leslie Ann begged him to stop, her ribs ached from laughing. Misty asked Leslie Ann to pass him a can of beer and enlightened them as to his philosophy regarding the healing powers of hops. Earl nodded sagely and decided he'd better have one too. After the first swallow, he got off to a brisk start on another of his travelogues.

"Little girl, you see those fields the other side a the windbreak? That there is your sugarcane . . ."

On either side of the road now wiliwili trees formed a green corridor of windbreaks rising twenty feet. They were tightly branched, tall narrow bundles of green really, and one after another they flexed in the wind creating the illusion of long vertical waves.

". . . so when they're ready to harvest the cane, see, they dozer themselves—"

"Dozer?" said Leslie Ann.

"Bulldozer, they use a bulldozer."

"Gimme another beer, Sugarcheeks."

"They dozer themselves a firebreak, then they torch the cane, to burn off all the leaves. Leaves is useless as tits on a toad."

"Old Earl," said Misty, raising his fresh can of beer as if to offer a toast, "a man of many words and none of them too pretty."

"Mist—Carl, cut it out."

"Am I right, Earl? You're just a salt-of-the-earth kinda guy."

"I guess that's true enough. Gimme another beer, will you, little girl? By the way, I want to pay my fair share. What'd this all come to?"

"Don't ask," said Leslie Ann.

"Don't worry about it, Earl," said Misty, "it's our treat."

"No, no," insisted Earl, "do I look like a cheapskate?"

It was difficult to say precisely what Earl *did* look like this morning sporting those long yellow sideburns and those tattoos, wearing raspberry trousers over his cowboy boots and a plum-colored T-shirt that he had bought that morning, waiting for the youngsters to show. On the back of the T-shirt it read: *I've been Mauied.* Good old Earl. His aftershave was as loud as his costume, something like the aroma of cotton candy on a midway. In fact, there was about him an air of transience and not so much meanness as durability, hardness, and some familiarity with deceit that is associated with carnies. That was where Earl belonged, thought Misty Carmichael, in a carnival. Sorry, Earl.

". . . so all that's left is the charred stalks, which they dozer them into piles, see, and load the piles onto flatbeds and the piles is still smoking. Big ol' rig going down the road, you see it smoking, that's your sugarcane, little girl. . . ."

Misty had not eaten any breakfast, just drank some coffee after a swim in the ocean (no hanky-panky this time), and he was looking forward to the picnic in the valley and watching Earl drink beer and most likely blather on, and watching too his precious thing, little Leslie Ann in her tight blue jeans and that scarlet halter top of some smooth material, satin maybe, something to be seen in the privacy of a bedroom, at least stirring that thought around in his mind, that thin veil over her perky womanliness. They were going to have a good time today.

Five A.M. and Izzy Stein could sleep no longer. He rolled from bed and phoned room service for a pot of coffee, drank it on his balcony overlooking the water. Light was just creeping into the sky and tinting the waves when Izzy Stein finished his second cup and decided to go jogging on the empty beach. Martin Combs wasn't scheduled to be relieved until eight, and Charlie Bolton was sleeping the sleep of lambs in the bed next to Izzy's.

Even though it was cool and breezy, he descended the elevator bare-chested and barefooted, wearing just a jockstrap and the plum shorts. He asked a night clerk to hold his key, told the young woman he would be back within a half hour. She insisted upon scribbling him a receipt for the key.

He walked through the lobby and onto the cobbled walkway and circled the hotel to reach the beach. In the troughs of the waves, strands of rosy light trickled and vanished, drowned by the explosion of water that frothed toward the shore. The shore itself smelled of stranded life, of small burrowing snails and clams, of crabs scrambling at a cockeyed pace toward the safety of the water, of brine and algae and whatever it was that composed the heart of an ocean. He broke into a trot where the sand was moist, moving north from the hotel, adjusting himself to the texture of the wet sand, then picked up the pace. It was not a surface he was accustomed to running upon, and he could feel it suck upon his muscles, the pull of it like the pull of the sea, insistent and strong and almost sensual in its grip, as if inviting him to submit to a superior, but benevolent, force. Dark in the early-morning light, gulls and terns dived and speared at the life in the water and on the wet sand, adding their creaky music to the noise of the waves crashing. Izzy Stein wished his parents had lived long enough to hear what he was hearing, see what he was seeing. He remembered the look of his mother in the Brooklyn Botanical Gardens and imagined how she would feel in a world such as this. He and Molly Carmichael owed it to the memory of his parents to share the cup of wine that was this place in the sea.

He pushed himself until he could feel his heart really working, then swerved ninety degrees and plunged into the ocean. The surf was building toward high tide and the strength of the current pummeled him, but he struggled out of it feeling cleansed and totally awake. He walked back to the hotel, pausing to rinse his feet at an outdoor shower, rode the elevator, and enjoyed a complete shower this time, with soap and shampoo, toweled off, and it was not yet seven when he drove the convertible less than a quarter mile to the complex where Molly Carmichael was staying. He found Martin Combs in the wine-colored Chrysler in a state of disbelief and frustration over what Charlie Bolton claimed to have witnessed on the balcony last night, Molly Carmichael in her birthday splendor.

"Martin," said Izzy, as gently as he could, "wake up Charlie. The two of you can sleep it off on the plane."

Martin Combs drove off in the wine-colored car, and Izzy rode the convertible down to the lower level, parked it where he would still have a view of the main entrance. He had with him a sack of doughnuts and a tall Styrofoam cup of coffee.

God, he thought, why don't you just walk up to her? Play it honest. But he didn't, because, in spite of the fact that each had deceived the other, he was still trying to maintain the figment of their innocence in this whole business.

So he nibbled the sweet rolls and sat in the convertible and waited for Molly to make herself visible.

The taxicab was red and white and blue and stopped at the western end of the complex, Molly having discovered an exit that didn't require riding the elevator, but trooping down five flights of concrete stairs and through another time-lock door. For her it was a pleasant exercise, with the additional perk of not having to smile at whomever was sitting the lobby. The driver was a long-haired blond man with skinny shoulders who surfed in the afternoons and kept a diary, aspiring to write a screenplay some day based upon his experience.

Izzy Stein might not have caught the transaction, except for the fact that he was transfixed by the shifting show of color on the water, and the flash of mahogany hair at one end of the drive distracted him. He cursed himself, and rightfully so, for not having paid stricter attention to the taxi when it first arrived, instead of now, when it was wheeling down the drive and turning north on Kihei. He accelerated out of the garage to follow it.

Five minutes later he was sitting in his parked car thinking big deal, the lady's just going shopping.

Molly Carmichael hauled two plastic shopping bags up through the western entrance, the one away from the lobby, feeling the climb up the concrete steps in her calves, accepting and even welcoming the faint sting of pain. She put away groceries and took a glass of apple-cranberry juice onto the balcony, to gaze across the street at the ocean.

Iz, she thought, where are you? Please call. Please call. I don't want to go on like this. I want you.

You, Iz.

I want to feel young once in my life, truly and freely, and only love does that.

The Iao Valley Road climbed and weaved among increasingly dense vegetation, and ahead of them they could see several lofty peaks and the gray, slashing evidence of rainfall up there, and Earl was saying, "Now this here is your typical rain forest, gets over four hundred inches of wet per year, whereas down on the coast where you folks is staying, lucky if you get ten inches."

"Tell you the truth, Earl, she's lucky to get six inches."

"Mist—Carl!"

"Son, you got a mind runs deep as a sewer, don't you?"

Misty laughed and called for another beer, and Earl thought he'd better have one too.

They passed a sign informing them that up ahead there was a rock formation that bore an unbelievable resemblance to the profile of the late president, John F. Kennedy, and Misty Carmichael spoke into his fist, affecting a tour guide's intonations: "Now, if you will look off to your right, ladies and gentlemen, the assman cometh."

"You should talk," said Leslie Ann from the back, "all the women you brag you been with."

"Hey, not bragging," argued Misty Carmichael, "but only to make a point. Out of them all, Sugarcheeks, you're tops. Didn't I say that?"

"Some comfort, with AIDS going around. I think you ought to be tested."

"Me, and not you?"

"Son, that ain't polite, say that to a woman."

"No Earl, he's right, that's only fair." She leaned forward to brush her fingertips on Misty Carmichael's cheek. "Both of us, baby."

"Shit," said Misty Carmichael, "I drove right past it. Whadda ya say, we'll catch JFK on the way back?"

"Sure," said Earl, "we got all the time in the world."

The peaks here did not measure up to Haleakala insofar as height, the loftiest rising to somewhere in the neighborhood of twenty-five hundred feet, but the lushness and variety of vegetation did not have to take a backseat to anyplace on the island. They stopped in a parking lot that featured a walk to a scenic view of something called Needle Rock, and after crossing a bridge and climbing some wide, shallow steps through the damp air, with flowers and thick leaves springing out at them at every turn in the path—nature's way of saying: gotcha!—they arrived at a stark structure with wooden seating, a ramada roof, and from here it was proposed there existed the best look at Needle Rock. To Misty it was just a pillar of dull stone or lava poked into some rainfall, but Leslie Ann Rice and old Earl exchanged enthusiastic observations, you'd have thought they were gazing upon the eighth wonder of the world.

Then they ambled back down, taking the long route because Leslie Ann Rice wanted to read all the signs that identified the flora, and of course old Earl seized the opportunity to read every sign aloud as if he were the hired guide. "Now this here's your plumeria, little girl," he said, pointing to a burst of spoon-shaped petals with butter-colored hearts, "which is what you make your leis from." The blossoms ranged from pink to mauve to white. They passed something called a hala, with a crown of long, slender, and abruptly drooping leaves, a sad and vulnerable-looking tree. And Earl introduced them to the kukui and the monkeypod with its branches twisted like something spun off in a centrifuge. They walked alongside a tumbling stream while Earl educated them in the ornamental uses of the black pods of the kukui, Leslie Ann saying, "Imagine that," encouraging the old fart. Misty Carmichael noticed that they were practically the only ones walking the paths without cameras and binoculars, but of course they had old Earl, and who could match that?

"I don't know about you two," he announced, trailing along behind them, "but I'm ready to eat."

The air was heavily misted, especially alongside the stream, and her sandals became damp and squeaked as she attempted to keep up with Earl, who kept a strong hand on her elbow, whispering to her whenever they were far enough ahead of Misty Carmichael.

"I don't know what you expect me to do," she pouted, trying to buy time, "when the money, I told you, is in the hotel safe deposit box."

"You're gonna listen is what you're gonna do. We're gonna throw a scare into that boy."

"Daddy, you're hurting my arm."

"Then listen. We get back this afternoon, you make an excuse to take a walk. On the beach or over to one a the stores, it don't matter, just so long as you're alone for a while. Then you come back, tell him you seen them guys you told me is chasing him. What's the first thing he's gonna do?"

She noticed for the first time in her life that her father said *thang* for *thing.*

"The money? Go for the money?"

"Bet your titties on it, little girl."

Then he said, *"Will you look at them clouds,"* and when Misty turned in the direction he was pointing, up toward the peak of Needle Rock, he whispered, "He goes for the money, then we go for him. Trust your daddy, our ship's coming in."

And that's when Misty Carmichael, unimpressed by whatever it was that had attracted Earl's eye, suggested they get on with their picnic. He proposed they stop at the site where there was supposed to be this JFK rock formation, but Leslie Ann protested, "There aren't any tables or anything there, I don't think."

"So what. This is a picnic. You want linen tablecloths?"

"I thought I saw a park, the something Gardens, Keepaweewee was it? I think I saw some tables with benches. Wouldn't you like that better?"

They had reached the rental car and Misty Carmichael unlocked it, looked across the roof at Earl and winked. "Women," he said, "they live for creature comforts. We're gonna have a picnic, not a goddamn suburban backyard barbecue. It'll be fun, see who can find Fast Jack's face in the rocks. Whadda ya say, Earl?"

"I say open a car and gimme a beer and let's do her."

So she relented and they drove out of the parking lot and back down the road they'd traveled, Earl regaling them with tales of life as a youth in the 1960's. It sounded unbelievably Eden-like to her, built upon a foundation of shit a mile high. Guys and girls walking around with flowers in their hair, what kinda fucking world they think they were living in—Disneyland? What the world was about, as Leslie

Ann Rice saw it, was making a buck and trying to have a good time in the process. What else was there? Politics was just a matter of who lied better on that particular day. Everybody sucked up and sold out. And the ones that got ahead grabbed for it. It was that simple. And maybe you find someone you like to fuck, enough to start a family, so you do that too. Big deal. The world wasn't pretty. It wasn't anything like the way she was feeling inhaling the scent of the Norfolk Island pine . . . no, the world was closer to her father threatening her if she ever uttered a word of where he kissed her when he felt bad about the spankings.

But why then did she feel so protective, so loyal, so willing to shield him from Misty Carmichael? Why was betrayal so difficult for her when so obviously easy for Earl?

Or was it so difficult? If Misty had been looking into her eyes, she bet, as they pulled over at the site to view the President's profile, he would have told her he could see the wheels turning.

They hauled the two Styrofoam coolers and chips from the car and crouched around them, using the cooler tops for tables, resting their beers and plates there, and speculated upon the various rock formations, and it was Earl who first identified the late President's rocky resemblance, and then Misty and Leslie Ann recognized it as well, the look of it absolutely uncanny. Then Misty scanned the slopes opposite and directed their attention to a blank slab of rock, saying, "Jesus, Earl, this place is crawling with presidential faces. Right there, that's George Bush."

And her father, with a mouth full of tuna fish, didn't let that stop him from blurting out, "Ain't a one of 'em worth a sack a shit," spewing bits of sandwich hither and yon.

She wondered what she was going to do with him. He was becoming not so much a forbidden pleasure as a complete and utter embarrassment. She knew for a certainty that her decision to stick with Misty Carmichael was the right one. But how, with the old goat thrusting this timetable upon her, was she going to frustrate his intentions on the one hand, without exposing her connection to him on the other? Life sure pressed in on you sometimes.

Earl finished two sandwiches and a heapful of potato salad and rocked back on his heels, squatting across from Misty Carmichael, working away at his teeth with a toothpick, then took it away to belch such that he startled several tourists across the road.

Misty Carmichael brushed his hands, a look of complete satisfaction on his gorgeous face. "Earl," he said, "I think I'm going to take a walk in the woods before my bladder busts. Care to join me?"

Earl rose to his feet and she could hear his knees creak. "You know what they say about beer, son. You don't buy it, you just rent it."

"That's what they say, huh? Sugarcheeks?"

"You go on. I'll put this stuff in the car. I didn't drink all the beer you two did."

They ambled off in the direction opposite the JFK profile and Leslie Ann Rice watched them navigate on the unfamiliar terrain, Earl in his plum shirt with the dopey sentiment on the back and Misty in his tight jeans that showed what a nice ass he had for a man and the butter-yellow shirt she had bought him in Phoenix. She watched them until they were swallowed up by the wealth of nature, and then she picked up the empty beer cans and plates and put them away with the uneaten food and put one Styrofoam cooler in the trunk and the other, the one with the remaining beer, behind the seat. Idly she listened to the remarks of the people across the road, the little shrieks of delight when someone discerned the face of the fallen President. Cars passed going both ways. Once she heard one of them backfire, and it rattled her, just as it did some of the people across the road, their faces swinging her way for an instant. All of them looking sheepish in the next instant, herself included probably. She glanced uneasily over at the curtain of fronds into which Misty and Earl had vanished, anxious to be moving, out of here, away from the memory of the pressure Earl was exerting. She skipped across the asphalt to bum a cigarette off a couple who said they were from Oregon, but hadn't met anyone yet on the island from Oregon. Was she from Oregon? She suppressed the urge to tell them no, she was from the fucking moon. She thanked them and crossed the road and climbed behind the wheel, inserted the key into the ignition and flipped the radio dial. The reception was poor what with the peaks. She puffed without inhaling, believing the cigarette might ease her anxiety—it had seemed to work on other occasions—although now it only made her feel queer and detached. And the smell of the smoke was awful. She gave up the effort to find a radio station and got out of the car and rested her fanny against the front fender, smoked and peered into the shifting shades of green out of which she expected Misty and Earl to emerge.

Then she saw Misty Carmichael shifting his weight like

a skier as he descended out of the greenery. His face looked dark and wary and determined, his arms out to balance himself, and when he had reached the dirt and the gravel, she saw upon his face what she had seen upon it in that instant in the Point, when he nearly jerked her off her feet, and she knew better than to ask questions, but got in the car and handed him the keys as soon as he was behind the wheel. His eyes went straight ahead as he turned the ignition. She butted the cigarette in the ashtray, and from some reserve of suspicion and self-preservation she managed to utter the admonishment: "Let's leave here slow and easy. Slow and easy, baby."

She would have bet her left breast it was not an automobile's backfire she and everyone across the road had heard.

He explained it to her with the windows down and the turbulence tossing her hair around, and she did not even think about how she looked, but concentrated upon hearing every word in the whip and the suck of the wind.

"I'm not stupid," he said, the first words he said to her when they were out of the valley and humming along Honoapililani Highway. He had one hand inside his shirt stroking the ugly wooden thing that hung there. "You think I don't see a connection?"

Leslie Ann Rice fought down her panic. "I don't know what you mean. Connection?"

"You didn't believe that sentimental crap he fed us last

night, how he decided to come to Maui on account we weren't. Did you?"

"I didn't . . . I didn't think about it, I guess."

"Uh-huh. Well I sure hope you come out of this a sharper lady."

"Where's Earl, Misty?"

"He's standing there shaking out his weenie and telling me all about the sixties, and I popped him right behind the ear. One shot," he added, and glanced at her. "You think *he* jumped. I must have cleared a country mile, straight back. Even dropped the fucking gun. It's no fucking picnic, shooting a guy up close like that."

Leslie Ann Rice shut her eyes tight and turned her face toward the open window.

Misty Carmichael continued, "Listen Sugarcheeks, if you didn't see a connection, let me explain it to you. Earl introduces himself with the lamest come-on since the Swiss started building watches. And what happens the first night with him, when he learns where we're staying? We have these assholes waiting for us at the hotel. They almost kill us. Kind of right after old Earl departs the scene. I didn't put this all together at first, or I'd never have called him on Oahu. But when he turns up on Maui with his bullshit story —what am I supposed to think? He's a point man for the assholes, can't you see that?"

She almost broke into laughter out of relief, although as sick as she felt in the pit of her stomach, she didn't dare exert herself that much.

What she said was, "Can we pull over? I'm not feeling too good."

And when he did, she pushed open the door and got sick right there alongside the road. As opposed to the pine, she thought, this is the way life smells—the terror of it, the meanness and the treachery and all the rest. She wasn't as tough as he thought she was, or that she thought she was for that matter.

CHAPTER 23

She didn't exactly snap right out of it, but she was coming around, stretched out there behind sunglasses on the plastic lounge chair in that purple bathing suit designed to suggest that it was about to burst from her attributes any instant. She didn't say much, and when she did speak, there was a stunned quality to her voice, a tone of detachment. As if she were uncertain as to her circumstances; as if she were in a foreign land and did not understand the language. But hadn't she been an ace back there, his precious thing, when he had gotten into the car with that hot dirty barrel stuck down his spine, his blood feeling like fire and there was not enough oxygen in the whole world to fill his lungs and she had calmed him with her voice, the strength within it? Her voice saying, *Slow and easy, baby.*

She did not want a drink.

She did not want to go into the water.

She wanted to lie there, she said, and watch him in the ocean, watch how beautiful he looked in the sun and watch him coming up to her dripping and smiling, the material of his trunks clinging to him. She said that was all she had the energy to do and she had no appetite for food.

She had brushed her teeth and he had brought her mouthwash from the market to gargle with, but the taste of sickness and death lingered, and right now she told him not an ocean of salt water would wash it away. But she loved him, and that is what carried her, would cure her.

So he dived into the pale-blue water that was a pure delight and frolicked in it, even flirted with an airline stewardess from Montreal with long dark hair, short like Leslie Ann, but with a set on her, she had to be a *D* cup minimum. She said her name was Emma, after some heroine in a famous French novel. He told her she looked about as much like an Emma as Maui looked like Cleveland. No, what she looked like, he told her, was a Kristy or a Nikki or a Farrah. She asked him if he knew about the Carpe Diem and he said are you kidding? She said she'd be there with a girlfriend around eight o'clock, and he said he could be there with a girlfriend around then, too. Maybe they'd see each other. After all, no relationship was carved in stone, was it? She laughed and he laughed, and then he said he had to go, the lady was waiting. And she said lucky lady. Then said later.

He dived into the surf once more and circled around

beneath the water, until his hands felt Emma's hips, and he came up behind her, staying low in the water. He blew the brine off his upper lip and bobbed there, keeping Emma between himself and the line of Leslie Ann's vision, Emma turning in the water so that he had a bone-hard view of the underside of her wonderful breasts.

"You know what my philosophy of love is?" he said, a look of absolute sincerity radiating from his face.

Molly Carmichael felt the lure of the sun and the water all morning and afternoon more strongly than any time in her life, but she avoided it still. If Iz had been with her, she would have relented, gone back on a lifetime's aversion. No, that was not being honest. She would not have relented, she would have initiated a visit to the shore. Knowing how much he enjoyed it, she wanted now to share that with him. My God, how she yearned to share it with him. To immerse themselves in that sweetly warm and stinging water. It brought tears to her eyes just thinking about it. And how they would emerge from it and let the sun bake the salt on them and come up here to be with each other.

But the phone didn't ring.

She spent hours practicing, as Abe had told her—a running monologue when she sat watching him clean his guns—was necessary, if she wanted to be comfortable with the gun, bringing it up and pointing it like a finger, dry firing it. Feeling foolish, she nonetheless persisted in the exercise, drawing and aiming at the television set or a book on the shelves, a lamp, a picture, her own faint reflection in the glass of the patio door. By late afternoon she was hungry, so she returned the bullets to the chamber, the smell of the lead almost intoxicating and at the same time making her faintly nauseous.

Izzy Stein followed her along the sidewalk to the restaurant that advertised itself as Italian in the upstairs half of the two-story strip of commercial property. There was a balcony that overlooked the ocean, and he could see her from the street at a table up there. He crouched beneath a palm tree watching her without benefit of binoculars, within a hundred yards by his calculation of his hotel and the condos adjoining it. The deep gray clouds that had descended from Haleakala, that had dirtied the light over the beach for the last couple of hours with the threat of ugliness, were drifting out to sea, rimmed with blazing light. Along the shore, heading his direction, a young woman in a purple one-piece suddenly collapsed to her knees and pitched forward, her chin flush against the sand.

Molly Carmichael ate, and as she ate, he believed he could see her as she chewed, every bite, enjoying the illusion that he was sitting across the table from her, seeing her eyes, her lips, the contour of her beautiful face, reading the pleasure of her satiation. There was nothing like it except maybe the captured moment in the scratchy photograph of his parents, his mother's gaze for his father. The frank and honest feeling there. The elemental connection.

The woman in the purple bathing suit was nowhere to be seen.

Confident that Molly Carmichael would be a while,

knowing how she liked to linger over her meal, savoring it, he walked down the street and crossed over, dined on two slices of Sicilian pizza containing enough cholesterol to stop a culvert, washed it down with a diet soda that tasted like an experiment gone bad. Standard stake-out fare.

When he was finished scrubbing the cheese from his chin, Izzy Stein pushed up the sleeve of his cream-colored sport coat and glanced at his watch. The sun was descending as he emerged from the little restaurant and crossed Kihei Road, dodging through gaps in the traffic. It felt good wearing the coat at this hour as the breeze was swinging in off the ocean. Under the coat he wore a gray T-shirt and some old, comfortable jeans. And the Smith & Wesson in a worn leather rig beneath his left shoulder.

Molly Carmichael was still up there, alone at her table. He leaned against the trunk of the palm tree and chewed on his thumbnail and watched the parade of automobiles go by, the banter between cars, everybody easy and full of merriment. Down the block the Carpe Diem enjoyed a boisterous crowd and above it in the distance the rugged cone of Haleakala sat like a fat black missile.

There was laughter and shouting and music up the steps in the Carpe Diem as Molly Carmichael strolled past in a royal-blue shoulderless sheath dress, hands clutching her elbows for warmth. She did pause to look up, but then moved on and turned her attention to the spectacle of the sun disappearing in the west. It had been her experience on islands in the sea that the exit of the sun was sudden and complete, as this one was, although she realized for the first time that this impression sprang from living in a city such as New York, where there were street lamps at dusk. Her world was the artificial one, and this was the real thing.

Inside the condo she kicked off her low heels, left her purse sitting on the breakfast bar, and scanned the bookshelves, choosing a volume of poetry that contained the works of W. B. Yeats. How long had it been since she had experienced the magic of Yeats? Years, decades, close to an era?

With the book in her hands, she stretched herself on the couch like a satisfied cat, and thought, Molly, Molly, you are one lucky lady.

The phones in the kitchen and in the bedroom rang.

"**H**ello?" she said. "Hello?"

Then a voice said, "You enjoying the weather, Molly?"

"Enormously."

"You got it?"

"I have it."

"Easiest ten grand you ever made, I'll bet."

She said nothing.

"No witty repartee tonight?"

"Misty, I'm your mother, not the other half of a lounge act. Recognizing that might go a long way toward waking you up. If that's possible."

"Too late, I'm afraid. I don't kowtow to people that scrubbed floors for a living. I'da preferred it if you'd been a professional hooker, instead of a social one. At least we'd have had some nice things. Of course, that's probably bullshit. You'd have spent it all going somewhere, wouldn't you?"

Molly sank to her knees and concentrated upon her breathing. She saw the bedroom as a moist blur.

"Be there at nine. I'll call, let you know where to bring it."

Molly Carmichael, still on her knees, heard the line go dead. Her breathing was harsh and shallow, exactly as if she'd been kicked in the stomach. It was a pain worse than childbirth. It was a kind of death.

Misty Carmichael let the receiver drop into the cradle, and there was a look of passionate satisfaction on his face, the relief of a long anger at last in the open. Mostly it was the anger of being left in the company of his grandparents, his only set of grandparents, and listening to them feud endlessly over whether Molly was a slut or his father was a heartless bastard. It was a big issue between them and probably what sustained the marriage, as neither would concede to the other. When Misty had grown older, he realized that the way they went at it had all the flavor of an argument between religious zealots.

The glass door that faced onto the ocean slid open, and Leslie Ann Rice stepped inside and Misty Carmichael, standing off to one side in the bright light of the kitchen mixing a batch of salty dogs, said, "Sugarcheeks, I was beginning to worry. Where you been—mudwrestling?"

The kitchen was off to the right of the door and faced into the living and dining area, a small patch of pale-white carpet, and the carpet continued into the two bedrooms that were on either side of the bathroom. Leslie Ann Rice padded straight toward the bathroom, saying, "I'm hungry. I feel better. Much."

Misty Carmichael brought salty dogs into the bathroom and set one of them on the counter next to the sink for Leslie Ann, who was standing in the shower stripping off her sand-encrusted bathing suit. Her skin was dusted with sand, even where it was sharply white, the secret sweetness of her that he intended to explore before they went out to dinner at Carpe Diem. Resting a hip against the countertop, he said, "Just needed the walk alone, huh?"

"I guess." She stepped out of the stall, her suit on the floor a purple heap amid what appeared to be the ruins of a modest sand castle. She adjusted the heat of the water, then stepped back inside, but did not close the stall door, so that she could look Misty Carmichael in the face. "I'm not . . . I'm not experienced . . . not in the habit of . . . I want to get out of here soon, Misty. I'm serious."

"How's tomorrow sound?"

"Really?"

"How's Australia sound, for openers?"

She turned her face to the pouring water, her eyes clenched, her lips tight and smiling. Then she looked down and with her toes nudged the bathing suit into a corner of the shower and said, "Why don't you take off those clothes and come in here with me?"

Misty Carmichael felt relaxed and confident, sitting in the restaurant portion of the Carpe Diem, looking into the eyes of his precious thing as she lifted her hair away from an eye. His nerves still tingled from the way she had worked him with her lips and her mouth, as if he had been plugged into an erotic network of power. He felt capable of anything.

The place reminded him in a vague way of Punch's, on Metropolitan Avenue. It was funky, not neighborhood funky the way Punch's was, but rather like an expensive bistro designed to give its customers the vicarious pleasure of slumming. It seemed to flaunt the absence of amenities.

Leslie Ann Rice ordered a tossed salad with blue-cheese dressing and crab legs with French fries. Misty Carmichael voted for the house dressing for his salad and went with the grilled salmon and baked potato, a side of sour cream. They drank beer with the meal.

As they finished eating, Misty Carmichael asked her how she was doing, and Leslie Ann Rice admitted she was feeling much better—than this afternoon, she hastened to say, because it would be hard to feel a whole lot better than she had felt there in the shower with him up inside her. A person couldn't feel much better than that feeling, unless there really was a heaven and it wasn't the kind of neutered dream that Christians seemed to live for. She said she never could understand a belief that strived to leave the body, and its needs, behind. Why else had God given it to them?

He said he didn't think about it a whole lot, but that she was right, it didn't get much better than what they had going in the shower.

Then he said, "How about we get outta here, go have a nightcap in the bar outside? Our last night on the island, we oughta celebrate. Besides, I need to do some business, and this is a nice, close place where you can party while I'm doing it."

"Sure, baby," she said, "whatever you say."

The bartenders—there were three of them, two men and a woman, all dressed casually in whatever they chose to show up in—worked behind an oval bar that looked sleek and dark, possibly polished walnut, beneath the track lighting. It was a good crowd, and there were television screens mounted around the premises, a baseball game on the screen, the Dodgers versus the Giants, and there seemed to be a solid contingent of supporters for both teams. Misty Carmichael found two bar stools for them on the outside railing with a view through the palm trees of the beach and the ocean. Starlight danced off the water as if choreographed for a movie, something with Cary Grant in it, Cary and some dreamy blond actress. A breeze sailed up at them off the sea, cool and fragrant.

A waitress threaded her way through the cluster of revelers and took their order. Leslie Ann Rice sat on her stool, elbows on the counter, her chin in her hands and her eyes taking in the black and starry night. She was wearing the red satin halter top that resembled a teddy and the same tight blue jeans, and she was shivering a little, so that Misty Carmichael stepped off his chair to stand behind her, to caress her arms. She pressed the back of her head against his chest and said, "Ummm, you do that so good, baby."

It wasn't more than a minute that he stood there squeezing her arms before he spotted the stewardess, Emma, at a table toward the rear with a party of people, the number of women and men about even, a happy, rowdy bunch if gesturing was any measurement. He leaned over Leslie Ann and said, "Enjoy the view, I need to see a man about a horse."

She reached up blindly to stroke his cheek, and he kissed the palm of her hand.

He walked toward the rear of the bar—the rest rooms were actually outside and down a sidewalk—and caught Emma's attention and she excused herself and followed him outside. They embraced next to a phone booth and their hands were frank about their intentions. Reluctantly, he released her lips and told her where his condo was, that he would meet her there in five minutes and would show her one half hour of ecstacy, take it or leave it. Because then he had business to conduct. Emma tugged her sweater back down over her naked breasts and said she'd take it.

In the bar he brushed his lips over Leslie Ann's neck and told her to wait there for him. He might be an hour, an hour and a half. But she should wait right there for him. He handed her a hundred-dollar bill and said that ought to cover it. She said she thought it would.

"Misty? Be careful, baby."

He reached beneath his shirt to finger the smooth cool object there. "You know what my philosophy is, Sugarcheeks?"

Little Emma with the long, straight dark hair and the incredible charms was waiting for him in a coral-and-white lounge chair, a drink in her lap that she had brought from the Carpe Diem. She extended her hand for him to assist her out of the lounge chair, and when she was standing, she said, "You use rubbers, don't you?"

"Emma, why spoil the pleasure?"

"It won't," she said, dipping her hand into a pocket of her tight white jeans and producing the foil packets. "You'll have all the pleasure you can stand. I guarantee it."

"Well well," he said, unlocking the door and sliding it open. "This could be interesting."

He led her across the pale carpet to the bedroom beyond the bathroom, not the one where he and Leslie Ann slept and had their moments. The walls were white and the bedspreads were cocoa and neatly made. Misty Carmichael made a mental note to straighten up when they were finished. No dawdler this little Emma, she walked directly to the nightstand between the beds and put her drink there along with the foil packets and turned around with a wanton smile for him, then inhaled sharply in order to unbutton her tight white jeans. "Leave the light on," she said, wrestling the jeans down over her hips. "I like to watch."

"The only way to go," he said, unbuttoning his shirt.

She kicked her jeans free and hooked her thumbs in her little white panties and stepped out of them, then crossed her arms to lift her sweater. The waist and button of her jeans had left their imprints in her flesh, a temporarily bright pink scar around her waist, as if she had been surgically joined there. It excited him. And then there they were, their pinkness at the ends staring him right in the face, pink as blushes, those breasts that would look big on an Amazon. She turned down the coverlet on the bed nearer the door while Misty Carmichael kicked off the last article of clothing and enjoyed the view of her ass as she bent over to slide between the sheets.

Naked he approached her, her arms spread for him, the wondrous perfume of her womanhood rising to greet him as he lifted the covers. Life didn't get any better than this.

"This is going to be good, Emma. Believe me when I tell you: I'm going to make you feel so good."

She reached for him and said, "Let's get this sucker in his diving gear, so you can show me."

The reluctance to part was sincere on both sides, but Misty Carmichael was running late as it was, so he promised Emma there was always tomorrow, if she would give him her phone number, which she did. They stood outside the sliding glass door locked in one last kiss and still groping each other with the kind of urgency they had experienced behind the Carpe Diem. And then she was gone and he was walking with an empty suitcase up the cobblestone entrance to the hotel and into the lobby and through it to the desk to complete the paperwork to enter the room of safe deposit boxes.

Ten minutes later he stood in the light of the bedroom he and Leslie Ann used, the suitcase open on the bed farther from the door, laying the .380 on the field of bills. Then he walked out to the kitchen, flipped on the light there, and dialed Molly's number.

When she answered, he said, "Just listen."

Familiar with the way the temperature dropped at the seashore at night, Molly Carmichael had brought along the jacket half of a blond silk suit, the jacket with a nubbed texture and lined. She put it on now, having scrubbed her face with hot water, and looked at herself in the mirror until her heartbeat returned to something within the range of normal. In the kitchen she opened her purse and made sure the safety was off. She snugged her feet into the L.A. Gears and locked the door behind her. Going down the five floors of concrete steps, she did not feel the effort or the impact of the concrete against her feet; she descended as if in a dream.

The air off the ocean slapped her cheeks gently, and it was a welcome sensation. She could almost taste the salt with her tongue. She walked beneath the tall palms down the drive without registering their majesty and crossed Kihei Road blindly, forcing traffic both ways to stop abruptly. She did not see the arms sticking out, the fists waggling forefingers and pinkies. She stopped when she reached the sand to remove her sneakers, burrow them into her handbag, careful to arrange matters so that the revolver was accessible. Continuing, she turned north, up the beach, her toes squeezing and pushing off from the sand in the moonlight. She did not see the figure behind her in a jacket as light as her own, moving warily down where the sand was moist.

She came up from the beach, passing the two lounge chairs that appeared to be striped in the shadowy light there, and knocked on the glass door and saw her son approaching out of light to the rear. He slid the door open and said, "Come on in."

They crossed pale carpet to a bedroom, and Misty Carmichael, who led the way, moved past the second bed and stood behind an open suitcase, facing his mother standing in the doorway, her gaze momentarily fixed upon the bed nearest her, unmade and no doubt showing the stains of lovemaking. That tickled him.

He chuckled. "The maid only comes around once a day. I tend to use a bed more often than that."

She raised her eyes to meet his. "Is that all the money there that you took from the loan shark?"

"Loan shark? I don't know what you're talking about. Anyway, I didn't invite you here to chitchat." He hoisted the banded package of bills that he had counted twice. "Here's the ten, Molly. Let's have the passport."

She reached into her purse. The smell of the oil on the gun oozed up at her, like the smell of some primal horror. It froze her momentarily.

But only momentarily.

She plucked out his passport and pitched it onto the bed beside the suitcase. Then she dug her hand once more into the purse. "I'm taking all of it," she said, holding the gun out in front of her as she had practiced it, although she couldn't stop the shaking. "I'm taking all of it, and that passport's your ticket out of here. There's almost two thousand dollars inside it, all I had in my account. This is the last mess I'm cleaning up for you."

He stood there staring at her, not believing any of it.

"Molly, what is this, an attack of PMS? Put the fucking gun down."

"The money's going back to the Scorcese family. Now close up the suitcase and hand it to me. Please don't be as big a fool as I'm afraid you are."

"Why you fucking bi—"

His hand was on the Colt when she shot him, drilled him right in the chest.

Following Molly Carmichael along the beach, he watched with some astonishment as she cut toward the cluster of condominiums that adjoined the very hotel in which he was staying. There was light in only one of the condos, the one on the southernmost end, and it was to this one that Molly went. Her son, that good-looking screwup, as complete an idiot as Frank Mears, was clearly visible in the light of the lamp above the door, greeting his mother with a smart-ass grin. Izzy Stein continued to shuffle along the sand until he reached the rocky promontory upon which the hotel stood. From there he could watch the patch of light in relative obscurity and wait for Molly Carmichael to come out. Once she was out of sight, he would pay the lad a visit, attempt to introduce him to reality. Molly might never know. The facade of their individual innocence might yet be salvaged.

He heard it and there was no question in his mind what he had heard.

Molly!

Running now, running across the sand in the moonlight, his legs pulling him at a pace that seemed maddeningly like he was standing still while his whole world was racing away from him—

Molly. Oh Molly.

Molly.

Molly.

Molly.

The impact of the bullet knocked him backward clutching his chest, and then he just stood there staring across the room at her. "You shot me," he said.

She could not quite believe it either as the terrifying sound of it lapped over her. She lowered the gun and it hung now at the end of her hand and her whole body was trembling and she seemed to be floating, floating in that instant of horror-filled time, trapped within it.

And then, and what made the horror greater, he was grinning. Misty Carmichael was standing across the room from her shot in the chest—she could see the hole in the butter-yellow shirt—and he was grinning. It was worse than a grin; it was a leer, and he was unbuttoning his shirt and she didn't understand it, because she was still trapped in the horror of that moment and she couldn't stop trembling.

She saw the bruise, the ugly purple welt on his chest, and realized she had done what she could not have done, given a thousand more opportunities: the bullet had struck the grigri, flattened itself there.

They both heard the door sliding open and she turned

instinctively to see, and saw that it was Izzy Stein coming through it and that there was a gun in his hand, and saw too her son reach into the suitcase.

There were two explosions and she saw Izzy spun around, falling.

She looked Misty Carmichael right in the eyes and emptied her gun. She was right. She didn't hit the grigri once.

CHAPTER **24**

In his business you did not stop thinking, not for one moment, and there was no room for love, because then you were feeling instead of thinking and something like this happened: you burst into a room with a gun forgetting to release the safety. And here you were.

Here he was indeed, lying on his hip and bleeding all over himself and the jacket and the carpet and Molly too, if she didn't listen to him. He had been hit once, for certain, in his left side, but the slug must have struck a rib and gone south, because blood was leaking from his back about at his waistline. His supply of adrenaline so far blocked the pain, the real teeth-clenching pain, but he was using it up fast and wanted Molly Carmichael out of there before it was on him and he couldn't think clearly, enough to persuade her to do the one thing that meant anything to him now.

She was kneeling beside him, trying to wrestle his shirt up to see where he'd been hit. She was crying and didn't seem to hear him, so he slapped her.

"There isn't time for this," he said. "Help me up, Molly."

The room swayed some, then settled solidly, although the air was hot and tasted evil. He saw the .22 where Molly had dropped it, on the carpet just beyond the door to the bedroom. He saw the open suitcase on the bed, but he did not see Misty Carmichael.

"Is he dead, Molly?"

"I . . . I haven't looked."

"We're going to look," he said, kneeling to retrieve the .22, "and then you're going to take my shoulder rig and my pistol and you are going to get the hell out of here."

"What—"

"Here." He handed her his room key from the pocket of his jacket. "I'm in the hotel next door. Put the gun and the rig in my room."

Misty Carmichael was lying on his back, his pretty face wrenched in a corner, a cheek pressed to his shoulder, and his arms outflung. His eyes were wide open, staring with what appeared to be furious disbelief through the tears standing in them. Molly Carmichael must have struck him with several rounds just beneath the rib cage, the wound there broad enough to have been done by a spear. Halfway between his fingertips and the bed, a gun lay on the carpet, and Izzy Stein saw not only what saved Molly's life, but no doubt what explained the expression on Misty's face: the grigri had failed him in the ultimate hour of his need. The poor putz's gun—neglected like everything Misty touched—had jammed.

They saw what was in the suitcase at the same time, and Izzy Stein said, "You know who that belongs to, take it to them."

Molly Carmichael looked at him and her face was composed. She was at once beautiful and a thousand miles away.

"In his passport there on the bed, it's almost two thousand dollars in cash. Tell the police he stole it from me, and you came here to retrieve it."

He was leaning heavily on her now and he loved her, because she was thinking, trying to do the thinking for the two of them. He smiled weakly. "They won't like the story. But they'll learn to like it. Just like they'll learn to like this twenty-two that just happened to be lying here."

He sat down heavily on the bed nearer the door. She knelt to pick up his gun from the living room, then came back to help him out of his pistol rig. Her hands were steady and her eyes purposeful and he breathed her perfume, trying to hang on. She put gun and rig in the open suitcase, closed and latched it, hauled it over to where he was sitting.

"You followed me here, didn't you? Somebody's been following me. Why?"

"I had a job to do."

"Was I just part of the job?"

"You know better."

"You lied to me."

"I won't argue. I never could win an argument with you, could I?" He squeezed his eyes shut for an instant. "I got nothing to apologize for, Molly. Neither do you."

She turned away with the suitcase dragging on her, straining to keep her shoulders erect inside the blond silk jacket, and he watched her royal-blue dress above her calves and bare feet pass through the open glass door and the light from the outside lamp catch fire in her hair, and watched her as she became a beautiful silhouette against the sand and the sea, until she was gone.

Then he forced himself to his feet and plucked the passport from the other bed, using his handkerchief to hold it. He inserted the document with the money inside into Misty's still-warm hand and folded the fingers over to press against the cover. He pinched a corner of the passport and lifted it out of Misty's hand and let it drop onto the bed. Several bills slipped free, fanning out on the bedspread. It looked good enough. Slowly he made his way to the kitchen and with a hand wet from his own blood lifted the receiver and dialed 911.

The ambulance made a hell of a racket when it arrived, but Izzy Stein didn't hear it.

Down the street, though, Leslie Ann Rice heard it and was happy to hear it as an excuse to escape the attentions of a tall guy named George, not a bad-looking guy really, who said he was ranked twenty-seventh in terms of earnings that year on the PGA circuit, which made him just about a millionaire, about halfway there. She told him she needed some air and what was the noise all about? He said life, it's just the noise and distraction of life, and he'd just as soon stay where he was and root for the Giants. She told him she'd see him around and got out of there.

Going down the steps of the Carpe Diem, she could feel the mix of alcohol and the shock of her daddy's death. The air off the ocean made her shiver, and when she looked in the direction of the rotating lights—some of them blue, some red—it wasn't only the air off the ocean that chilled her. She wobbled across Kihei Road and approached the condominiums where she and Misty were staying, in time to see two shapes being wheeled out on gurneys, one of them appearing to receive oxygen and blood, the other in a body bag. She swayed there and rested her hand on a palm tree and lifted her hair away from her eye. She could see policemen everywhere entering and emerging from the southernmost unit of the condominiums.

This time she was stronger.

She found George where she had left him, on a stool along the railing, glancing at the ballgame on television and making remarks that had the waitress in stitches.

"You were right, George. It wasn't anything."

He looped a long arm over her shoulders. "Any*thang?*" he said.

"Do I really sound like that?" she said. "Do I, George?"

He reached down to squeeze her ass and she knew she was home free.

It was difficult to say from minute to minute, hour to hour, whether Zelda Stein was conscious of anything, for her most comprehensible connection with the world of the living was the ability to blink.

In the chair beside her bed Molly Carmichael read aloud the final pages of the tragedy that was the Civil War. Almost three days had passed since she had returned from Maui and delivered the suitcase to Joe Scorcese and told him looking into his eyes in the back of the van that if he didn't take his hand off her *now*—she would kill him.

She did not kill him and he did not pay her a penny of what he had promised for the return of his money, summarily evicting her from the van on a dubious street corner in Flatbush.

That was fine. She did not want his money. She wanted something more lasting.

The light in the room was bright, almost starchy, like a nurse's uniform, and Molly Carmichael ceased reading just prior to Lee's arrival at Appomattox. Zelda was staring at the ceiling and her mouth was open, unmoving. She had not uttered a word since her brief, enigmatic enunciation of "Florida."

Molly glanced at her watch. Abe was due to arrive shortly. She leaned over the bed and applied makeup to Zelda's warm and wasting face.

The door opened.

Abe Stein stood there like a big bear with paws he

didn't know what to do with, and then he came across the threshold, fingers pushing at his eyes.

"Iz didn't make it, Molly."

Beyond the open door came the sound of footsteps and of someone softly crooning a love song. But the lyrics made no sense to Molly Carmichael, issuing as they did from a world as far away as paradise.